ISBN 978-1-332-75874-6
PIBN 10433370

1 MONTH OF
FREE
READING

at
www.ForgottenBooks.com

By purchasing this book you are eligible for one month membership to ForgottenBooks.com, giving you unlimited access to our entire collection of over 1,000,000 titles via our web site and mobile apps.

To claim your free month visit:

www.forgottenbooks.com/free433370

English
Français
Deutsche
Italiano
Español
Português

www.forgottenbooks.com

Mythology Photography **Fiction**
Fishing Christianity **Art** Cooking
Essays Buddhism Freemasonry
Medicine **Biology** Music **Ancient
Egypt** Evolution Carpentry Physics
Dance Geology **Mathematics** Fitness
Shakespeare **Folklore** Yoga Marketing
Confidence Immortality Biographies
Poetry **Psychology** Witchcraft
Electronics Chemistry History **Law**
Accounting **Philosophy** Anthropology
Alchemy Drama Quantum Mechanics
Atheism Sexual Health **Ancient History**
Entrepreneurship Languages Sport
Paleontology Needlework Islam
Metaphysics Investment Archaeology
Parenting Statistics Criminology
Motivational

EASY LESSONS IN READING.

WITH AN

ENGLISH AND MARATHEE

VOCABULARY.

———————

BOMBAY:

AMERICAN MISSION PRESS.

E. A. WEBSTER, PRINTER.

————————

1841.

31,550

CONTENTS.

CONTENTS,

EASY LESSONS.

LESSON I.

HOW SCHOLARS SHOULD READ.

The first thing little boys and girls should think of, when they begin to read, is, whether what they read can be plainly heard by every one in the room. You know, children, that you may be heard, and yet not be *plainly* heard.

I have known some children read in such a way, that when I was sitting at the other side of the room, their voices sounded much like the buzz of a humble-bee, and I could not tell what they were reading about.

The next thing in reading is, to place the emphasis on the right words. Perhaps you do not know, what *emphasis* means. I will tell you. When you place the emphasis on a word you speak it more strongly than the other words.

If you were sent to the door, to call a-boy whose name was James, perhaps you would say, "James, the teacher says you must come in." Here you would place the emphasis on the words *James* and *in*. The words on which the emphasis is placed, are called the *emphatical* words.

One thing more I wish you to remember; and that is, to notice the stops. At a comma, you should make quite a short stop: not longer than you would be in speaking the word — *and*. At a semicolon, or a colon, you should stop a little longer than at a comma; and at a period, longer still.

1

You will not often find a book, in which all the stops are just as they should be; you should therefore make the same stops when you read, as when you talk. You should also speak your words, when reading, as when talking.

LESSON II.

THE GIRL WHO ATE TOO MUCH.

Bess was a fine girl of eight years old, who could run, and jump, and play, for hours. She was strong and well, and might have been so for a long time, if she had been good and done as she was bid. But she was too fond of cakes, and would eat all she could find; and she would eat fruit that was not ripe.

Her mother bid her not to eat so much, or some day she would be made sick by the trash she put down her throat; but Bess would not mind her. one day she became very sick, and was put to bed and she had pills to take, which she did not like.

She was sick eight long days, and lay in bed all that time in a dark room. She had such a pain in her head, that she could not bear to see the light, or hear, the birds sing. When she got up at last, she could, not stand or walk, she was so weak. She could not, run, or jump, or play, for a long time; nor could she, run in the fields, or eat ripe fruit with the good boys, and girls.

But while she was ill, and could not sleep at night she thought a great deal; and she found that those, who told her not to eat too much were good friends to her, and that she had done wrong not to mind them.

When Bess was quite well, she took great care about what she ate, and to do all that she was bid to do: so she grew strong, and was soon able to walk and run again.

What was Bess too fond of? What could she eat? Was she sick? How long? What did she think of while she was sick?

LESSON III.

DEFINITIONS.

Weak, not strong. Impudent, saucy. Fierce, furious, cruel. Prints, pictures.

What is the opposite of Sick? Of Tall? Of Hard? First? Down?

LITTLE CHARLES.

Charles was eight years old, and did not know how to read or write; this would have been a great shame, had it been quite his own fault; but it was not. His old aunt, in whose house he was, lay sick in bed more than half the year, and was too weak to teach him, nor did she send him to school, till her maid, Grace, told her that he was grown so impudent that she could not bear him.

Then his aunt told Grace to take the boy out with her, and leave him at school. The first day he went with good will; but when he was there, and found what he had to do, he did not like it. So the next day, when Grace put on her cloak to go with him, he said, " I will not go to school; I will play with the cat at home."

Grace said, " You must go," and took his hand. But he gave her a hard slap, and said, " No, I won't. " So Grace said no more, but went out of the room, and soon came back with a great, tall, strong man, to whom she said " take up that child and come with me."

The man did as he was bid; and Charles did not dare to strike him, for he had a fierce look and a large stick. So Charles was brought to school in the man's arms; and it made all the boys laugh to see him put down on the floor like a bag of corn.

Grace said it was the way he should go the next day, if he was not a good boy. Charles saw there

was no help for him, so he thought it best to do at
once what he was bid.

At last he found out it was a good thing to go to
school and learn; for his poor old aunt was so glad,
when she heard he could spell and read, that she
gave him books with prints in them, of men, and
beasts, and birds, and trees.

When Charles had got so far that he could write
and cipher, his aunt was so kind as to buy a horse
for him to ride in the fields, and up and down the
hills that were near her house. So he found it was
well for him to do as his aunt wished to have him.

LESSON IV.

THE LITTLE GIRL WHO WAS KIND TO OTHERS.

Ann was a child of five years old, who was good
and kind to all. The girls who went to school with
her were fond of her; and the beasts and birds a-
round the house would come when they heard her
voice. All the fowls in the yard would run to her
as soon as they saw her: and she was glad when she
had leave to feed them.

One day when she came home from school she met
her mother, who gave her a cake; and as it was a fine
day she went to the field at the back of the house to
eat it.

She had just sat down by the fence, when a poor
thin dog came to look at her; she gave him a small
bit of her cake, and saw him eat it and wag his tail.
Then an old man came out of a poor hut to call
the dog; and Ann saw that he too was thin, and pale,
and sick.

So she gave him a large piece of her cake; and he
said, "Thank you, good child!" and ate it, and told
her that it did him good. The old man and his dog
then went back to the hut and Ann ate the small bit

of cake that was left, and felt much better than if she had eaten the whole.

Yet she was fond of cakes; and I am not sure, if the old man and his dog had been fat and strong, that she would have thought of giving them a bit, as they did not ask for it; but she saw that they were in great want, which put her in mind to share with them.

It was not long before Ann had another cake. As soon as she had got it, she went to look for the old man and his dog, but could not find them; and she met a boy who told her that they were grown fat and well, and were gone to their own home, a great way off.

LESSON V.

THE GIRL WHO TOLD LIES.

Rose was a sad girl. She did not tell the truth; no one could trust to a word she said; and she had got such a bad name, that if some one said, " Rose told me the grapes were ripe," some one else would say, 'Then I am sure they are not ripe, for Rose does not tell the truth.'

One morning when there was a hard frost, as she ran by the road side, her foot slid on some ice, and she fell down. She felt a great pain in one leg, which made her scream and cry out; and she could not move that leg, nor stir from the spot where she lay.

A man who came that way in great haste said, "Are you hurt?" and Rose said "Oh! yes: I have broken my leg." But when the man saw who she was, he thought she did not say the truth, and so he went away.

Then came a girl with a milk-pail on her head, and Rose said, " Pray help me; my leg is broke." And the girl put down her pail; but she came near and saw it was Rose who spoke: then she said, " I

1*

dare say this is not true, and I have no time to lose." So she took up her pail and went on.

Poor Rose was in great pain, and she told two or three more, who came by, the sad state she was in; but as they all knew her, they thought it was false, and would not stop. So she lay there for two hours with no one to help her, and thought what a sad thing it was that nobody would believe her.

At last a man came that way who did not know Rose, and said, "Why do you cry and moan so?" She said, "I have broken my leg, and no one will help me or take me home." This good man then said, " Poor child! do not cry so; I will take you home. "

So he took Rose in his arms, and brought her home ; and though he went slow, and took care not to hurt her, yet she felt great pain, and it made her cry and moan by the way.

Her friends wept when they saw her so much hurt. Her leg had grown stiff in the two hours she lay on the ground; she felt great pain when the bone was set, and she had caught a bad cold.

She had to lie in bed a long time; and could not run or jump for four months; but in this time she thought a great deal ; and when the cough shook her and hurt her leg, she felt that if she had been known to tell the truth, she might have had no cough.

All this made Rose think what a bad thing it was to tell lies ; and when she got well she did not tell any more. And her friends were all very glad, and grew very fond of her, when they found that they could trust her word.

LESSON VI.

DEFINITIONS.

Wise, judicious. Gather, to bring together. Idle, lazy, not busy.

Tell me the opposite of Big. Higher. Pleasant. Went. Pull. Come. Build. Well. Good.

THE IDLE BOY WHO BECAME A GOOD BOY.

There was a little boy; he was not a big boy, for if he had been a big boy, I suppose he would have been wiser! but this was a little boy, not higher than the table, and his papa and mama sent him to school.

It was a very pleasant morning; the sun shone and the birds sung on the trees. Now this little boy did not much love his book, for he was but a silly little boy as I told you; and he had a great mind to play instead of going to school.

And he saw a bee flying about, first upon one flower, and then upon another; so he said, Pretty bee! will you come and play with me? But the bee said, No, I must not be idle; I must go and gather honey.

Then the little boy met a dog; and he said, Dog! will you play with me? But the dog said, No, I must not be idle; I am going to drive the pigs out of my master's garden.

Then the little boy went by a hay-stack, and he saw a bird pulling some hay out of the hay-stack; and he said, Bird! will you come and play with me? But the bird said, No, I must not be idle; I must get some hay to build my nest with, and some moss, and some wool. So the bird flew away.

Then the little boy saw a horse, and he said, Horse! will you play with me? But the horse said, No; I must not be idle; I must go and plough, or else there will be no corn to make bread of.

Then the little boy thought with himself, what, is nobody idle? then little boys must not be idle. So he made haste, and went to school, and learned his lesson very well and the master said he was a very good boy.

LESSON VII.

DEFINITIONS.

Neat, cleanly. Careful, watchful. Cleanse, to make clean.

Tell me the opposite of Remember. Whole. Smooth. Little. Dirty. Go.

ABOUT BEING NEAT.

I have sometimes seen a child go to school with dirty hands, a dirty face, and a dirty book; but I do not remember that I ever heard such a child read very well, and I am sure nobody could like to look at him.

A neat scholar will wash his face and hands before he comes to school, and be very careful to keep his clothes and books free from dirt. And he will want to have the school room kept very neat. He would sweep it himself, almost every day, rather than have the floor covered with leaves and dirt.

If he has a writing-book, you will not see a single blot in the whole of it. The corners of the leaves will not be rolled over, like a dog's ears, but will be kept smooth and clean. A neat scholar will not go into a house without cleaning his shoes, if they are dirty. He will spit as little as may be; and will not whittle chairs or benches.

LESSON VIII.

DEFINITIONS.

Gnaw, to wear away by biting. Delighted, much pleased. Allow, to permit.— Children are not allowed to be noisy at school. Troublesome, giving trouble.—A scholar who does not come to school in season, is troublesome; because he disturbs others. Sip, to drink a little at a time. Angry, very much displeased. Persuade, to make another willing, by talking to him or treating him kindly. Presently, soon. Thrust, to push. Appear, to be in sight. Valuable, worth a great deal.

Tell me the opposite of better. Of Always. Mistress. Loved. Summer. Nothing. Danger. Carry. Found. Sorry. Mother.

MARY AND HER KID.

Kids are little goats. Goats do not like to live in the streets and houses, like the dogs. Goats love to run and jump about in the woods, and to gnaw the bark of trees. A goat is a little larger than a sheep.

It is between two and three feet high; that is about as high as a table. Goats give very good milk. People carry them to sea, because they are smaller than cows, and do not take up so much room in the ship.

The skins of goats are made into leather. The skins of kids make very nice gloves. Handles for knives and forks, are made of goats' horns. Their flesh, tallow, and hair are also valuable.

Mary, a little girl, who lived in a place where there are many goats, taking a walk one day, found a little kid; its mother, the old goat, had left it; it was almost dead.

Mary felt sorry for the poor little kid; she took it up, hugged it in her arms, and carried it home with her. She begged her mother to let her keep the kid for her own. Her mother gave her leave. Mary got a basket full of clean straw, and laid it on the warm hearth, for a bed for the kid. She warmed some milk and held it to him to drink. The kid drank it, and licked Mary's hands for more. Mary was delighted when she saw him jump out of the basket, and run about the room; presently, he lay down again, and took a comfortable nap.

The next day Mary gave her kid a name; she called him Capriole. She showed him to all the family, and allowed her little brothers and sisters to pat him.

Capriole soon followed Mary all about the house; trotted by her side into the yard; ran races with her in the fields; and fed out of her hand. He soon grew troublesome, and thrust his nose into the meal tub. Sometimes he got a blow for sipping the milk.

Capriole's little horns soon began to appear, and a white beard soon sprouted at the end of his chin. He grew bold enough to fight when he was angry, and sometimes threw down Colin, Mary's little brother, into the dirt. Every body said, " Capriole is getting too saucy ; he must be sent away, or be taught to behave better. "

Mary always took his part, and let him do as he pleased. Capriole loved his little mistress dearly. Near to Mary's house, were some large fields, and some tall rocks ; a little further off was a high hill.

One fine summer's day, Mary had finished her morning's work, and wanted to play with her kid. She looked about the house door and could not see Capriole. She then ran to the field, and called aloud "Capriole! Capriole!" expecting to see him come running towards her. No Capriole came.

Her heart began to beat. "What can have become of him? Somebody must have stolen him. Perhaps the neighbours' dogs have killed him. Oh my Capriole! my dear Capriole! I shall never see you again."

Mary began to cry; but she still went on, looking all around, and calling "Capriole! Capriole!" After a while she heard the voice of Capriole. She looked up, and saw her little goat, standing on the edge of a high rock ; she was afraid to call him, lest he should jump down and break his neck.

There was no danger; Capriole had run away from his mistress; he liked the fields and the rocks better than he liked Mary. She waited for him, however, till she was tired, and then went home, and got her little brothers to go back with her, to the foot of the hill. They carried some bread and milk for Capriole, but they could not persuade him back again: he had found a herd of goats, and they were playing together. So Mary bade him good bye.

What is a kid? What do goats love to do! How high are goats? Where carried? Of what use are their skins? Horns? The skins of kid? What did Mary do with the kid she found? What else? What did he soon become? What was said of him? What became of him?

LESSON IX.

DEFINITIONS.

Depend, to rely on. Affronted, provoked. Determined, resolved. Convenience, ease, accommodation.
Tell me the opposite of Lend. Willing. Proper. Lost. Run. Night.

MARY AND SARAH.

Mary. I wish you would lend me your thimble, Sarah, for I can never find mine when I want it.

Sarah. And why can you not find it, Mary?

Mary. I am sure I cannot tell, but if you do not choose to lend me yours, I can borrow of somebody else.

Sarah. I am willing to lend it to you, but I should like to have you tell me why you always come to me to borrow when you have lost any thing?

Mary. Because you never lose your things, and always know where to find them.

Sarah. And how, think you, do I always know where to find my things?

Mary. How can I tell? If I knew I might sometimes contrive to find my own.

Sarah. I will tell you the secret if you will hear it. I have a set place for every thing, and after I have done using a thing, I always put it in its proper place, and never leave it to be thrown about and lost.

Mary. I never can find time to put my things away; and who wants, as soon as she has used a thing, to have to run and put it away, as if one's life depended upon it?

Sarah. Your life does not depend upon it, Mary, but your convenience does; and let me ask, how much more time will it take to put a thing in its proper place than to hunt after it when lost, or borrow of your friends?

Mary. Well, I will never borrow of you again, you may depend upon it.

Sarah. Why, you are not affronted, I hope.

Mary. No but I am ashamed, and am determined before night to have a place for every thing, and to keep every thing in its place.

How can one always know where to find things? What depends on doing this? What else? *The convenience of others.*

LESSON X.

DEFINITIONS.

Meadow, moist level ground, covered with grass and flowers. Cluster, a bunch. Affectionate, fond, tender. Trouble, uneasiness. Playful, sportive, lively. Overjoyed, much pleased. Caper, to jump about playfully. Dispute, to say a thing is not so. Credit, honor, character. Intend, to mean. Wholesome, healthy. Fruit, apples, pears, cherries, &c. Greedy, eager to eat.

Tell me the opposite of Large. Ripe. Pleased. Happy. Ran. Best. Glad. Agree. Foolishly. Kind. Great. Carried. Sick.

JACK AND HIS SISTERS.

There was a large grape vine that ran up an oak tree in a meadow, about half a mile from the house. The vine hung full of grapes, in large clusters. When they were ripe and very fine, Jack invited his sisters to go there with him one fair day, and get some. The little girls were so pleased with going that they were ready in two minutes.

Their mother smiled to see them go off so brisk and happy, and so affectionate to each other. "Little birds," she said to herself, as they went out through the gate, "they have no trouble or care."

Amnon, the pet lamb, ran playfully along after the children, and Mary said they could let him go as well as not. Jack let down the bars for the girls, and the lamb skipped through with them.

When little Betsey came under the vine, and saw the great bunches of grapes over her head, she jumped and hallooed, "O! O! O! I never did see such a sight, in all my life. What a parcel! O, I wish my ma was here, to see this grape tree."

The pet lamb cared nothing about the grapes; but, seeing Betsey so overjoyed, seemed to think she was playing with him. He began to hop up and down too, and they both jumped and capered very much alike.

The grapes were indeed very fine. Mary said they were nearly as large as robins' eggs, almost as sweet as honey, and that she had never tasted any half so good. The color was dark purple. The vine ran over the whole of the oak tree.

Jack climbed up among the branches, and the girls held their aprons to catch the beautiful clusters, as he threw them down, till they got their aprons heaping full. Then he scrambled down to the lower limb, and jumped from that to the ground.

"Now, girls," said he, "I will tell you what we will do. We will spread these grapes on this clean grass, and sort them and pick out the very best bunches to carry home to pa and ma." "O yes," said Mary, "that is right; so we will."

"Yes, brother Jack," said little Betsey, "you are a good boy." She was pleased about giving the best grapes to her father and mother, though the little parrot could hardly speak all her words.

"They will be glad," said Jack," to see that we think so much about them." "Yes," said Mary; " and another thing; let us agree never to quarrel and be cross to each other."

" If you see me get angry, and act foolishly, do you tell me of it, so that I may leave it off, and behave better, and I will do the same with you; because it is very bad for brothers and sisters to dispute, and you know father and mother are always so pleased, when they see us kind to each other."

" Yes, I know that," said Jack: " We can never pay our parents all we owe them, for being so good to us; but we ought to do all we can to make them happy and keep up the credit of our family." The little girls both said they would try with all their might.

" Yes," said Jack, " that is what all good children should do. When I become a great man, pa and ma will be old grey-headed people, and have wrinkles in their faces, like old Mr. Allen and his wife; and then I intend to take care of them."

When they carried home the grapes to their mother, Mary said, "Did you ever, in your life, ma, taste any thing so good?" " They are very fine, indeed, my dear," said Mrs. Halyard. " We picked out all the best, ma," said Mary, " for you and pa." " Ah, my children, " said their mother, " then I shall tell your father of that good action, when he comes, and he will like the grapes very much."

" Ma" 'said Jack, " are not grapes very wholesome to eat?" " Yes, my son," said she, " most kinds of fruit are wholesome, if they are ripe ,and eaten a little at a time."

" The best thing may become hurtful, when taken to excess; and children frequently make themselves sick, with good things, by being too greedy. To be sure, people must eat, in order to live; but I wish my children always to remember that eating is not the chief thing they are to live for."

LESSON XI.

DEFINITIONS.

Hut, a poor small house. Vegetable, a plant, an herb. Coachman, one who drives a coach. Pious, religious. Amuse, to please with harmless play. It sometimes means to deceive artfully. Innocent, that which does not hurt. Infant, a very young child. Food, victuals.

Tell me the opposite of Able. Of Near. Open. Busy. Poor. Honest. Often. Old. Found. Cold. Out. Asleep. Some. Useful. Fetch.

THE OLD MAN AND LITTLE PETER.

There was once a poor old lame man; he had been a soldier, and had almost lost the use of one leg, so he was not able to do much work. He built himself a little hut, and made a garden where he planted potatoes, beans, and such other vegetables as he wanted to eat.

All the money he got was given to him by people for opening a gate near his hut. People riding in coaches do not like to have the coachman leave the horses to open a gate; they are willing to give any body a few cents to do it for them.

The money which the poor man got in this way was enough to buy him clothes, and such other things as he wanted. This poor man was very honest, so every body thought well of him. He was pious, too; he prayed to God every night and morning; he thought of God often, and he tried to please God.

This old man, in a walk one day found a little kid, that had lost its mother, and was almost starved. He took it home, and fed it, and nursed it, so that it grew very large and strong. He called the goat Nan.

Nan loved her master; she ran after him like a little dog, and ate the grass which grew round his door.

She often played very prettily, so that she amused her master with her innocent tricks. The old man would lift up his eyes and thank God, that he had given him this faithful creature.

One cold night in the beginning of winter, the old man thought he heard a child cry; he got up, lighted a candle, went out at the door, and looking all about, he soon found a little baby lying on the ground. The old man knew not what to do.

"I can hardly take care of myself," said he; "what shall I do with a poor infant? If I leave it here, the little creature will die before morning. I will take it in, and give it some food."

Saying this he took up the little boy, who was covered with only a few rags. The infant smiled, and stretched out his arms towards the old man. When he had brought it into the hut, he called his goat, Nan; her little kid was just dead, and she had milk to spare.

Nan was quite willing to nurse the little boy; he sucked till he had enough, and then fell asleep. The old man took the child to his bosom, and went to bed. He felt happy, because he had done a good action. Early next morning, he waked, and gave the infant some of Nan's milk.

"Who knows," said the old man, "but this child may live to be a man, and that God will make him good and happy. When he grows bigger he will be a comfort to me; he will learn to be useful, to fetch my wood, and dig in the garden."

The little boy grew fast, and loved the old man dearly; and he loved the goat too. She would lie down, and little Peter would crawl on his hands and knees close to her, and go to sleep in her bosom.

In a short time Peter could walk, and he soon learned to talk a little. He called the old man " Daddy," and the goat he called " Mammy." He used to run about after his Mammy.

At night the old man would take Peter upon his knee, and talk to him while their supper was boiling over the fire. When Peter grew bigger, he opened the gate for his Daddy, and learned to get the breakfast and dinner. The old man used to tell Peter stories, and amuse him very much.

Can you tell me something you are able to do? Something else? Something you are not able to do? Something which is work? Something else? What is better than money? Why? Who makes doors? Of what? The hinges? Of what? How? What is iron made of? What are candles made of? What else gives light?

LESSON XII.

DEFINITIONS.

Desire, wish. Grieved, made sorrowful. Grateful, feeling that another has been kind. Daddy, a child's name for father.

Tell me the opposite of Faithful. Of Crying. Fast. Lady. Long. Gave. Day.

MORE ABOUT LITTLE PETER.

The old man had a great desire that his darling should learn to read and write, but he had neither books, nor pens, nor paper. In the summer the old man would sit at his cottage door, and draw letters in the sand; he taught Peter their names, and taught him to make them. Peter soon learned all the letters of the alphabet, and he soon learned to put them together, in syllables and words.

About this time Peter's faithful nurse, Nanny, died. While she was sick, Peter took great care of her; he tried to make her take food, and held her head upon his little bosom. All would not make her well; she died, and Peter was very much grieved.

The poor goat was buried in the garden; Peter would go there, and call upon his mammy, and ask her why she had left him. One day as he was calling

2*

Nanny, and crying, a lady came along in a carriage: she overheard Peter.

As soon as Peter heard some one call, "open the gate," he ran as fast as he could. The lady asked him whom he was calling, and why he cried so. Peter answered, it was for his poor mammy, that was buried in the garden.

"How did your mammy get her living?" asked the lady. "She used to eat grass," said Peter. The lady did not know what he meant; but the old man came out of his hut, and told her the whole story of Peter.

She looked at the boy, who had dried up his tears, and was playing at the coach door; she was much pleased with him. "Will you go with me, little boy?" said she; "I will take care of you if you behave well."

"No," said Peter, "I must stay with daddy; he has taken care of me for a long time, and now I must take care of him." The lady was pleased with this answer; it showed Peter to be a grateful boy.

She put her hand in her pocket, and took out her purse; she found half a dollar in it, which she gave to Peter, and bid him buy some shoes and stockings; then she went away.

Peter knew how to use money; he had been sent to buy bread, and such things as his daddy wanted; but he did not know much about shoes and stockings. He had seen them upon others, but he had never worn any in his life. The next day the old man made him go to the town and lay out his money.

Peter had not been gone long, before his daddy saw him come back, without his shoes and stockings. "What have you done with your money, Peter?" said the old man.

"Daddy," answered Peter, "I went to the store, and just put on shoes and stockings, but I did not like them; so I laid out the money for a warm waistcoat for you; winter is coming, and you will be cold."

Did Peter have any books? How did he learn to read? What became of Nanny? What can you tell me of the lady? Was

Peter willing to go home with her? Why? What did this show him to be? What did she give him? For what? Did he buy them? What did he buy?

Can you name something which you have a desire to do? Something else? Something else? Something you have a desire not to do? Should we always be grateful to those who take care of us? Who takes care of you? Of all people? Are children grateful who do not mind their parents? Their teachers? Who do not thank God for taking care of them? If Peter had chosen to buy warm clothes for himself, while the old man who took care of him had none, what would he have been?

LESSON XIII.

DEFINITIONS.

Obedience, doing as one is told. Difficult, hard, not easy. Fatigued, tired. Patient, willing to wait quietly.

LITTLE HARRY.

"Grandmother, when do you think mother will be at home?" said little Harry, as he seated himself upon the floor at her feet.

"It will not be long before we shall see her," said his grandmother, "as it is almost dark."

"I wish it would grow dark faster," said Harry, "for I want to tell her about my shoes, and all that lady said."

"You must try to be patient, my little boy," said his grandmother; and she took off her spectacles, and laying aside the apron she was mending for Harry, took him up in her lap. This little boy loved his grandmother, and always liked to sit in her lap.

"What is the reason, grandmother, that you wear spectacles? I should not think you could see to work or read with them. When I put them on, I can but just see you; and you look so funny, that I can hardly tell where your eyes and nose are."

"My eyes are not so good as yours are, Harry, and

I could not see to work at all without these spectacles."

"But I thought old people could do every thing a great deal better than little boys, said Harry."

"They know a great deal better how to do things, but they often cannot do them as well," said his grandmother: "they often cannot see as well, or hear as well, or walk as well ; but then they can teach little boys a great deal, and tell them what they can do with their eyes, and their ears, and their l.mbs, to make them useful before they grow old."

"What can I do with my eyes, grandmother, that is useful ?" said Harry.

"A great many things, my dear ; you can find my needle when I happen to drop it, and you know you have learned to thread it for me ; and when my spectacles are out of the way, you know I say, 'come, Harry, bring my spectacles for me ;' and when you come and use your eyes for me, you make them useful, and make me very happy to think that besides my own eyes, I have a pair in your little head."

"I hope, grandmother, you will always let me thread your needles for you," said Harry ; "and I dare say there are some other things I might do for you if you would let me."

"There are other things that you already do for me," said his grandmother ; "besides helping me with your eyes, you sometimes also use your feet for me. Don t you remember when I was sick the other day, you went to the Doctor's for me ? and often when my old limbs are tired, you use your young ones, and bring me what I want, while mine are resting."

While Harry and his grandmother were talking together in this pleasant way, the time which Harry thought would be so long, was passed, and his mother came home.

As soon as Harry saw her, he jumped down and ran to her saying, "Mother, mother, I have got a pair of shoes ; now may I not go to school ?"

" I am too tired to attend to you now, Harry," said his mother ; " so run off."

Harry was grieved at his mother's not hearing the long story he had to tell her about his shoes ; but he left her as soon as she bid him, and did not say a word. Harry had learnt the best lesson a little boy can learn, which is obedience, and he did not find it so difficult to be quiet, as some children might suppose.

Harry's mother was strong, and had been out doing a hard day's work, and w s s much fatigued that she felt too sick to talk till she had taken her supper. When she felt better, she said, " now Harry, you may come and tell me about your shoes ; how did you get them ?"

Harry now began to tell his mother all about the lady who had been there in the morning, and brought him the shoes.

" It was the same lady, mother, that came the other day, and told you about that school, where they teach children to read and count, and show them pictures and tell them stories. Now, mother, may I not go ? for the lady said she wanted me to go, and she brought me these shoes on purpose."

" Yes, child, you shall go, and I will bless them that keep you out of mischief, and give you more learn- ing."

- When Harry had got his mother's leave to his go- ing to school, he went to bed. He did not yet know that when he lay down to sleep, the Being who made the sun to shine, took care of him in the night, and always watched over him. He had not yet learned that when he was good, he pleased this good Being, who made the whole world and every thing in it.

What can you tell me about little Harry ? About his grand- mother ? Mother ?

Should children always try to be patient when they have to wait for what they want ? Should children practise obedience ? To whom ? To whom else ? When do they not practise it ? Can you name something which you would find difficult ? Do you never get fatigued ? When ? Who makes the sun to shine ? Who made the world ?

LESSON XIV.

DEFINITIONS.

Enter, to go in. Repeat, to say over. Attentively, carefully. Quiet, still.

Tell me the opposite of Much. Of Black. Ask Right. Forget.

MORE ABOUT LITTLE HARRY.

The wished-for morning soon came, and Harry awoke full of life, and was soon in readiness to go to school with his mother, who was glad to take her little boy to a place where so good care would be taken of him.

And now we suppose Harry in a school-room for the first time. When he went in, he felt a little troubled at seeing so many faces he did not know; and he thought he should rather be in his grandmother's lap than even in this school, where he had so much wished to come.

But the school-mistress spoke very kindly to him and showed him some pictures; and after she had talked with him a little while, Harry was willing to stay, and in a short time felt as happy as he expected to feel.

It so happened that he was seated on a bench with a little boy he knew, and this made him feel quite at home. After a little while, all the boys and girls were seated in their different places, and when all was quiet, the school-mistress spoke to the children all together, and asked them if they would like to repeat their morning hymn.

All that were old enough then stood up, and repeated something which Harry did not quite understand. They were singing a morning hymn. He did not know what a morning hymn meant. It was not long, however, before Harry understood that a morning hymn was a song of praise God to for taking care of us through the night, and for letting us enjoy another day.

After this the school-mistress went to a large black slate, and with a piece of white chalk made some letters. Harry noticed every thing she did. When she made one letter, she asked the children its name. They almost all said, A.

Harry looked at this letter very attentively, and saw that it seemed to stand upon two legs and had a little bar across it. She then made another letter that was like a ring, and this was O. And another which looked like a gate, and this was H.

Harry kept his eyes all the time on the slate, and noticed the difference in the letters, so that he might remember them when he saw them again. The school-mistress saw how attentive Harry had been, and when the lesson was over, she went up to him and said, "your name is Harry, is it not, my little boy?"

"Yes ma'am," said Harry.

"I shall remember, then," said she, "and always call you by your right name, Harry and n t Billy, or Tommy, and you must try to remember to call all my letters by their right names ; I hope the next time you see them you will not forget their names, and I will try not to forget yours."

What troubled little Harry when he first went into school? How did the mistress speak to him? Whom did he sit with? What did the scholars repeat? What is meant by morning hymn? How did the teacher show the children the letters?

LESSON XV.

DEFINITIONS.

Differ, to be unlike. Pouch, a small bag. Chap, (*pron. chop*) the upper or under part of an animal's mouth. Down, soft feathers. Jaw, the bone of the mouth in which the teeth are fixed. Torpid, dull, stupid. Gluttonous, fond of eating a great deal. Food, victuals. Surface, the outside.

Tell me the opposite of Wet. Of lazy. Under. Empty. Downwards.

Do you know why the rain does not make the birds very wet? Why, it is because their feathers are oily, so that the rain does not easily soak through them. Their wings are very strong. A swan could break a man's leg with his wing.

THE PELICAN.

The Pelican is a large bird weighing over twenty pounds. It differs from all other birds in its bill, and the great pouch under it.

The pouch hangs at the lower edge of the chap, and will hold fifteen quarts of water; it reaches the whole length of the bill to the neck : this bag is covered with a very soft down, and when empty can scarcely be seen, as the bird wrinkles it up into the lower jaw.

These birds are very torpid and very gluttonous. When in search of food they fly over the water with one eye turned downwards, and as soon as they see a fish near the surface, they dart down swiftly, and are almost sure to seize it and store it up in their pouch.

Why do not birds get quite wet when it rains? How much will a pelican weigh? How much more than a hen? Four or five times as much. What hangs at the lower edge of the pelican's under chap? How much will it hold?

LESSON XVI.

DEFINITIONS.

Ambition, desire of honor. Jovial, merry. Resolute, bold, determined. Tattling, apt to tell tales.

Major Wilson had a son, named Isaac, about ten years old, and Isaac was inclined to be quite idle, and childish. His father was very anxious to have him do well; but was afraid he would never make a man of honor and usefulness.

Isaac was a stout, hearty boy; but he seemed to have no manly ambition. In the winter he would sit moping in the corner, without reading so much as a newspaper, or caring whether Canada was North or South from the United States.

The neighboring boys, one cold day in February, had a jovial time, skating, and sliding down hill on their sleds. Some of them ran, as brisk as squirrels, to ask Major Wilson to let Isaac come and play with them. "O yes, by all means," said Major Wilson: "I was once a boy myself:

> "Yes, I'm for the lad that's active in play,
> "And thorough at work; that's much the best way."

"Go Isaac, by all means, and have a lively time with your mates:" but Isaac, scowling, shrugged up his shoulders and said he did not want to play in the cold. "Poor little child," said Solomon Belmot, "he wants his hands wrapped up in his mamma's warm apron." So these boys ran back to the rest to enjoy their sport.

"Halloo, boys," said the others, "where is Isaac?" "O," said Solomon, "he is sitting in the corner to keep the cat from eating the tongs. That is all he will ever be good for: the ninny is too lazy even to play."

This Solomon Belmot lived at a place called "Briar Hill," on account of the multitude of black-berries which grew there. Solomon was an active lad among the boys, and heartily earnest, in whatever he engaged; but he was so very fond of a joke, that he would often say things a little improper, in order to make people laugh.

This turn of mind was unfortunate, and sometimes created difficulty, where he did not intend it. He was more inclined to practise this harshness of speech because his mother did so, though she was a good sort of a woman in other respects, and had the name of

3

making the best cheese of any farmer's wife about "Briar Hill."

Major Wilson was mortified, at having such an idle lubber as Isaac for a son. He was much troubled to determine what to do with him. After some time he thought of Jack Halyard, and concluded that the best thing he could do, would be to get so good a scholar to come and live a while at his house.

Jack's father agreed to let him go home with Major Wilson: but told him to be careful not to spend his time in boyish play with Isaac, and do him more hurt than good. This was in the month of May.

Jac stayed five weeks, and in all that time went home only once. During these five weeks, Isaac was so altered, he hardly appeared to be the same boy.

He was more active, more resolute, more manly in his conduct, had better ideas of things, and began to love learning.

Before that time Isaac was afraid to go out alone after dark; but Jack cured him of that foolish whim, and many others. He used to make up a pitiful face, and think he was almost killed, if he hurt his finger or toe; but after Jack had been with him, he was ashamed to snivel or squeal for every trifling affair.

One day, as they were in a pasture together, Isaac was frightened almost to death, at the sight of a rattle snake. He ran and screamed, as if the terrible creature was going to swallow him alive; but Jack, without being at all afraid, got a good stick and killed the snake.

What sort of a boy was Isaac? What did Solomon say of him? What kind of a boy was Solomon? What mortified Major Wilson? Whom did he send for? Is it a good thing to be resolute? Why? Of what did Jack cure Isaac?

LESSON XVII.

MORE ABOUT ISAAC WILSON.

"These animals," said Jack, "I have heard my father say, are like tattling, mischief-making people: they are very poisonous; but dangerous only when they creep in secret, and bite before they are seen."

When Jack had been at Major Wilson's about a week, he met Solomon Belmot in the road, and the following dialogue took place.

Jack. Good morning, Solomon.

Solomon. Good morning, Jack: I see you are going about with Isaac Wilson, and the people say you have come to live there a while, and try to make something of him.

Jack. I expect to stay there, till my father begins his haying and harvest.

Sol. You will find Isaac very much like the jockey's horse, that had but two failings.

Jack. What were those two?

Sol. One was, the horse was bad to catch.

Jack. What was the other?

Sol. When they had caught him, he was good for nothing.

Jack. I hope Isaac is not so bad as the horse you tell of; he will make a very decent man yet, if he will try in earnest.

Sol. Ay, there is the difficulty, my good fellow, who can change that bag of sand into a smart boy?

Jack. I should hardly think that any young lad would be such a dolt, as not to try to make himself respectable in the world.

Sol. You might as well teach a fish to eat grass in the fields, as to make any thing of that lazy fellow.

Jack. We should be very careful, Solomon, about speaking evil of our neighbors. Good bye.

Sol. Good morning.

Jack talked much and very sensibly with Isaac and took great pains to teach him by example, which his father had told him was the best teaching in the, world.

Among other things which the boys read together, was the thirteenth chapter of the first book of Corinthians. St. Paul says, "When I was a child, I spoke as a child; I thought as a child; I understood as a child : but when I became a man, I put away childish things."

Isaac began to wake from his babyish dreams, and to think of becoming a man of talents and merit. He told his father he was determined to exert himself in all that was good. He found that he slept better, and felt altogether better, when he had been well employed through the day.

Major Wilson was so much pleased with the change in his son, that he said Jack Halyard was worth five times his weight in gold ; and he made him a present of a likely colt, which was just weaned. Jack thanked him very politely ; but said this was much more than he had any reason to expect. Major Wilson insisted on his taking the colt.

" My good little friend," said the Major to Jack, —and he almost shed tears while he said it,—" the great happiness of parents is seeing their children do well. If Isaac should ever make an honorable man, it will be in part owing to what you have done for him, and I should not regret giving ten times as much. Take this colt. I hope, my dear fellow, you may live to ride him to Congress.

Can you tell any thing which Jack and Solomon said to each other ? How did Major Wilson like the change in his son ? What did he give to Jack ? What was the reason of Isaac's becoming a better boy ? Are we always apt to be like those whom we are often with ? Whom then should we choose for our friends ? Those who know most and behave best. What is the great happiness of parents ?

LESSON XVIII.

THE LITTLE PHILOSOPHER.

Mr. L. was one morning riding by himself, when, dismounting to gather a plant in the hedge, his horse got loose and galloped away before him. He followed, calling the horse by his name, when he stopped, but on his approach set off again. At length a little boy in the neighboring field, seeing the affair, ran across where the road made a turn, and getting before the horse took him by the bridle, and held him till his owner came up.

Mr. L. looked at the boy, and admired his ruddy, cheerful countenance. Thank you, my good lad ! (said he) you have caught my horse very cleverly. What shall I give you for your trouble? (putting his hand into his pocket.)

Boy. I want nothing, sir.

Mr. L. Don't you? so much the better for you. Few men can say as much. But pray what were you doing in the field?

B. I was rooting up weeds, and tending the sheep that are feeding on the turnips, and keeping the crows from the corn.

Mr. L. And do you like this employment?

B. Yes sir, very well, this fine weather.

Mr. L. But would you not rather play?

B. This is not hard work; it is almost as good as play.

Mr. L. Who sent you to work?

B. My father, sir.

Mr. L. Where does he live?

B. Just by, among the trees, there, sir.

Mr. L. What is his name?

B. Thomas Hurdle, sir.

Mr. L. And what is yours?

B. Peter, sir.

Mr. L. How old are you?

B. I shall be eight, thanksgiving day.

Mr. L. How long have you been out in this field?

B. Ever since six in the morning, sir.

Mr. L. And are you hungry?

B. Yes, sir, I shall go to my dinner, soon.

Mr. L. If you had six-pence now, what would you do with it?

B. I don't know ; I never had so much in my life.

Mr. L. Have you no playthings?

B. Playthings? what are they?

Mr. L. Such as balls, nine-pins, marbles, tops, and wooden horses.

3*

B. No, sir; but our Tom makes foot-balls to kick in the cold weather, and we set traps for birds; and then I have a jumping pole and a pair of stilts to walk through the dirt with; and I had a hoop, but it broke.

Mr. L. And do you want nothing else?

B. No, I have hardly time for those; for I always ride the horses to the field, and bring up the cows, and run to the town on errands, and that is as good as play, you know.

Mr. L. Well, but you could buy apples or ginger-bread, at the town, I suppose, if you had money.

B. O, I can get apples at home; and as for gingerbread, I don't mind it much, for my mother gives me a piece of pie now and then, and that is as good.

Mr. L. Would you not like a knife to cut sticks?

B. I have one — here it is — brother Tom gave it to me.

Mr. L. Your shoes are full of holes—don't you want a better pair?

B. I have a better pair for Sundays.

Mr. L. But these let in water.

B. O, I don't care for that.

Mr. L. Your hat is all torn too.

B. I have a better hat at home, but I would as soon have none at all, for it hurts my head.

Mr. L. What do you do when it rains?

B. If it rains very hard, I get under the fence till it is over.

Mr. L. What do you do when you are hungry before it is time to go home?

B. I sometimes eat a raw turnip.

Mr. L. But if there are none?

B. Then I do as well as I can; I work on, and never think of it.

Mr. L. Are you not dry sometimes, this hot weather?

B. Yes, but there is water enough.

Mr. L. Why, my little fellow, you are quite a philosopher.

B. Sir?

Mr. L. I say you are a philosopher; but I am sure you do not know what that means.

B. No sir — no harm, I hope.

Mr. L. No, No! Well, my boy, you seem to want nothing at all, so I shall not give you money to make you want any thing. But were you ever at school?

B. No sir, but Father says I shall go, after harvest.

Mr. L. You will want books then.

B. Yes sir, the boys all have books.

Mr. L. Well, then, I will give you them — tell your Father so, and that it is because I thought you a very good contented boy. So now go to your sheep again.

B. I will, sir. Thank you.

Mr. L. Good bye, Peter.

B. Good bye, sir.

Now children, what do you think of little Peter? You see he was contented with every thing. Was not this much better than if he had complained of having to work, and of not having more playthings? In the next lesson you will see how a child appears, who cries at every trifle.

What was Peter doing in the field? Did he like to work? What did he have to play with?

LESSON XIX.

THE LITTLE GIRL WHO WAS CROSS.

"What is the matter, Mary? What makes you throw your pretty patchwork on the floor, and stamp on it so?" Mary's cheeks were very red; for she felt a little ashamed, that her mother should see her behave so; and she said, "It is very ugly patch work, mother. very ugly indeed; and the needle is very ugly too, It pricks my fingers every minute."

"That is because you do not feel very good-natured, my dear, not because the needle is naughty," said her mother. "You push the needle in such a hurry, that it pricks your fingers."

"I do not love to sew. May I get my playthings, mother?" asked little Mary. Her mother told her she might get them. So Mary brought out her wooden lion and lamb, and her waxen doll, and her little milk-maid with her churn.

Then Mary twitched the string that kept the milk-maid churning, and it broke, so that she could not raise her arm up and down any more, and Mary cried. "What is the matter?" asked her mother.

"She is a very ugly milk-maid,' said Mary, "I cannot make her churn any more." "That is because you were cross, and pulled the string so hard that you broke it," said her mother.

Before Mary could dry up her tears, her father, and her little cousins, George and Charlotte, came in.

When her father asked what made her eyes look so red, her mother said, "little Mary is cross to-day."

"O no, I am not cross," said Mary; and she was just going to cry again; but her father looked at her very kindly; and though her lips trembled a little, because she was very much grieved, she did not cry aloud.

And she ran to find her very little pail, full of pretty corn, that she might shew it to Charlotte. And Charlotte brought her a very little swan, and a piece of steel; the swan's mouth was made of magnet.

Now magnet loves steel dearly, and will run towards it. So they put the swan in a basin of water; and when they held the steel a little way off from the bird, he would swim all round the water to catch the piece of steel.

Mary laughed very much, to see him fly round so; and put a piece of bread on the steel, and held it to him and said, "Come, biddy come." And the bird swam round after the bread, just as he would if he had been alive and hungry.

Then Charlotte told her that she must not hold the steel too near the swan's mouth, for if she did, it would fasten on it, and she could not pull it off. Then

George and Charlotte ran into the next room, to play with her cousin's bow and arrow, and her little pail of corn.

While they were there, Mary held the steel too near the bird; and his mouth and the steel fastened together, just like two pieces of wax; and because Mary could not pull the steel off, she screamed with all her might, for she forgot that when her father looked kindly at her, she did not mean to cry any more that day.

"What! crying again?" said her mother. "Why, mother, I did not mean to cry any more; and I should not have cried — but this swan is so very ugly, he will not let go this piece of steel."

"It is not the swan that is naughty," said her father. "It is my own little Mary, who is not very goodnatured. You put the steel too near the bird, and then because it fastened on his mouth, you screamed."

"Why did not you, like a patient little girl, say, Mother, will you be so good as take this off? Would it not have been much better than to cry so?" Mary said that it would have been much better; and then she meant to be pleasant all day.

But George came running in with a dead butterfly which he had found on the window; and he struck his foot against Mary's little pail and spilled all the corn on the floor. "O dear," said Mary, "What an ugly pail." And she cried again.

When George had picked up all the corn, and Mary was quiet, Charlotte asked her aunt if she would be so good as to cut out some houses, and trees, and dogs, from some nice white paper, she held in her hand: and her aunt cut out a great many pretty things and made some little boats, and cocked-up hats for her and Mary.

After that, Mary's father went down into the library; and her mother said she was going to her chamber, a moment; and she said, "You must be very kind to each other, and I hope I shall not hear Mary cry again to-day."

What can you tell me of Mary? Of her troubles? &c.

LESSON XX.

MORE ABOUT THE GIRL WHO WAS CROSS.

Now Mary's mother had told her a great many times never to put any thing in her nose and ears ; but when little girls are cross, they never know what to do with themselves ; so Mary rolled up some of the paper, and stuffed it in her ears ; and after she had done it, she was frightened, because her mother had told her it might hurt her very much.

So she cried, and ran to the foot of the stairs, and called out —"Mother, mother, I've got a cocked-up-hat in my ear." And her father and mother both came very quickly ; for she called so loud, that they thought she was half killed ; and when they heard what she said, they laughed very much ; and that made Mary cry louder.

Her mother took the paper hat out of her ear, and dried up her tears; and when Mary looked round, she saw Charlotte sitting in her father's lap ; and she puckered up her lip, and looked up to her mother with a very grieved face.

Her mother shook her finger at her, — so she did not cry ; but her voice trembled very much, as she said, " Mother, Charlotte is sitting in my father's lap."

" That is because Charlotte is a good girl, and does not cry," said her father. " If little Mary had been a good-natured girl, she would have sat in my lap, too." Mary could not bear that ; for she loved her father very dearly, — and she laid her head down in her mother's lap, and sobbed.

" Mary is very sick, I am sure," said her mother. " Charlotte, will you ring the bell, that I may tell Susan to take her to the nursery ? She is too sick to sit up, I am sure."

" Oh no, I am not sick ; I am not sick ; but I do want to cry," said Mary. But she knew it was naughty to do so ; and in a few moments she took her mother's handkerchief, and wiped her face quite dry.

A gentlemen came in, and began to talk with her father; and by-and-by, her father showed him one of Mary's picture books, and asked him to take it home, to show it to one of his little girls.

He put it in his pocket; and then Mary thought she should burst out crying again; but she remembered that her father had said she must not sit in his lap if she cried, — so she crept up softly behind his chair and said, " Father, that is my book."

" I know it, my dear; and you shall have it again," whispered her father. In a few minutes, the gentleman went away, with the book in his pocket; Mary tried very hard to keep the tears from coming into her eyes.

She shut her mouth tight, and winked her eyes; and so she kept from crying. When she looked up, she saw her father was very much pleased with her, for trying to be so good.

He took her up in his lap, and kissed her, and said, " Now little Mary shall sit with me, because she did not cry, when she wanted to very much indeed."

And Mary said " I never mean to cry so much again. My playthings break, and nobody loves me, and I feel sadly when I am so cross."

She was a better girl, for she was always afraid that her mother would be obliged to tell her father again, " Little Mary is cross to-day."

What was in Mary's ear? What was it made of? What was done with one of Mary's picture books? Should children be willing that others should read their pretty books? Is it foolish and wrong to cry at every trifle? Would you rather be like Mary, or Peter?

LESSON XXI.

THE WAY NEVER TO CRY.

When little Robert Smith was about seven years of age, he was sitting one day on a little step, before the door of his father's house crying very much.

Just at that time, Robert's uncle came to take him to play with his little cousins; but as soon as his uncle saw his red eyes, and how dirty he had made his face, by wiping the tears away with his dirty hands, he thought he would not take Robert that day, but would rather wait, and see if he would not be a better boy.

"For," said his uncle to himself, "I cannot walk through the streets with a naughty boy; and I am sure he must have been naughty, or he would have no cause to cry."

When his uncle came up to the little step where Robert sat, he said, "Well, Robert, are you always crying? — What is the matter?"

"Dear uncle," answered Robert, sobbing and rubbing his face again with his dirty hands; "I cry almost all day long."—"Where is your pocket handkerchief?" said his uncle: "you should not wipe your face with those dirty hands."

"I have lost my handkerchief," answered Robert. "Did any one take it out of your pocket?" asked his uncle. "No," said Robert: "I laid it down somewhere, and when I wanted it, I could not find it: I am sure it must be lost."

"But, my dear Robert," said his uncle, "whenever you use your pocket handkerchief, you should never lay it down, but always put it in your pocket: for if you do not know where you have put it, you can never know where to find it."

Robert cried and sobbed still louder than before; and stammered out as well as he could, "Dear uncle, do not you find fault with me too: every body huffs and reproves me all day long.

"When I go to the school, my master punishes me for not saying my lesson; when I come home, the maid says, 'O you naughty boy, what a house you make with your dirty feet;' when I go into the parlor, my father says, 'Why do you not shut the door after you?

"My brothers and sisters are angry, and quarrel with me, whenever I break or lose any of their playthings : and now I have been turned out of the room, because I did not go to dinner when the servant called me, but staid to finish my game at ball with that little boy you met as you came. — Is it not very hard, dear uncle, — is it not very sad ?"

When Robert had done, his uncle said, " Yes, my dear little boy, I dare say you find it very hard to be huffed and found fault with ; but you should remember, my child, that nobody ever finds fault with good children, and that if you were to try and never do wrong, nobody would ever huff you or make you cry.

" Now I think it would be better, when you come from school in the afternoon, if you were never to go to play, till you have learned your lesson for the next morning.

" The next morning read it carefully over again before you go to school ; and when you have said your lesson well, your master will not punish you, but will say that you are a good boy, and that you will be a clever man.

" When you come from school, stop at the door, and scrape your feet ; not carelessly, but in a careful manner : then go to the mat and rub them until they are clean ; and then the maid will say, ' Here comes our little Robert ; he is a good boy — do you not hear how he scrapes and rubs his feet ? '

" When you go in or out of a room, shut the door every time after you. When you are with your brothers and sisters, never touch or take away any of their playthings, without first asking leave.

" If they let you have any thing, take care not to break it or lose it, and then your brothers and sisters will never quarrel with you, but will love you and lend you any thing they have.

" I would have you try and do all this, for a few days, and I am sure, when I come again, you will tell me you have had no cause to cry."

Little Robert remembered what his uncle had said to him, and tried to be a good boy ; he became every day better and better, and cried every day less and less.

In about a week, Robert's uncle came again. Robert ran to meet him at the garden gate.

"O," said Robert, "what a good uncle you are, you have made me quite happy. I have tried and done all that you told me; now I never cry, and every body loves me."

"I am very glad to hear it, my dear child," answered his uncle; "now you shall go with me. The last time I came, you should have gone; but as I found you a bad boy, I could not take you."

LESSON XXII

DEFINITIONS.

Absent, away, not at home.   Instrument, a tool.

THE GIRL WHO SWALLOWED FRUIT-STONES.

Ellen Martin had a habit of swallowing the stones of fruit. She once made herself so ill with cherry-stones, that her mother would not allow her to eat any more cherries that season.

But notwithstanding, as soon as plums came, she began to swallow plum-stones; and at last she thought of trying to get down the stone of a peach. So she put one into her mouth, intending to take it out again, if she found it too large.

Just at that moment she happened to look out of the window near which she was standing, and she saw her father arrive at the door, after having been absent several weeks on a journey.

She was so glad to see him return, and she ran down stairs to meet him in such haste, that she forgot the peach-stone in her mouth. In running she shook it down into her throat, where it stuck so fast that it could not be moved.

It choked and hurt her so dreadfully, that she thought she was going to die. Her face turned black with pain, and her eyes looked as if they were going to start from her head.

Her father and mother were shocked when they saw her. She could scarcely speak so as to make them understand what was the matter.

A Doctor, who lived next door, was sent for, and with great difficulty he pulled out the peach-stone by putting an instrument down her throat, which was sore for a long time after; it having been so scratched and scraped that she spit up blood.

She never again swallowed fruit-stones.

Can you name a boy who is absent from school? A girl? Can you name an instrument for cutting wood? For mending a pen? Should you be choked if you had no air to breath? How much air do you inhale in a day? About one hundred hogsheads.

LESSON XXIII.
THE LEOPARD.

The Leopard is an animal of the cat kind. The back of this animal is as high as the head of a child of two years old, and his body is as long as a bench on which four or five children can sit.

He is about two feet and a half high, and a little more than four feet and a half long. His shape is like that of the cat and the tiger. His head is small; his ears short; his body long, and his legs short and strong.

His color, along the back, is yellowish brown, spotted with black; his head, face, and throat are pale brown, and his breast pale yellow. Every part of his skin is spotted with black.

When this animal is quiet in his cage, and no one goes near him, he looks mild and innocent, like a cat. But if any person goes to him when he is eating, or strikes at him with a whip, he growls, shows his teeth, and looks very fierce and dangerous.

The Leopard is not so cruel or ferocious a beast as the tiger. He is more kind to his keeper than the tiger, and will not always bite when he is touched with the hand.

He can even be tamed when taken quite young, and treated with kindness. Some Leopards have been so tame as to follow their masters like the dog, and when patted on the head, to purr like the cat.

He is however a dangerous animal, when ever so tame, for he will sometimes get angry and fly at his master and try to tear him in pieces. This animal is found in the greatest numbers in Africa; but he also lives in China.

The Leopard lives on such animals as he can catch, by springing upon them in the woods. But sometimes, when he is hungry, he will leave the woods, and go to the sheep-yards, where he makes terrible destruction, often killing a whole flock in one night.

The hunting Leopard is not so large as the common Leopard. He is sometimes tamed and taught to catch other animals for his master. He is taken into the woods in a cage, and when his master sees a deer, he takes the Leopard out and shows it to him. The cunning animal creeps along slyly, like a cat, until he gets near his game; he then springs upon it, and holds it fast for his master. The skin of the Leopard is very beautiful, and sells at a high price. The flesh of the Leopard is useful in Africa, where he is eaten by the poor negroes.

Is a sheep *ferocious?* Is a dog, when angry, ferocious?—How large is the Leopard? What is his color? How does he look when no one is near him? When he is eating? Can he be tamed? What does he live on? Of what use is the Leopard?

LESSON XXIV.
DEFINITIONS.

Anecdote, a short story. Provider, one who provides or furnishes. Sheep-fold, a pen where sheep are kept. Robbery, theft done by force. Contend, to quarrel. Pursue, to go after.

Can you tell me the opposite of Pleasure? Of Peace? Contented? Wrong? Right?

ANECDOTES OF THE LEOPARD.

The Leopard, like other beasts of this kind, shows no mercy to such living creatures as he can master. He kills what he does not want, and so long as he can have the pleasure of destroying, he does not even eat.

Thus, he often kills great numbers, without eating any. Mr. Kolbe says, that two Leopards, with their three young ones, stole into a sheep-fold one night at the Cape of Good Hope, and killed nearly a hundred sheep. It seemed, from the short time they had to make all this destruction, that they did not eat any thing until all the sheep were killed.

The old ones then took three sheep, that were dead, and laid them before their young ones to eat, and having all ate as much as they wanted, the parents, like good providers for their family, each took a whole sheep in their mouths, and began to move towards the woods.

They however paid dearly for this night's robbery; for the people, finding what had happened, pursued, and destroyed them all, except the old male, who escaped to the woods, in spite of all they could do.

Mr. Kolbe also says, that the Leopard will not, like the wolf and hyena, eat flesh that has been long killed, nor will he touch any meat that has been killed by other animals.

Leopards are so selfish and quarrelsome, that they cannot live in peace even with each other. When two are shut up together in a cage, one seems to wish the other dead, so that he can have all the food that is given them.

When they have a piece of meat thrown in for both, they cannot be contented to divide it, and each take his part, but they both want the whole, so that they keep growling and striking each other, as long as any of their food is left.

When it is all eaten up, and there is nothing to contend about, they again become good-natured and friendly, and lie down together in peace.   But they are always ready to fight again if there is any thing to quarrel about.

I have seen some children, who like the Leopards, were always ready to quarrel, or even to fight, when they could not have every thing they wanted. Such children are much worse than Leopards, because these dumb beasts do not know good from evil, and therefore do not know that it is wrong to fight.

But children know good from evil.   They are taught by their parents, and at Sunday Schools, that it is not only mean and shameful to quarrel and fight, but that it is wicked in the sight of God.

Now let every child, when he is angry, say to himself, If I quarrel and fight I shall be no better than a leopard or a dog ; but I ought to be better than these animals, for God has given me power to speak, to know good from evil, which power he has not given to the beasts.

Let him think, also, that if other children quarrel, and do wicked things, this is no excuse for him, and that it is better in the sight of all good people, and in the sight of God, to suffer wrong than to do wrong

What is said of the Leopard's showing mercy? What of those who broke into a sheep-fold? How will two Leopards appear when shut up in a cage together?   What is said of children who are always ready to quarrel? What should every child say to himself when he gets angry?   What is better than to do wrong?

LESSON XXV.

DEFINITIONS.

Delicious, highly pleasing to the taste.   Attracted, engaged. Ascend, to go up. Arrive, to get to a place Recover, to get back again.

Can you tell me the opposite of Began? Possible? Quick? Slyly? Behind? Returned? Thinner? Narrow? Safe?

HOW TO MAKE THE BEST OF IT.

Robinet, a very poor man, after a hard day's work, was returning home with a basket in his hand. What a delicious supper I shall have! said he to himself.

This piece of kid well stewed down, with my onions sliced, thickened with my meal, and seasoned with my salt and pepper, will make a dish fit for the Governor. Then I have a good piece of a barley loaf at home to finish with. How I long to be at it!

A noise in the hedge now attracted his notice, and he spied a squirrel nimbly running up a tree, and popping into a hole between the branches. Ha! thought he, what a nice present a nest of young squirrels will be to my little nephew! I'll try if I can get it.

Upon this, he set down his basket in the road, and bagan to climb up the tree. He had half ascended, when casting a look at his basket, he saw a dog with his nose in it, ferreting out the piece of kid's flesh.

He made all possible speed down, but the dog was too quick for him, and ran off with the meat in his mouth. Robinet looked after him — Well, said he, then I must be content with a soup without meat — and no bad thing either.

He travelled on, and came to a little public house by the roadside, where an acquaintance of his was sitting on a bench, drinking beer. He invited Robinet to take a draught. Robinet seated himself by his friend, and placed his basket on the bench by him.

A tame raven, which was kept at the house, came slyly behind him, and perching on the basket, stole away the bag in which the meal was tied up, and hopped off with it to his hole.

Robinet did not perceive the theft till he was on his way again. He returned to search for his bag, but could hear no tidings of it. Well, says he, my soup will be thinner, but I will boil a slice of bread with it, and that will do it some good at least.

He went on again, and arrived at a little brook, over which was laid a narrow plank. A young woman coming up, to pass at the same time, Robinet offered her his hand.

When she had reached the middle of the plank, either through fear or sport, she shrieked out, and cried she was falling. Robinet hastning to support her with his other hand, let his basket drop into the stream.

As soon as she was safe over, he jumped in and recovered it but when he took it out, he perceived that all the salt was melted, and the pepper washed away. Nothing was left but the onions.

Well! says Robinet, then I must sup to-night upon roasted onions and barley bread. Last night I had the bread alone. To-morrow morning it will make no difference what I had. So saying, he trudged on, singing as before.

What can you tell me of Robinet and his losses? Can you name something which you think is delicious? Something else? Is wormwood delicious? What will attract a horse? A cat? What ascends the chimney? Does rain ascend? Can birds ascend? Where shall you arrive soon after school is out? Can you recover your time, if you spend it idly? Are those persons the most happy who make the best of every thing.

LESSON XXVI.
THE LITTLE MISER.

Mr. and Mrs. Anderson had four children; and William was one them. He would never spend a cent; but used to put all the pocket-money that was allowed him, and all the money that any body gave to him, into an old garden pot.

The garden pot was covered over with a piece of wood, and hidden in a corner of the garden, under some earth and brick-bats; so that no one could see it, or know where to find it.

The greatest pleasure William had was to count over his money, and to cover it up again.

When William and his brothers and sisters were seated, one morning, at breakfast, his father said, "Children, do you know that last night, while we were all sleeping safely and quietly in our beds, there was in another part of the town a dreadful fire which has burnt the house, and the clothes, and the furniture, of a number of very poor, but very honest people?"

"O, poor creatures, that is very shocking : I wonder what they will do?" said Sophy. "I am going to tell you, love," said the father. After there has been a fire, there are always many people who go to see the ruins."

"What do you mean by ruins?" asked Edward.

"After a house has been burned, so as to fall down, there remains in the place where the house stood, a great heap of the brick-bats, and wood, and mortar, of which the house had been made, and even sometimes there remains still a part of the house: now this, all together, is called the ruins.

"Do you all understand me, children?" asked the father. The children said they understood it very well; and he went on.

"Now I was telling you, that many people go to see these ruins. There stands a man near the place, with a box or a plate in his hands, and he holds the box or plate to the people who go, and they put money into it; and this money is given to the poor people whose things have been burnt.

"Your mother and I are going to take a walk to the place to-day, and if any of you like to go with us, we will wait till you all come from school."

The children thanked their father, and said they should like to go ; and as soon as breakfast was over, the children went to school. At 12 o'clock they all came home again, and found their father and mother ready to go ; and Sophy asked her mother, whether she intended to give any thing to the poor people .

The mother said, she went there on purpose to give them something. "Your father," said she, "will give for himself and me." Sophy said she had three sixpences, and that she would give one of the sixpences to her father, that he might give it for her.

Edward said, he could not give any thing, because he had given as much as he could afford the day before, to a poor woman who went to the hospital. Little Anna, the youngest child, said " pray, father, do you think that three cents will do the poor people any good?"

"Three cents alone, my child," said the father, " would do but little good; but when we think that many persons will give three cents a-piece, who cannot afford to give any more; and that all these cents together will make a large sum of money, I think you will do well to give it to them."

William stood in the corner of the room ; but he did not say a word, or offer to give any thing. " William," said the mother, " now you may do good with some of the money you have. I am sure you must have a great deal, for I believe you never spend any thing."

' "No," said William, "I never spend any. I have all my money safe."

" And for what purpose do you keep it, my dear ? What do you intend to do with it ? "

" I do not intend to do any thing with it; I like to keep it, and get more to put to it."

William's father told him, that money was of no use, except when we would do good with it, either to ourselves, or to those who are in want of it. " If you saved your money to do any thing with, or to buy any thing with, or to give to any body, I should think you did right; but, as it is, William, I think you act very wrong."

When William's father had said this, they all set out; and when they came to the place where the fire had been, they found many poor people, and many poor children.

Some were sitting half naked, because all their clothes had been burnt; and many poor children were crying for their fathers and mothers who had been burnt; or who had broken their arms or legs, in jumping out of the windows to save their lives.

When Mr. Anderson, the children's father, put the money, which he and their mother gave, into the box which the man held in his hand, Sophy said softly to her brother William, "If you could only be half as happy as we are, from thinking that what we give to these poor people will help to make them more happy, you would not mind giving them all you have."

"There is no need of my giving them any thing," said he. "Did not you see how many people there were who gave them money?"

"But," said Sophy, "suppose every body, instead of giving them something, had said, 'O, there will be people enough to give; I have no need to give,'—do you not think they would have had very little?"

William had not had time that day to look at his money and count it; and therefore, as soon as they all got home, he went into the garden, to the place he always kept it in, and lifted up the brick-bats which covered his garden pot.

He then lifted up the bit of wood which lay over the pot — but how vexed and sorry he was to find his money all gone, and a parcel of little stones instead of it, and a little piece of paper, on which was written —

"Foolish boy! you have only lost that which you did not use; and stones will do as well to count as money."

What can you tell me about little William? Should we always try to help those who are in trouble? Is it best to do any thing, if we can help them but little? Why? Is it best to spend money for things which do no good, while many poor people have no way to get food? Would you rather be like William or Sophy?

LESSON XXVII.

DEFINITIONS.

Obstruct, to hinder in passing. Ferry, to carry any one over water in a boat. Habitation, a place to live in· Hospitable, kind to strangers and visitors, without ask ing pay.

THE MAN WHO WAS HOSPITABLE.

As Judge Hall was returning from one of the Western States, he was overtaken by the night, and found his path obstructed by a river. Seeing a house on the opposite side, he called for help.

A half-naked fellow came down, and with some trouble ferried him over. The Judge followed him to his habitation. It was of the meanest kind, being made of logs, and having but one room. There were seven or eight persons in the family, and every thing looked as if they were very poor.

"After drinking a bowl of milk," says the Judge, " which I merely called for by way of excuse for paying him a little more for his trouble, I asked to know his charge for ferrying me over the water ; to which he good-humoredly replied, that he never took money for helping a traveller on his way.'

" Then let me pay you for your milk."

" I never sell milk."

" But," said I, " I would rather pay you ; I have money enough."

" Well," said he, " I have milk enough ; so we are even. I have as good a right to give you milk, as you have to give me money."

Can you obstruct the burning of a fire ? How ? What kind of habitations do people have here ? What are they made of ? Where do squirrels make their habitation ? Would the poor man have been hospitable if he had asked a great price for helping the other man ? Would it have been right ? Do you think little William uld have asked pay, if he helped any body ? Why ?

LESSON XXVIII.

DEFINITIONS.

Debate, a dispute. Resign, to give up. Enslave, to make another a slave. Shaft, the pole of a carriage.

THE HOG AND OTHER ANIMALS.

A debate once arose among the animals in a farm-yard, which of them was most valued by their master. After the horse, the ox, the cow, the sheep, and the dog, had spoken, the hog took up the discourse.

"It is plain," said he, "that the greatest value must be set upon that animal which is kept most for his own sake, without expecting from him any return of use and service. Now which of you can boast so much in that respect as I can?

"As for you, horse, though you are very well fed and lodged, and have servants to attend upon you and make you sleek and clean, yet all this is for the sake of your labour.

"Do not I see you taken out early every morning, put in chains, or fastened to the shafts of a heavy cart, and not brought back till noon? when after a short respite, you are taken to work again till late in the evening. I must say just the same to the ox, except that he works for poorer fare.

As for you, Mrs. Cow, who are so dainty over your chopped straw and potatoes, you are thought worth keeping only for your milk, which is drained from you twice a day to the last drop, while your poor young ones are taken from you, and sent I know not whither.

"You poor innocent sheep, are turned out to shift for yourselves upon the bare hills, or penned up with now and then a withered turnip, or some musty hay.

"You pay dearly enough for your keeping, by giving up your warm coat every year, for want of which you

5

are liable to be frozen to death on some of the cold nights before summer.

"As for the dog, who prides himself so much on being admitted to our master's table, and made his companion, that he will scarcely condescend to reckon himself one of us, he is obliged to do all the offices of a servant by day, and to keep watch during the night, while we are quietly asleep.

"In short, you are all of you creatures maintained for use — poor things, made to be enslaved or pillaged. I, on the contrary, have a warm stye and plenty of provisions, all at free cost.

"I have nothing to do but grow fat and follow my amusement; and my master is best pleased when he sees me lying at ease in the sun, or filling myself."

This was not long before winter began. It proved a very scarce season for fodder of all kinds, so that the farmer began to consider how he was to maintain all his live stock till spring.

"It will be impossible for me," thought he, "to keep them all; I must therefore part with those I can best spare. As for my horses and working oxen, I shall have business enough to employ them; they must be kept, cost what it will.

"My cows will not give me much in the winter, but they will in the spring. I must not lose the profit of my dairy.

"The sheep, poor things, will take care of themselves as long as there is a bite upon the hills; and if deep snow comes, we must do with them as well as we can, by the help of a few turnips and some hay, for I must have their wool at shearing time.

"But my hogs will eat me out of house and home, without doing me any good. They must be killed, that's certain; and the sooner I get rid of the fat ones, the better."

So saying, he singled out the orator as one of the fattest among them, and sent him to the butcher the very next day.

When shall you have a respite from study ? Ought you to have one before you have learned your lesson ? Can you name something to which you are liable ? Something else?

LESSON XXIX.

THE LISTENER.

Charlotte Walden had a constant desire to hear what every body was saying, and she was so mean as to listen at doors, and to hide herself, that she might hear things that were not intended for her to know.

Charlotte's mother often told her that a listener is almost as bad as a thief. A thief steals money or property that belongs to other people, and a listener steals the secrets of others.

All persons that are in the habit of listening, make themselves appear mean, and deserve to be punished.

Charlotte's father and mother sent her out of the room, when they were going to talk of any thing that they did not wish her to hear, but she always remained listening at the door with her ear close to the key-hole.

One of her curls once got entangled in the key, and when her father suddenly opened the door, she fell forward into the room, and hurt her nose so that it bled.

When she knew that her mother had visitors in the parlor, or that her father had gentlemen there with him on business, she would quit her lessons or her playthings, and come softly down stairs and listen at the door; or would slip into the garden and crouch down under the open window, that she might hear what they were saying.

Once when she was stooping, half double, under the parlor window, her father, not knowing that she was there, and finding that a fly had got into a glass of beer that he was going to drink, went to throw out the beer, and emptied the tumbler on Charlotte's head.

Once when she heard her mother say, that she expected two ladies at three o'clock on particular business, Charlotte went into the parlor before the time of their arrival, and hid herself under a bed that stood there.

Here she lay till the ladies arrived, and her mother came down to them. A dog belonging to one of the ladies ran directly to the bed, and began to snuff and scratch as if he had found something.

The lady said, "I think Carlo must have smelled a cat under the bed." Mrs. Walden got up to look, but before she reached the bed, the dog had lifted the bed-clothes with his nose, and discovered the naughty girl, who hid her face with her hands.

Her mother called one of the maids, desiring her to take Charlotte and lock her up in a back chamber, for the remainder of the day.

One evening, after she was old enough to put herself to bed, her little lamp blew out as she was going up stairs, and she went down to the kitchen to get it lighted. When she came near the door, she found that the servants were talking with some of their acquaintances about families in which they had formerly lived.

Being very desirous of hearing all they said, she did not go into the kitchen to light her lamp, but slipped into the cellar, which had two doors, one opening into a little entry, and one into the kitchen itself.

Leaning her head against this door, which had a very wide crack, she seated herself on a large log of wood, and listened for a while with great attention, till she began to doze, and at last fell fast asleep.

When the servants were going to bed, they bolted both the cellar doors, not knowing that any person was there, and went upstairs, leaving Charlotte in a deep sleep.

Some time in the middle of the night she awoke by falling off the log backwards, upon a heap of coal.

The back of her neck and head were very much hurt, and began to bleed.

When she first awoke, she did not know were she was, or what had happened to her ; but when she found herself alone at midnight in the dark cellar, and felt the pain of the bruises and cuts in her head and neck, and knew that the blood was trickling from them, she began to scream violently.

The loudness of the noise awoke her father and mother ; and Mr. Walden, putting on his flannel gown, and taking the night lamp, ran up into Charlotte's room, knowing the voice to be hers. To his great surprise, he found she was not there, and that there was no appearance of her having been in bed that night.

The screams grew louder, and louder and Mr. Walden found that they came from the cellar. By this time every one in the house was up ; and the women stood at the head of the stairs, while the servant man followed Mr. Walden.

When they came to the cellar, they found Charlotte stretched on a bed of coals, her white frock blackened by the coal dust, and stained with blood, her face deadly pale, and herself altogether in a sad condition.

Her father took her in his arms, and it was some time before she could speak to tell how she came into the cellar. He carried her to her mother, who was much shocked to see her in such a wretched state.

Charlotte's soiled and bloody clothes were taken off, and she was washed, and a clean night-gown put on her. The wounds in her head and neck were dressed with bandages, and she was carried to bed crying, and faint with the loss of blood. She had a high fever and could not sleep, and her mother sat by her bed, side all the rest of the night.

By the time Charlotte Walden got well of her hurts, she was entirely cured of her inclination for listening, and never again showed a desire to over-hear what people were talking about or to pry into secrets.

Is it mean to listen at doors? What does a listener steal ?

What do those who are in the habit of listening deserve? What happened to Charlotte when listening at the key-hole? Under the window? Under the bed? At the cellar door?

Can you name something which you are desirous of doing? Which you are not desirous of doing? What is the meaning of *remain*? When you are sent to do an errand, should you remain after it is done?

LESSON XXX.

LETTER FROM A LAD AT SEA, TO HIS MOTHER.

Ship Fair Trader, June 14th, 1812.

My Honored Mother,

We have had boisterous and wet weather, and I have been very sea-sick, since we left New York; but it has been pleasant, yesterday and to-day, and I am now much better. This sea-sickness is the most distressing feeling that I ever knew. I could hardly hold up my head.

For several days I ate nothing except one or two of the biscuits you gave me. I don't know but I should have starved, if it had not been for them; for I could not bear the sight of the ship bread. I do not mean to complain, I only want to tell you just how it is. In a little time, I believe, I shall get hardened, and begin to eat of the sailors' fare with a good relish.

Nothing very remarkable has happened to us, so far on our passage. Two or three vessels passed us at a great distance; and yesterday, an English ship came near us. The Captain hailed them, with his speaking trumpet. They said they were out twenty-one days from the city of Bristol, bound to Kingston in Jamaica.

They were freighted with nails, window glass, hollow ware, dry goods, and crockery; and expected to carry back a cargo of sugar, molasses, and pimento; with a few boxes of limes and lemons.

One thing I could not help noticing. As a ship approached us, at a great distance, it appeared like a speck on the surface of the water. We saw at first only the top of the sails; because the sea, like a bow, rose up between them and us; but as we came nearer, we could see lower and lower down the mast, till the whole body of the ship hove in sight.

This shows plainly that the world is round. It was as if one little fly was creeping towards another, on an orange. They would first peep over the rounding part, and just see each other's back; and so, by degrees, down to the feet.

It is now fifteen days that I have been out of sight of land. It appears as if the sun rose out of the sea in the morning, and sunk into it again at night. I should be very glad to get a sight of hills and trees once more, and sleep in a house that will stand still in its place, instead of rolling about, and making my head so dizzy.

Though I have been but a short time from home, I want very much to see you all. When I get to Liverpool, I will write again.

Please to give my best respects to uncle Jacob, and all our good friends.

Your dutiful son,
JACK HALYARD.

LESSON XXXI.

LETTER FROM THE SAME, TO HIS BROTHER.

On board the ship Fair Trader, June 15th, 1812.

My dear brother,

I wrote a letter yesterday for our kind mother. I thought we should meet some vessel that would carry it to the United States, and that she would wish to hear how I make out in this new business of ploughing the water with a ship. It has been a pretty hard time with me; but I hope the worst is over. When I get home I will tell you more about it.

You may be sure I shall not make wry faces for trifles; but, if I am any judge in the case, I have taken a pretty thorough seasoning with sea-sickness. I believe you don't know much about what that means. You will know very well, my good fellow, if you ever try it, though Captain Mitchell says people do not often die with it.

Just after I finished the letter to my dear mother, we saw a very large Whale, lying on the smooth sea. As our ship came near him, he began to spout and flounce, raising a great foam in the water, and soon dove out of sight.

I remember reading of whales, in many books; but I did not think they were of such monstrous size. This one was as long as our garden, or as Mr. Buskirk's great barn in New-Jersey. These huge creatures were called, in old time, Leviathans. There has lately been a high dispute whether they are fish or not; because they differ so much from the rest of the water tribes.

One of our passengers, a very learned man, who has been acquainted with many whales, says they have warm blood, like land animals. Proper fish have cold blood. Whales have lungs, and breathe the air, like an ox or a horse: and can stay only a short time under water.

I used to think they remained deep in the sea; but they live on the top of it, and would drown if they could not come up to breathe. The female whales nurture their young, as sheep do their lambs; but this is not the way with shad and trout. Their young ones must take care of themselves, as well as they can, or be eaten up by the large fish.

Our learned passenger is an eminent Natural Philosopher. He says, all creatures are divided into different classes, according to their leading qualities.

The class of dogs is called the canine family, because the Latin word *canis* means dog.

Wolves are nothing but wild dogs, and every wild dog becomes, in fact, a wolf. They have the same kind of teeth and paws. Foxes also belong to this class of quadrupeds, and bark in the same manner.

Lions, and tigers, and panthers, are only large cats; and rats and mice are small ones. They have whiskers, and soft feet, and long sharp claws, like each other, and they all belong to the cat family; but more about this another time.

Present my best love to those two little frolicsome girls at home. Give each of them forty-five kisses for me, on each cheek, and see how many that will make.

Your affectionate brother,
JACK HALYARD.

LESSON XXXII.

DEFINITIONS.

Rush, to move with violence. Attack, to fall upon violently. Wound, a hurt. Approach, to draw near. Carcass, the dead body of an animal. Float, to swim on the surface of the water. Fin, the wing of a fish. Blubber, the fat of whales. Defend, to protect.

THE WHALE.

The Whale is the largest animal of which we can give any certain account. The Greenland Whale measures from fifty to eighty feet in length; those found in the South Seas are said sometimes to measure one hundred and fifty.

The head is one third of the whole animal; the mouth is very wide, and the under lip broader than the upper one.

The tongue is very large, and yields five or six barrels of oil. There are two holes in the middle of the head, through which it spouts water to a great height, with a great noise.

Whales are shy and timid, having no way to defend themselves, except with their tails. When they see a boat coming, they generally dive; but sometimes they rush against a boat, and dash it in pieces with one stroke of the tail.

Many ships are employed in the Whale Fisheries. Each ship carries six or seven boats; each boat has a harpoon, several lances, and a very long line. Thus prepared, they attack the Whale.

As soon as the Whale is struck with a harpoon, he darts down into the water, dragging with him the harpoon and the line which is fastened to it. If the line were to become entangled, it would either snap like a thread, or overset the boat. That this may not happen, a man attends to the line, to see that it goes out regularly.

When the Whale comes up to breathe, the harpooner gives him a fresh wound, till at last he grows faint from loss of blood. The men then venture to approach him, and a long lance is thrust into his breast, which soon puts an end to his life.

When the carcass begins to float, they cut holes in the fins and tail, and having put ropes through them, they fasten him to the ship. They then cut out the blubber and whale-bone, and let the carcass float away.

There have sometimes been more than two hundred and fifty British ships employed in the Whale Fishery. In the year 1814, seventy-six British vessels procured over fourteen hundred Whales.

How long is the Whale? How long is this room? How much longer is the Whale? How much oil is made from its tongue? Are Whales bold? How are they caught? What is taken out of them? Can fish live without air? *They cannot; every portion of water contains air.* Can the Whale live with what air he gets in the water?

LESSON XXXIII.

THE OSTRICH.

The Ostrich is a bird of great size, very strong, and having the finest and most beautiful feathers, black and white. Yet it is by no means a handsome bird, as it has very few feathers upon it, and a large part of the body is quite naked.

Ostriches live in the deserts of Arabia and Africa, feeding chiefly upon vegetables; leading a social and harmless life. They lay forty or fifty eggs in a season, in the sand, where they are often forgotten by the mother, or destroyed by the wild beasts. The eggs are very large, being four or five inches in thickness.

This animal devours leather, hair, grass, stones, oyster-shells, lead, iron, or any thing that is given to it, and is always ready to eat. Its size is very great, being from seven to eight feet high when the head is raised, and it is strong enough to carry a *stout man* on its back.

The Ostrich runs with great swiftness, its legs being long, and as large as a young colt's; its wings also serve as sails and oars to help it along. It never tries to fly, for the feathers are not like those of any other bird; they are not close together but loose, and all very soft and downy.

It has on each wing two curious spurs, which, it is said, are of use by bleeding the animal as the wings flap against its sides, when it runs and becomes overheated; for it is naturally very hot-blooded, and might, but for this means of relief, be suffocated.

The head is small, the neck very long, and being covered with very small feathers, you can observe any thing large that it swallows, passing in a winding way down to the body.

The eyes are bright, large, and round, with eyelashes, the thighs without feathers, the legs covered

EASY LESSONS.

with scales, and each foot has two large toes; the inside one, the largest, is about seven inches long, with a claw at the end, with which it strikes a very severe blow.

It fights with its feet, and has been known to rip open the body of a man with a single blow. When roused it makes a grand appearance; the head is thrown up, the breast forward, and the wings stretched out and quivering in a beautiful manner.

When pursued, it leaves behind the swiftest Arabian horses, but in a hunt of five or six hours is worn out. The Ostrich is noted for its neglect of its young, and as being a stupid creature, and very timid.

I saw one some time since, which, when it was to be moved from one place to another, became so frightened that it could not walk, and had to be carried by two or three men, its weight being equal to a barrel of flour.

How many eggs will an Ostrich lay in a season? How large are the eggs? What do Ostriches eat? How high are they? How high is this room? Is the Ostrich strong? How heavy is it? Are men usually as heavy?

LESSON XXXIV.

LOVE AND DUTY TO PARENTS.

My Father, my Mother, I know
    I cannot your kindness repay;
But I hope, that as older I grow,
    I shall learn your commands to obey.

You lov'd me before I could tell
    Who it was that so tenderly smil'd;
But now that I know it so well,
    I should be a dutiful child.

I am sorry that ever I should
    Be naughty, and give you a pain;

I hope I shall learn to be good,
    And never so grieve you again.

But for fear that I ever should dare
    From all your commands to depart,
Whenever I'm saying my prayer,
    I'll ask for a dutiful heart.

LESSON XXXV.

DEFINITIONS.

Impatient, hasty, uneasy, fretful. Gradually, a
little at a time. Protected, kept from injury. Guarded, protected.

THE CHESTNUT BURR.

One fine pleasant morning, in the fall of the year,
the Master was walking along towards school, and he
saw three or four boys under a large chestnut tree,
gathering chestnuts. One of the boys was sitting
upon the ground, trying to open some chestnut burrs
which he had knocked off from the tree. The burrs
were green, and he was trying to open them by
pounding them with a stone.

He was a very impatient boy, and was scolding, in
a loud and angry tone, against the burrs. He did
not see, he said, what in the world chestnuts were
made to grow so for. They ought to grow right out
in the open air, like apples; and not have such
prickly skins on them, just to plague the boys.

So saying, he struck, with all his might, a fine
large burr, crushed it to pieces, and then jumped up,
using, at the same time, profane and wicked words.
As soon as he turned round, he saw the Master standing very near him. Then he felt very much ashamed and afraid, and hung down his head.

"Roger," said the Master, (for the boy's name
was Roger,) "can you get me a chestnut burr?"

6

Roger looked up a moment, to see whether the Master was in earnest, and then began to look around for a burr.

A boy who was standing near the tree, with a red cap full of burrs in his hand, held out one of them.

Roger took the burr and handed it to the Master, who quietly put it in his pocket, and walked away without saying a word.

As soon as he was gone, the boy with the red cap, said to Roger, "I expected the Master would have given you a good scolding for talking so."

"The Master never scolds," said another boy, who was sitting on a log pretty near, with a green satchel in his hand, "but you see if he does not remember it."

Roger looked as if he did not know what to think about it.

"I wish," said he, "I knew what he is going to do with that burr."

That afternoon, when the lessons had been all recited, and it was about time to dismiss the school, the boys put away their books, and the Master read a few verses in the Bible, and then offered a prayer, in which he asked God to forgive all the sins which any of them had committed that day, and to take care of them during the night.

After this he asked all the boys to sit down. He then put his hand into his pocket and took out the chestnut burr, and all the boys looked at it.

"Boys," said he, "do you know what this is?"

One of the boys in the back seat, said in a half whisper, "it is nothing but a chestnut burr."

"Lucy," said the Master, to a bright eyed little girl sitting near him, "what is this?"

"It is a chestnut burr, sir," said she.

"Do you know what it is for?"

"I suppose there are chestnuts in it."

"But what is this rough prickly covering for?"
Lucy did not know.

"Does any body here know?" said the Master.

One of the boys said he supposed it was to hold the chestnuts together, and keep them up on the tree.

"But I heard a boy say," replied the Master, "that he thought they ought not to be made to grow so. — The nut itself, he thought, ought to hang alone on the branch, without any prickly covering, just as apples do."

"But the nuts themselves have no stems to be fastened by," answered the same boy.

"That is true, but I suppose this boy thought that God could have made them grow with stems and that this would have been better than to have them in burrs."

After a little pause, the Master said he would explain to them what the chestnut burr was for, and wished them all to listen attentively.

Who heard Roger use wicked words? Who else? Who else? What does the Bible say of him who takes God's name in vain? What kind of men use wicked words?—What did the Master do? Who expected he would give Roger a scolding? What did another boy say? Can you tell what chestnut burrs are for?

LESSON XXXVI.

WHAT THE CHESNUT BURR IS FOR.

"How much of the chestnut is good to eat, William?" asked he looking at the boy before him.

"Only the meat."

"How long does it take the meat to grow?"

"All summer, I suppose."

"Yes; it begins early in summer, and gradually grows and swells until it has become of full size and is ripe, in the fall. Now suppose there was a tree out here near the school-house, and the chestnut meats should grow upon it without any shell or covering; suppose, too, that they should taste like good

ripe chestnuts at first, when they were very small.
Do you think they would be safe?"

William said, "No! the boys would pick them,
and eat them before they had time to grow."

"Well, what harm would there be in that? would
it not be as well to have the chestnuts early in summer as to have them in the fall?"

William hesitated. Another boy who sat next him,
said, "There would not be so much meat in the
chestnuts, if they were eaten before they had time to
grow."

"Right," said the Master, "but would not the boys
know this, and so all agree to let the little chestnuts
alone, and not eat them while they were small?"

William said he thought they would not. If the
chestnuts were good, he was afraid they would pick
them off and eat them, if they were small.

All the rest of the boys in the school thought so
too.

"Here, then," said the Master, "is one reason
for having prickles around the chestnuts when they
are little. But then it is not necessary to have all
chestnuts guarded from boys in this way : a great many of the trees are in the woods, which the boys do
not see; what good do the burrs do there?"

The boys hesitated. Presently the boy who had
the green satchel under the tree with Roger, who was
sitting in one corner of the room, said, "I should
think they would keep the squirrels from eating
them."

"And besides," continued he, after thinking a moment, "I should suppose, if the meat of the chestnut
had no covering, the rain might wet it and make it
rot, or the sun dry and wither it."

"Yes," said the Master, "these are very good
reasons why the nut should be carefully guarded.
First, the meats are packed away in a hard brown
shell, which the water cannot get through ; this keeps
them dry and away from dust, and other things which
might injure them.

" Then several nuts thus protected grow together closely, inside this green prickly covering, which grows over them and guards them from the larger animals and the boys. When the chestnut gets its full growth, and is ripe, this covering you know splits open, and the nuts drop out, and then any body can get them, and eat them."

The boys were then all satisfied that it was better that chestnuts should grow in burrs.

" But why," asked one of the boys, " do not apples grow so ?"

" Can any body answer that question ?" said the Master.

The boy with the green satchel said that apples had a smooth tight skin, which kept out the wet, but he did not see how they were guarded from animals.

The Master said it was by their taste. " They are hard and sour before they are full grown, and so the taste is not pleasant, and nobody wants to eat them, except sometimes a few foolish boys, who are often punished by being made sick.

" When the apples are full grown, then they change from sour to sweet, and become mellow ; then they can be eaten. Can you tell me of any other fruits which are preserved in this way ?"

One boy answered, strawberries and blackberries, and another said, peaches and pears.

Another boy then asked why the peach-stone was not outside of the peach, so as to keep it from being eaten. But the Master said he would explain this another time. Then he dismissed the scholars, after asking Roger to wait till the rest had gone, as he wished to see him alone.

What good does the chestnut burr do? What else ? Why do not apples grow so ? Who want to eat apples before they are grown ? How are they often punished ? Why do you suppose the Master kept Roger after the rest had gone ?

6*

LESSON XXXVII.

THE TWO PEAR TREES.

Betsy Bloom was a fine, straight, well-made child ; and she had a very beautiful face. The servant, who used to dress her in the morning, when she got up, and to undress her at night, when she went to bed, would often say to her, "What a beautiful, fine Miss you are! I am sure, not one of your play-fellows. is half so beautiful."

There was an old woman, who had nursed Betsy, that used to come and see her, and almost every time she came, she used to say to Betsy, "What a pretty face, my sweet Miss! I am sure I think you grow prettier every day."

Betsy heard so much about her prettiness, that she began to think she was better than other children, who were not so pretty.

If any of her school-fellows were homely, Betsy would not speak to them : at last, she became so naughty, that she would sometimes mock them, and give them nick-names.

Betsy's father and mother were very fond of her ; and paid so much attention to her, that they saw all her faults, and always tried to make her a good girl ; "for," said they, when they were talking to each other alone, "we are sure, although our Betsy is such a pretty child, every body will dislike her, if she is not also good-natured and obliging."

One day Betsy was walking in the garden with her father and mother, when little Gertrude, a neighbor's child, came into the garden. Gertrude ran up to Betsy's father and mother, gave each of them a hand, and said, "If you please, I will stay a little while and play with Betsy."

They told her she was welcome to stay as long as she pleased; and Betsy's mother stooped down and kissed her, and said, "Come whenever you like, my dear — you know we are always glad to see you."

Now Gertrude's face was very much scarred and pitted with the small pox: she had very red weak eyes; and, besides this, she was very short for her age; for she was as old as Betsy, and not so tall, by more than a head; and she had a hump on her back.

But Gertrude was very sensible; she was always in good humor with every body; she was never seen angry; and she was so attentive to her lessons, that every body who knew her loved her.

Little Betsy loved her too; but since she had thought so much of her own beauty, she was ashamed to be seen with such a homely child as Gertrude.

Betsy therefore took very little notice of Gertrude, and would not play with her at all; so that Gertrude, who thought Betsy was not in good humor, said she would go home, and come again another day.

Betsy was glad when she was gone and ran up to her father and mother, who were still in the garden. They were standing near a fine, straight, high pear tree; there were many pears growing upon the tree; — the pears were of a fine yellow color, and one side of them was as red as a cherry.

Betsy came running up to her father and mother: "O," said she, "how beautiful those pears are: I think they must now be quite ripe; will you be so kind, father, as to give me one?"

The father picked off one of the most beautiful looking pears that he could find, and gave it to Betsy. "Thank you, father," said she, and bit a piece directly out of it; but when it was in her mouth, she did not know what to do.

It was as dry as a bit of stick, and so hard and rough, that she would have spit it out, but she thought, as her father had picked it for her, he would take it ill if she did not eat it.

"Do you not like the pear?" asked Betsy's mother, who saw what a face she made. "I do not think I can eat it," said Betsy.

"You may throw it away, then," said her father; "but I thought you would have liked it, because of its beauty: you know, my dear, you like every thing that is handsome, and dislike whatever is homely."

He then led his daughter to an old, crooked pear tree, which looked almost as if it would fall down: the pears that grew on it were not beautiful; and they looked so green, that Betsy said she thought they were not half ripe. Her father gave her one of them, and told her to taste it: as soon as she bit it, her mouth was filled with fine juice, and she cried out, "O, father, what a nice pear! I never tasted any thing so nice before!—How full of juice it is! —What a fine taste it has!"

"Are you sure that you like the pear?" asked her father; "for it is not a beautiful pear." Betsy said she liked it, though it did not look pretty.

"Pray, then, my dear," said her father, "if I were to make you a present of a pear tree for yourself, which would you choose—the old crooked tree upon which these pears grow, or the beautiful looking tree yonder, upon which the others grow?"

Betsy said she should choose the ugly looking, crooked tree, with the green pears. Her father asked her why? "Because," said Betsy, "the one bears nice pears, that I can eat; and the other would be of no use, for I could not eat one of the pears."

"Then, I suppose," said her father, "you think things that are good and useful, better than things that are beautiful and of no use." Betsy said yes, that was what she thought.

"But, my dear child," said her father, "if you think so, how could you be so unjust, and so cruel, to poor little Gertrude, as you were a little while ago? You know she is very good; and how can you be so cruel to some of your play-fellows, whom you despise because they are not so handsome as you are?—though they are better than you, for they despise no one."

Betsy stood quite ashamed, and did not dare to look up to her father: the tears run down her cheeks; but she took her father's hand, although she could not speak a word.

" Do you think you have been wrong and naughty? —and are you resolved to mend?" asked her father, in a kinder voice than that in which he had before spoken.

"I am very sorry," said Betsy, "that I should have behaved so ill; but if you will forgive me, my dear father, I am sure I shall never do so any more —for I now see, that the most beautiful things and people, are not always so good as those things, and those people that are homely."

What bad things did Betsy do? Do you know what the Bible says of some children who mocked a good old man? Who came to see Betsy? Was she sensible? What does that mean? Did Betsy treat her kindly? Why? Was this right? Which pear tree bore the best pears? Are handsome people better than others? Are they worse, if more proud?

LESSON XXXVIII.

DEFINITIONS.

Haughty, proud. Mien, look. Mild, gentle. Submissively, humbly, without pride. Frankness, fairness. Argue, to reason, to dispute. Revenge, the injuring one who has injured us. Deny, to contradict.

THE WAY TO FIND OUT PRIDE.

Pride, ugly pride, sometimes is seen,
In haughty looks, and lofty mien;
But oft'ner it is found, that pride
Loves deep within the heart to hide,

And, while the looks are mild and fair.
It sits and does its mischief there.

Now, if you really wish to find
If pride is lurking in your mind,
Inquire if you can bear a slight,
Or patiently give up your right.
Can you submissively consent
To take reproof and punishment,
And feel no angry temper start
In any corner of your heart?

Can you with frankness own a crime,
And promise for another time?
Or say you've been in a mistake,
Nor try some poor excuse to make,
But freely own that it was wrong
To argue for your side so long?

Flat contradiction can you bear,
When you are right and know you are;
Nor flatly contradict again,
But wait, or modestly explain,
And tell your reasons, one by one,
Nor think of triumph, when you've done?

Can you, in business, or in play,
Give up your wishes or your way;
Or do a thing against your will,
For somebody that's younger still?
And never try to overbear,
Or say a word that is not fair?

Does laughing at you in a joke,
No anger nor revenge provoke?
But can you laugh yourself, and be,
As merry as the company?
Or when you find that you could do
To them, as they had done to you,
Can you keep down the wicked thought,
And do exactly as you ought?

} ut all these questions to your heart,
And make it act an honest part ;
And, when they've each been fairly tried,
I think you'll own that you have pride ;
Some one will suit you as you go,
And force your heart to tell you so ?
But if they all should be denied,
Then you'are too proud to own your pride !

LESSON XXXIX.

THE LITTLE APPLE TREE.

" Look here, Lucy," said little Charles to his sister, " and tell me what this is that is coming up out of the ground."

Lucy ran to see ; it was a green thing that looked a little like a leaf. Lucy did not know what it was.

" I will ask papa," said she, " he is coming along by here."

She asked her father to look at it, and he stopped a moment, and said that it was a little apple tree which was growing up from a seed, but that he was in haste, and could not stop to talk about it.

" A little apple tree !" said Charles, as his father passed on. " What is a little apple tree ? Do you know Lucy ?"

Lucy said she did not — there was an apple tree in the garden, but it was a great high tree, and besides, it did not look at all like that.

" We will wait till papa can tell us."

The next morning Charles came running in to call Lucy to look at the little apple tree. They went out together, and found that it had changed a great deal in the night. The green thing was up entirely out of the ground, and looked like two little leaves upon a stem.

" I wonder what makes it grow up so," said Lucy.

" I don't know," said Charles. Would not you dig it up and see ?"

" O no, I would not; I am afraid it would not grow any more."

" O, we can put it back again exactly as it was before ; and it would be so good to find out what it is which makes it grow."

Lucy at last consented, and they dug away the earth with a stick, and took the little apple tree up. Its stem reached down only a little way, and there was nothing at the end of it, but a littte root. They dug all about there, but could not find any thing which made it grow.

At last Charles said he would give up — he did not believe he could find out — he did not believe any body knew. So they began to fill up the hole, and tried to fix the little apple tree in its place again. They dirtied the top of it in handing it with their dirty fingers, and though they pushed it this way and that way, they could not fix it exactly as it was before. At last they left it, and went in to ask their mother about it.

She told them that she knew what made it grow.

" What is it ?" said Lucy.

" It is God. He makes every thing grow — the grass, and the tress, and every thing."

" But, how can he make every thing grow at the same time ?"

" Because he is present every where, and he is able to do any thing which he pleases. He is always with you and Charles; and makes your hair and your fingers and your whole body grow."

" Then he is always in us, and all about us."

" Yes, and he sees you at all times; he notices when you do wrong and when you do right."

Charles and Lucy then went away thinking that they ought to be careful not to do any thing wrong. The next morning they went to see the little apple tree, and found it wilted and dead.

How did Charles and Lucy try to find out what made the apple tree grow? Who did make it grow? Does he make any thing else grow? Where is God? What does he notice?

LESSON XL.

THE TWO BOOKS.

"Mind how you touch my gilded cover," said a fine book to a very plain one that happened to lie near him. "I wonder how such a ragged fellow can dare to take such liberties."

"It is true," said the plain book, "I do not look so fine as you do, but I have no rags that I need be ashamed of; for while you have been doing nothing these six years on the shelf, I have been read a hundred times.

"Besides, although my cover is nearly worn out, my leaves are sound, and worth a new cover; but when your fine cover is eaten off by the worms, you will never get another I fear."

"I am glad you like your rags," said the fine book, "but I will thank you to stand a little farther off, for I do not like them so well."

"For my part," said the poor book, "I would rather be worn out in doing good, than rust in idleness. But here comes our master."

The master came in, and seeing the two books together, the thought struck him that it would be well to put the good cover upon the book which was used, and the old one upon that which nobody read.

No sooner said than done. They were sent to the book-binder's, and before night changed covers.

He that would be useful in the world, must expect sometimes to wear out his coat, and suffer abuse from the idle and selfish.

LESSON XLI.

THE BLACKBERRY GIRL.

" Why, Phebe, are you come so soon,
    Where are your berries, child ?
You cannot, sure, have sold them all,
    You had a basket pil'd."

" No, mother, as I climb'd the fence,
    The nearest way to town,
My apron caught upon a stake,
    And so I tumbled down.

" I scratched my arm, and tore my hair
    But still did not complain ;
And had my blackberries been safe,
    Should not have cared a grain.

" But when I saw them on the ground,
    All scattered by my side,
I pick'd my empty basket up,
    And down I sat and cried.

" Just then a pretty little Miss
    Chanc'd to be walking by ;
She stopp'd, and looking pitiful,
    She begg'd me not to cry.

' Poor little girl, you fell,' said she,
    ' And must be sadly hurt'—
" O, no, I cried, but see my fruit,
    All mix'd with sand and dirt !"

' Well, do not grieve for that,' she said :
    ' Go home, and get some more.'
" Ah, no, for I have stripp'd the vines,
    These were the last they bore.

"My father, Miss, is very poor,
  And works in yonder stall;
He has so many little ones,
  He cannot clothe us all.

"I always long'd to go to church,
  But never could I go;
For when I ask'd him for a gown,
  He always answer'd, 'No.'

'There's not a father in the world
  That loves his children more;
I'd get you one with all my heart,
  But, Phebe, I am poor.'

"But when the blackberries were ripe,
  He said to me one day,
'Phebe, if you'll take the time
  That's given you for play,

'And gather blackberries enough,—
  And carry them to town,—
To buy your bonnet and your shoes,
  I'll try to get a gown.'

"O Miss, I fairly jump'd for joy,
  My spirits were so light:
And so, when I had leave to play,
  I pick'd with all my might.

"I sold enough to get my shoes,
  About a week ago;
And these, if they had not been spilt,
  Would buy a bonnet too.

"But now they're gone, they all are gone,
  And I can get no more,
And Sundays I must stay at home
  Just as I did before."

"And, mother, then I cried again,
  As hard as I could cry;

And, looking up, I saw a tear
　　Was standing in her eye.

" She caught her bonnet from her head—
　　' Here, here,' she cried, ' take this !'
" O, no, indeed — I fear your 'Ma
　　Would be offended, Miss."

' My 'Ma ! no, never ! she delights
　　All sorrow to beguile ;
And 'tis the sweetest joy she feels,
　　To make the wretched smile.

' She taught me, when I had enough,
　　To share it with the poor ;
And never let a needy child
　　Go empty from the door.

' So take it, for you need not fear
　　Offending her, you see ;
I have another, too, at home,
　　And one's enough for me.'

" So then I took it, here it is—
　　For pray what could I do ?
And, mother, I shall love that Miss
　　As long as I love you."

What is a stall ?　What is it to beguile the sorrow of others ?　Who are meant by the wretched ?

What happened to little Phebe ? Why did she cry ? Who pitied her? Why did Phebe want a gown? Why did not her father get her one ? When blackberries were ripe, what did he say to her? Did she get the shoes ? The bonnet ? How ? &c.

LESSON XLII.

WHAT THE BLACKBERRY GIRL LEARNED AT CHURCH.

"What have you in that basket, child?"
  "Blackberries, Miss, all pick'd to-day;
They're very large and fully ripe;
  Do look at them, and taste them, pray."

"O, yes; they're very nice, indeed,
  Here's fourpence — that will buy a few;
Not quite so many as I want—
  However, I must make it do."

"Nay, Miss, but you must take the whole,"
  "I can't, indeed, my money's spent;
I should be glad to buy them all,
  But I have not another cent."

"And if you had a thousand, Miss,
  I'd not accept of one from you.
Pray take them, they are all your own,
  And take the little basket too.

"Have you forgot the little girl
  You last year gave a bonnet to?
Perhaps you have — but ever will
  That little girl remember you.

"And ever since, I've been to church,
  For much do I delight to go;
And there I learn that works of love
  Are what all children ought to do.

"So then I thought within myself,
  That pretty basket, Billy wove,
I'll fill with fruit for that dear Miss,
  For sure 'twill be a work of love.

" And so this morning up I rose,
　　While yet the fields were wet with dew,
And pick'd the nicest I could find,
　　And brought them, fresh and sweet, for you.

" I know the gift is small indeed,
　　For such a lady to receive ;
But still I hope you'll not refuse
　　All that poor Phebe has to give."

What did the little girl give to the young lady who gave her
the bonnet? What does *going to church* mean? What did
the girl learn at church? What are *works of love?* Ought
you to do such works? If the little girl had taken pay for her
berries, would she have been grateful? Did you ever read of
a little boy who was grateful? Of one who was a miser?
Would a miser give away clothes?

LESSON XLIII.

HOW TO BEHAVE AT MEETING.

It often happens that children who go to meeting
sit in the gallery, away from their parents. And
sometimes they play in time of worship, which is very
wrong. It has been said, that " parents know, that
when their children sit together, and out of their
sight, they will play ; and that no parent who wishes
them to do otherwise, will send them into the gallery
to sit by themselves."

It is hoped, however, that this is not true of all
parents whose children do not sit with them at meeting. Perhaps they do not always think enough a-
bout it.

If any of the children who read this book, when
they attend public worship, do not sit with their parents, or other friends who are older than themselves,
they must remember that God is displeased with those
who play, while others around them are worshipping

Him — it may be well for them to show this lesson to their friends at home.

When young people go to church, they should make as little noise as possible, in shutting doors, and in walking to their seats.

They should not be paring their finger-nails, or be otherwise busy with their penknives; but should attend closely to what is said, and try to remember it.

People ought not to sleep at meeting; though good people have sometimes been known to do it.

A man, whom we will call Mr. Arnum, once heard one of his neighbors use bad words. Mr. Arnum knew this to be wrong.

He therefore went to the person, and said to him, "My friend, when a man sees his neighbor doing what is wrong, don't you think he ought to go to him and tell him of it?" "Certainly," answered the man; "have you known me do any thing that was not right?"

"Yes," replied Mr. Arnum; "not long since I heard you use bad language." "Did you? indeed!" said the man; "well, I thank you for your kindness, and will try to leave off doing so."

Soon after, on the Sabbath, Mr. Arnum fell asleep at meeting. The man who had been reproved by him for using bad words, sat at the other side of the house. He saw that Mr. Arnum was nodding, and rose from his seat and went to him.

He then put his hand on his shoulder, and gently shook him, saying, "Mr. Arnum, when a man sees his neighbor do wrong, don't you think he ought to go to him and tell him of it? — I think it is wrong to sleep when we meet to worship our Maker."

Mr. Arnum was much mortified, as almost every one in the house was looking at them. Perhaps, also, he felt ashamed that this man should have reason to reprove him, when, but a short time before, he had gone to the man to tell him of his fault.

Is it right to play at meeting? To be paring your finger-nails &c.? Do you think the Blackberry Girl played at
meeting? Why do you think so? What can you tell me of
Mr. Arnum? What is it to reprove a person? Are those
who kindly reprove us for our faults, our best friends? Should
we be offended with them?

LESSON XLIV.

THE LITTLE SIN.

Thomas Barker went one day to a neighbor's house,
and when he returned, his mother observed he had a
new board-nail in his hand. She inquired where he
obtained it, and found that he had picked it-up at
the neighbor's house, and brought it home without
leave.

She told him he had done very wrong, and made
him go and carry it back again. Thomas did not do
any such thing again for some days; but after a
while he brought home three or four apples, and
confessed they were not given to him. At this time
his mother sent him to return them, and whipped
him besides.

Now perhaps some children think his mother was
cruel, to whip little Thomas for only getting a few
apples not worth a cent. But let us think about it
a moment.

She had often told her little son, that it was wrong
to take any thing which was not his own, without
having leave; and when he took the nail, she reproved him, and made him return it.

But Thomas forgot all this, or would not mind it
and went and took the apples. He was then more
wicked, than if he had not done so before, or if his
mother had not taught him and reproved him.

She was afraid he would do the same thing again
and again, if she let him alone, till he should become

very wicked, and steal goods and money, and be sent to the State's prison as a thief.

So she took a rod and chastised him betimes, as the wise man says, to drive his wickedness away. She did right, and it was very good for Thomas. " The rod and reproof give wisdom."

He was afterwards tempted to take things that he wanted, when people did not see him. But he remembered the smart which the rod gave him : that brought to mind his mother's instructions and warnings ; he thought that the eyes of God were upon him ; and he did not steal any more.

He grew up a good boy ; and when he became a man, he was virtuous and respected.

Now, children, do not say that Thomas committed a little sin, and one that was not worthy of notice. It is true that the nail and apples were little things. But then Thomas was a little boy ; and with such little fellows, little things are as important as great things are to men and women.

No doubt Thomas thought as much of his apples as a man would of three dollars. And would it not be wrong for a man to steal three dollars ? Besides, none of us should do any thing wrong because it is little. God does not allow of little sins.

We should always ask, Is it right ? or Is it wrong ? We should not ask, whether it is less wicked than some other wicked thing ; but whether God will or will not be angry. Sin is hateful, whether it be great or small ; children should no more commit a little sin, than they would take a little poison.

By doing wrong in little things, when they know it to be wrong, children cast off the fear of God and make their hearts hard. By and by they become bolder ; and if they are not restrained by punishment, they become very wicked.

Many poor creatures who have been hung for murder have confessed that they began with small offences, and went on from one wickedness to ano-

ther, till they became thieves and robbers.   They
did not love and obey their parents, when they were
small children.

They did not keep holy the Sabbath day.   Afterwards they stole some little things, and then things
of more value.   They told lies about their playthings
to one another ; then about other things to their parents ; and finally became great liars, whom nobody
could trust.

They first got angry about their sports ; after
some time they would strike and push one another ;
before they were men, they would quarrel and fight
in the streets ; and it is no wonder they were at last
hanged for murder.

What did Thomas first steal?   What did his mother do?
Did he steal again?   What did his mother then do?   Was she
cruel?   What was she afraid he would do, if she did not
punish him?   What did Thomas remember, when he afterwards wanted to steal?   Do you think he ever would have
been a good man, if he had not been punished?   What should
we ask ourselves about actions?   When we are not certain
whether a thing is right, what should we ask? Ans.   *Is there
any harm in letting it alone?*   What have those often confessed,
who have been hung?

LESSON XLV.

FRANK LUCAS,

Mrs. Corbon kept a village school in the State of
New York.   She had a noble mind, and was a friend
to all good children.   One cold morning in the winter, a small boy came along, with a saw on his arm,
and wanted this lady to hire him to saw wood.

She said that one of her neighbors, a trusty man,
would like to saw the wood, and she did not wish to
hire any body else.   "Oh dear," said the boy, "what
shall I do!"   "Why, little fellow," said she, "what
is the matter?"

He answered, " My father is blind, mother is sick, and I left my sister crying at home, for fear poor 'ma will die. I take care of them as well as I can ; but they have nothing to eat. I want to work, and get something for them."

Mrs. Corbon had never seen this lad before, and did not know what his name was, till he told her; but she perceived he was a boy of uncommon good-ness, because he was so kind to his parents and sister.

He shivered very much with the cold ; for he was but thinly dressed, and his ear locks were white with frost. The lady asked him to come in and warm himself. As he sat in a chair by the fire, she saw the tears run down his cheeks, and she tried to com-fort him.

" It is not for myself," said Frank, " that I cry. I don't mind a little cold, but I can't help thinking of the family at home. We used to be very happy ; but a sad change has happened in our house."

" Are you not hungry ?" said Mrs. Corbon.

" Not much, ma'am : that is not what troubles me. I had some potato for dinner yesterday." " Did you not have supper last night ?" " No, ma'am." " Nor breakfast, this morning?" " Not yet: but no mat-ter ; I shall get some by and by. — If I try to do well, God will protect me : for so my precious mother says. I believe she is the best woman in the world. If I did not think she was, I would not say so."

" You are a fine boy," said the lady : " I will be your friend, if you have not another on earth ;" and the tears sparkled in her eyes, as she gave him a bis-cuit with a piece of meat, on a small plate.

" Thank you, ma'am," said Frank ; " if you please, I will keep them to carry home. Don't you think, ma'am, that any body will hire me to saw wood ?"

" Yes, my dear little fellow," she answered, " I will give you money to saw mine." He thanked her again, and ran to the wood pile to begin his work.

The lady put on her cloak, and went out among her neighbors.

She told them Frank was one of the best boys she had ever seen, and she hoped they would do something to help the little fellow to provide for the family.

So they came to her house, where he was, and one gave him a six cent piece, another a shilling, and a third twenty-five cents, till they made up nearly three dollars.

They gave him a loaf of bread, part of a cheese, some meat and cake, a jug of milk, and some apples to roast for his sick mother; with a little basket to put them all in; so that he had as much as he could carry.

He told them he was very much obliged to them indeed; but he did not wish to be a beggar. He chose to work and pay for what he had, if they would let him; but they said he must not stay now. He might see to that another time.

"We are going," said Mrs. Corbon, "to send the things to your mother; because she is such an excellent lady; and I should like to go and see her myself."

Frank hurried back, tugging his load, and the whole family cried for joy. "Bless your dear little heart," said his poor blind father; "come here and let me get hold of you. I hope, my son, you will never be unable to see the friends you love: but we must not complain, nor forget the favors we receive, because we cannot have every thing as we wish."

It is thirty years since this affair happened; and the same Frank Lucas is now a Judge, and one of the first men in the county where he lives. His father is dead.

Judge Lucas is married, and now has five children. They go to school; and their father tells them, if they intend ever to be useful, they must learn well while they are young: if they expect to be happy in this world, or the next, they must love God, honor their parents and teachers, and be kind to all ; and that, in this free country, the way for a poor little boy to become a great and happy man, is, to be honest, industrious, and good.

Why did Frank want to saw wood? Was he hungry? What had he eaten? What did he say of his mother? What did the lady give him? What did he wish to do with it? Did she hire him to work? What did the lady then do? What did the neighbors give to Frank? What did he say to them? Were the family glad when Frank came home? What did Frank afterwards become? What did he tell his children they must do, if they wished ever to be useful? If they expected to be happy?

LESSON XLVI.

DEFINITIONS.

Indolent, idle, lazy. Flourishing, increasing, prosperous. Comical, funny. Commercial, connected with trade. Navigable, suitable for the passing of ships or boats.

THE IDLE SCHOOL BOY.

I will tell you about the laziest boy you ever heard of. He was indolent about every thing. When he played, the boys said he played as if the master told him to. And when he went to school, he went creeping along, like a snail, with a satchel on his back. The boy had sense enough; but he never learned any thing — he was too lazy to learn any thing.

When he had spelled a word, he drawled out one syllable after another, as if he were afraid the syllables would quarrel, if he did not keep them a great way apart. Once, when he was saying a lesson in Geography, his Master asked him, "What is said of

8

Hartford?" He answered, "Hartford is a flourishing, comical town."

He meant it was "a flourishing, *commercial* town;" but he was such a stupid fellow that he never knew what he was about. When asked how far the Kennebec was navigable, he said it was "navigable for boots as far as Waterville." The boys all laughed, and the School-master could not help laughing too. The idle boy colored like scarlet.

"I say it is so in my book," said he; and when one of the boys showed him the Geography, and pointed to the place where it was said, that the Kennebec was navigable for *boats* as far as Waterville, he stood with his hands in his pockets, and his mouth open, as if he could not understand what they were all laughing at.

You can easily guess what luck this idle boy had. His father tried to give him a good education, but he would be a dunce; not because he was a fool, but because he was too lazy to give his attention to any thing. He had a considerable fortune left him, but he was too lazy to take care of it; and now he goes about the streets, with his hands in his pockets, begging his bread.

How did the lazy boy spell his words? What did he say of Hartford? Of the river Kennebec? What made him a dunce? What became of his fortune? What is a *fortune*?

LESSON XLVII.

THE LITTLE BEGGARS.

"I think poor children must be very unhappy," said little Octavia, as she sat dressing her doll in muslin. "If I were as poor as those little children who came here begging yesterday, I should not take the least comfort in the world."

"My little daughter is mistaken," said her mother. "Poor children are just as happy as rich ones, except when they are suffering from cold. or hunger; and that very seldom happens in America. Our Father who lives in heaven, takes care of them, as well as of you."

God has given them hearts and minds; and good feelings and good thoughts alone make both great and little folks happy; it is no matter what clothes they wear, what food they eat, or what toys they play with.

When you have been a naughty girl, your waxen doll, and your glass bird, and your gold musical box, do not make you feel happy; and when you have been a good girl, you can be very happy without them.

So you see it depends upon your thoughts and feelings, whether you are happy or not; and poor children have as good and as kind feelings as rich ones. That little boy who came here to beg yesterday, who was so small he could hardly reach the latch of the door, is a very good boy; and therefore I know he is a very happy boy.

A piece of cake, or candy would be a great rarity to him, and he would love them very much; yet when I offered him a few cents the other day, for going on an errand, he said, "No ma'am, I would rather not take it; you have been too kind to my mother."

Octavia thought a little boy who loved his mother better than himself, must be happy; and she asked leave to walk with her mother, the next time she went to see the beggar children.

When they went, Octavia found one little girl five years old, building a house with some dirty blocks she had picked up in the streets; while her little sister, about three years old, knocked it down, and laughed so loud that she made the room ring again. Presently the little boy, her mother had spoken of, came in with a saucer half full of boiled rice.

" Where have you been, John ?" asked his older
sister.

" I have been in to give Bob Rowley some of my
dinner," answered the boy ; " he has been out begging all day, without getting any thing to eat ; so I
have given him half of my rice."

Then John sat down on a cricket, and ate up his
morsel of rice with a good relish. He scraped the
saucer very clean, and looked at the spoon, as if he
wished there had been more. But he put it away
with a cheerful look, and said to his mother, " Is there
any thing I can do for you, this afternoon, mother ?"
and in obedience to her he ran off to pick up chips,
whistling and singing as he went.

" Well my dear Octavia, do not these children seem
happy ?" asked her mother, as they walked homeward.

" Yes ma'am," replied the little girl ; " their dirty
blocks seemed to amuse them as much as my doll
does me."

" From this, my daughter, learn that God is good
to the poor, as well as to the rich," said her mother.
" God has ordained that every body shall be happy,
who is good; and he helps every one to be good
who earnestly wishes to be so.

" Little John wanted all his dinner sadly ; but he
gave it to a boy who needed it more than he did.
He put down a selfish feeling, and he encouraged
a kind feeling ; and that is the reason he is happy."

What makes people happy ? Whom did Octavia go with her
mother to see ? What were the children doing ? Where had
John been ? What did he say of Bob Rowley ? What did
Octavia think of these children ? What has God ordained?
Whom does he help to be good? Why was little John
happy ?

LESSON XLVIII.

THERE IS NOTHING LIKE TRYING.

Mary Jones and her brother Edmund, had no father or mother ; but they had a sister who was older than themselves, and who was very kind to them.

She used to teach them every day, to read and write ; besides that, she wished them to learn lessons in Colburn's Arithmetic.

Perhaps some of my little readers may not have met with this book ; and it may seem hard that Mary and Edmund should be desired to study any thing so difficult as arithmetic ; but you must remember, that their sister was very kind to them, and, therefore, would not be likely to give them any thing to learn, which was too hard for them.

Edmund was eight years old, and was able to answer any of the first questions in fractions ; such as, " Seven fourths of twelve, are how many times six ?" and he had attended so closely to it, that he understood the relations of numbers very well.

But Mary, who was seven years old, was, I am sorry to say it, unable to answer, " How many are two and five," or any of those simple questions. She had not attended, as her brother had done ; and this was the reason she had not succeeded in learning as well.

" Sister, have you the head-ache to-day ? You look sick," said Mary, affectionately.

" Yes, my dear, my head does ache ; but I will try to teach you, notwithstanding, about your lesson, and, if you are attentive, I can make you understand it in a few minutes. What is your lesson to-day ?"

Mary's face lengthened very much, as she answered dolefully, " It is, how many gills in a quart ? and, sister, I cannot find it out ; I've been studying a great while, and I know I never shall understand it."

Her sister took a slate and pencil and marked out a circle, which, she said should stand for a quart ; then

8*

she drew a line through the middle of it, and divided the circle into two parts.

" One of these halves, Mary, is a pint; you know two pints make a quart. Now, I will divide this pint into two parts and each part, you know, is half a pint; in a half-pint there are two gills, — make a dot for each gill — now divide the rest, as you have seen me do this." `

" I cannot, sister."

" Well, Mary, then I will do it. I place a dot for each gill — now count the gills; there are eight. I think you understand now, Mary ?"

" Yes, sister, I think I do; may I take my spelling-book ?"

" Very soon — now tell me, lest you forget it. Mary, how many gills in a quart ?"

" I don't know — I never shall learn those hard questions ;" and Mary looked very red, — for she was very much ashamed of her inattention, while her kind sister had been trying to teach her.

She looked up in her sister's face, and saw that she looked very ill, and her eyes were full of tears.

Mary would much rather she had spoken harshly to her, than to look so grieved ; and her own heart told her she had done very wrong to try the patience of one who had been so good to her.

But she did not like to say that she was sorry; so she took her spelling-book, and bent her head over it to study very hard.

In a little time, Edmund was ready to repeat his lesson : it was short, but he understood it fully, and answered every question readily : his sister kissed him and she said, " Mary, you remember that little fan of mine with the ivory handle, that you like so much; if you will commit your lesson in arithmetic, perfectly. for a week, you shall have it for your own."

Mary did not say a word, but she hid her face in her spelling-book, and the tears dropped thick and fast from her eyes. It was a long time before she could command her voice sufficiently to say, " I do not wish for the fan."

" Not wish for it Mary ? I thought you did wish for it very much."

" I mean," said Mary, " I wish to learn my lesson, to please you, and because I ought to do so, — and not for the sake of the fan ; and I do not want you to give it to me, if I do get my lesson. Indeed, sister, I will try to learn better, if you will not look so sorry."

Her sister did not look sorry then ; but she kissed Mary, and told her, if she pleased, she might come and attend that moment to her arithmetic lesson. When the explanation was finished, Mary answered the question " How many gills in a quart ?"—" Eight."

In a few months she understood all the mysteries of her arithmetic ; if at any time her lesson seemed too difficult, she recollected the time when she learned the number of gills in a quart, and would say, very gravely, to her brother, " After all, Edmund, there is nothing like trying.

I find when I really try, that I can learn any thing — any thing, I mean, in fractions, and spelling ; and I remember, when I did not get my lessons perfectly, it was always because I was thinking of something else.

I was always thinking of our blocks, and how we should make a temple, and put the kitten inside, or something else that had nothing to do with the lesson. I tell you this, Edmund," she concluded, with a dignified air, " so that you may know how to correct yourself if — if you should not study well. Come, let us go build a pagoda."

Did Mary and Edmund have parents to teach them ? Who did teach them ? What did she wish them to learn? What simple question could not Mary answer ? Why ? What was the lesson, which Mary thought so hard ? How did her sister try to make her understand it ? Did Mary attend to what her sister was saying ? Was this being grateful ? How did her

sister look ?　What did she offer to give Mary if she would get
her lessons well for a week ?　Would Mary take it ?　Why ?
Did she in a few months understand her lessons ?　What did she
say to Edmund ?　Why did not she get her lessons before ?

When Mary was crying, she could not command her voice ;
what does that mean ?　Do you commonly succeed in getting a
lesson, when you study hard ?　When you are thinking about
something else ?　What is a circle ?　Can you make one with
a pencil ?　When Mary looked dignified, did she laugh ?　Cry ?
Look silly ?　What are pagodas ?　Temples in the East Indies,
where idols are worsihpped.—What are idols ?

LESSON XLIX.

DEFINITIONS.

Solitary, having no company. Combat, a battle. Select, to pick out. Victim, something destroyed. Prey,
that which is taken by force to be devoured. Resemble, to be like.

THE TIGER.

The Tiger is from three feet and a half, to four feet
high, and from eight to ten feet long.

His shape is very much like that of the cat ; but
his legs are thicker, and stronger in proportion to his
body, than those of the cat. His ears are small ; his
mouth is wide ; and his teeth and claws are long and
terrible.

The color of this animal gives him a most beautiful
appearance. It is deep yellow, striped around the body
with black.

The Tiger is the most ferocious and blood-thirsty
of all beasts. He is so cruel, as never to be contented with slaying, so long as he sees any living creature
near him.

His rage for destroying is such, that he does not
eat, so long as he can have the pleasure of killing.
Even when he is not hungry, he delights in tearing
other animals in pieces.

This animal has seldom or never been so far tamed as to make it safe for a stranger to go near him, when full grown. Young Tigers have, however, permitted dogs to live with them.

Neither the kindest, nor the most severe treatment, has ever subdued this ferocious animal. When he is starving, he will often bite the hand that feeds him, just as soon as he will one that strikes him.

In his rage, he will attack every living beast except the elephant and the rhinoceros, and even these he does not always avoid.

He is so bold and fierce, that he does not even fear the face of man ; but will attack the solitary traveller, wherever he can find him, or at a single bound, select his victim from a group of men.

The Tiger seizes his prey exactly as the cat does. The cat does not seize her prey by running it down like the dog, but she watches until the poor little mouse comes along, when she springs upon it at once.

Just so the huge Tiger does. He hides himself where the buffalo or other animals come to drink, and when one comes near him, he gives a bound, and seizes it with his terrible claws and teeth.

It is said that the Tiger is so amazingly strong, that after having killed a buffalo, an animal larger than an ox, he throws it across his back, and holding it with his teeth, runs off, just as a fox runs away with a goose.

These animals are so fierce and spiteful, that they never can agree to live in peace, even among themselves : and hence they never run in droves, nor do they assist each other in their combats with other animals.

The shape of the Tiger and the Leopard are very nearly the same. Their colors are also alike. The Tiger is yellow, striped with black, while the Leopard is yellow, spotted with black.

The size of the Tiger is much larger than that of the Leopard ; he is also more fierce and cruel. The

Leopard can be tamed so as to be glad to see his master ; but the Tiger is seldom glad to see any thing which he cannot tear in pieces and devour.

The skin of the Tiger, on account of its singular beauty, is valuable, and sells at a high price, but no other part of the animal is of any use.

If the Tiger himself, is of little use, his history perhaps may be useful ; for we must not believe that any thing has been made without a good design.

If it should be asked, for instance, why the most beautiful of quadrupeds should be at the same time one of the most ferocious and hateful of all animals, in his actions, we may answer that the Creator, perhaps intended to show us how little value we ought to set upon beauty, by thus bestowing it on the worst of creatures.

In not permitting such strong and cruel animals to run in droves, the Creator's wisdom, and his kindness towards man, are plainly to be seen. For did Tigers herd together, the people where they live would either be destroyed by them, or be obliged to go constantly with guns or spears in their hands to defend themselves, and save their lives.

Thus we see that the ferocity of Tigers, being such as not to admit of their running in droves, is the very means by which their causing wide destruction is prevented.

Is the Tiger as long as this room ? How high is he ? What is his shape ? Color ? Is he cruel ? Can he be tamed ? How does he seize his prey ? How large is a buffalo ? Can the Tiger lift a buffalo ? Do Tigers live in peace among themselves ? What animal does the Tiger resemble in his looks ? Is he spotted ? Is the Tiger of any use ? Why may we suppose so hateful an animal made so beautiful ? What shows that the Creator is wise, and kind to man ? When do children resemble Tigers ?

LESSON L.

DEFINITIONS.

Conceited, having a high opinion of one's self. Pert, bold, saucy. Flatter, to coax. Permission, leave. Encourage, to give courage to ; to make bold.

THE CONCEITED BOY.

When little Henry had finished his lesson, Mrs. Kitty came into the study, and asked her master's leave to go, in the afternoon, to see her sister, who lived about a mile distant, and to take Master Henry with her.

" You have my leave to go yourself, Kitty," said Mr. Dalben ; " but as to taking Henry, I think he will do you no credit; his spirit will rise, he will begin to chatter, and I fear that you will not check him as you ought."

" Indeed I will, Sir," said Mrs. Kitty ; " I always do speak to him when he is rude."

" And I will be very good," said Henry.

" And I will keep him out of all mischief, Sir," said Kitty.

" And I will do every thing which Mrs. Kitty bids me," said Henry.

" And I am sure little Master will be good," added Mrs. Kitty.

" And so I suppose I must give my permission," said Mr. Dalben ; " but I trust to you, Kitty, if he does not behave well, that you will never ask leave to take him out again."

Thus the matter was settled ; and as soon as dinner was over, Master Henry took leave of his uncle, and walked off with Mrs. Kitty over the fields towards Mrs. Green's cottage.

Mrs. Green, who expected her sister, was dressed in her best gown and apron ; and her two daughters had also put on their best. At sight of Henry and

Mrs. Kitty, they came out at the door, and gave them a hearty welcome.

"And so, Master Milner," said Mrs. Green, "this is very kind in you, to come so far to see us poor folks Come, Master Milner, please, Sir, to be seated; you must have the big chair.

"Nay, sister," said Mrs. Kitty, in a whisper, "do not make too much of the child; he will grow troublesome; and master will blame me."

Mrs. Green, however, still kept flattering him. She and her daughters gave him the first and best at supper, till the young gentleman, by degrees, grew very pert, and began to chatter at a great rate.

After he had talked for some time, as the party were sitting around the table, a large frog came sprawling over the little narrow walk, which ran from the house door to the gate.

"Ah!" said Kitty, "look at that frightful creature: sister Green, I wonder you don't clear your garden of those frogs! I would as soon meet a thief in the dark, as a frog."

Mrs. Green laughed, and said, "O, they do no harm; why should you be afraid of them?"

Master Henry now took it upon himself to show how much he knew. "Those creatures do no harm," said he; "they are of the class amphibia; that is, of the third class; some of that class are very mischievous; but frogs never hurt any one."

"Amphibia!" said Mrs. Kitty: "what a word is that, Master Henry! how can you use such words?"

"It is not English, Mrs. Kitty," said Henry, "you don't understand it, I know; but I do; it means the creatures who live half on land and half in water, as frogs and toads do."

Mrs. Green looked at her sister, and said,

"Dear me! do hear how he talks!"

"There are six classes of living creatures," said Henry, being encouraged by Mrs. Green; "first, those which feed their young ones with milk, such as cows, and dogs, and cats, and rats, and sheep; and then there is the second class, birds; and the third, amphibia; and the fourth, fish; and the fifth, insects, as butterflies; and the sixth, worms."

"There, again," said Mrs. Green, " what words are those to come out of the mouth of such a boy! Did you ever hear the like?"

Mrs. Kitty was pleased that Henry should be able to do himself so much credit before Mrs. Green; but she said, " You know, sister, he does not find out these things, but that Master teaches him; and so you know it is no wonder, if he knows more than we do."

" Oh !" said Mrs. Green, " but it is a wonder how such a young creature should be able to keep all these things in his head, and speak them so properly as he does."

Where did Mrs. Kitty and Henry go? What did Henry promise? How was Mrs. Green dressed? What did she say to Henry? Did she flatter him? What did he soon become? What soon came in sight? What did Kitty say? What did Henry? What did he say about the amphibia? About the first class of living creatures? The second? Third? Fourth? Fifth? Sixth? How came Henry to know more than the women? Was it right to be proud of it? Can you name an amphibious animal?

LESSON LI.

THE CONCEITED BOY'S TROUBLES.

By this time Henry was become so conceited, that he could not sit still; so, having eaten and drank as much as he could conveniently swallow, he got up, stalked about the room, and then went out into the garden, having been told not to go beyond the fence.

The first thing he did, was, to pursue Mrs. Green's ducks round the house, calling out, " Quack, quack, quack," as they waddled before him, till they made their escape through the fence into the next field.

He then espied an old owl, hid in a tree. As soon as Henry saw him, he began to call to him, making a low bow, and saying, " Your servant, old gentleman ; your nose is exactly fit for a pair of spectacles."

The owl, however, being used to the human voice, took no notice of Henry ; whereupon he began picking up sods to throw at him ; this was very cruel sport.

Being soon tired of this, he looked around again for something to amuse him ; and seeing a ladder set up against the side of the house, he climbed up it, and scrambling along the roof, he reached the very highest part of it, astride of which he set himself, and trying to fancy that the house was an elephant, he pretended, to be driving it forward, as if it were really moving.

When Mrs. Kitty was ready to go home she sent her nieces to call Henry. He was mounted on the top of the house, and had the pleasure of hearing himself called for, and saw them running here and there to find him.

Neither of them thought of looking for him where he really was. This pleased Master Henry mightily, and he kicked his elephant, and rode away famously, in his own conceit. Mrs. Kitty and Mrs. Green came out, and called Master Henry so loudly, that they might be heard a quarter of a mile distant.

After a while Henry called out, " O ! O ! Henry Milner, where are you, where are you, Sir? Don't you hear the people call you ?"

At the sound of his voice, the women looked up and said, " O, Master Milner! you little rogue! how you have frightened us; and how did you get up there ?" Henry then came down, and they started for home.

They took a different path from that by which they had come ; it led them down a long, narrow lane, at the end of which was a little brook, which they were to cross by a narrow wooden bridge. Mrs. Green and her daughters went with them part of the way.

Master Henry soon became very rude, and Mrs. Kitty grew angry, and tried to catch hold of the naughty boy; but he ran down the lane, got upon the wooden bridge, and stood jumping upon it with all his might.

On seeing this, Mrs. Kitty scolded, Mrs. Green screamed, and her daughters ran forward with all speed, but all in vain. The plank broke in the very centre, and Henry came tumbling into the brook, bringing the bridge down with him.

The water was not indeed very deep, but there was enough of it to wet the little boy to his knees, as he stood up. He was not hurt, but was covered with mud up to his shoulders.

Mrs. Kitty was much vexed and frightened; however, she and her nieces soon contrived to pull the little boy out of the water, and passing over the brook as well as they could, some of the party made the best of their way towards home.

Mr. Dalben was walking in his garden, when Mrs. Kitty and her younger niece appeared, leading Master Henry between them; for Mrs. Green and her oldest daughter had gone back.

The whole party were well bedaubed with mud, and Mrs. Kitty looked rather ashamed; neither was Master Henry in quite so high spirits as when he was explaining his *six classes* to Mrs. Green and her daughters.

"Why, Kitty," said Mr. Dalben, "what is the matter? Where have you all been? Henry, my boy, what can you have been about? have you been improving your acquaintance with the amphibia?"

"O, Sir!" said Mrs. Kitty, "Master Henry would not mind what I said to him; and he broke down the bridge, Sir; and he has been in the brook."

"Well, well," said Mr. Dalben, "I told you how it would be; but make all possible haste now; take off his clothes and warm his bed, and I will come in a few minutes with something for him to drink."

Mr. Dalben soon returned with something which was very bitter; Henry drank it without saying a word; for he knew he had behaved ill, and deserved punishment.

When Henry had done eating, what did he do? Do you think he did right to climb to the top of the house? Why? Do you think he had a comical look when he came out of the brook? A haughty look? What is found at the centre of an apple? At the surface? Do you think Henry was delighted with the bitter drink? Was it delicious? What will make children conceited?

LESSON LII.

DEFINITIONS.

Generous, ready to give. Convince, to make one believe by showing good reasons. Reverence, love and respect. Sustenance, victuals, food. Furnished, supplied. Deceived, made to believe a lie.

FIRST OF APRIL.

Joseph and Charles were both of them blessed with excellent parents. Both of them attended the Sabbath School; and both were good scholars.

Charles was pleasant, affectionate and kind; Joseph was good, generous and just. Charles loved a good story: Joseph was a lover of truth. On the first of April, Joseph asked leave to spend the evening with his friend. His mother cheerfully gave him leave.

"Charles," said he, as he entered the door, "I am tired of the first of April."

Charles. Why, what is the matter, Joseph? You don't object, I hope, to a little fun.

Joseph. Yes, Charles, I object to such fun as I have seen to-day. I object to lying.

Charles. Why, the first of April we are always allowed to fool people, and I don't see that there is any harm in it. Every body does so.

Joseph. I know that every body sins against God; but still, sin is wrong, and God will call us to account for it. Is it no harm to tell a lie? Besides, Charles, I can tell you things which I have seen to-day, that will convince you that I am right.

Charles. Well, Joseph, I am willing to be convinced, if I am wrong.

Joseph. I saw an old gentleman riding on horse-back, — I should think he was sixty years old, — the few hairs upon his head were gray. For such men we ought always to feel a great reverence. The boys had wrapped up some sand in a paper, on the out-side of which was written *Sugar*, and put it in the muddiest place in the road.

The old gentleman stopped his horse, and got off in the mud, and was about to pick up the bundle, when my heart was touched, and I said to him, " Sir, the boys are trying to fool you." Then all the boys shouted "April fool," and one of them wanted to fight with me for spoiling their sport; but I refused to do it, and walked away.

Charles. That was really too bad to make sport of such an old gentleman, who had done them no harm.

Joseph. There was another cruel thing that I saw. Some boys had taken pains to heat a horseshoe very hot, and laid it upon a stone by the side of the road. A traveller passing along in a wagon, with his wife, saw the shoe, and got out to pick it up; in doing which he burnt his hand very severely.

The boys, at the same instant, shouted, " April fool," which frightened the horse, so that he ran away with the wagon, and upset it, scattering the traveller's things all along the road. The woman, in attempt-ing to jump from the wagon, fell upon her face, and was very much injured.

Charles. That was cruel indeed. How did the boys feel?

Joseph. At first they laughed : when they saw the horse running, they trembled ; and when the woman was hurt, they were afraid and ran away. I saw many other tricks, where no serious damage was done, but where a great many lies were told ; and sometimes the " fool " came upon the boys themselves.

Charles. Yes : I saw one trick of that kind, and a pretty good one too. A little boy, whose mother was very poor, was sent with half a dollar to buy flour. Several of the boys had fooled him, and he thought he would have a little sport.

He stopped at the coppersmith's and got a hole bored in the half dollar, and put a string into it ; then laying the piece down before a store, stood behind the door, and when any person attempted to pick it up, he twitched it in. The string near the money was covered with dust, so that it could not be seen.

He succeeded in fooling a number of people in this way. At last, a drunken man came along, who understood the trick, and stepped on the string, and broke it, and got the money, and told the boy he was an " April fool," and spent the money in drinking.

Joseph. For my part, I am resolved never to play " April fool " again ; for I think it the worst kind of lying. Here we see old age made sport of ; human life put in danger ; a poor widow deprived of her sustenance ; and a drunkard furnished with the means of getting drink ; — all this, and a great deal more, to gratify foolish children.— Now Charles, who are the greatest fools, the boys who tell the lies, or those who are deceived by them ?

Charles. Well, Joseph, I am of your opinion. I never before knew the evils to be so great.

Joseph. Let us both, then, set our faces against this vile practice. Let us do all we can to put a stop to it.

What mischief was done by the boys to the traveller and his wife ? What does the Bible say about lying ? Ans. It says, " Lie not one to another." Who are the greatest fools, those who tell lies, or those who are deceived by them? Did you ever read of a little girl who told lies? Do you remember what happened to her? Can a person act a lie? Is it right to make sport of old people? Are you furnished with books? What furnishes people with milk?

What happened to the boy who was sent to buy flour? Who succeeded in getting away his half dollar? What did the man do with the money? What do you suppose he drank? Why do you suppose so? Would it have been better to throw away the money? Why?

LESSON LIII.

DEFINITIONS.

Mirror, a looking-glass. Cricket, a low stool. Reflect, to think. Deprive, to take away from.

LITTLE TYRANTS.

"Mary, Mary, if you behave so rude and don't mind me, when I tell you to stop, I shall not let you go with me to-morrow to pick currants in that beautiful garden," said Ellen Wilson to her sister, a little romping girl, four years younger than herself.

Mary stopped her play of jumping from the table, and looking at her sister, half laughing, a little saucily replied, "I guess, Miss Ellen, I shall go; because mother has promised me, and you know she always performs her promises."

"Yes I know she does; but did she not add, if you were a good girl?"

"Well, you know I have been a good girl, Ellen."

"No, I don't, Mary; for I have been trying this long time to make you stop jumping from the table, and you would'nt mind me until now: and if you won't mind me here at home, I shall not dare to take you where there are so many things you can injure by touching."

"Well, Ellen, I will mind you; I won't jump there any more."

Ellen was a gentle and very amiable child ; though, like all children, sometimes fond of a little authority.

Mary played some time very prettily with her doll ; but spying a new book on the table, she took it, and, delighted with the pictures, refused to resign it to her sister, who said, " Give it to me, Mary ; 'tis a borrowed book ; and you know mother does not allow you to have borrowed books."

" Well, Ellen, only let me see this one picture ; it is so pretty ! O ! here is another, prettier yet."

But Ellen, fearing the book would not be resigned until she had seen all it contained, said, " Very well, Mary, I must go to mother."

The eager little girl was so much engaged looking at the picture of a colored butterfly on the back of a mouse, she did not notice immediately that her sister had gone. As soon as she missed her, she put up the book, and running to the door, called. " Ellen, Ellen, I have put it up." But Ellen did not hear ; she was in the room with her mother. ·

Mary followed, quite ashamed of herself ; for she knew that her mother wished her to mind her sister, who was usually very gentle and kind to her.

" Mother," said Ellen, " Mary has the book William borrowed yesterday ; and will not let me have it."

While Ellen was speaking, Mary entered the room, saying, " I have put it up, mother ; but Ellen hurried me so."

" My dear," said Mrs. Wilson, " you did very wrong not to mind your sister. She is older than you are, and knows better than you do what is proper and right ; and as you did not choose to resign the book when she asked you for it, I shall not take the trouble of showing you all the pretty pictures it contains, and explaining them to you. Now you may go to your play. I trust you will not be so rude again."

" Mother," said Ellen, " is it best Mary should go to that beautiful garden with me, to-morrow ? I know she won't mind me; and she may step on the flowers, and do something wrong."

"I should be sorry to deprive her of so much innocent enjoyment, Ellen; but if you think you cannot agree together, I shall certainly keep her at home; though if you are kind, and don't attempt to tyrannize over her, my dear, I think she would be a very good, obedient little girl."

"Tyrannize! Mother, I don't know what that means."

"Tyranny means an unjust, unkind, or cruel use of power. You know what power means, Ellen."

Yes, mother, the President has power; and you and father have power, and can reward or punish us. But I heard William .reading something to you about a king, who was a tyrant; can little girls and kings be alike?"

"If a little girl makes bad use of all the power she has, she will be as tyrannical as a king, who makes a bad use of all the power he has. A little girl has but little power; so she can do but little harm. It is probable, if her power were increased, it would increase her desire to tyrannize."

"But mother, I never tyrannized over Mary in my life."

"Are you sure of that, Ellen? Perhaps you do not yet clearly comprehend the word; I will tell you of two little girls, though they are young ladies now, the eldest of whom, I think, tyrannized over her sister. I was on a visit to their mother.

LESSON LIV.

THE LITTLE TYRANTS,—AGAIN.

One afternoon, I was writing in a room next to the one in which the children generally sat. Mrs. Norton left me, and went up stairs for something, leaving the door open. I was perfectly still, and the little girls did not know of my being near.

'Caroline,' said the eldest, 'bring me that book on the table.'

'O Julia, I can't get up,' said little Caroline. 'Don't you see my lap is full?'

I could see them both in the large mirror that hung opposite. The dear little chubby girl was seated on her cricket in the corner; her white apron spread over her small lap; her little hands arranging her many-colored squares for patch-work.

'See, Julia,' said she, in a beseeching tone, 'all my pretty patch-work that I have been so long lay-ing out to baste together, will be tumbled on the floor, if I get up.'

'Nonsense,' said her sister, 'make haste; I have done this volume and want the other immediately.'

'How can you be so cross, Julia? you are doing nothing at all. I am sure I would not plague you so, for any thing.'

'You know, Caroline, mamma tells you to mind me.'

'But I am sure she would'nt, Miss Julia, if she knew how cross you are to me sometimes.'

'There comes mother,' said Julia, hearing her steps on the stairs; 'we'll see, Miss Caroline, if you won't mind.'

The little girl jumped up and got the book. I saw many of her pretty squares fall on the carpet; and the rest were tumbled in a heap in her lap. Julia took the book and began her reading again.

Mrs. Norton came through the room in haste, with-out noticing the big tears that filled the bright blue eyes of her little girl; who, wiping them away with the corner of her apron, began her work anew with a patient sweetness, that quite won my love."

"O! mother, what a cross sister," said Ellen.

"Yes, my dear, she was tyrannical. I think, my daughter, you understand the meaning of tyranny now. You perceive that Julia tyrannized over her sister.

"Yes, mother."

"Mrs. Norton, thinking Julia, as she was so much older, capable of guiding her sister, and of being useful to her in many ways, had given her power, which she abused ; and though her mother found it out in time to prevent its injuring the gentle Caroline, Julia grew up with a desire to tyrannize, and her manners are far less pleasing than her sister's who is now the mother of just such a little lively girl as Mary."

"Did I ever see her mother? Does she live in this town?"

"No, my dear, she lives a great way off; I wish she was near us; for I love her much."

"Ellen, I will tell you how you can always have almost absolute power over your sister ; absolute power means power to make her do just what you wish her to do,—and such power you can have over Mary without tyranny, and without harshness."

"How, mother?"

"By being perfectly good. You think I am mistaken, I dare say ; but if you will reflect a moment, you will remember many times when your manner of asking her has been improper, your look impatient, and your voice too loud. To-day, my daughter."

"Indeed, mother! I was not impatient to-day ; but waited until she had seen four pictures."

"I suppose you waited a moment, my dear ; but had you been perfectly kind, you would have thought how much little folks love pictures, and what a temptation such a beautiful book is, and instead of saying, ' You must not have it, Mary,' you should have said, ' It is a beautiful book, I know : and I will show you all the pictures as soon as I have done my work ; but you know mother will be displeased if you disobey her, and take a borrowed book in your hand.' Don't you think, if you had spoken thus, she would have resigned the book to you willingly?"

"Yes, mother."

"But now, my dear, you have deprived her of the pleasure of seeing its contents. Remember, my dear child, I give you some power over your sister, not merely because you are older, but because I think you her superior; because I think you capable of guiding her right, often when her frolicsome disposition would lead her into mischief. Is it not important, then, that you should always show yourself capable of guiding her by the patient gentleness of your manners, and by your obedience to the commands and wishes of your parents?"

"Oh yes, mother, and I do try to be good."

I think you do, Ellen, and I am certain, my child, that you know how to apply to God for aid and strength, when you feel your weakness. 'And remember, you are never fit to command, until you know how to obey.'"

Ellen threw her arms round her mother's neck. Her eyes were full of tears, and her young heart full of kind feelings. She said, "I will take Mary with me to-morrow, mother; for I shall be so gentle and affectionate to her, that she will love to mind me."

"Keep that resolution, my dear, and you will be certain of her ready obedience, and an agreeable visit."

Does this book *contain* pictures? Does it contain pretty stories? Does *enjoyment* mean the same as pain? What is the opposite of pain?—Is it *probable* that idle scholars will learn much? — Do you *increase* in strength as you grow older? Can you mention a person who is your *superior?* — Another? What does *impatient* mean? Is it right to be *impatient*, when taking care of a little sister?

LESSON LV.

THE RHINOCEROS.

The Rhinoceros is about five and a half, or six feet high, and from twelve to fourteen feet long.

This animal's body is very long and large; his legs are short, but thick and clumsy; his ears are broad, and stand upright; his upper lip is long, and hangs over the lower one; his eyes are small; his skin lies in great folds, like a thick, stiff piece of cloth, his nose is long, and is armed with a great, strong horn; and his feet are short, ending in three toes each.

The Rhinoceros uses his horn to defend himself against the lion, elephant, and other animals. It is so strong, that he can run it through a small tree, just as easy as a boy runs an awl through a small stick.

The Rhinoceros lives on grass, and the small twigs of trees; he also eats thorns, sugar cane and all sorts of corn.

He gathers his food with his upper lip, which ends in a point, and which he can stretch out a foot or more.

He is a harmless beast, when let alone; but when attacked by other animals, or pursued by men, no animal is more fierce or more dangerous. He is so strong, and fights with so much skill with his horn, that even the elephant cannot master him, and the tiger would rather attack the elephant than the Rhinoceros. His skin is so thick and hard, that it is a good defence against the claws of the lion and tiger.

The color of the Rhinoceros is a dark, bluish brown. He has no hair except on the tail and ears.

This animal runs wild in Asia and Africa, where he lives in low, muddy places, for he loves to wallow in the mire like the hog.

The Rhinoceros can be so far tamed as to be quiet in confinement, and to do a few things at his master's bidding. But he is not a docile animal, and under instruction behaves more like a pig than like any other beast.

He is a solitary beast, and loves best to be alone. He seems too stupid to take any pleasure in company, and is contented if he can wallow in the mire, get enough to eat, and then go to sleep.

The Rhinoceros is said to hear uncommonly well.

He will listen with great attention to any sound, which he has not often heard before. Even while he is eating, if a drum is beat, he will raise his head, and hearken to it a long time.

The flesh of this animal is eaten by the Indians and Africans, and is said by them to be excellent. His skin makes the hardest, and for some uses, the best leather, in the world. His horn is sometimes used by ignorant people as a medicine.

At a single thought, it might be difficult for us to conclude, for what use such a huge and disgusting creature as the Rhinoceros was made : but if we reflect a moment, we shall see, that in the country where he lives, he may be a great blessing to the poor negroes, who might perhaps, starve without his flesh. Nor is it difficult to see that the Creator has been kind to this poor stupid beast, for He has given him a horn, with which to defend himself, and without which, he would easily be beaten to death by the elephant, or become the common prey of the lion and tiger.

How large is the Rhinoceros? What is his shape? What food does he live on? Is he a harmless animal? What is his color? Where is he to be found? Can he be tamed? What makes him contented? What other animal does so? Can the Rhinoceros hear well? Of what use is he?

LESSON LVI.

ANECDOTES OF THE RHINOCEROS.

Many years ago, a Rhinoceros was sent from India to London, and although he was only two years old, the cost of his living, during the voyage, was upwards of four thousand dollars. He was fed on rice, sugar, and hay.

He had, three times a day, seven pounds of rice, mixed with three pounds of sugar, besides large quantities of hay and herbs. This animal was of a peaceable disposition, and would let a person touch any part of its body, without being angry. When he was hungry, or when struck by any one, he became very furious, nor would he become tame, and mild again, until something was given him to eat, when he would again become harmles as before.

When angry, he would spring about in a very strange manner, and often raise himself up on his hind feet, at the same time pushing most furiously against the sides of his cage. His motions were quick, and nimble, although he was so stupid and lazy in appearance.

Dr. Parsons, who writes the substance of the above account, says that he does not believe this creature can ever be tamed, so as to obey his master, and that when offended, he believes he would destroy every person who happened to be near him.

Mr. Kolbe, who went into the country where the Rhinoceros lives, says that this animal, in his wild state, does not often attack men, unless they provoke him, or wear a red dress. Why a red dress should make him angry, we cannot say; but on seeing it, he becomes very furious, and pursues after the man who has it on, and will destroy him, if he can.

But Kolbe says it is very easy to escape him, although he runs with great swiftness, for this beast cannot see any thing that is not right before him. Therefore the man whom he is pursuing must stand still until the Rhinoceros comes very near him, when he must suddenly jump one side, and then run away. The animal keeps on for a while, but not seeing the man, stops, not knowing which way to pursue; and thus the man has time to get out of his way.

Now can we not see the goodness of the Creator towards man, in having made the sight of this huge animal less perfect than that of other animals? For, could he see all around, like the cow and horse, no person could escape his fury, who should be pursued by him.

Does the Rhinoceros eat a great deal ?   What color does he is like ?   Is it easy to escape him ?   Why ?

LESSON LVII.

MY BROTHER.

Who often with me kindly play'd,
And all my little playthings made,
My kite or ball — though still unpaid ?
                              My Brother.

Who made a sled when winter came,
With little ropes to draw the same,
And on its sides carv'd out my name ?
                              My Brother

Who after him my sled would tow,
Swift o'er the ice, where'er I'd go,
And mark'd the gliding wave below ?
                              My Brother.

Who lov'd to soothe my childish fear,
And wip'd away the falling tear,
When the cold ice crack'd loud and near ?
                              My Brother.

And who was it that taught to me
The seeds of learning, A, B, C,
On paper mark'd them out for me ?
                              My Brother.

Who to the school my books would bear,
And lead me o'er the bridge with care,
And lessons find for me when there ?
                              My Brother.

Who gathered apples from the tree ?
Chestnuts and walnuts too — for me,
Who cheerful did all this but thee,
                              My Brother ?

These joyful days have had an end;
But oh! to me thy kindness lend,
And still remain my dearest friend,

My Brother.

And may I ever grateful be
For all thy kindness shown to me,
And ne'er withdraw my love from thee,

My Brother.

LESSON LVIII.

DEFINITIONS.

Splendid, very bright, showy. Brilliant, shining. Estimation, regard. Entertainment, a feast, diversion, Nuisance, that which gives trouble. Disgusting, provoking dislike. External, outward.

THE PEACOCK.

The common Peacock is about five feet long, the tail being three feet and a half, and the body one foot and a half.

This bird is very beautiful. The head is small, and crowned with a crest, consisting of a few straight feathers; the neck is long and small; the body is of a considerable size; the wings short, and the tail very large and long.

Its colors are very splendid. The back and wings are of a slight ash color, mingled with black; the head, neck, and breast are greenish blue, with a gloss, which, in the sun, appears exceedingly brilliant; the eyes are set between two stripes of white; the feathers of the tail are a mixture of green, blue, purple, and gold; the bird can spread its tail into the form of a half circle, when it becomes one of the most beautiful objects imaginable.

Among the Romans, Peacocks were held in the highest estimation; and the person who first used

them at his table, as an article of food, became so
celebrated on this account, that his name is known to
this day.

After their first introduction to the table, it soon
became fashionable among the great men at Rome to
eat Peacocks ; not probably on account of their good-
ness, but because most people were unable to furnish
so costly a dish ; so that the man who first undertook
the business of fattening them for the markets, made
his fortune by the trade.

In Greece, at one period, these birds were so highly esteemed, that the price of a pair of them was more
than a hundred dollars of our money ; and we are told,
that when Alexander the Great was in India, he was
so struck with their beauty, that he laid a heavy fine
and punishment on any person who should in any
manner wound or injure them.

At that time, when a pair was carried to Athens,
the rich went from all parts of Greece, for no other
purpose than to behold so great a curiosity ; each
person paying a certain sum for the sight.

In what manner the Romans cooked Peacocks, we
are not informed ; but at the present day, after the
highest seasoning, their flesh is still black, tough, and
far inferior to that of other birds.

How long Peacocks were considered a delicious, as
well as a costly article of diet, does not appear ; but
in the time of king Francis First, of France, rather
more than three hundred years ago, these birds were
still used at the entertainments of the great, though
they were not eaten.

At that time, the fashion was to take off the skin,
and then, having prepared the flesh with spices and
salt, the skin was again drawn on, so that the bird
appeared in full plumage.

Thus fitted up it was kept for many years, to be
set on the table in full dress, on great occasions. At
weddings and other like times, they filled the beak

and throat of the bird with cotton and camphor, which was set on fire for the entertainment of the company.

For beauty of plumage, few of the feathered race can compare with the Peacock. But this poor bird can boast of nothing but outside show. His voice, which is a kind of scream, is unpleasant, and even shocking to the ear; his legs are black, and so homely, that it is said he will never look at them himself. He is a voracious eater, and devours plants, seeds, corn, and insects. In gardens and planted fields, he is such a nuisance, that his owner is often obliged to pay money for the damage he does.

The bad conduct of this bird, therefore, makes him a disagreeable companion, notwithstanding his beauty. So that those who are well acquainted with him, take little notice of his dress, his character being a matter of much more consequence to them than the fine appearance of his feathers.

Let this be a lesson to those who expect that beauty and external show, rather than good qualities, will gain them respect and influence in the world. The truth is, that personal beauty, like the Peacock's plumage, after being a little while admired, if not combined with other charms, is every where soon forgotten or despised.

Let a person be ever so gaudily dressed, and ever so handsome, if he is disgusting in his manners, and overbearing in his conduct, he will soon find himself shunned and hated by every body; whereas a person of amiable and obliging manners, though neither handsome in person, nor dressed in fine clothes, will always be beloved, and always have influence, wherever he goes.

How long is the Peacock's body? His tail? Is it beautiful? Are Peacocks good to eat? Why then did the Romans eat them? Is it foolish to eat things because they cost a great deal of money? What would it be better to do with the money? What is all this bird can boast of? What is better for children than outside show?

LESSON LIX.

THE LAW OF GOD.

In the State of Massachusetts, the law requires that all the instructors of youth shall " use their best endeavors to impress on the minds of children and youth committed to their care and instruction, the principles of piety, justice, and a sacred regard to truth."

In other States, where there may be no such law, teachers owe it as a duty to God and their country, to see that their pupils have a knowledge of these great principles. This cannot be done, while they are ignorant of

THE TEN COMMANDMENTS.

1. Thou shalt have no other gods before me.

2. Thou shalt not make unto thee any graven image, or any likeness of any thing that is in heaven above, or that is in the earth beneath, or that is in the water under the earth ; thou shalt not bow down thyself to them nor serve them : for I, the Lord thy God, am a jealous God, visiting the iniquity of the fathers upon the children, unto the third and fourth generation of them that hate me and showing mercy unto thousands of them that love me and keep my commandments.

3. Thou shalt not take the name of the Lord thy God in vain ; for the Lord will not hold him guiltless that taketh his name in vain.

4. Remember the Sabbath day, to keep it holy ; six days shalt thou labor and do all thy work ; but the seventh day is the Sabbath of the Lord thy God ; in it thou shalt not do any work, thou, nor thy son, nor thy daughter, thy man-servant, nor thy maid-servant, nor thy cattle, nor the stranger that is within thy gates ; for in six days the Lord made heaven and earth, the sea, and all that in them is, and rested

the seventh day: wherefore the Lord blessed the Sabbath day, and hallowed it.

5. Honor thy father and thy mother: that thy days may be long upon the land which the Lord thy God giveth thee.

6. Thou shalt not kill.

7. Thou shalt not commit adultery.

8. Thou shalt not steal.

9. Thou shalt not bear false witness against thy neighbor.

10. Thou shalt not covet thy neighbor's house, thou shalt not covet thy neighbor's wife, nor his man-servant, nor his maid-servant, nor his ox, nor his ass, nor any thing that is thy neighbor's.

What is a law in Massachusetts? What is the duty of teachers in all places? Why? Can you repeat the first commandment? The second? &c.

LESSON LX.

A TALK ABOUT THE COMMANDMENTS.

BETWEEN A FATHER AND HIS CHILDREN.

Father. Children, how many commandments are there?

All the Children. Ten.

Father. Where do you find them, Benjamin?

Benjamin. I do not know.

Father. Do you know, Ann?

Ann. In my primer.

Father. *True*, they are in your primer, and in many other small books for children. But I mean to ask in what part of the Bible they are. Can you tell me, George?

George. They are in the 20th chapter of Exodus.

Father. That is right. Are they in any other part of the Bible, Lucy?

Lucy. I believe not.

Father. What do you think about it, James?

James. They are in the fifth chapter of Deuteronomy.

Father. That is right, my son. They are all recorded together in these two places, but no where else in all the Bible. They are mentioned singly, or several of them together, in other places, some of them frequently. But if you want to find the ten commandments in one place, you must look in one of these two chapters. Can you tell me whose commandments they are, or who gave such commandments?

All. God.

Father. Whom does God command?

George. The children of Israel.

Benjamin. Us.

Ann. All the children.

James. Every body.

Lucy. All mankind.

Father. You all answer differently; but you all say the truth. But, George, what made you think that these commandments were for the children of Israel?

George. Because, when Moses was alone with God in the mount, God wrote them on two tables of stone, and Moses carried them down to the children of Israel, and gave them to that people, as God bade him.

Father. You are right. God gave them first to the children of Israel, and they kept them laid up among their sacred things from age to age; one generation taught them to their children, and they to their children, and so they have been preserved among the Israelites, or Jews, to this very day. But, Lucy and James, why do you suppose that these commands are for "every body," or "all mankind?"

Lucy. Because, all the Jewish Scriptures, "the law and the prophets," make part of the Bible; and the Bible is intended for every "creature under heaven," and ministers are "to go into all the world and teach it."

Father. That is true; and is it by such means we have the Bible, with all its precious commandments and ordinances?

Lucy. Yes, Sir. You have told us that the Old Testament books were preserved among Christians after the time of Christ, as well as those of the New; and that the Old Testament has been translated from the Hebrew into the English, and the New Testament from the Greek; and that all together make our English Bible, which we have been taught to read ever since we could read at all.

Father. Yes. The sacred books were brought in ancient times, from the south-east part of Europe to Great Britain; and when our fathers came to this western wilderness, they brought them with them. And now, in this land of liberty and plenty, almost every child may read and hear in his own tongue, the wonderful works of God. Now James, can you tell me any other reason why the ten commandments are for " every body," besides the fact that the books of Exodus and Deuteronomy make part of our English Bible?

James. Christ and his apostles, I believe, quote the commandments, and speak of them as the commandments of God, and as binding on Jews and Gentiles, and all people.

Father. They do so; and it would be a pleasant and profitable exercise, if we could refer to a number of such places, and read and remark on what they wrote. But we have no time this evening, for I want to talk with you more about the commandments themselves. They are indeed designed for " all the children," as, Ann said, and " us," as Benjamin said. Now I want any of you to tell me, what these commandments are sometimes called.

Lucy. The decalogue.

James. The moral law.

George. The law of God.

Father.   You all say right.   Lucy, why are they called the " decalogue" ?

Lucy.   Because there are just ten of them.

Father.   Why is that a reason for the name ?

Lucy.   I do not know.

Father.   Then I will tell you.   The word " deca•logue" means any thing which consists of ten words, or ten speeches.   It is also called a " law," or " the law of God," because it contains what God requires and forbids, and threatens punishment to those who disobey.   It is called the " moral law," to distinguish it from another which bears the name of the " ritual, or ceremonial law."   That was a law which told the Israelites about the sacrifices, and the holy days, and the modes of worship at the temple.   This law relates to the heart and the conduct through every day of our life ; and contains in a few words all that God requires of men, and what he forbids, both towards him and towards one another.

George.   I have been thinking, Pa, why these ten commandments should be called the great law of God ; did he never give but ten commandments to mankind ?

Father.   Yes, my son, he has given a great many more.   But, as I was just now saying, these ten are the great commands, given in few words, so that we may easily remember them ; but in other parts of the Bible, they are explained at greater length, and applied in a great many particular cases.   And if any body should obey these ten, and love them with all the heart, he could not hate or disobey one of all the words of God in the Bible. He would, like the Psalmist, " have respect unto all God's commandments," and to him " every word of God" would be pure, and lovely, and sweet.   Our Lord Jesus even reduced the number below ten.   Having said, " Thou shalt love the Lord thy God with all thy heart," he added, " This is the first and great command ; and the second is like unto it, Thou shalt love thy neighbor as thyself. On these two commandments hang all the law and the prophets." Do you think, children, if a man or a child loved God with all his heart, he could have any other gods before him, or worship images ?

All. No, Sir.

Father. If a man or a child loved every body as well as he did himself, could he kill any body in anger, or for money ?

All. No, Sir.

Father. Could such a man steal, or bear false testimony, or even desire to get away what belonged to another ?

All. No, Sir.

Father. Could a child that had such love, ever disobey or grieve his parents ?

All. No, Sir.

Father. Now we will talk no more at present. But I want you to commit all the ten commandments to memory, if you do not know them now, so that at another time I may see how well you understand them.

LESSON LXI.

ABOUT COLUMBUS.

All the great and good men, who have ever lived, became great and good by their own efforts. Christopher Columbus was one of these great men ; and though he lived about four hundred years ago, and was at first a poor boy, people now love to talk about Columbus, and praise him.

He was born at Genoa, a city of Italy, in 1435. His father was a wool-comber, and it is likely was not able to let his son go to school as much as most boys go now.

Mr. Irving, who has written a large book about Columbus, tells us that he became a good scholar by " diligent self-schooling," and by studying, when perhaps, other boys or young men of his age were at play.

Some boys, when they go to school, and have to learn a lesson in Geography, think it very hard, and cannot see of what use it will be, to remember so many hard names. But Columbus loved to study Geography, and he thought about what he read.

And when he had learned all that he could from books, he wanted to know more about the earth. He did not feel satisfied with the accounts given of the shape of the earth. He thought it was round like an orange, and that men could sail round it.

Columbus wanted to try to find another continent by going west. But he could not build a ship, and hire men to help him, without money. So he applied to the sovereigns of his own country for aid. But they refused to help him.

He then went to the king of Portugal; and the king pretended to think it a foolish scheme; but he privately sent some ships himself, that he might have all the honor and benefit of the voyage. Perhaps the king was advised to deceive Columbus by his counsellors, and would have acted right, if they had not urged him to do wrong. But like most people who do wrong, he did not succeed. Columbus soon left him, and went to the king of Spain.

The name of this king was Ferdinand, and that of his queen, Isabella. The queen was much pleased with the plan of Columbus, and she hoped he would find the country he expected to find. She persuaded the king to let him have ships and men and money; and Columbus engaged to let the king have most of the valuable things he might find.

Before they sailed, Columbus and his men prayed to God, that he would take care of them, and give them success. They then began their voyage, on the 14th of August, 1492.

On losing sight of land, the sailors felt as though they had taken leave of the world. They despaired of ever again seeing their homes. Many of them shed tears.

Columbus tried to soothe their distress, promising them land, riches, and many other things. He did not do this in order to deceive them ; for he really believed he should fulfil his promises.

When they were far out at sea, the sailors were still more afraid, and wanted to go back, and treated Columbus with great disrespect. But he persuaded them to continue the voyage a few weeks longer, and at length they discovered land.

Their first act on landing, was to return thanks to God, with tears of joy. They called the island on which they landed, *San Salvador.* Columbus soon after returned to Spain.

The king and queen were very glad when they heard of the new country he had found. They sent him back again with many other ships. They then discovered the islands which are called the West Indies.

Columbus afterwards made another voyage, and discovered the continent, and was sent home in chains by those who envied him. The ill treatment he now received, afflicted him so much as to hasten his death, which took place in 1506.

Columbus intended to use the vast gains he expected from his discoveries for the relief of the poor, and for religious purposes. He was a good man. Mr. Irving says of him, " The Sabbath was to him a day of sacred rest ; on which he would never sail from a port, unless in case of extreme necessity." " His language was pure, and free from all gross or irreverent expressions."

" He has been extolled for his skill in controlling others, but far greater praise is due to him for the firmness he displayed in governing himself." Now, if you would have a character like that of Columbus, you must imitate his good qualities.

Where was Columbus born? How long ago? What was his father? How did Columbus become a good scholar? What did he want to do? To whom did he apply for help? To whom next? How did the king of Portugal treat him? Was this right? Why? Of whom did he at last obtain help? What did queen Isabella persuade the king to do? What did Columbus and his men do before they sailed? How did the men feel when they lost sight of land? How did Columbus *soothe* them? What does *soothe* mean? How did they treat Columbus when they had gone still farther? What did they do when they discovered land, and went on shore? Did Columbus afterwards make another voyage to the New World? Another? How was he treated then? How did this affect him? What did he mean to do with the gains he expected to make? How did he regard the Sabbath? What kind of language did he use? Do good men use bad language? Should you imitate good men in doing what is right?

APPENDIX.

पुरवणी.

NOTES AND EXPLANATIONS.

सुचना आणि व्याख्या.

(Page. 2. l. 4.) You should speak the words when reading as when talking.

सर्व शब्द जसें संभाषण करतांना बोलत असतां तसें वाचतांना बोलावें.

(p. 2. l. 30.) She found that she had done wrong, not to mind them.

त्यांस न मानण्याने तिने वाईट केलें असें तिच्या समजण्यांत आलें.

(p. 3. l. 9.) This would have been a great shame had it been quite his own fault.

जर केवळ त्याचाच दोष असला तर मोव्या लाजेची गोष्ट असती.

(p. 5. l. 1.) —and felt much better than if she had eaten the whole.

तिने सर्व खाल्लें असतें त्यापेक्षां तिला आतां सुख वाटलें.

(p. 6. l. 4.) — the sad state she was in, (म्हणजे) the sad state in which she was, *or*, her sad state.

आपली दुर्दशा.

12

(*p.* 8. *l.* 23.) He will spit as little as may be.

अगत्य नसलें तर तो थुंकणार नाहीं.

(*p.* 10. *l.* 25) What can have become of him ?

त्यांचें काय झालें असेल.

(*p.* 11. *l.* 29.) And how, think you, do I always know how to find my things ?

माझ्या वस्तू कोठें सांपडतील हें मला नेहमी ठाऊक आहे हें कसें झणून तुला वाटतें ?

(*p.* 16. *l.* 26.) Who knows, said the old man, but this child may live to be a man, and that God will make him good and happy ?

म्हातारा बोलला कोण जाणे हें लेंकरूं कदाचित वांचून प्रौढ होईल आणि परमेश्वर त्याला चांगलें व सुखी करील.

(*p.* 16. *l.* 31.) The little boy grew fast.

तो लहान मुलगा लवकर वाढला.

(*p.* 18. *l.* 12.) She looked at the boy who had dried up his tears and was playing at the coach door.

तो मुलगा जो आपलीं आसवें पुसून टाकून गाडीच्या दाराजवळ खेळत होता त्याकडे तिने पाहिलें.

(*p.* 21. *l.* 1.) I am too tired to attend to you now.

मी दमल्यें तुझें ऐकवत नाहीं.

(*p.* 28. *l.* 37.) He followed calling the horse by his name when he stopped, but on his approach set off again.

तो घोड्याच्या पाठीमागें चालून त्याचें नाव घेऊन हाका मारीत गेला तेव्हां तो (घोडा) उभा राहिला, परंतु तो (Mr. L.) जवळ येतां (घोडा) पुन्हा निघाला.

(*p.* 29. *l.* 40.)—ran across where the road made a turn, and getting before the horse took him by his bridle, and held him till the owner came up.

जेथे रस्ता वळला तिकडे मधून धांवला आणि घोड्याच्यापुढें होऊन व ळगाम धरून धनी येईपर्यंत त्याला धरिलें.

(*p.* 29. *l.* 10.)—so much the better for you.

एवढें तुझें घरें आहे.

(*p.* 29. *l.* 18.) But would you not rather play ?

परंतु त्यापेक्षां खेळणें तुला आवडत नाहीं कीं काय ?

(*p.* 29. *l.* 23.) Just by, among the trees there.

जवळ त्या झाडामध्यें.

(*p.* 30. *l.* 21.) But these let in water.

परंतु यांत पाणी शिरतें.

(*p.* 30. *l.* 2.4) I would as soon have none at all (no hat at all)

मला नसली तर सारखेंच.

(*p.* 30. *l.* 27.) If it rains very hard, I get under the fence till it is over.

जर झड लागती तर उघडेपर्यंत मी कुंपणाखालीं बसतों.

(*p.* 30. *l.* 32.) But if there are none ?

कांहीं नसलें तर ?

(*p.* 30. *l.* 33.) Then I do as well as I can. I work on, &c.

तर जसें माझ्याने होईल तसें करितों. मी काम करीत करीत जातों &c).

(*p.* 30. *l.* 38.) Why you are quite a philosopher.

झ्यास नूं फार विवेकी आहेस.

(*p.* 43. *l.* 12.)—to finish with, (म्हणजे) with which to finish.

(*p.* 43. *l.* 17.) I'll try if I can get it.

तें मला मिव्हेल कीं काय, हें पाहीन.

(*p.* 44. *l.* 11.) As soon as she was safe over, &c.

ती पार गेली तेव्हां तो लागलाच इ०).

(*p.* 46. *l.* 34.) If you saved your money to do any thing with, or to buy any thing with, I should think you did right.

जर कांहीं करण्यासाठीं किंवा कांहीं विकत घेण्यासाठीं आपला पैका ठेविला असता तर तूं नीट करतोस अर्सें मला वाटलें असतें.

(*p.* 50. *l.* 1.) You are liable to be frozen to death.

तुला थंडीने मरून जाण्याचा लाग आहे.

(*p.* 50. *l.* 11.) I, on the contrary, have a warm stye and plenty of provisions all at free cost.

मला तर निवाऱ्याचा गोठा आणि अन्नाची ऊरपूर हीं सर्व फुकट आहेत.

(*p.* 50. *l.* 13.) I have nothing to do but grow fat and follow my amusement.

पुष्ट होणें व कर्मणूक करणें इतकेंच काम मला आहे.

(*p.* 52. *l.* 20.)—to get it lighted.

तो लावण्यासाठीं.

(*p.* 54. *l.* 15). This sea-sickness is the most distressing feeling that I ever knew.

हा समुद्रावरचा विकार यासारखा असा कांहीं कंटाळवाणी माझ्या अनुभवास कधीं आला नाहीं.

(*p.* 54. *l.* 23.) I shall get hardened.

मला सराव होईल.

(*p.* 55. *l.* 1.) One thing I could not help noticing.

एक गोष्ट माझ्या लक्षांत सहज आली.

(*p.* 55. *l.* 13.) It is now fifteen days that we have been out of sight of land.

भूमि दृष्टीस पडली नाहीं, आज पंधरा दिवस झाले.

(*p.* 56. *l.* 4.) I have taken a pretty thorough seasoning.

मला पक्का सराव झाला.

(*p.* 59. *l.* 31.)—but for this means of relief.

चैन पडण्याचा हा उपाय नसतां.

(*p.* 60. *l.* 12.) The ostrich is noted for its neglect of its young, and as being a stupid creature, and very timid.

शहामृग आपल्या पिलांचा संभाळ करील नाहीं आणि तो मयाळी व फार भेकूड आहे असा प्रसिद्ध आहे.

(*p.* 61. *l.* 22.) He did not see what in the world chestnuts were made to grow so for.

Chestnuts हे असे कशाला उत्पन्न झाले हे मी समजत नाहीं, असें त्याने सांगितलें.

(*p.* 62. *l.* 36.) Do you know what it is for?

हें काय कामाचें आहे हें तुला ठाऊक आहे काय?

(*p.* 66. *l.* 35.) They told her she was welcome to stay as long as she pleased.

तुझी मर्जी होईल, तोंपर्यंत राहा, असें त्यांनी तिला सांगितलें.

(*p.* 67. *l.* 5.)—she was very short for her age.

ती फार ठेंगणी होती.

(*p.* 68. *l.* 32.) Betsy said, yes, that was what she thought.

Betsy म्हणाली होय, मला तेंच वाटतें.

(*p.* 73 *l.* 22.) I would rather be worn out in doing good than rust out in idleness.

रिकामी असून आपणावर जंग चढावें त्यापेक्षां उपयोगी पडण्याने झिजून जाणें हें मला बरें वाटतें.

(*p.* 73. *l.* 29.) No sooner said than done.

बोलला इतक्यांत केलें.

(*p.* 76. *l.* 8.) All sorrow to beguile.

सर्व दुःख निवारण करायास.

(*p.* 76. *l.* 15.)—for you need not fear offending her you see.

कारण कीं तिला राग येण्याचें भय नाहीं बरें.

(*p.* 76. *l.* 20.) For pray what could I do?

तर मला काय करायाचें होतें बरें ?

(*p.* 80. *l.* 31.) He was then more wicked than if he had not done so before, or his mother had not taught him and reproved him.

जर त्याने पूर्वीं असें केलें नसतें अथवा आपल्या आईने बोध व निषेध केला नसता तर तो एवढा दोषी झाला नसता.

(*p.* 81. *l.* 28.)—but whether God will or will not be angry.

परंतु देव रागें भरेल किंवा नाहीं.

(*p.* 81. *l.* 30.) children should no more commit a small sin than they would take a little poison.

जसें लेंकरांस थोडकें विष प्यायाचें नाहीं तसें त्यानी हलकें पाप करायाचें नाहीं.

(*p.* 85. *l.* 22.) I will tell you about the laziest boy you ever heard of.

इतका आळसी मुलगा तुमच्या ऐकण्यांत कधींच झाला नसेल त्या- विषयीं मी सांगतों.

(*p.* 85. *l.* 23.) when he played the boys said he played as if the master told him to.

जेव्हां खेळत होता तेव्हां पंतोजीने हुकूम दिल्यासारिखा तो खेळतो भसें मुलगे झणाले.

(*p.* 88. *l.* 1.) Where have you been.

तूं कोठे गेला होतास.

(*p.* 88. *l.* 5.)—he has been out begging all day without getting any thing to eat.

तो दिवसभर भीक मागत फिरला परंतु कांहीं खायास मिळालें नाहीं.

(*p.* 96. *l.* 19.) I wonder you do'nt clear your garden of those frogs.

त्या बेडकांस तुह्मी आपल्या बागांतून काढून टाकीत नाहीं हें मला आश्चर्य वाटतें.

(*p.* 102. *l.* 34.) Let us both, then, set our faces against this vile practice.

तर ही दुष्ट चाल मोडावी झणून आह्मी दोघे जन जीव लावूं.

(*p.* 110. *l.* 10.) At a single thought it might be difficult to conclude, for what use such a huge and disgusting creature as the Rhinoceros was made.

गेंड्यासारखें अवजड व ओंगळ जनावर कशासाठीं उत्पन्न केलें हें प्रथम मनांत विचारितांना पहिल्याने सांगायास अवघड आहे.

(*p.* 122. *l.* 38.) on losing sight of land, the sailors felt as though they had taken leave of the world.

जेव्हां खलासी लोकांस भूमी दिसेनाशी झाली तेव्हां त्यास जग सो-डल्यासारखें वाटलें.

(*p.* 123. *l.* 7.)—far out at sea.

पाण्यावर लांब असतां.

ABBREVIATIONS AND EXPLANATIONS.

संक्षेप आणि व्याख्या.

---

a. stands for adjective. .... गुणविशेषण.

a. याचा अर्थ adjective असा आहे.

ad.   „   adverb. ....….... क्रियाविशेषण.

conj.   „   conjunction .... उभयान्वयी.

interj.   „   interjection. .... केवलप्रयोग, काकु.

n.   „   noun *or* substantive.. नाम.

n. p.   „   proper noun........ विशेष नाम.

p. p.   „   passive participle.... कर्मणी कृदंत.

prep.   „   preposition .... उपसर्ग.

pret.   „   preterite *or* imperfect tense.......... } भूतकाळ.

pron.   „   pronoun.............. सर्वनाम.

v. a.   „   auxiliary *or* helping verb. .... } सहायकारक क्रियापद.

v. i.   „   intransitive *or* neuter verb.......... } अकर्मक क्रियापद.

v. t.   „   transitive *or* active verb...... ...... } सकर्मक क्रियापद.

in comp. „   in composition...... संयुक्त असतां.

pl.   „   plural............... बहुवचन.

(*invers.*) before a Marathí verb denotes that what is the nominative case in English, is in the oblique case in Marathí, *and* what is the nominative case in Marathí is in the oblique case in English. *Examples. I think,* मला वाटतें. *I do not see him,* तो मला दिसत नाहीं. *I can read,* मला वाचतां येतें. *I know,* मला ठाऊक आहे. *1 have a book,* मला एक पुस्तक आहे.

(*invers.*) or (*inv.*) हें मराठी क्रियापदाच्या मागून असतां असें दाखवितें कीं इंग्लिश भाषेंत जो त्या क्रियापदाचा कर्ता आहे, तो मराठी भाषेंत कर्म होतो, आणि मराठी भाषेंत जो कर्ता तो इंग्लिश भाषेंत कर्म होतो. (मागलीं उदाहरणें पाहा).

m.	after a Marathi noun denotes		....	*masculine gender.*
f.	,,	,,	,, ...	*feminine gender.*
n.	,,	,,	,, ...	*neuter gender.*
m.	हें मराठी नावाच्या पुढें असतां त्याचा अर्थ....			पुल्लिंग.
f.	,,	,,	,, ,, ...	स्त्रीलिंग.
n.			,, ...	नपुंसकलिंग.

VOCABULARY.
कोश.

A *a.* एक. — a while कांहीं वेळ.

able *a.* समर्थ, शक्तिमान. — to be able, शकणें, (*inv.*) शक्ति भसणे-होणे, येणे. उ. I am able to read, मी वाचूं शकतों *or* मला वाचतां येतें *or* माझ्याने वाचवतें.

above *prep.* वर, वरतीं.

above *a.* वरता, वरचा, वरला. (२) मागला (लिहिण्यामध्यें.) उ. I think the above story is true मागली गोष्ट खरी आहे, असें मला वाटतें.

about *prep.* भोंवतां, आसपास. (२) विषयीं. — to be about work, कामांत असणें. What are you about तूं काय करितोस? He has gone about his business तो आपल्या कामावर गेला.

about *ad.* सुमारें, सरासरी. (२) चहुंकडे, इकडे तिकडे. (३) गरगर. (४) जवळ. (५) उन्मुख, टेंकला. उ.—about to die मरणोन्मुख, मरायास टेंकला, — about to go गमनोन्मुख, जाणारच, जायास टेंकला.

absent *a.* गैरहजीर, असमक्ष, अपरोक्ष नाहीं, एथें नाहीं.

absolute *a.* स्वतंत्र, मुखत्यार, निश्चयाचा, निश्चित, मोकळाच, कोणाच्या ताबेदार नाहीं.

absolutely *ad.* निश्चयें, निश्चयाचा, परिच्छिन्न, अगत्य, अगदी, अवश्य.

abuse *n.* (एब्युस) खुंदळणें *n.* धुसडा *m.* (२) शिवीगाळी *f.* शिंवी *f.* (३) अपव्यय *m.*

abuse *v. t.* (एब्युज) खुदळणें, कुदळणें, हाल करणें, पुसडणें, वदळ करणें. (२) चांगल्या कामास न लावणें. (३) शिवी देणें.

accept *v. t.* घेणें, अंगीकारणें, स्वीकारणें.

accommodation *n.* सोई *f.* स्वस्थता *f.*

account *n.* वर्णन *n.* गोष्ट *f.* हकीकत *f.* (२) हिशोब *m.* झडती *f.* जमाखर्च *m.* —to call to account झडती घेणें. — on account of मुळें, करितां, साठीं. —of no account विशाद नाहीं, हलका, कामाचा नाहीं.— of great account भारी, मोठा.

account v. t. मोजणे, गणणे, मानणे.

account (for) v. i. कारण दाख-
विणे, सबब लावणे. (२) (inv.)
कडे असणे, जिम्मेस असणे.

ache v. i. दुखणे, ठणकणे, कसक-
सणे.

ache n. दुःख n.

acquaint (with) v. i. ओळख पाड-
णे, ओळखवणे, कळवणे, सांगणे,
विज्ञापणे. — to be acquainted
with ओळखणे, जाणणे, (inv.)
कळणे, ठाऊक असणे, माहित अ-
सणे.

acquaintance n. ओळख f. परि-
चय m. माहितगारी f. (२)
ओळखीचा m.

across prep. आडवा, पार, मधून.

act n. क्रिया f. कृत्य n. कर्म n.
करणें n.

act v. i. कार्य करणे, करणे. (२)
चालणे, आचरणे, वर्तणे.

action n. व्यापार m. व्यवहार m.
कर्म n. क्रिया f. करणें n. आ-
चार m. चाल f. — in action
चालता, खेळता, जागृत.

active a. चपळ, हुशार. (२)
सावध.

add v. t. मिळवणे, जोडणे, लावणे.
(२) अणखी सांगणे.

admire v. t. अनुमोदणे, अनुमोद-
न देणे, आर्चवा करणे, (inv.)
मानवणे, फार आवडणे, आश्चर्य
वाटणे.

admit v. t. येऊं देणे, कबूल करणे,
मान्य करणे, अंगीकारणे, कबूल
-मान्य-होणे. — to admit of
देणे, होऊं देणे, (invers.) होणे.

adultery n. जारकर्म n.

advise v. t. मसलत देणे, उपदेश
देणे, बोध-उपदेश-करणे.

affair n. गोष्ट f. काम n. खटला
m. प्रकरण n.

affect v. t. लागणे.

affection n. ममता f. प्रीति f. प्रे-
म m. माया f. (२) वासना
f. मनोवृत्ति f.

affectionate a. प्रीतिमान, मायाळू,
ममताळू, स्नेहाळू, प्रेमाळू.

affectionately adv. प्रीतीने, मम-
तेनें.

afflict v. t. दुःख देणे, पीडणे.

affliction n. दुःख m. पीडा f. हा-
ल m. खेद m.

afflicted a. & p. p. दुखित, दुःख
पावलेला, पीडित.

afford r. t. देणे. (२) देण्यास
शक्तिमान असणे, (invers.) शक्ति
असणे.

affront v. t. राग उठविणे. — to be
affronted रुसणे, रागें भरणे.

afraid a. भयभीत. — to be afraid
भिणे, (inv.) भय वाटणे.

Africa n. p. आफ्रिका खंड.

African a. & n. सिद्दी m. हब-
्शी m.

after prep. नंतर, वर, मागें, या-
गून, पुढें. (२) साठीं. उ. I
have come after a book मी
एका पुस्तकासाठीं आलों. (३)

प्रमाणें. उ. After this manner याप्रमाणें.

afternoon n. दुपारून, परतवेळ f. — this afternoon आज दुपारून. — that afternoon त्या दिवसीं दुपारून.

afterwards adv. मागें, पुढें, त्यानंतर, उपरांत, मग.

again ad. फिरून, पुनः, पुनरपि, आणखी, परतून, माल्याने. — back again परत, माघारें. — again and again वारंवार, वरचेवर.

against prep. विरुद्ध, वर,-ला,-सीं. — over against समोर.

age n. वय n. उमर f. क्षीण f.m. — of age पक्त, पोक्ता, जाणता, प्रौढ. (२) युग n पिढी f. — from age to age पिढींच्या पिढी.

ago ad. मागें, झाला, लोटला. उ. a year ago एक वर्ष झालें-लोटलें, or एक वर्षामागें.

agree v. i. जमणें, मिळणें, (inv.) जम-जमाव-मेळ-होणें. — to agree to कबूल-मान्य-होणें, कबूल-मान्य-करणें. — to agree with जमणें, मिळणें, (invers.) जमाव होणें. (२) मानवणें, भावणें. — I agree with you तुझें मत माझें मत आहे.

agreeable a. मंजूर, आवडता, संतोषक, रम्य, सुखकारक, प्रिय.

ah! inter. हां.

aid n. साह्य n. मदत f. कुमक f. पाठ f. (२) सहाय m. f.

aid v. t. साह्य-मदत-कुमक-करणें, पाठ-हात-देणें, (inv.) सहाय असणें.

air n. हवा f. वारा m. वायु m. (२) आकाश n. m. अंतराळ n. — in the air अधांतरीं. (३) चेहेरा m.

Alexander n. p. पुरुषाचें नाव.

alike a. सारिखा, एकसारिखा.

alive a. जिवंत, जिता, सजीव.

all a. अवघा, सगळा, सर्व, सारा, मात्र. — not at all अगदीं नाहीं. — all about, all round चहुंकडे, इकडे तिकडे.

all n. माकल्य n. सगळें n.

Allen n. p. माणसाचें नाव.

allow v. t. देणें, होऊं देणें, परवानगी-हुकूम-देणें, सोसणें (पाग).

almost ad. बहुतकरून. — to be almost लागास-असणें-येणें, जवळ-असणें-येणें. उ. He is almost here तो जवळ आहे. He is almost dead तो मरण्याच्या लागास आहे. It is almost ten o'clock दाहा वाजायास आलें. My work is almost done माझें काम थोडें वेळांत होईल. It is almost ready आतां तयार होईल.

alone a. एकटा, एकला, नुसता. (२) केवळ, मात्र, च. — to let alone असूं-राहूं-देणें.

along ad. पुढें. उ. Go along पुढें जा, चल. — all along अखंड.

aloud ad. मोठ्याने.

alphabet *n.* वर्णमाला *f.* मूळ अ-क्षरें.

already *ad.* आतां, अगोदरहि.

alter *v. t.* बदलणे, पालटणे, बद-ल-फेर-करणे, वेगळा करणे.

alter *v. i.* फिरणे, पालटणे, (*inv*) फेर होणे, वेगळा होणे.

although *conj.* जरी.

altogether *ad.* अगदीं, यावत, नि-स्तूक.

always *ad.* सर्वकाळ, नेहमीं, हमेशा, सर्वदा, नित्य, सदासर्वदा, सदो-दीत.

am *v. i.* (be पाहा) आहें.

amazingly *ad.* अत्यंत, पराकाष्ठेने, आश्चर्याने, फार.

ambition *n.* हौंस *f.* जिगीषा *f.* मानाची इच्छा *f.* ईर्षा *f.*

amiable *a.* प्रियकर, प्रियपात्र.

Ammon *n. p.* पुरुषाचें नाव.

Amnon *n. p.* पुरुषाचें नाव.

among *prep* मध्यें, आंत.

amphibia *n.* भूजलवासी, उभयचर.

amphibious *a.* भूजलवासी, उभय-चर.

amuse *v. t.* गमत करणे, करम-णूक करणे, आवडणे, मौज वाटणे.

an *a.* (a पाहा) जर a याच्या पुढें स्वर येतो तर तो an असा शब्द होतो, आणि h याचा उच्चार जेव्हां होत नाहीं तो पुढें आला असतां तेव्हांहि an होतो. उ. an ox, an hour, &c. परंतु जेव्हां दीर्घ u याचा उच्चार पुढें येतो तेव्हां a याचा कांहीं बदल

होत नाहीं. उ. a union, a ewe lamb.

ancient *a.* प्राचीन, पुरातन, पूर्वी-ल, पुराणा, चिरकाळी.

and *conj.* आणि, व.

Anderson *n. p.* माणसाचें नाव.

anecdote *n.* नक्कल *f.* फरडूक *n.* फरडूक *n.* चुटका *m.* गोष्ट *f.*

anew *ad.* फिरून, मार्ग्यान, पर-तून, नवीन.

anger *n.* राग *m* कोप *m.* क्रोध *m.* रोष *m.*

angry *a.* क्रोधायमान, रागें भरला. —to be angry, रागें भरणे, ह-सणे.

animal *n* जनावर *n.* प्राणी *m.*

Ann *n. p.* स्त्रियेचें नाव.

another *a.* दुसरा, आणखी एक, अन्य, परका, वेगळा. — one.... another एक....एक. — one another एकमेक, परस्परें.

answer *n.* उत्तर *n.* जबाब *m.* जा-ब *m.* प्रत्युत्तर *n.*

answer *v. t.* उत्तर देणे, जबाब देणे, ओ करणे. (२) बरें लागणे, ज-मणे, पुरें असणे — I will answer for that तें मजकडे आहे, *or* तें माझ्या जिम्मेस आहे.

anxious *a.* चिंताग्रस्त, चिंताक्रांत, चिंतातुर, इच्छायुक्त.

any *a.* कांहीं, कोणी, कोणीएक, को-णीनरी. — any more आणखी.

apart *ad.* अंतराने, फरक, दूर. (२) एकीकडे. — to take apart वेगळे करणे, निराळे करणे, उ-

लगउणें, उख्खळणें (यंत्र इ.)—
wide apart विसकळ, व्यस्त.

apiece *ad.* दरएक, हरएक, एक
एक.

apostle *n.* प्रेषित *m.*

appear *v. i.* दिसणें, दृश्य-असणें-
होणें, दृष्टीस पडणें, प्रगट होणें,
उमटणें. (२) भासणें, वाटणें.
(३) समक्ष होणें,-येणें.

appearance *n.* वेश *m.* रंग *m.* मु-
द्रा *f.* दर्शन *n.* झकल *n.* घोर-
ण *n.*

apple *n.* एका प्रकारचें फळ.

apply *v. i.* लागणें.—to apply
for मागणें (साह्य इ.)

apply *v. t.* लावणें, देणें.

approach *n.* आगम *m.* आगमन
n जवळ येणें.

approach *v. i. t.* जवळ येणें.

April *n.* चवथ्या महिन्याचें नाव.

apron *n.* उपरणा *m.*

apt *a.* प्रवीन, सुजाण.— to be apt
सवंकणें, घोरण-ओढ-चट-सवई-
भसणें, भसणें. उ. This horse
is apt to kick हा घोडा लात
मारायास सवकतो, हा घोडा ला-
त मारीत असतो—त्याला लात
मारायाची सवई आहे—त्याला
लात मारण्याची चट आहे. He
is apt to do so तो भसें करीत
भसतो.

are *v. i.* (be पहा) आहों, आहां,
आहेत.

argue *v. i. t.* वादविवाद करणें, अ-
नुमान करणें, प्रमाण दाखविणें.

arise *v. i.* उठणें, होणें, उत्पन्न होणें.

arithmetic *n.* गणित *n.* (२) हि-
शोबाचें पुस्तक.

arm *n.* भुज *m.* बाहु *m.* हात *m.*
—arms हत्यार *n.* हातेर *n.*

arm *v. t.* हातेर बांधणें, शस्त्र देणें,
सज्ज करणें.

armed *a. & p. p.* हतेरबंद, हत्या-
रबंद, शस्त्रपाणि, सज्ज.

Arnum *n. p.* माणसाचें नाव.

arose *pret. of* arise.

around *prep.* सभोंवता, चहुंकडे,
भोवता, भासपास.

around *ad.* चहुंकडे, इकडे तिक-
डे, आजूबाजूस, चहुफेर.

arrange *v. t.* रचणें, मांडणें (यथा-
स्थित, बरोबर), व्यवस्था करणें,
बंदोबस्त करणें, अनुक्रमाने-वि-
ल्हेवार-लावणें.

arrival *n.* पोहंचणें *n.* आगमन *n.*

arrive *v. i.* पोहंचणें, पावणें, येणें.

art *n.* युक्त *f.* युक्ति *f.* हुनर *m. f.*
(२) कला *f.*

artfully *ad.* हिकमतीनें, युक्तीनें,
तर्कबुद्धीनें, हुनरानें.

article *n.* जिन्नस *m.* पदार्थ *m.* व-
स्तु *n.*

as *ad.* जमा....तसा, प्रमाणें. उ.
Do as you are told जसें तुला
सांगितलें आहे तसें कर *or*
तुला सांगितल्याप्रमाणें कर.
—(२)जेव्हां....तेव्हां, तेव्हां, असतां.
उ. I saw him as I came out
of the city मी नगरांतून बा-
लों, तेव्हां म्या त्याला पाहिलें *or*

नगरांतून येत असतां, म्या त्याला पाहिलें. As I came near, he ran away मी जवळ येत असतां (or आल्यावर) तो पळून गेला.   As it was a fine day, she went to the fields (p. 4.) सुदिन असतां, ती शेतांत गेली.

— (३) कां कीं, यास्तव, झणून. उ. She will come soon, as it is almost dark (p 19) ती लवकर येईल, कां कीं रात्र जवळ आहे.   As they all knew her, they thought it was false (p. 6) त्या सर्वांनीं तिला ओळखिलें यास्तव हें खोटें असें त्यांला वाटलें.   As my work was done I went away माझें काम झालें झणून मी गेलें.

— (४) असा,-रूप, स.रिखा.   उ. I regarded him as a son म्या त्याला पुत्र असें मानिलें, or म्या त्याला पुत्रासारिखें मानिलें, or तो मला पुत्ररूप होता. — As for you, as for me, &c. तुजविषयीं,मजाविषयीं, इ.   He eats as if he was hungry, भुकेल्याप्रमाणें तो खातो. — such....as, जे....तें.   उ. Such as love God will be happy जे देवावर प्रीति करितात, ते सुख पावतील.

ascend v. i. वर जाणें, चढणें.

ashamed a. लज्जित, लज्जायमान.
—to be ashamed लाजणें, शरमणें, (invers.) लाज-शरम-वाटणें.

ashes n. pl. राख f. रक्षा f. भस्म n.

ash-colored a. राखेच्या रंगाचा.

Asia n. p. आशीखंड.

aside ad. एकीकडे.—aside from, शिवाय, खेरीज.

ask v. t. विचारणें, पुसणें, मागणें.

asleep a. निद्रिस्त, निजला, झोंपीं गेला.

ass n. गाढव m. f. n.

assist v. t. साह्य करणें, मदत करणें, पाठ करणें, कुमक करणें, हात देणें, (inv.) सहाय असणें.

astride ad पाय फांकून (बसणें).

a prep -स,-ीं,-कडे,-जवळ.—उ. at Bombay मुंबईस.—at home घरीं.   Look at me मजकडे पाहा.—at the door दाराजवळ, दारासीं.— At a comma, make quite a short stop जेथे comma आहे तेथे केवळ थोडेसें थवसान करावें. — not at all अगदीं नाहीं, नाहींच.— At ten o'clock दाहा वाजतां. — He is at work, तो काम करीत आहे or तो कामांत आहे. — at once एकदम, तेव्हांच.

ate pret. of eat.

attack n. हल्ला m. उचल f. दरवडा.

attack v. t. हल्ला करणें, उचल करणें, अंगावर येणें-जाणें.

attempt n. प्रयत्न m. यत्न m. लाग m. उद्योग m.

attempt v. t. i. प्रयत्न करणें, यत्न करणें, लागणें, उद्योग करणें.

attend *v. t. i.* लक्ष लावणे, लक्ष दे-
णे, जपणे. (२) येणे, हजीर
होणे, जाणे. उ. to attend
meeting देवळांत-जाणे-येणे
(भजन करण्यासाठीं). to at-
tend a meeting मंडळीस-जाणे-
येणे, *or* सभेंत हजीर होणे. to
attend school साळेंत-जाणे-
जात असणे.

attention *n.* लक्ष *n.* सावधगिरी *f.*
(२) सत्कार *m.* स्वागत *n.* ता-
रतीम *n.* बरदास्त *f.*

attentive *a.* एकचित्त, सावध, हु-
शार, सावधान, एकाग्र.

attentively *ad.* काळजीने, सावधप-
णाने, जपून, एकाग्रतेने.

Athens *n. p.* एका शहराचें नाव.

attract *v. t.* आकर्षणे, ओढणे, लक्ष
ओढणे, (*inv.*) लागणे (लक्ष).

August *n. p.* आठव्या महिन्याचें नाव.

aunt *n.* बापाची किंवा आईची बहीण,
आत *f.* मावशी *f.* चुलती *f.*
मामी *f.*

authority *n.* सत्ता *f.* अधिकार *m.*
मुखत्यारी *f.* भल्त्यार *m.* जो-
रा *m.* (२) आधार *m.* गम-
क *n.* ऐश्वर्य *n.* प्रमाण *n.*

avoid *v. t.* चुकविणे, वर्जणे, वर्जित
करणे,-पासून दूर जाणे, जवळ
न येणे,-पामून राहणे.

awake *a.* जागा, जागृत, निद्रिस्त
नाहीं, न निजतां, निजला नाहीं.
— to be awake जागणे.

awake *v. i.* जागा होणे, उठणे.

awake *v. t.* जागा करणे, उठविणे.

away *ad.* एकीकडे, दूर (एथून),
नाहीं. उ. He is away तो
एथें नाहीं. — to go away
जाणे, वाटेस लागणे, निघणे,
निघून जाणे. — to send a-
way वाटेस लावणे, धाडणे, र-
वाना करणे. — to take away
काढणे, घेऊन जाणे. — to run
away पळून जाणे. — to put a-
way सोडणे. (२) ठिकाणीं ठे-
वणे, ठेवणे. — to fly away उ-
डून जाणे. — far away दूर,
लांब. — to get away *v. t.* हि-
रून घेणे. (२) *v. i.* जाणे,
दूर-पलीकडे होणे.

awoke *pret. of* awake.

B.

Baby *n.* तान्हा, बाळ *n.* बालक *n.*

babyish *a.* तान्ह्यासारिखा.

back *n.* पाठ *f.* पृष्ठभाग *m.* माग-
ला भाग *m.*

back *ad.* माघारा, पाठीमागें, परत.

back *a.* मागला.

backwards *ad.* पाठीमागें, माघारा.

bad *a.* वाईट, दुष्ट, कुत्सित, खेर, दु-
र (*in comp.*) उ. दुर्भाषण,
दुर्गुण, इ. bad language,
bad qualities *or* propensities.

bade *pret. of* bid.

bag *n.* थैला *m.* थैली *f.* पिशवी *f.*
पोतें *n.*

ball *n.* चेंडू *m.* गोळा *m.* गोळी *f.*
पिंड *m.* गुंजडी *f.* (दोऱ्याची इ.)
गुंडाळी *f.*

band age *n.* बंद *m.* पट्टी *f.*

bare *a.* नागवा, बुचा, उघडा, नुस्ता.
— bare-footed अनवाहणी.—
bare-headed, बोडका.—bare
hill, माळडोंगर.

bark *n.* साल *f.* त्वचा *f.* सालपट *n.*

bark *v. i.* भोंकणे, भुंकणे.

bark *v. t.* साल-काढणे-करंडणे.

barley *n.* जव *m.* यव *m.* सातू *m.*

barn *n.* कोठी *f.* कोठार *n.* चाळ *f.*

basin *n.* तबक *n.* बासन *n.*

basket *n.* पांटी *f.* टोपली *f.* करं-
डा *m.* टोकरी *f.*

baste *v. t.* शिवणे (लांब टांकानी,)
लाकणे.

battle *n.* लढाई *f.* युद्ध *n.* संग्राम *m.*
— battle field समरांगण *n.*

be *v. i.* असणे, होणे.

beak *n.* चोंच *f.* टोंच *f.* टोंक *f.*

bean *n.* एक प्रकारची भाजी; ज-
सी चवळी, घेवडा, इ.

bear *n.* अस्वल *n.* रींस *n. m.* भा-
लूक *f.*

bear *v. t.* सोसणे, साहणे, सहन क-
रणे. (२) नेणे, वाहणे, (*inv.*)
येणे. उ. this tree bears
fruit या झाडाला फळें येतात.—
to bear a name (*invers.*) ना-
व असणे.—to bear testimony
or witness साक्ष देणे. — to
bear children प्रसविणे, जन्म-
विणे, (*invers.*) लेंकरें होणे.

beard *n.* दाढी *f.* (२) काडी *f.*
(ओंबीची).

beast *n.* पशु *m.* जनावर *n.*

beat *v. t.* मारणे, पिटणे, ताडणे,
जिंकणे, बडवणे.

beat *v. i.* भडभडणे, धडकणे, ठण-
ठणणे, ठसठसणे.

beautiful *a.* सुंदर, रूपवान, शो-
भायमान, सुरूप, सुरेख.

beauty *n.* सुंदरपण *n.* चांगुलपण *n.*
शोभा *f.* सुरेखाई *f.* लावण्य *n.*

because *conj.* कारण कीं, कां कीं.
— because of, *prep.* मुळें, क-
रितां.

becomes *v. i.* होणे.

become *v. t.* साजणे, शोभणे.

bed *n.* बिछाना *m.* शेज *f.* अंथरू-
ण *n.* अंथरूण *n.* शय्या *f.*
(२) तळ (नदीचा). (३) वा-
फा *m.* तक्ता *m.* (बागामध्ये).—
Go to bed निजायाला जा.

bedaub *v. t.* मळविणे, लेपणे, लिप-
णे, —to be bedaubed, भरणे
(चिखलाने).

bee *n.* मोहोळ माशी *f.* मधमाशी *f.*
मधुमक्षिका *f.*

been *p. p. of* be.

beer *n.* जवाचें शर्बत *n.*

before *prep.* पुढें, मोहरें, आगाऊ.
(२) समोर, समक्ष, देखत, प्रत्य-
क्ष, जवळ, हुजूर. (३) मागें,
अगोधर, पूर्वीं.—It was not
long before he came पुष्कळ
वेळ झाला नव्हता तेव्हां तो आला
or थोड्या वेळानंतर तो आला.

beg *v. t.* भीक मागणे, मागणे, विनं-
ती करणे, विज्ञापना करणे.

began *pret. of* begin.

beggar n. भिकारी m. भिक्षुक m. याचक m. (२) रंक m.

begin v. t. i. प्रारंभणे, आरंभणे, लागणे, सुरू करणे, चालू करणे, प्रवर्तणे, आरंभ करणे.

beginning n. आरंभ m. प्रारंभ m. सुरवात f. अथ.— from beginning to end अथेति, साद्यंत.

beguile v. t. फसविणे, मोहणे, भुलविणे, भुलताप-देणे-टाकणे. — to beguile away time गमत करणे, करमणूक करणे.

behave v. i. वागणे, वर्तणे, चालणे, आचरणे, वर्तणूक करणे, (inv.) वर्तणूक असणे.

behind prep. & ad. मागें, मागां, पाठीमागें, परोक्ष, खालीं.

behold v. t. i. पाहणे, निरखणे, निरखून पाहणे, लक्षणे, देखणे.

being n. स्थिति f. भाव m. अवस्था f. (२) सत्व n. प्राणी m. व्यक्ति f.—The Supreme Being परमेश्वर, परमपुरुष.

believe v. t. विश्वासणे, विश्वास ठेवणे, भरवसा ठेवणे, समजणे, (inv.) वाटणे.

Belmot n. p. माणसाचें नाव.

belong v. i. -ला - कडे - चा - असणे. उ. This book belongs to him हें पुस्तक त्याचें आहे.

beloved a. प्रिय, भावडता, जीवलग, प्राणसखा.

below prep. खाली, खालती, खालचा.

bench n. बांक m.

bend m. वांक n. वांकडेपण n. वळण n.

bend v. i. लवणे, नमणे, वांकणे, वांकणे, वळणे, (inv.) वळण-वांक-असणे.

bend v. t. वांकविणे. — to bend down खाली करणे (डोकें इ.)

beneath prep. & ad. खालता, खालतो, खालतें, खालीं.

benefit n. लाभ n. उपकार m. उपयोग m. हित n. नफा m. फायदा m. फलश्रुति f.

benefit v. t. लाभ देणे, उपकार करणे, हित करणे, (invers.) लाभ हेाणे.

Benjamin n. p. पुरुषाचें नाव.

berry n. एक प्रकारचें लहान फळ (जसें करवंद, बकूळ, इ.)

beseech v. t. याचणे, मागणे, प्रार्थणे, विनंती करणे, विज्ञापना करणे.

beseeching a. काकुळतवाणा, दीन, दीनवाणी.— beseeching toue काकऱ्त f. करुणास्वर m.

beseeching n. याचना f. प्रार्थना f.

beside prep. जवळ, बाजूला.

besides or beside prep. वांचून, शिवाय, खेरीज, वेगळा.

besides ad. यांखेरीज, याशिवाय, अणखी, दिगर.

Bess n. p. स्त्रीचें नाव.

best a. सर्वांहून चांगला, उत्तम, वरिष्ठ, श्रेष्ठ, उत्कृष्ट.— to make the best of it, त्यामध्यें (or त्याचें) जितकें होईल तितकें करणे.

bestow v. t. देणे.

betimes *ad.* वेळवारीं, यथाकाळीं, मोव्या पाहटेस.

Betsy *n. p.* स्त्रीचें नाव.

better *a.* अधिक चांगला.

between *prep.* मध्यें, भतर (*in comp.*)

beyond *prep. & ad.* पलिकडे, पार, पैलीवर, पुढें.

Bible *n. p.* देवाचें शास्त्र.

bid *v. t.* सांगणे (कांहीं करायाला), आज्ञा देणे.—to bid good bye, सलाम सांगणे (जाल्ये वेळेस), निरोप देणे.

bid *prep. & p. p. of* bid.

biddy *n.* कोंबडें *n.* कोंबडी *f.*

big *a.* मोठा, थोरला, थोर.

bigger *a.* अधिक मोठा.

bill *n.* चोंच *f.* टोंच *f.* चुंच *f.* टोंक *f.* (२) हुंडी *f.* (३) हिशोब *m.* याद *f.*

Billy *n. p.* पुरूषाचें नाव.

bind *v. t.* बांधणे, कसणे, बेंटणे.

binding *n.* बेंटाळणी *f.* पुष्टिपत्र *n.* बंद *m.* बंध *m.* बंधन *n.*

binding *a.* लागत, लागू, मानणें प्राप्त. उ. this law is binding on all हा हुकूम सर्वांला लागत आहे *or* मानणें प्राप्त आहे.

bird *n.* पक्षी *m.* पांरबर *n.*

biscuit *n.* पोळी *f.* पोपली *f.* लहान भाकर *f.* पीगी *f.*

bit *n.* तुकडा *m.* शाकल *n.* घांस *m.* कांहीं, तीळभर *n.* लवलेश *m.* तुकडी *f.*

bite *n.* चावा *m.* दंश *m.* डंस *m.*

तुकडा *m.* तुकडी *f.* लोचका *m.* लचका *m.* थोडाच *m.*

bite *v. t.* चावणे, खाणे, डसणे, दंशणे. —to bite out, चावून घेणे. — to bite out a piece, लोचका-तोडणे-घेणे-काढणे.

bitten *p. p. of* bite.

bitter *a.* कडू, कडवट, कटु.

black *a.* काळा, काळवट.

black *v. t.* काळा करणे.

blacken *v. t.* काळा करणे.

blackened *p. p.* काळा झाला.

blackberry *n.* एक प्रकारचा मेवा (तुतासारखा).

blame *n.* दोष *m.* अपराध *m.* अन्याय *m.*

blame *v. t.* अपराधी ठरविणे, दोष ठेवणे, दोषारोप करणे.

bled *pret. & p. p. of* bleed.

bleed *v. i.* रक्त निघणे.

bleed *v. t.* रक्त काढणे.

bless *v. t.* आशीर्वाद देणे, दुवा देणे, वर देणे.

blessed *a.* आशीर्वादित, धन्य, सुखी. (२) सुवंदित.

blessing *n.* आशीर्वाद *m.* दुवा *m.* वर *m.* (२) सुवंदन *n.* स्तुति *f.*

blew *pret. of* blow.

blind *v. t.* झांकणे, झांपणे (डोळ्यांस).

blind *a.* अंध, अधळा.

blind *n.* झांपडी *f.* झांप *m.*

block *n.* ठोकळा *m.* फांटें *n.*

block up *v. t.* बंद करणे, भइथळणे, अटकावणे, कोंडणे.

blood n. रक्त n. रुधिर n. रगत n.

blood-thirsty a. घातकी.

bloody a. रक्तवॉर्णाळ, रक्तांपीळ. (२) घातकी.

bloom v. i. फुलणे, उमलणे, विकासणे, प्रफुल्लित होणे.

blot n. डाग m. बट्टा m. ठिपका m. ठपका m.

blot v. i. फुटणे (कागद, शाई).

blot v. t. डाग पाडणे, शाई पाडणे, ठपका ठेवणे. — to blot out, खोडून टाकणे, पुसून टाकणे.

blow v. i. t. फुंकणे. (२) सुटणे, वाहणे (वारा). (३) फुलणे, विकासणे.— to blow out v. i. विझून जाणे. (२) फुलणे. v. t. विझविणे, विझवून टाकणे. —to blow the nose नाक शिंकरणे.

blubber n. बुडबुडा m. (२) माशाची चरबी f. मर्दि n.

blue a. निळा, श्याम, आस्मानी.

bluish a. निळसर.

board n. तखता m. तक्ता m. फळी f. (२) खाणें n. अन्न n. परान्न n. (३) on board a vessel or ship तारवांत, तारवावर.

boast n. वल्गना f.

boast v. i. वल्गना करणे, आपणाला वाखाणणे, आपणाला नावांजणे.

boat n. नौका f. लहान तारूं n. गलबत n. नाव f. मचवा m. होडी f.

Bob n. p. पुरुषाचें नाव, Robert या नावाचा संक्षेप.

body n. कुडी f. शरीर n. देह m. कलेवर n. अंग n. — every body, जनलोक m. सर्व लोक. —some body, कोणी, कोणीएक.— any body, कोणी, कोणी तरी.—no body, कोणी तरी नाहीं.

boil n. फोड m. कैसतोड n.

boil v. i. शिजणे, उकळणे, (invers.) कढ येणे, उकळी येणे, अभण येणे.

boil v. t. शिजविणे, रांधणे, उकळणे, ऊन करणे, तापविणे.

—to boil down, आळविणे.

boiled p. p. & a. शिजविलेला.

boiled rice, भात.

boisterous a. वादळाचा, जवळी (समुद्र, दिवस), दांडगा, अडबाड.

bold a. निर्भय, हिमती, धैर्यवान, निधोस्त, जवानमर्द, निइशंक. (२) बेशक, धीट, निर्लज्ज, उद्धाम.

bolt n. खीळ f. खिळा m. कोयंडा m. अर्गळ f. m. अगळ m. f.

bolt v. t. अमळ लावणे, अडसर घालणे, बंद करणे.

bone n. हाड n. अस्थि n. f. हाडूक n. हडकी f.

bonnet n. टोपी (स्त्रियांची).

book n. पोथी f. पुस्तक n. ग्रंथ m. वही f.

book-binder n. वही बांधणारा m.

boot n. ऊंच जोडा m. पोटरी जोडा m. गुडघेजोडा m.

bore v. t. विंधणे, भोंक पाडणे.

bore pret. of bear.

2

bore n. छिद्र n. छेद m. विंध n. भोंक n. वेज m.

born p. p. of bear.

borrow v. t. उसनें घेणे, उभार घेणे, कर्ज घेणे-काढणे, कर्जावर घेणे.

borrowed a. उसना.

bosom n. ऊर m. छाती f. वक्षस्थ-ळ n. (२) हृदय n.

both a. उभयता, दोन्ही, दोघे, दोन.

bound n. उडी f. झपाटा m. उड्डा-न n.(२)मर्यादा f. सीमा f. ह-द्द f. (३) उसळणे n. उसळी f.

bound v. i. उडी मारणे, फांदणे. (२) उसळणे, उसळी खाणे, उस-ळून वर येणे.

bound v. t. सीमा सांगणें. (२) सीमा असणे.

bound pret. & p. p. of bind. —to be bound (by an oath, or obligation, बंदा खालीं वसणे, बांधलेला असणे. (२) (to any place), जाणारा, जाया-चा, (invers.) जायाचें.

bound a. बांधलेला, बंद.

bountiful a. उदार, दाता.

bow (बॉ) n. धनुष्य n. कमाण f. कमटा m.—bow and arrow, तीरकमठा m. धनुष्यबाण m.

bow (बौ) n. नमन n. नमस्कार m

bow (बौ) v. i. t. नमणे, थोणवणे, लवणे.

bowl (बोळ) n. प्याला m.

box n. पेटी f. हडपा m. करंडा m. उवा m. उवी f. (२) चपराक f.

boy n. मुलगा m. पोर m. कुमार m.

boyish a. मुलासारखा, पोरगळ.

—boyish play, बाळक्रीडा f.

brain n. मगज m. मीर m. गर m.

branch n. खांदी f. शाखा f. फां-दी f. फांटा m. फांटी f. (झाडाची, नदीची, इ.)

brave a. शूर, बहादूर, हिमतीचा, धैर्यवान.

break v. i. तुटणे, फुटणे, मोडणे, मोडून जाणे.—to break down, मोडून पडणे, कोसळणे. — to break up, उठणे, (सभा इ.), मोडून जाणे.

break v. t. मोडणे, फोडणे, तोडणे. — to break down, मोडून-पाडून-टाकणे. —to break up, उबळणे. (२) उठविणे.

breakfast n. न्याहारी f. सकाळचें खाणें-जेवण n.

breast n. छाती f. ऊर m. वक्षस्थ-ळ n. दुग्ध m. (२) हृदय n.

breath n. दम m. श्वास m श्वासो-श्वास m.

breathe v. i. t. दम टाकणे, दम घे-णे, श्वास टाकणे.

Briar hill n. p. जागेचें नाव.

brick n. ईट f.

brickbat n. इटकर f. n. टोळ m. रोडा m. इटकूर n.

bridge n. पूल m. दादर m.

bridle n. लगाम m.

bright a. ढाळदार, तेजस्वी, लकल-कीत, चकचकीत, सोज्वळ; निव-ळ (डोळे, अभाळ), भडक. (२) हुशार.

brilliant *a.* झळझळीत, चकचकीत, लकलकीत, तेजवंत, तेजस्वी.

bring *v. t.* आणणें, घेऊन येणें.—to bring forth (voung) प्रसवणें, विणें; (fruit) देणें, उपजवणें.

brisk *a.* चलाख, चंच, चंचुवाग, च-पल.

Bristol *n. p.* एका शहराचें नाव.

British *a.* इंग्लिश, इंग्लंड राज्याचा.

broad *a.* रुंद.

broke *pret. of* break.

broken *p. p. of* break.

broken *a.* फुटका, तुटका, मोडका.

brook *n.* नाळा *m.* ओघळ *m.* ओ-हळ *m.* ओघ *m.* लहान नदी *f.* ओढा *m.*

brother *n.* भाऊ *m.* बंधु *m.*

brought *pret. & p. p. of* bring.

brown *a.* तपकिरी, पिंगट, कपिल, भुरा, भोरा.

bruise *n.* खोंक *f.* खोंप *f.* वळ *m.* जखम *f.* खोंच *f.*

bruise *v. t.* चेंचणें, टेंचणें, चेंचर-णें, चेंगरणें, वळ वठवणें.

buffaloe *n.* म्हैस *f.* रेडा *m.* रे-डी *f.* टोणगा *m.* हेलगा *m.*

build *v. t.* बांधणें, रचणें, उभारणें.

bunch *n.* घड *m.* गुच्छ *m.* पुंज-का *m.* घोंस *m.* (२) गुळुंब *m.* वळ *m.* टेंगळ *n.* टेंगूळ *n.*

bundle *n.* गांठोडें *n.* पुडा *m.* पुडी *f.* पेंडी *f.* जुडा *m.* भारा *m.* गठा *m.*

burn *v. i.* जळणें, पोळणें, हुरप-ळणें, भाजणें, भडकणें, भडभडणें.

burn *v. t.* जाळणें, हुरपळणें.

burnt *pret & p. p. of* burn.

burr *n.* कांटि-टरफळ *n.*

burst *v. t.* फोडणें. — to burst open, फोडणें.

burst *v. i.* फुटणें. — to burst out crying किंकळी मारणें-फोडणें. —to burst out laughing, मो-ठ्याने हासूं लागणें.

burst *pret. & p. p. of* burst.

bury *v. t.* पुरणें, माती देणें, गाडणें.

bushel *n.* एक माप (कैली).

business *n.* काम *n.* धंदा *m* उ-द्योग *m.* काज *n.* व्यापार *m.* व्यवहार *m.* कार्य *n.* कसब *n.*

busy *a.* उद्योगी, काम करतांना, आळसी नाहीं, कामी, कामसू. — to be busy कामांत असणें.

but *conj.* परंतु, पण, मात्र, केव-ळ, फक.

but *prep.* खेरीज, वाचून, शिवाय.

butcher *n.* कसाई *m.* खाटक *m.* कसावी *m.*

butter *n.* लोणी *f.* मस्का *m.* न-वनीत *n.*

butterfly *n.* पतंग *m.* पाकोळी *f.* वेंगा *m.*

buy *v. t.* विकत घेणें, खरीदी क-रणें. (२) (invers.)-कडून मि-ळणें.

buzz *n.* भणभण *f.* गुंजारव *m.*

buzz *v. i.* भणभणणें, गुंगणें, गुं-जारव करणें.

by *prep.* जवळ, जवळून, पासीं. (२)-कडून,-ने. (३)-पर्यंत, पाबेतों.

— by and by, अमळ्याानी, थोड्या वेळनंतर.

— by himself, एकट्या.

bye *ad.* good bye, सलाम, सुगती, (जाल्ये वेळेस).

C

Cage *n.* पिंजरा *m.* पंजर *m.*

cage *v. t.* पिंजऱ्यांत घालणे.

cake *n.* पोळी *f.* पक्वान्न *n.*

call *n.* हाक *f.* पाचारण *n.* भेट *f.*

— to make a call, भेट घेणे.

call *v. t.* म्हणणे, नांव देणे. (२) बोलावणे, आमंत्रणे, आवर्तणे, पाचारणे. (३) हाक मारणे, पुकारणे, हांकरणे.

— to call for, मागणे.

— to call to mind, ध्यानांत आणणे.

— to call on the name of, नावाने हाक मारणे,-ची प्रार्थना करणे, धावा करणे.

— to call to account झडती घेणे.

called *p. p.* नामक, नांवे, म्हणून.

came *pret. of* come.

camphor *n.* कापूर *m.* कर्पूर *m.*

can *v. a.* शकणे. शक्यरूपार्चे सहाय क्रियापद, वर्त्तमान काळ. शक्यता किंवा मोकळ्वीक अहे अर्थ दाखविते. उ. I can read, मला वाचतां येतें *or* मला (माझ्याने) वाचवते *or* मी वाचूं शकतों. I will do as well as I can, शक्तिप्रमाणे (यथाशक्ति) मी करीन. You can go if

you plense, खुशी असली तर तुझी जावें. It cannot be so, नसेलच, नसावें.

Canada *n. p.* एका देशाचें नाव.

candle *n.* वत्ती *f.* दिवा *m.*

candy *n* चिकी *f.* खडीसाखर *f.*

canine *a.* श्वानस्वभाविक, कुत्रेजात, कुत्र्यासारखा.

canis *n.* श्वान संज्ञा.

can't, cannot याचा संक्षेप.

cap *n.* टोपी *f.*

capnble *a.* शक्तिमान, समर्थ, कावील, दुकसबी, दक्ष.

cape *n.* भूशलाका *f.* भूमीचें टोंक *m.*

caper *n.* चेष्टा *f.* खिदजा *m.*

caper *v. i.* खिदळणे, वागउणे, शिंगावणे.

Capriole *n. p.* करजाचें नाव.

captain *n.* सरदार *m.* अधिकारी *m.* तांडेल *m.* नाखवा *m.*

carcass *n.* कुडी *f.* कलेवर *n.*

care *n.* चिंता *f.* (२) काळजी *f.* खवरदारी *f.* जतन *f.* (३) संभाळ *m.* रक्षण *n.* (४) हवाल्य *m.* जिम्मा *f.* (५) बंदोवस्त *m.*

— to commit to the care of, -च्या हवालीं करणे,-स-ला सोपणे, हवालणे.

with care, संभाळून, जपून, काळजीने, जतन.

care (for) *v. i.* चिंता करणे, व काळजी करणे-धरणे, चिंतणे, संभाळणे, (*invers.*) चिंता असणे.

careful *a.* खवरदार, सावध, चिंता-

क्रांत, चिंताग्रस्त.— to be careful, संभाळणे, जपणे.

carefully *ad.* काळजीने, खबर-
दारीने, जपून, संभाळून, जतन.

careless *a.* निष्काळजी, गफलती.

carelessly *ad.* हयगयीने, निष्काळ-
जीने, उगींच.

cargo *n.* भरगत *n.* लादणी *f.* बार-
दान *n.*

Carlo *n. p.* पुरुषांचें नाव.

Caroline *n. p.* स्त्रियांचें नाव.

carpet *n.* सतरंजी *f.* जाजम *n.* गा-
लिचा *m.*

carriage *n.* रथ *m.* गाडा *m.* गाडी
f. यान *n.* (२) गति *f.*

carry *v. t.* वाहणे, घेऊन जाणे, नेणे.
— to carry on (work, busi-
ness, trade), चालविणे, निर्वाह
करणे.— to carry (in arithmetic) हातचा भरणे.

cart *n.* गाडा *m.* गाडी *f.*

cart *v. t.* गाडीवर वाहणे-नेणे.

carve *v. t.* कोरणे, खोदणे.
— to carve out कोरणे.

case *n.* गवसणी *f.* म्यान *n.* (२)
गोष्ट *f.* दशा *f.* अवस्था *f.* स्थिति
f. (३) उदाहरण *n.* (४) वि-
भक्ति *f.* (५) मुकदमा *m.* खटला
m. —in that case, असें असतां.

cast *n.* जात *f.* ज्ञात *f.* वर्ण *m.* प्र-
कार *m.* आकार *m.* रंग *m.*
रूप *n.*

cast *a.* भोंतीं.— cast down, उ-
दास, तोंड उतरलेला.

cast *v. t.* टाकणे, त्यागणे, फेंकणे,

पाडणे.— to cast up accounts,
हिशोब करणे.

— to cast a look, दृष्टि लावणे.

— to cast lots, पण घालणे.

— to cast down, पाडणे.

cast *pret. & p. p. of cast.* —
to be cast down, उदास होणे.

cat *n.* मांबर *n.* मांजरू *n.* बोका *m.*

catch *v. t.* धरणे, झेलणे. — to
catch away, हिसकून घेणे, हिरा-
वून घेणे.— to catch cold, (*invers.*) सरदी लागणे, पडसें येणे.

catch *v. i.* अडकणे, गुंतणे.

cattle *n. pl.* गुरें *n.* ढोरें *n.*

caught *pret. & p. p. of* catch.

cause *n.* कारण *n.* आदिकारण *n.*
निमित्त *n.* हेतु *m.* प्रयोजन *r.*
मूळ *n.* सबब *f.* — without
cause सहज, उगींच, निष्कारण.

cause *v. t.* करणे, करवणे, (*invers.*) नें-करून होणे, उत्पन्न
होणे.— याबद्दल मराठी क्रिया-
पदांत, व, वि, इव, घालतात. उ.
to go, चालणे. to cause to go,
चालविणे. — to bring, आणणे.
to cause to bring, आणविणे, इ.

celebrate *v. t.* वाखाणणे, स्तवन-
स्तुति-प्रशांसा-करणे, नावांजणे,
कीर्ति करणे, वर्णणे.

celebrated *a. & p.p.* कीर्तित, कीर्ति-
मान, नामांकित, विख्यात.

cellar *n.* तळघर *n.* भुयार *n.*
बळद *n.* पेंव *n.*

cent *n.* एक प्रकारचें नाणें, पै-
सा *m.*

2*

centre n. मध्य m. मध्यर्बिंदु m. केंद्र n.

ceremony n. क्रिया f. कर्म n रीत f. संस्कार m.

ceremonial a. रीतीचा, क्रिया-संबंधी. (२) कर्मनिष्ट, कर्मशील, कर्मठ.

certain a. फलाणी, अमुक, अमका, किल्येक, कोणी एक. (२)नि-श्चयाचा,निर्भ्रांत,खचीत,निश्चित

certainly ad. अवश्य, निर्धर्यं, ख-चीत, अगत्य, भलवत.

chain n. सांखळ f. सांखळी f. शृं-खला f. बेडी f. जंजीर f.
— in chains बेड्या घातलेला, सांखळ्या घातलेला.

chain v. t. सांखळ ल्रवणें-घालणें.

chair n. खुरशी f.

chalk n. खडू m.

chalk v. t. खडूने अंकणें.

chamber n. कोठडी f. म्याडी f.

chance n. दैवयोग m. सहजगती f
— by chance सहज, सहज-गतीनें, उगींच, एरवीं.

chance v. i. घडणें, सहज होणें.

change n. बदल m. पालट m. फेर m. फेरफार m. (२) खुर्दा m.

change v. i. बदलणें, फिरणें, पाल-टणें, वेगळा होणें, (inv.) फेर होणें.

change v. t. बदलणें, फीरविणें, पालटणें, वेगळा करणें, फेर क-रणें, -चे करणें.

chap n. मुसकूट n. जबडा m.

chap n. गडी m. बच्चाजी m. वा-प्या m.

chap v. i. फुटणें (टांच, साल, इ.) (invers.) चीर पडणें.

chapter n. अध्याय m. पर्व n. स्कंध m. प्रकरण n.

character n. स्वभाव m. भाव m. प्रकृति f. (२) आब्रू f. हुरमत f. प्रतिष्ठा f. (३) अक्षर n. हरफ m. लिपी f.

charge n. हवाला m. दिम्मत f.
— to commit to the charge of,-ला, सोपणें-निरवणें-गुदरणें-गुजरणें. (२) हुकूम m. आज्ञा f. (३) किम्मत f. मोल n. हेल m. हिशोव m. (४) वार m. (५) हल्ला m.

charge v. t. जमाखर्च लिहिणें, हिशोबांत मांडणें. (२) हेल सांगणें, किम्मत-मोल ठरवणें-सांगणें. (३) घालणें, करणें, (दोष, दोषारोप, इ.) (४) बजा-वणें, बजावून सांगणें, ताकीद करणें, हउसून सांगणें, आज्ञा-हुकूम देणें.

Charles n. p. पुरुषार्चें नाव.

Charlotte n. p. स्त्रियांचें नाव.

charm n. सौंदर्य n. सुंदरपण n. रमणीयता f. (२) मंत्र m. मोहनी f.

charm v. t. भावडणें, मंत्रणें, मंतरणें, मोहणें, रंजन करणें.

charming a. रंजक, मनोरम, म-नोहर, मनोहारी, दिव्य, रम-णीय.

chase *v. t.* पाठलाग करणे, पा-
ठीस लागणे.

chasten *v. t.* शिक्षा देणे.

chatter *n.* बडबड *f.* बकणी *f.*
बकवा *m. f.*

chatter *v. i.* बडबडणे, बकणे,
बकणी करणे.

check *n.* अडथळा *m.* आटोप *m.*
हरकत *f.* विघ्न *m.* अटकाव *m.*

check *v. t.* आटोपणे, अटकावणे,
अडथळणे, आवरणे.

— to be checked, भडणे, अ-
डकणे, गुंतणे.

cheek *n.* गाल *m.* गल्ल *m.* कपो-
ल *m.*

cheerful *a.* हस्तमुख, आनंदी, सं-
तोषी, खुशी, राजी, हास्यमुख.

cheerfully *ad.* संतोषाने, आनं-
दाने, हास्यवदनेंकरून, खुशीने.

cheese *n.* चका *m.* मठा *m.* ख-
वा. *m.*

cherry *n.* एक प्रकारचें झाड आणि
त्याचें फळहि.

chestnut *n.* एक प्रकारचें झाड
आणि त्याचें फळहि.

chief *n.* मुख्य *m.* मुकदम *m.*
शिरोमणि *m.*

chief *a.* मुख्य, श्रेष्ठ, प्रथम, प्रमुख,
अग्रगण्य, अग्रसर.

chiefly *ad.* विशेषेकरून, बहुतक-
रून, फारकरून.

child *n.* लेंकरूं *n.* बाळक *n.*
बाळ *n.* मूल *n.* पोर *n.* मुलगा
m. मुलगी *f.* बचा *m.*

childish *a.* पोरसमजुती, पोरस-

भावी, लेंकरासारखा, लेंकु-
रवा, बाल्यबुद्धीचा, पोरगळ.

children *pl. of* child.

chimney *n.* धुराडें *n.* धुराणे *n.*

chin *n.* हनवटी *f.* हनु *f.* अन-
वटी *f.*

China *n. p.* चिन देश.

chip *n.* खलपी *f.* खलपट *n.* ख-
लपा *m.*

choke *v. t. i.* गुदमरणे, दम कों-
डणे.

chop *n.* जबडा *m.* (२) मास्याचा
तुकडा *m.*

chop *v. t.* कापणे, तोडणे, छेदणे.

choose *v. t.* निवडणे, निवडून घेणे,
वेचणे, इच्छिणे, (*inters.*) इच्छा
असणे, भावणे.

chose *pret. of* choose.

chosen *p. p. of* choose.

Christ *n. p.* खीस्त, अभिषिक्त.

Christian *a.* खिस्ती.

Christopher *n. p.* पुरुषाचें नाव.

chubby *a.* ठिलू, बाळसें झालेला.

church *n.* खिस्ती लोकांची मंडळी
f. (२) खिस्ती लोकांचें देऊळ *n.*

churn *n.* माथण *f.*

churn *v. t.* मथणे, घुसळणे, मंथन
करणे.

churning *n.* घुसळण *n.* मंथन *n.*

circle *n.* मंडळ *n.* वाटोळें *n.* व-
र्तुळ *n.* चक्र *n.*

cipher *n.* पूज्ञ *n.* शून्य *n.*

cipher *v. i.* हिशोब करणे.

class *n.* वर्ग *m.* गण *m.* जात *f.*
वर्ण *m.* प्रति *f.*

class *v. t.* वर्ग करणें, आप आप-ल्या वर्गांत ठेवणें-मांडणे, प्रतींत लावणे.

claw *n.* नख (पाखरांचें), पंजा (वाघाचा, मांजराचा, इ.)

clean *a.* साफ, स्वच्छ, शुद्ध, नि-र्मळ, निवळ.

clean *v. t.* (cleanse या शब्दा-ला पाहा).

cleanly *a.* निर्मळ, चकपक, स्वच्छ, शुद्ध.

cleanse *v. t.* साफ करणें, स्वच्छ करणें, निर्मळ करणें, धोषणें, पवित्र करणें, शुद्ध करणें.

clear *a.* उघडा, मोकळा. (२) स्वच्छ, निर्मळ. (३) स्पष्ट.

clear *ad.* अलाद, अचानक, अल-ग. (२) स्पष्ट.

clear *v. t.* धोषणें, निर्मळ करणें, निवळवणें, साफ करणें. (२) सो-उणें, मोकळा करणें.

— to clear out *v. t.* उजेरणें, काढणें, बाहेर लावणें. *v. i.* जाणे.

— to clear away *v. i.* उघडणें (अभाळ). (२) *v. t.* काढणें.

clear *ad.* स्पष्ट, बरोबर.

clever *a.* कसबी, चतुर, काबील, हुशार, शहाणा, चांगला, युक्ति-वान, सुगर.

cleverly *ad.* हुशारीने, शहाण-पणाने, कसबाने, बरें, युक्तीने.

climb *v. t. i.* वेंघणें, चढणें (झाडा-वर इ.)

cloak *n.* घुगी *f.* झांकण *n.* उ-गलें *n.*

cloak *v. t.* झांकणें, (लाक्षणीक).

clock *n.* एक प्रकारचें घड्याळ *n.*
— What o'clock is it? किती वाजलें ? It is four o'clock, चार वाजले.

close (क्लोज) *n.* शेवट *n.* अखेरी *f.* समाप्ति *f.* परिणाम *m.*

close (क्लोज) *v. i.* संपणें, भरणें (आयुष्य, वेळ.) (२) लागणें, मिटणें.

close (क्लोज) *v. t.* बंद करणें, ला-वणें, मिटणें. (२) सिद्धीस नेणें, संपविणें, समाप्तीस आणणें, भरटी-पणें, जुळणें (हिशोब).

close (क्लोस) *a.* दाट, घट्ट. (२) जवळ, पासीं, सन्निध.
— close at hand जवळ.
— to be close (air of a room, weather), उबणें, उबावणें.

closely (क्लोसली) *ad.* जवळ, सान्नि-ध्यतेने, गच्च, लागोपाठ.

cloth *n.* कापड *n.* फडका *m.* पां-घरूण *n.* चिरगूट *n.* — broad cloth सखलत *f.* बनात *f.*

cloth *a.* कापडी.

clothe *v. t.* वस्त्रें देणें, नेसवणें, पां-घरविणें.

clothes *pl. of* cloth. वस्त्रें *n.* पो-षाक *m.* चिरगूट पांघरूण *n.*

clumsy *a.* अवडधोंवड, बेढौल, अडाणी, हेंगाडा, ऐवट.

cluster *n.* घड *m.* घोंस *m.* गुच्छ *m.* झुवका *m.*

cluster *v. i.* एकत्र मिळणें.

coach *n.* रथ *m.* गाडी *f.*

coachman *n.* सारथी *m.* गाडीवान *m.* सुत *m.* रथ हाकणारा *m.*

coal *n.* कोळसा *m.*

coat *n.* अंगरखा *m.* उगलें *n.* (२) लेप *m.*

coax *v. t.* फुसलावणे, घुलावणे, भुलथाप देणे, लुलूपन् करणे. (२) गोंजारणे, समजावणे.

cocked up, *a.* मुरडलेला (टोपी).

Colburn *n. p.* माणसाचें नाव.

cold *n.* थंडी *f.* हिंव *n.* शीत *n.* हिम *n.* गारठा *m.* (२) पडसें *n.*

cold *a.* थंड, गार, शीतळ.

Colin *n. p.* माणसाचें नाव.

color *n.* रंग *m.* वर्ण *m.*

color *v. t.* रंग देणे, रंगवणे, रंगणे.

colored *a.* रंगदार, रंगलेला, रंगविलेला.

colon *n.* लिहिण्यांतील ही खूण(:)

Colonel *n.* (सैन्यांतील एक किताब), पलटणीचा सरदार *m.*

colt *n.* शिंगरूं *n.* शिंगरट *n.*

Columbus *n. p.* पुरुषाचें नाव.

comb *n.* फणी *f.*

comb *v. t.* विंचरणे, पिंजणे.

combat *n.* लढाई *f.* रण *m. n.* झुंज *n.* युद्ध *n.* संग्राम *m.*

combat *v. t.* लढणे, युद्ध करणे, झुंजणे.

combine *v. t.* जोडणे, मिसळणे, एकत्र करणे, मिळविणे, (*invers.*) आंत असणे.

combine *v. i.* मिळून असणे, कट करणे, मिळणे, एकत्र होणे.

combined *a.* संयुक्त, जोडलेला.

come *v. i.* येणे.— to come out, निघणे.— to come up, उगवणे, हुडणे (झाडें इ.) (२) वर येणे.

— to come to pass, पूर्ण होणे, होणे, प्रत्ययास येणे.

comfort *n.* चैन *n.* सुख *n.* समाधान *n.* शांति *f.* शांतवन *n.*

comfort *v. t.* शांतवन करणे, शांतवणे, सस्तावणे, समजवणे.

comfortable *a.* समाधानी, समाधानयुक्त, शांत, स्वस्थ, खुशाल, बरा, सुखी.

comical *a.* तऱ्हेचा, तऱ्हेवाईक, तऱ्हेदार, थट्टेबाज, मौजेचा.

comma *n.* एक विरामाची खूण अशी (,).

command *n.* हुकूम *m.* आज्ञा *f.* तैनात *f.*

command *v. t.* हुकूम देणे, आज्ञा देणे, आटोपणे.

commandment *n.* हुकूम *m.* आज्ञा *f.*

commerce *n.* व्यापार *m.* उदीम *m.* व्यवहार *m.* वहिवाट *f.*

commercial *a.* व्यापारिक, व्यापाराचा, व्यापारसंबंधी.

commit *v. t.* करणे. उ. to commit wickedness, वाईट करणे. (२) सोपणे. उ. I commit this child to your care, हें लेंकरूं तुझ्यास सोपून देतों *or* तुमच्या हवालीं करितों.

— to commit to memory, पाठ

करणे, मुखोद्रत करणे, घट्-
मुखपाठ करणे.

common *a.* साधारण, सामान्य,
मुमाराचा, नेमस्त. (२) स-
माईक. (३) रूढ (शब्द).
(४) ओवळा.

commonly *ad.* सामान्यत:, बहुत-
करून, फारकरून, उर्फ.

communicate *v. t.* सांगणे, अर्पणे.

communicate *v. i.* लागणे. (२)
(*inv.*) वहिवाट असणे.

companion *n.* सोबती *m.* संगती
m. सखा *m.* गडी *m.* सर्वगडी
m जिवलग *m. f.* प्राणसखा *m*

company *n.* टोळी *f.* मंडळी *f.*
संगत *f.* सोबत *f.* मेळा *m.* ज-
माव *m* जमात *f.* थवा *m.*

compare *v. t.* तोलणे, ताडणे,
तुलनेस आणणे, लावून पाहणे,
उपमा देणे.

compare *v. i.* (*invers.*) उपमा
लागणे, उपमा असणे.

compel *v t.* जुलूम-जबरदस्ती-
जबरी करणे.

complain *v. i.* फिर्याद करणे, दाद
लावणे, गऱ्हाणे सांगणे, नालिस्त
करणे, दोष देणे. (२) शोक
करणे, रडणे, हुरहुरणे, गऱ्हाणे
करणे, दुःख सांगणे.

complaint *n.* दाद *f.* फिर्याद *f.*
गऱ्हाणे *n.*

comprehend *v. t.* समजणे, (*invers.*)
कळणे, ध्यानांत येणे.

conceal *v. t.* लपविणे, छपविणे,
दावणे, गुप्तांत ठेवणे.

conceit *n.* अहंकार *m.* अहंभाव *m.*
अभिमान *m.* गुमान *m.* पत्राज *f.*
दिमाख *m.* मीपण *n.* (२) मान *m.*

conceited *a.* अहंकारी, गुमानी,
अभिमानी, दिमाखदार, भत्या-
भिमानी.

conclude *r. t. i.* ठरावणे, निश्चय
करणे, मत स्थापणे. (२) संप-
विणे, शेवटीं बोलणे, (*invers.*)
शेवट असणे. (३) अनुमान करणे.

condescend *v. i.* मेहरबानी करणे,
कृपा करणे.

condition *n.* दशा *f.* अवस्था *f.*
गति *f.* स्थिति *f.* (२) पदवी *f.*

conduct *n.* वर्तनूक *f.* वागणूक *f.*
आचरण *n.* वहिवाट *f.* चाल *f.*

conduct *v. i.* वागणे, वर्तणे, चालणे.

conduct *v. t.* वहिवाटणे, वहिवाट
करणे, चालविणे, निभावणे. (२)
वाट दाखविणे, पोंहचविणे, वाटो-
च्या असणे.

confess *v. t.* कबूल करणे, कबूल
होणे, मान्य करणे, पदरीं घेणे,
भंगीकारणे.

confinement *n.* बंद *m.* कैद *f.*
(२) प्रसुति *f.* (स्त्रियेची).

confusion *n.* अंधाधुंदी *f.* घालमेल
f. वचवच *f.* पौंटाळा *m.*

Congress *n. p.* राजमंडल *n.* राज-
दरबार *m.* राजसभा *f.*

consent *n.* रुकार *m.* सम्मत *n.*
पत्कार *m.* मान्यता *f.* होकार *m.*

consent *v. i.* पत्करणे, रुकारणे,
कबूल होणे, पसंत करणे, अनु-
मोदन देणे.

consequence n. परिणाम m. कार्य n. (२) मान m. मोजणी f. गणना f.

consider v. t. i. विचार करणे, कल्पणे, मोजणे, मानणे, गणणे, (invers.) वाटणे.

considerable a. थोडाबहुत, कांहीं-सा मोठा, मध्यम.

consist v. i. होणे, सिद्ध होणे, संभवणे,-चा भसणे.

consistent a. संगत, संभाव्य, सुयुक्त.— to be consistent, संभवणे. (२) प्रमाणें असणे.

constant a. नित्य, एकाग्र.

constantly ad. नित्य, नेहमी, हमेश, निरंतर, हरवख्त, सर्वकाळ.

contain v. t. धरणे (पेटी, भांडें, इ.), (invers.) मावणे, आंत भ-सणे. उ. This box contains books, या पेटींत पुस्तकें आहेत.

contend v. i. भांडणे, लढाई करणे, तंटा करणे, वादविवाद करणे, भांडण-कज्जा करणे.

content a. (contented या श-ब्दाला पाहा).

content n. तृप्ती f. समाधान n. खुशी f. खुशाली f. — contents pl. मजकूर m. अनुक्रमणिका f. (पुस्तकाची, प-त्राची, इ.), जें आंत आहे तें, (पेटीमध्यें, पुस्तकामध्यें, इ.).

content v. t. पुरवणे, तृप्त करणे.

contented a. समाधानी, तृप्त, खुश, संतुष्ट.

continent n. महाद्वीप n. खंड m.

continue v. i. पुढें चालणे-जाणे. (२) राहणे, टिकणे, भाझून असणे.

continue v. t. चालवणे, आणखी बोलणे. उ. He continued his discourse, त्याने आपली गोष्ट पुढें चालविली.

contradict v. t. विरुद्ध बोलणे, ना-कारणे, प्रतिकूल बोलणे.

contradiction n. नाकार m. हठ-वाद m.

contrary a. हट्टी, हटवादी, प्रतिकूल, विपरीत. (२) उलटा.—on the contrary, उलटें.

contrivance n. युक्ति f. युक्तिप्रयुक्ति f. यंत्र n. कला f. तजवीज f. इलाज m.

contrive v. i. t. योजणे, योजना करणे, कल्पिणे, तजवीज करणे, युक्ति-हिकमत करणे.

control v. t. आटोपणे, आवरणे.

convenience n. योग्यता f. सोई f. अनुकूलता f.

convenient a. योग्य, सोईवार, शि-स्तवार, सोईचा.

conveniently ad. योग्यतेने, सोईनें.

convince v. t. समजविणे, समजूं देणे, निशा करणे, खातरी देणे-करणे, खातरीस आणणे. (invers.)-कडून खातरी होणे,-कडून समजूत होणे. —to be convinced, खातरी झाले-ला असणे, (invers.) खातरी होणे.

convinced p. p. कायल, कबूल.

cook n. सैंपाकी m. स्वंपाकी m. स्वंपाकीण f. आचारी m.

cook *v. t.* रांधणे, सैंपाक करणे, शिजवणे, भाजणे.

copper *n.* तांबें *n.*

copper-smith *n.* तांबट *m.*

Corbon *n. p.* माणसाचें नाव.

Corinthian *n. p.* कोरिंथकर.

corn *n.* दाणे *m.* धान्य *n.* मका *f.*

corner *n.* कोपरा *m.* कोन *m.* पदर *m.* (वस्त्राचा).

correct *a.* शुद्ध, ठीक, नीट, सरळ, अचूक, शिस्त.

correct *v. t.* शुद्ध करणे, नीट करणे, निटावणे, सुधारणे. (२) शिक्षा करणे.

cost *n.* किम्मत *f.* मोल *n.* खर्च *m.*

cost *v. t. (invers.)* -साठीं लागणे-पडणे, किम्मत असणे. What did that cost? त्याची किम्मत काय होती? — Cost what it will, किम्मत किती तरी असो.

cost *pret. & p. p. of* cost.

costly *a.* मोलवान, किम्मतदार.

cottage *n.* झोंपडी *f.* झोंप *f.* खोपट *n.* पर्णकुटी *f.*

cotton *n.* कापूस *m.* रू *m.* रूई *f.*

cough *n.* खोकला *m.*

cough *v. i.* खोकणे.

could *v. a.* शक्यरूपाचें सहाय क्रियापद, भूतकाळ, शक्यता असा अर्थ फारकरून दाखवितें. उ. I could say my lesson yesterday, काल माझा धडा मला झणतां येत होता. — On examination I found that those boys could not recite their lesson, परिक्षा घेते वेळेस माझ्या पाहण्यांत असें आलें कीं त्या मुलांस आपला धडा झणतां येव नाहीं. — I told him I could not go, माझें जाणें होत नाहीं *or* मला जाववत नाहीं, असें म्या त्याला सांगितलें. — I told him I could not do it, म्या त्याला सांगितलें कीं, तें मला करितां येत नाहीं. — I asked him if he could do this, he said he could, हें तुला करितां येतें कीं काय, असें म्या त्याला विचारिलें. तो झणाला, मला करितां येतें. — I ran as fast as I could, मी आपल्या सर्व शक्तीनें धांवलों. — I did as much work as I could, माझ्याने जितकें काम करवलें, तितकें म्या केलें. — I could do no more, माझ्याने आणखी करवलें नाहीं. — What more could he say? त्याला आणखी काय सांगायाचें होतें. — I thought this story could not be true, ही गोष्ट खरी नसेल, असें मला वाटलें. — He could not speak, त्याच्याने बोलवेना. — He could not see, त्याला दिसेना. — I told him I would do it if I could, म्या त्याला सांगितलें कीं जर मजकडून होईल तर मी करीन. — I told him I would go if I could, जर मला जाववेल तर मी जाईन; असें म्या त्या-

ला सांगितलें. — Could he know this he would come quickly, हें त्याला ठाऊक भ- सतें तर तो लवकर येता.— If he had asked me I could have told him, त्याने मला वि- चारिलें असतें तर मीं त्याला सां- गायास शक्तिमान होतों.— Oh that I could know what to do! काय करावें हें मला ठाऊक असतें तर बरें असतें!— I think it could not have been he, तो नसेल असें मला वाटतें.— I looked all round, but could not see him, म्या चहूंकडे पा- हिलें परंतु तो कोठें दृष्टीस पडला नाहीं or दिसला नाहीं. — I looked for it but could not find it, म्या त्याचा शोध केला परंतु त्याचा शोध लागला नाहीं. I told him, I could not find it, तें मला सांपडत नाहीं असें म्या त्याला सांगितलें. — 1 thought he could not speak, त्याला बोलतां येत नाहीं असें म- ला वाटलें.— I wish I could do it, मला करतां येतें तर ब- रें or करावें असी माझी इ- च्छा आहे.— You could not do me a greater favor, या- पेक्षां मजवर एक मोठा उपकार तुमच्याने होणार नाहीं.— What could have been the cause of that ? यांचें कारण काय झालें असेल ?— He came before I

could get ready, मला तयार होण्याचा अवकाश नाहीं इतक्यांत तो आला.

counsellor n. मंत्री m. प्रधान m. मसलतदार m. मसलत देणारा m. अमात्य m.

count v. t. गणणें, मोजणें, हि- शोब करणें.

countenance n. तोंडवळा m. तों- ड n. मुख n. चेहेरा m. चर्या f. सुरत f.

countenance v. t. भंग देणें, पाठ देणें.

country n. देश m. प्रदेश m. प्रां- त m. मुलूख m.

county n. जिल्हा m. परगणा m. सुभा m.

courage n. धैर्य n. हिम्मत f. म- र्दी f. मर्दुमी f. पराक्रम m.

cousin n. चुलत भाऊ m. बहीण f. मामे भाऊ m.-बहीण f. आ- ते भाऊ m.-बहीण f. मावस भाऊ m.-बहीण f.

cover n. झांकण n. ढांपण n. पुष्टिपत्र n. आच्छादन n.

cover v. t. झांकणें, ढांपणें, आं- च्छादणें, भरणें (चिखलानें इ.) — to cover up, झांकणें, लपविणें.

covered p. p. झांकला, व्याप्त, आच्छादित, गुप्त.

covering n. झांकण n.

covet v. t. लोभ ठेवणें, इच्छणें.

cow n. गाय f. धेनु f.

crack n. भेग f. चीर f. फूट f. तडा m.

3

crack *v. t.* चीर पाडणे. (२)
(a whip) कडाखा वाजविणे.

crack *v. i.* उलणे, उकलणे, तड-
कणे.

— to crack open, उलणे, इ.

— to be cracked, चीर गेली
असणे, तडा गेला असणे, चीर
पडणे, फुटणे.

cracker *n.* फटाका *m.* (२) फट-
कारा *m.* कडाखा *m;* (३)
एक प्रकारची लहान भाकर *f.*

crawl *v. i.* रांगणे (बाळ). (२)
सर्पटणे, सर्पटत चालणे, उराने
चालणे, (सर्प).

create *v. t.* उत्पन्न करणे, निर्माण
करणे.

creator *n.* उत्पन्न करणारा *m.* नि-
र्माण करणारा *m.*

creature *n.* प्राणी *m.* जनावर *n.*
जन *m.*

credit *n.* पत *f.* हुरमत *f.* नेक *f.*
सचोटी *f.* साख *f.* प्रतिष्ठा *f.* आब्रू
f. (२) भरवसा *m.* खातरी *f.*
विश्वास *m.*

credit *v. t.* विश्वासणे, विश्वास ठेव-
णे, भरवसा धरणे, (invers.)
खातरी-भरवसा असणे.

creep *v. i.* सर्पटणे, सर्पटत चाल-
णे, (साप, यांडवळ, इ.) रांगणे.
(बाळ). (२) चोरून येणे
(मांजरासारिखा).

crept *pret. of* creep.

crest *n.* तुरा *m.* किरीट *mn.* मुगु-
ट *m.*

cricket *n.* झिंळी *f.* राळ *f.* (२)

पादपीठ *n.* चवरंग *m.* (पायां-
साठीं).

crime *n.* अपराध *m* गुन्हा *m.*
पाप *n.* दोष *m.* तक्शीर *f.*
अन्याय *m.*

crockery *n.* मृन्मयपात्र *m.*

crooked *a.* वांकडा, तेडा, तिडा,
वक्र, नीट नाहीं, सरळ नाहीं.

cross *n.* वधस्तंभ *m.* क्रुस *m.* (२)
अडचण *f.* अडकाठीं *f.*

cross *a.* खास्ती, कर्कश, खंक,
कैदी, दाष्टीक, द्राष्ट, विपरीत,
रडका, किरकिरा, तिडतिडा, तु-
सडा. (२) आडवा.

cross *v. t.* ओलांडणे, उल्लंघणे. (२)
अटकावणे, आडवा येणे. (३)

— to cross out, खोडणे.

crouch *v. i.* दबणे, ओणवणे, वां-
कणे, दब्ब करणे, लवणे.

crow *n* कावळा *m.* काक *m.*
काग *m.*

crow *v. i.* आरडणे (कोंबडा).

crown *n.* किरीट *m.* मुगुट *m.*
(२) माथा *m.*

crown *v. t.* मुगुट घालणे.

— to be crowned, (invers.)
वर असणे (मुगुट).

cruel *a.* क्रूर, निष्ठुर, दुरात्मा,
कठोर, निर्दय.

crush *v. t.* चुरडणे, चुरणे, चेंच-
रणे, चिरडणे.

— to crush to pieces, चुरडणे.

cry *v. i.* रडणे, ओरडणे, आक्रोश
करणे. (२) दवंडी पिटणे. (३)
कूकारणे, पुकारणे.

cunning *a.* धूर्त, चतुर.

cunning *n.* धूर्तपण *n.* कावा *m.*

cure *v. t.* निरोगी करणें, बरा कं-रणें, सुधारणें.

cure *n.* रोगहरक *m.* औषधोप-चार *m.* वैद्योपचार *m.* (२) रोगहरण *n.* रोगपरिहार *m.* आरोग्य *n.*

curiosity *n.* नवल *n.* चमत्कार *m.* आश्चर्य *n.* विस्मय *m.* नवलाई *f.*

curious *a.* विलक्षण, चमत्कारीक.

curl *n.* झुलूप *n.* वेटाळें (केसांचें).

— in curls, कुरळ, मुरटा.

curl *v. i. t.* पीळ घालणें, पिळवटणें, कुरळ करणें, वेटोळें घालणें, मु-रटा करणें.

currant *n.* एक प्रकारचें फळ.

custom *n.* रीत *f.* चाल *f.* धारा *m.* वस्तूर *m.* परिपाठ *m.* वहि-वाट *f.* पद्धत *f.* प्रघात *m.*

cut *n.* घाय *m.* धाव *m.* जखम *f.* (२) तोड *f.* (३) चित्र *n.*

cut *v. t.* कापणें, तोडणें, कातरणें.

— to cut out, कापून काढणें.

— to cut off, कापणें, छेदणें (शीर), कापून टाकणें, काटणें.

— to cut down, तोडून टाकणें.

cut *pret. & p. p of* cut

D

Daddy *n.* बाप *m.*

dainty *a.* गोड्यांशा, सांगळ, ना-जुक, खोडकर, कंटाळखोर.

dairy *n.* दुग्धें *n.*

Dalben *n. p.* माणसाचें नाव.

damage *n.* नुकसान *n. f.* नाश *m.* तोटा *m.* उपद्रव *m.*

damage *v. t.* नाश करणें, नुक-सान करणें, नासविणें, नासणें.

damage *v i.* नासणें, खराब होणें.

damp *a.* दमसर, दमट, ओलसर, ओलट,

— to be damp, दमटणें.

danger *n.* धोका *m.* संकट *n.* जो-खीम *m. f.* भय *n.*

dangerous *a.* भयंकर, ज्याचा धोका लागतो तसला, भयावह.

dare *v. i.* धजणें.

— I dare say, मला सांगता येतें.

dark *n.* अंधार *m.* काळोख *m.* रात्रि *f.* (darkness पाहा).

dark *a.* काळोखमय, तामस, अंधा-र्युक्त, अंधारी (रात्र), अंधार (*in comp*). उ. अंधारकोंडी. (२) काळ्य, काळसर, (रंग इ.)

darkness *n.* अंधार *m.* काळोख *m.* रात्रि *f.* काहूर *n.* (२) काळिमा *f.* काळेपण *n.*

darling *n.* लाडका *m.* छावडा *m.* जिवाचा जाईत *m.* प्रीति *f.* प्रिय, जिवलग, जिवडा *m.*

dart *n* भाला *m.* (२) झपेट *f.*

dart *v. i* झपाटा करणें, झपेट करणें, (घार इ.) झपाट्याने जाणें.

dash *v. t.* आपटणें.

— to dash in pieces, फोडणें.

— to dash on, away, &c. झ-पाट्याने टाकणें.

dash *v. i.* आपटणें, खळवळणें.

dash *n.* रेघ *f.* रेषा *f.*

daughter *n.* कन्या *f.* मुलगी *f.*

day *n.* दिवस *m.* रोज *m.* every day, रोज, रोजरोज. — day's work, मजुरी *f.* — day's wages, रोजी *f.* — day by day, नित्य, रोज, प्रत्यहीं.

dead *a.* मेला, मयत, वारला, मेलेला.

deal *n.* वांटा *m.* भाग *m.* — a great deal, पुष्कळ, फार.

deal *v. i.* व्यापार करणें. (२) वागणें, वर्त्तणें, (कोणी एकासीं). उ. — to deal well by any one, कोणी एकासीं चांगल्या रीतीनें वर्त्तणें.

— to deal ill by any one, कोणी एकासीं वाईट रीतीनें वर्त्तणें.

deal (out) *v. t.* वाटणें, (अन्न इ.)

dealing *n.* व्यवहार *m.* घेवदेव *f.* व्यापार *m.* उदीम *m.* व्यवसाय *m.*

dear *a.* प्रिय, आवडता, लाडका, (२) महाग.

— O dear! बाबा! (दुःखामुळें, आनंदामुळें).

— dear me! अरेरेरे!

dearest *a.* सर्वाहून प्रिय, अति प्रिय. (२) सर्वाहून महाग.

dearly *ad.* पुष्कळ, फार. (२) प्रीतीनें, ममतेनें. (३) महागाईनें.

death *n.* मरण *n.* मृत्यु *m.* — to beat to death, पिटून पिटून जीवें मारणें.

debate *n.* वादविवाद *m.* तंटा *m.* वाद *m.*

debate *v. t. i.* वाद घालणें, वाद- विवाद करणें, तंटा करणें, वि- चार करणें (आपल्या मनांत).

decalogue *n.* देवाच्या दाहा आज्ञा, दशवचन.

deceive *v. t.* फसविणें, ठकविणें, वं- चणें, दगाबाजी करणें.

— to be deceived, फसणें, ठकणें.

decent *a.* प्रतिष्ठित, समयांद, भला, चांगला, साजरा.

declare *v. t.* सांगणें, निवेदन क- रणें, वदणें, निरूपणें.

deep *a.* खोल, सखल. (२) गाढ (झोंप).

deer *n.* हरण *m. f. n.*

defence *n.* शरण *n.* रक्षण *n.* संरक्षण *n.* राखण *n.* आश्रय *m.*

defend *v. t.* राखणें, संरक्षण क- रणें, शरण करणें, सांभाळणें.

defer *v. t.* चालढकल करणें, हेल- सांड-दयगई करणें.

define *v. t.* अर्थ सांगणें, वर्णन करणें, ह्मणजे काय ह्मणून सां- गणें.

definition *n.* व्याख्या *f.* वर्णन *n.* लक्षण *n.* अर्थ *m.*

degree *n.* परिमान *n.* मान *m.* (२) अंश *m.* — by degrees, उत्तरोत्तर.

deliberation *n.* मनसुबा *m.* वि- चार *m.* मसलव *f.* (२) सा- वकाशी *f.*

delicate *a.* नाजूक, कोमळ, मुकु-
मार, सोंगळ.

delicious *a.* रुच्य, रुचिकर, स्वा-
दिष्ट, गोड.

delight *n.* आनंद *m.* संतोष *m.*
मनोरंजन *n.*

delight *v. i.* आमोदणें, आनंद पा-
वणें.

— to delight in, (*invers.*) आ-
वडणें, मन बसणें.

delight *v. t.* आनंदविणें, रिझविणें,
संतोषविणें, फार आवडणें.

depart *v. i.* जाणें, निघून जाणें.

— to depart from, सोडणें.

depend *v. i.* टांगणें, लटकणें.

— to depend upon, अवलंबणें,
अवलंब करणें, आश्रय भरणें, प-
दरीं पडणें, — वरून होणें, (*ir-
vers.*) आधार असणें. (२) भ-
रवसा धरणें, मदार असणें, खा-
तरी ठेवणें. (३) संबंधीं असणें.

dependent *a.* अंकित, आश्रित, प-
रतंत्र, परस्वाधीन, ताबेदार.

dependent *n.* अंकित, आश्रित, अ-
नुग *m.* अनुचर *m.*

— dependants *pl.* परिवार *m.*

deprive (of) *v. t.* काढून घेणें, न
देणें, हरविणें.

— to be deprived of, मुकणें.

derive *v. t.* मिळविणें, पावणें, (*invers*) मिळणें.

desert *n.* रान *n.* जंगल *n.* ओस
जागा, ओसाडी *f.* भरण्य *n.*

desert *v. t.* सोडणें, सोडून जाणें.
उ. This sepoy deserted his
regiment, हा शिपाई आपली
पलटण सोडून गेला.

deserve *v. t.* योग्य असणें, जोगा
असणें, पात्र असणें, लायक अ-
सणें.

design *n.* बेत *m.* हेतु *m.* उद्देश *m.*
निमित्त *n.* मनसुबा *m.* — by
design, दादून, बुद्ध्या, समजून
उमजून.

design *v. t.* उद्देशणें, भवांकणें,
कल्पिणें, योजणें, (*invers*) मनां-
त असणें, बेत असणें.

desire *n.* इच्छा *f.* हव्यास *m.* कां-
क्षा *f.* वांच्छा *f.* सोस *m.*

desire *v. t.* इच्छिणें, सोस करणें,
हव्यास करणें, मागणें.

desirous *a.* इच्छायुक्त, (*invers.*)
इच्छा असणें, उत्कंठित.

— to be desirous, इच्छिणें,
(*invers.*) इच्छा असणें. उ.

— I am disirous of doing
this, हें करायास मी इच्छितों.

desk *n.* एका प्रकारचा चौरंग *m.*

despair निराशा *f.*

— to be in despair, निराशा
असणें.

despair (of) *v. i.* निराशा होणें, आ-
शा सोडणें, निराशा असणें.

despise *v. t.* तुच्छ मानणें, हलका
मानणें, धिक्कारणें, तिरस्कारणें.

destroy *v. t.* नाश करणें, नासणें,
बुडविणें, मारून टाकणें, नाहींसा
करणें, नष्ट करणें.

— to be destroyed, नाहींसा
होणें, नाश पावणें, लयास जाणें.

destroying a. नाशक, नाशा, पात
क.

destruction n. नाश m. पात m.
निःपात m. लय m.

determine v. t. निश्चय करणे, सं
कल्प करणे, मनसुवा करणे.
(२) फैसला करणे, ठरविणे.

determined p. p. निश्चित. (२)
निश्चयक, धीर, निश्चयाचा.
— to be determined, निश्चयें
भसणे, (intens.) निश्चय भसणे.

Deuteronomy n. p. नेमप्रकरण,
(खिस्ती शास्त्रांतील पांचवें पु
स्तक).

devour v. t. खाऊन टाकणे, पस्त
करणे.

dew n. देव n. देंवर n. वांहिंवर n.

dialogue n. संभाषण n.

dictionary n. कोश m. शब्दकों
श m.

did pret. of do.

die v. i. मरणे, वारणे, मरणी पाव
णे, प्राण सोडणे, (invers)
जीव-प्राण जाणे.

diet n. भन्न n. आहार m. (२)
पथ्य n.

diet v. i. पथ्य करणे.

differ v. i. वेगळा भसणे, न जम
णे, न मिळणे, (invers.) भेद
भसणे, भंतर पडणे-भसणे.

difference n. भेद m. फेर m. भं
तर n. तफावत f. तारतम्य n.
फरक m.

different a. वेगळा, निराळा, वेग
व्ळा, दुसरा, वायला, दुंजा, भिन्न.

differently ad. वेगलें, निराळें.

difficult a. सोपा नाहीं, अवघड, क
ठीण, विकट, दुर्घट.

difficulty n. अडचण f. कठीणपण
n. श्रम m. पेंच m. लचांड n.
कचाटी f.

dig v. t. i. खणणे, खांदणे, खा
णणे, खोंदणे, उकरणे.
— to dig up, खणून काढणे.

dignified a. थोरवट, थोर, थोर मा
नला.

dignify v. t. थोर करणे, थोर मा
नणे.

dim a. मंद (दृष्टि), अभ्यक, पुसका.

dimple n. वण (देवीमुळें), खोलगा
(गालवर इ.).

dimple v. t. वण पाडणे, खोलगा
करणे.

dimpled a. वण पडलेला, खोलगा
झालेला.

diligent a. उद्योगी, मेहनती, भन
लस, कामसू, अभ्यासी.

dinner n. जेवण n. भोजन n. (दु
पारचें).

directly ad. सरळ, नीट. (२)
लंवकर. (३) तत्काळ, लाग
लाच.

dirt n. मळ m. मावी f. केर m.

dirty a. मळीण, मळकट, साफ नाहीं.

dirty v. t. मळविणे, मळ घाणे.

disagreeable a. ओंयळ, कंटाळवा
णा, नावडता.

discourse n. गोष्ट f. भाषण n. क
था f. उपदेश m.

discourse v. i. गोष्ट करणे.

discover v. t. उमगणे, शोधून काढणे, काढणे, मार्ग काढणे, प्रगट करणे, पाहणे, दाखविणे, (invers) शोध लागणे, सांपडणे, थांग लागणे.

discovery n. उमग m. शोध m. थांग प्रगट करणें n. मार्ग लावणें.

disgust n. कंठाळा m. तिटकारा m. तिरस्कार n. शिसारी f. किळस f. m. चिळस f.

disgust v. t. कंठाळा आणणें, (invers) कंटाळा करणे, कंटाळणे.

disgusting a. कंटाळेवाणा, ओंगळ.

dish n. भोजनपात्र n. ताट m. तबक m. (२) खाणें, पदार्थ (खाण्याचा).

dislike v. t. नावडणे, नावडता मानणें, तिरस्कारणे, तिरस्कार करणे, (invers.) नावडणे, भावड नसणे, गोड न लगणे, कंठाळा असणे-वाटणें.

dislike n. नावड f. तिटकारा m. विणका m. अप्रीति f. अभक्ति.

dismiss v. t. रजा देणे, सुटी देणे, बरतरफ-रवाना करणें, वाटेस लावणे.

dismount v. t. उतरणें, (घोड्यावरून, इ.).

disobey v. t. न मानणे, न ऐकणे.

display n. डौल m. थाटमाट m.

display v. t. दाखविणे, प्रगट करणे, थाटणे, मिरविणे.

displease v. t. राग आणणें, कोपावणे नावडणे.

— to be displeased, रागें भ-

रणे, रुसणे, नाखुश असणे, मन तुटणे, गैरखुशी असणे.

displeasing a. नावडता, वाईट, ओंगळ, (वाटणें).

disposition n. स्वभाव m. वासना n. भाव m. प्रकृति f.

dispute n. तंटा m. वाद m. वाद-विवाद m. कलह m. पखेडा m. कळजा m.

dispute v. i. t. तंटा करणें, कलह करणे, वाद घालणे, वादविवाद करणे, नाकारणे, नाहीं म्हणणे, पखेडा करणे.

disrespect n. अमर्यादा f. हेळणा f. भर्त्सना m. धिक्कार m. अव्हेर m. अपमान m. n.

— to treat with disrespect, अव्हेरणे, हेळणे, धिक्कारणे, भनादर करणे.

distance n. लांबी f.—at a distance, दूर.

distant a. दूर, लांब, दूरचा.

distinguish v. t. भेदणे, भेद करणे-पाहणे.

distress n. खेद m. दुःख n. हैराणी f. संकट n. गजब m. n. पेंच m. आउचण f.

distress v. t. दुःख देणे, दुःखविणे, हैराण करणे, गांजणे.

distressing a. दुःखदायक, दुःखकारक, शोककारक.

disturb v. t. त्रासणे, त्रास देणे, उपद्रव देणे, श्रमी करणे, श्रम देणे, हलविणे.

dire *v. i.* गुचकळी मारणे, गुडी मारणे, गुटकुळ्यें मारणे.

divide *v. i.* विभागणे, विभाग करणे, भागणे, भागाकार करणे, दुभागणे, छिन्न करणे, छिन्न छिन्न करणे.

dizziness *n.* भोवळ *f.* भोंड *f.* गि॰ रकी *f.*

dizzy *a.* भोवळयुक्त,

—to make dizzy, भोवळ आणणे.

do *v. t.* करणे.

— I have nothing to do with you, मला तुजशीं संबंध नाहीं. — That will do, तें पुरें आहे. (२) तें बरें आहे, तें बरें लागतें, तें चांगलें वसतें-आहे. — How do you do? तूं कसा आहेस? तुझी प्रकृति कसी आहे?

do *v. a.* (निश्चयार्थक), -च, ज, I *do* read, मी वाचतोंच *or* मी वाचतों आहें. — I *do* study, मी शिकतोंच *or* शिकतों आहें. — I *did* speak, मी बोललोंच.

—(२) (प्रश्नवाचक). ज॰ Do you read? तूं वाचतोस कीं काय? *or* तुला वाचतां येतें कीं काय? — Does this road lead to Poona? हा रस्ता पुण्यास जातो कीं काय? — Where does this road lead to? हा रस्ता कोणीकडे जातो? — What did he say? त्यानें काय सांगितलें? — What do you think? तुला कसें वाटतें?

—(२) (प्रश्नांच्या उत्तरांमध्यें सर्व क्रियापदांवदल लावलें आहे). ज॰ Do you go to day? उत्तरें. I do *or* I do not, (झणजे) I do go *or* I do not go. तूं आज जातोस कीं काय? (उत्तर) मी जातों *or* मी जात नाहीं. — Did you see him? I did, त्या त्याला पाहिलें कीं काय? पाहिलें.

— Did he come yesterday? He did. तो काल आला कीं काय? आला.

—(४) (निषेधार्थ), ज॰ I do not know, मी जाणत नाहीं, *or* मला ठाऊक नाहीं. — He does not come, तो येत नाहीं. — He did not go, तो गेला नाहीं. — Do not go, जाऊं नको-नका-नये. — Do not do so, असें करूं नको-नका-नये.

—(५) (कोणती तरी क्रिया तुळणेस झणली आहे, तेव्हां कर्धींकभीं सर्व क्रियापदांवदल लावितात). ज॰ He walks as fast as I do, झणजे, He walks as fast as I walk, तो माझ्या इतका लवकर चालतो. — I can read as well as he does, झणजे, I can read as well as he reads, मी त्याच्या इतका चांगला वाचतों. *or* मला त्याच्या इतकें चांगलें वाचतां येतें, *or*, त्याच्यासारिखें मला चांगलें वाचतां येतें. — He can write better than I do (than I write), माझ्यापेक्षां त्याला चांगलें लिहितां येतें. — Do as

I do, जसें मी करितों तसें तसें नूं कर.—I think as he does, जसें त्याला तसें मला वाटतें.—Read as I do, नूं माझ्यासारिखें वाच. or जसें मी वाचतों तसें तूं वाच.—Do not tell lies as bad boys do, तूं वाईट मुलांसारिखा लबाड बोलूं नको. — It does not rain to day as it did yesterday, कालच्यासारिखा आज पाऊस पडत नाहीं. — He does not go as well as he did before, पूर्वींसारिखा तो चांगला चालत नाहीं.

—(६)(क्रियापद भावरूपांत असलें, आणि do लावलें, तर हा शब्द काकूळती दाखवितो). व. Do tell me, कृपाकरून मला सांग.—Do give me that book, तूं कृपाकरून तें पुस्तक मला दे. — Do let me go, कृपाकरून मला जाऊं दे.

docile a. विनीत, नम्र, सुबोध, गरीब.

Doctor or Dr. n. वैद्य m. (२) ह्यास्ती m.

dog n. कुत्रें m. कुत्रा m. श्वान n.

done p. p. of do & a. झाला, समाप्त, केला, सिद्ध.

dolefully ad. शोकाने, काकूळतीने, दुःखाने, दुःखशब्दाने.

doll n. बाहुली f. पुतळी f.

dollar n. एक नाणें, (सुमारें दोन रूपयां मोलाचें).

dolt n. टोणा m. टोणपा m. नंदी m.

dont, do not, याचा संक्षेप.

door n. दार n. द्वार n. दरवाजा m. कवाड m.

dot n. बिंदु m. टिंब n. ठिपका m.

dot v. t. टिंब देणे, ठिपका देणे.

double n. दुपट, दुहेरा, दुणा.

double v. t. दुमटणे, दुपट करणे, दुणणे.

doubt n. संदेह m. संशय m. शंका f. आशंका f. भ्रांति f. दिकल f.

doubt v. i. t. कल्पना-संशय येणे, (invers.) संशय वाटणे, मनांत संशय असणे.

dove (दव) n. पारवा m. खबुतर m.

dove (दोव) pret. of dive.

down ad. खालीं, खालतें, खालतीं. (२) वरून.
— to fall down, पडणे.
— to throw down, पाडणे, टाकणे.
— to lie down, नीजणे.
— to write down, मांडणे, लीहून ठेवणे.
— to sit down, बसणे.
—to put down, उतरणे, ठेवणे.

down n. लंव f.

downwards ad. खालीं, खालतीं, खालतें, खोल.

downy a. लंवेचा, लंवेसारिखा, मऊ.

doze n. डुकली f.

doze v. i. गुंगणे, पेंगणे. (२) डुकली खाणे, (invers.) डुकली येणे.

Dr. (Doctor, याचा संक्षेप). वैद्य *m.*

drag *v. t.* ओढणे, खेंचणे.

drain *n.* पाट *m.* मोरी *f.* नाला *m.* नळ *m.*

drain *v. t.* पाट काढणे, निथळणे, पाझरू देणे.

drain *v. i.* पाझरणे, थबथबणे, झरणे.

draught *n.* घोट *m.* घोटभर *m.* (२) ओढ *f.*

draw *v. t.* ओढणे, आंकर्षणे. (२) अंकणे, रेखाटणे, काढणे, चितरणे.

— to draw out, off, &c. काढणे, लांबविणे, निथळणे (पाणी, इ.)

— to draw back *v. i.* मागें सरणे, हटणे. *v. t.* सारणे, हटविणे.

— to draw near *v. i.* जवळ येणे, नेटणे, भिडणे. *v. t.* जवळ आणणे.

— to draw together, गोळा करणे.

drawl *v. t.* हेल काढणे, हेल काढून वाचणे-बोलणे, इ. नादांने बोलणे.

dreadful *a.* भयंकर, क्रूर, उग्र, अघोर, पराकाष्ठिचा, मनस्वी.

dreadfully *ad.* अतिशयें, फार, पराकाष्ठेंने, पराकाष्ठा.

dream *n.* स्वप्न *n. m.*

dream *v. i.* स्वप्न पडणे, स्वप्नहोणे.

dream *v. t.* स्वप्न पाहणे, स्वप्नांत पाहणे.

dress *n.* पोशाक *m.* पेहराव *m.*

वस्त्र *n.* पांघरूण *n.* वस्त्रप्रावरण *n.*

dress *v. t.* पोशाक घालणे, वस्त्र नेसणे.

dried *pret. & p. p. of* dry.

drink *n.* जें प्राशनीय तें, पानीय *n.* प्राशनीय, पाणी *n.*

drink *v. t.* पिणे, प्राशन करणे.

— to give to drink, पाजणे, प्यायास देणे.

drive *v. t* हांकणे, चालविणे. (२) मारणे, ठोकणे, (खिळा, मेख इ).

— to drive away, off, हाकून लावणे.

drone *n.* घरडुकर *n.* आळशी.

drop *n.* बिंदु *m.* ठिपका *m.* थेंब *m.* बुंद *m.* टिंब *n.*

drop *v. i.* पडणे, टिपकणे, गळणे, थबथबणे.

drop *v. t.* पडूं देणे, हरवणे, पाडणे.

drove *n.* कळप *m.* थवा *m.* मेळा *m.* जमाव *m.*

drove *pret. of* drive.

drown *v. t. i.* बुडून मरणे, बुडणे, गुदमरणे, (पाण्याने).

drum *n.* ढोल *m.* ढोलकी *f.* ढोलकें *n.* डिमकी *f.* नगारा *m.* नौबद *f.*

drum *v. t.* ढोल-टिमकी इ. वाजविणे, पिटणे.

drunk *a.* गुब्ध, गुंग, (दारूने), मस्त.

— to be drunk, तारवटणे, गुंगणे, भुळणे, मस्त असणे.

drunkard *n.* दारूबाज *m. f.* मद्यपी *m. f.* अमली *m. f.*

drunken a. धुंद, गुंग, (दारूने), मस्त.

dry a. कोरडा, शुष्क, सुखा, सुका, वाळलेला. (२) तान्ह्राळू, तन्हेला. — dry goods, कापड चोपड.

dry v. i. सुकणे, वाळणे, अटणे. — to dry up, अटणे, ओसरणे.

dry v. t. सुकविणे, वाळविणे, शोषणे. — to dry up, पुसणे, (भसवें), अठविणे.

duck n. बदक n.

due a. देण्याचा, देणें, येण्याचा, यथायोग्य, यथार्थयोग्य.— in due time, यथाकाळीं, योग्य वेळेस, सुकाळीं.

due ad. — due east, west, &c. पूर्वेकडेच, पश्चिमेकडेच इ.

due n. देणें n.

dug pret. & p. p. of dig.

dull a. बोथा, बोंथट, धार नाहीं असा (चाकू इ.). (२) मंद, जड, जडबुद्धि

dull v. t. धार बसविणे, खांड पाडणे.

dumb n. मुका. — dumb beast, जनावर n.

dunce n. टोणपनाथ m. नंदी m. बैल m. दगड m. फत्तरफोड m.

during prep. पर्यंत, भर, आंत, पावेतों, (वेळाविषयीं).

dust n. धूळ f. माती f. रज n. m.

dutiful धार्मिक, आज्ञा धारक, आज्ञांकित.

duty n धर्म m. (२) जकात f. कर m. पट्टी f. हाशील m.

E

each a. प्रत्येक, एक एक.— each other, एकमेक, परस्पर.

eager a. अगत्यवादी, अस्तैशिक, तत्पर, उत्सुक, उत्कंठित.

ear n कान m. कर्ण m. (२) कणीस n.

early ad. मोठ्या सकाळीं, प्रातःकाळीं, मोठ्या पाहटेस, झुंझुरका, यथाकाळीं, योग्य वेळेस, लवकर. (२) आरंभीं, पहिल्या दिवसीं.

early a. आगस, हळवा, पहिला.

earnest a. अगत्यवादी, एकनिष्ट, तत्पर. — in earnest, मनाने, थट्टेने नाहीं, एकनिष्टेने, अगत्यवादी, एकनिष्ट.— earnest money, इसार.

earnestly ad. एकनिष्टेने, खरेपणाने, अगत्याने, सर्ग मनाने.

earth n. पृथ्वी f. भुमी f. मही f. (२) जमीन f. माती f.

ease n. चैन n. समाधान n. सुख n. शांति f. स्वस्थता f. — at ease, शांत, अढेद्य, निवांत, निर्घोर, निसूर. — with ease, सहज, अनायासें, अनायासाने, श्रमावांचून.

easily ad. सहज, अनायासाने, अनायासें, अढेश. (२) लवकर.

east n. & a. पूर्व f.

East Indies n. p. आशी खंडाचा पूर्व दक्षिण भाग.

easy *a.* सोपा, सुगम, मुलभ, सहज, अवघड नाहीं, सवघड. (२) स्वस्थ, सुखी, शांत, समाधानी.

eat *v. t. i.* खाणे, जेवणे, भक्षणे, भोजन करणे.

— to eat up, खाउन टाकणे, खाणे, पस्तखाणे, ग्रासणे.

— to eat off, करउणे.

eaten *p. p. of* eat.

cater *n.* खाणारा *m.*

eating *n.* जेवणे, भक्षणे, खाणें. (२) भक्ष *m.* खाणें *n.* अन्न *n.* आहार *m.* जेवण *n.*

edge *n.* धार *f.* (हत्याराची, सुरीची इ.). (२) कांठ *m.* किनारा *m.* कड *f.*

— to be set on edge (teeth), अंबणे.

Edmund *n. p.* पुरुषाचें नाव.

education *n.* विद्याभ्यास *m.* शिद्धा *f.*

Edward *n. p.* पुरुषाचें नाव.

effort *n.* यत्न *m.* प्रयत्न *m.* नेट *m. n.* लगट *m. f.* उद्योग *m.* आयास *m.*

— to make effort, नेटणे, यत्न-प्रयत्न करणे.

egg *n.* अंडें *n.* आंडें *n.*

eight *a.* आठ.

either *a.* एक (दोहोंतून), द्वि. — either or, किंवा. — either one or the other, दोहोंतून एक.

elder *a.* वडील, ज्येष्ठ, पूर्वज.

elephant *n.* हत्ती *m.* गज *m.*

Ellen *n. p.* स्त्रियेचें नाव.

elopement *n.* चोरून जाणें.

else *ad.* नाहीं तर, एरवीं, अन्यथा.

— or else, नाहीं तर.

else *a.* इतर, दुसरा, अणखी, अन्य.

eminent *a.* प्रतिष्ठित, नामदार, विख्यात, थोर, नामांकित, संभावित.

emphasis *n.* सरस *m.* जोर *m.* (शब्द उच्चारण्यांत), उंचस्वर.

emphatical *a* सरसयुक्त.

employ *v. t.* कामांत लावणे, काम देणे, ठेवणे (चाकरीस), रचवणे, वहिवाटणे, वापरणे, चाकरी देणे.

— to be employed, कामांत असणे, रुधणे, गुंतणे, उद्योग करणे, उद्योगीं असणे.

employment *n.* उद्योग *m.* काम *n.* कसव *n.* व्यवहार *m.*

— out of employment, रिकामी.

empty *a.* रिकामा, रिता, खाली, सुना, शून्य, निरर्थक, पोकळ.

empty *v. t.* रिचवणे, रिता करणे, रिकामा करणे.

empty *v. i* मिळणे (नदी).

encourage *v. t.* आश्वासणे, धीर-दिलासा-आश्वासन-पाठ-विश्वास-अवसान देणे. (२) वाळगणे.

end *n.* शेवट *m.* अग्र *m.* अवसान *n.* पार *m.* परिणाम *m.* शेंडा *m.* — from begining to end, सार्धांत, भयेति, अर्धंत, सर्व.

end *v. t.* संपविणे.

end *v. i.* शेवटीं असणे, (*invers.*) शेवट असणे.

endeavour *v. i.* प्रयत्न-यत्न करणे, लगट करणे, शक्ति-मन लावणे.

engage (to do, &c.) *v. i.* कबूल करणे, करार करणे, वचन देणे, निश्चय सांगणे, प्रतिज्ञा करणे. (२)
— to engage (in work, business, trade, &c.), करणे, चालविणे, लागणे, करूं लागणे, मन लावणे, मनावर घेणे, शिरणे.

engage *v. t.* भरणे, (invers.) लागणे (मन, लक्ष, इ.). (२) रंधवणे, कामांत घालणे-लावणे, काम देणे, लादणे, ठेवणे, चाकरीस ठेवणे, भाड्याने ठेवणे, (invers.) कबूल करणे, करार करणे.
— to be engaged, रंधवणे, गुंतणे, कामांत असणे, लागणे, लीन-निमग्न असणे.

Euglish *a.* इंग्लिश.

enjoy *v. t.* भोगणे, अनुभवणे, उपभोगणे, उपभोग-अनुभव घेणे.

enjoyment *n.* भोग *m.* उपभोग *m.* सुख *n.* अनुभव *m.*

enough *a.* पुरा, पुरता.

enough *ad.* पुरें, पुरतें.

enough *n.* पुरें, पुरतें, जितकें पाहिजे तितकें.

enslave *v. t.* दास करणे, दास्यांत ठेवणे हस्तगत करणे.

entangle *v. t.* गुंतवणे.
— to be entangled, गुंतणे.

enter *v. t.* शिरणे, आंत जाणे-येणे, प्रवेश करणे, पुसणे, रिघणे, शिरकणे. (२) टिपणे, टिपण करणे, मांडणे, (टिपणामध्यें).

enter (in, into) *v. i.* शिरणे, आंत जाणे-येणे. (२)—to enter into, upon, (business, work, trade, &c.), शिरणे, लागणे, करूं लागणे, मन लावणे, मनावरघेणे.

entertainment *n.* संतोषविणें *n.* करमणूक *f.* (२) मेजवानी *f.* वरदास्त *f.* पाहुणचार *m.* पाहुणेर *m.* गमत *f.*

entirely *ad.* अगदी, पस्त, बिलकुल, निपट, निस्तूक, झाडून, निखालस, निश्शेष.

entrance *n.* प्रवेश *m.* प्रवेशन *n.* (२) आंत जाण्याची जागा, दार *n.* दरवाजा *m.*

entry *n.* प्रवेश *m.* (२) प्रवेशस्थान *n.* शिरण्याची जागा, (घरांत). (३) लिहून ठेवणे, टिपणें, मांडणें, (वहीमध्यें इ.)

envy *n.* हेवा *m.* अदेखाई *f.* मत्सर *m.* ईर्षा *f.* असोशी *f.* असूया *f.*

envy *v. t.* हेवा-ईर्षा करणे, (विषयीं) अदेख-मत्सरी असणे.

equal *a.* बरोबर, समान, तुल्य, सारिखा, (in comp.) सम.

errand *n.* जासुदी *f.* संदेश *m.* निरोप *m.* काम *n.* (दुसऱ्या ठिकाणीं जाऊन कांहीं सांगण्याचें किंवा करण्याचें).

escape *n.* मोकळीक *f.* सुटका *f.* सुटणें *n.*
— to make an escape, पळून जाणे, जाणे, सुटणे.

escape *v. i. t.* चुकविणे, वांचणे, तरणे, निभावणे, (*invers.*) ट-ळणे. (२) सुटणे, निघून जाणे, पळून जाणे, सुटून जाणे.

espy *v. t.* पाहणे, दुरून पाहणे, अकस्मात पाहणे, (*invers.*) दृष्टीस पडणे.

esteem *n.* गणना *f.* मान *m.* मो-जणी *f.*

esteem *v. t* गणणे, मानणे, मो-जणे, भावणे, लेखणे, जुमानणे.

estimation *n.* अजमास *m.* सुमार *m.* पाड *m.* केवा *m.* मान *m.* गणना *f.* अटकळ *f.*

Europe *n. p.* युरोप खंड *m.* वि-लायत *f.*

even *ad.* हि, देखील.

even *a.* सम, उमान, सपाट, बरो-बर, सारिखा. (२) बेकी.

even *n.* संध्याकाळ *m.*

evening *n.* संध्याकाळ *m.* सायंकाळ *m.* सांज *f.*

event *n.* गोष्ट *f.* (घडलेली). (२) शेवट *m.* परिणाम *m.* व्यवस्था *f.*

ever *ad.* नेहमी, हमेशा, सर्वकाळ, कर्षीं, निरंतर.

. — ever since,-पामून आतां-पर्यंत, (वेळाविषयीं).

— ever so (much, great, many, long), केवढा तरी, कि-ती तरी.

— ever so little, कितीहि थोडें -लहान.

every *a.* प्रत्येक, सगळा, सर्व, स-मग्र. (२) दर, हर.

evil *a.* वाईट, दुष्ट. (२) दैवहिन, हतभाग्य, कुत्सित.

evil *n.* वाईटपण *n.* दुष्टाई *f.* दुःख *n.* हतभाग्यपणा *m.* अरिष्ट *n.* अनर्थ *m.*

exactly *ad.* ठिकला, तंत, बरोबर-च, खास,-च, नेमका. उ.

The wind is exactly west, वारा खास पश्चिमेचा झाला. —

It is exactly ten o'clock, दाहा वाजत आहेत or बरोबर दाहा वाजले.

— exactly .... as, जसा-तसाच.

example *n.* उदाहरण *n.* मासला *m.* दाखला *m.* दृष्टांत *m.* किता *m.* उपमा *f.* नमुना *m.*

exceedingly *ad* पराकाष्ठेने, फार, अति, निपट, अतिशयें, मनस्वी.

excellent *a.* उत्तम, नामी, फार चांगला, चोख, मजेदार, खाशी, उत्कृष्ट.

except *prep.* वांचून, शिवाय, खे-रीज, मौजून, नाहीं तर.

except *v. t.* सोडणे.

excess *n.* अतिशय *m.* पराकाष्ठा *f.* अतिरेक *m.* ऊर *f* शेष *m. n.* उरलें *n.*

excuse (एक्सक्यूस्) *n.* निमित्त *n.* निमित्य *n.*

excuse (एक्सक्यूज) *v. t.* सोडणे, क्षमा करणे, (अपराध इ.). (२) रजा देणे, सुटका देणे, सोडिला असा मानणे.

exercise *n.* सहल *f.* व्यायाम *m.* व्यवहार *m.* काम *n.* उद्योग *m.*

अभ्यास m. धंदा m. तालीम f.
कसरत f.

exercise v. i. t. सहल घेणे, अभ्या-
स करणे, काम-व्यायाम-उद्योग
करणे, कसरत करणे.

exert v. t. लावणे (मन, शक्ति, इ.)
— to exert one's self, mind,
strength, &c.), प्रयत्न-यत्न क-
रणे, झटणे, नेटणे, नेट लावणे,
मन लावणे.

exertion n. यत्न m. प्रयत्न m. नेट
m. n.

Exodus n. p. निघणें, (ख्रिस्ती शा-
स्त्रांतील दुसरें पुस्तक).

expect v. t. वाट पाहणे, प्रतीक्षा
करणे, आशा धरणे, पाहणे, हो-
ईल झणून समजणे, (invers.)
सरणे, आशा असणे.

expense n. खर्च m. व्यय m. वेंच m.

explain v. t. समजविणे, दाखविणे,
बोधविणे, कळविणे, उलगडणे.

explanation n. तपशील m. व्या-
ख्या f. बोध m. अर्थ m. टीका
f. अर्थांतर n.

expression n. वाक्य n. बोल m.
वचन n. उक्ति f. (२) स्वरूप n.
रूप n. धोरण n.

external a. बाहेरील, बाहेरला, बा-
हेरचा, बाह्य.

extinguish v. t. विझवणे, शांत क-
रणे, नाहीसा करणे.

extol v. t. कीर्ति सांगणे, वाखा-
णणे, नावाजणे.

extreme n. पराकाष्ठा f. शेवट m. n.
निदान n.

extreme a. अति, आत्यंतिक, परा-
काष्ठेचा, फार, अत्यंत, मनस्वी,
अंत्य, शेवटील.

eye n. डोळा m. नेत्र m. दृष्टि f.
लोचन n. (२) नेढें n. नाक n.
भोंक n. (सुईचें इ.) (३) लक्ष
n. विचार m.

eye v. t. रोखणे, निरखून पाहणे,
न्याहाळून पाहणे.

eyed a. डोळ्याचा. उ. bright-
eyed, निवळ डोळ्यांचा.

eye-lash n. पापणीचे केस.

F

Face n. तोंड n. मुख n. (२) पा-
ठ f. (पृथ्वीची.)
— on the face of the ocean,
-deep, समुद्रावर, सागरावर.
— to fall upon the face, उ-
पडा पडणे.

face v. t. नाकासमोर जाणे.

fact n. सत्य n. भूत n. m. जें झा-
लें तें, जें आहे तें, प्रमाण n.
गोष्ट f. — in fact, खरेंच, वा-
स्तविक, खचीत.

fail v. i. उणा पडणे, कमी होणे,
चुकणे, सरणे, खपणे.

failing n. अवगुण m. दुर्गुण m.
खोड f. क्षुद्रक n. उणें n. न्युन-
ता f. मर्म n.

faint a. शक्तिहीण, क्षीणबळ, ग्लान,
मूर्च्छित. (२) फिका, अभ्रक,
मंद.
— to grow faint, थकणे, (invers) कलम येणे, कलमलणे.

faint v. i. मूर्च्छणें, (invers.) क-
लम येणें, कळमळणें, मूर्च्छना
येणें. (२) थकणें.

fainting n. मूर्च्छना f. कलम m.
ग्लानि f.

fair a. गोरा, रूपवान, उजळ, दे-
खणा, सुरूप. (२) अनुकूळ
(वारा). (३) उघडा, निरभ्र
(दिवस). (४) प्रमाणिक, चां-
गला, ठीक, योग्य.

fair n. मेळा f. बाजार m. हट्ट m.

fairly ad. यथायोग्य, यथास्थित,
बरोबर, प्रमाणिकपणाने, खरे-
पणाने. (२) खरेंच, अगदी.

fairness n. प्रमाणिकपण n. चांगु-
लपण n. सालसाई f. साळसुदी
f. (२) गोरेपण n. सुरूपता f.

faith n. विश्वास m. इमान n. इत-
बार m. भाव m. भरवसा m.
खातरी f.

faithful a. विश्वासू, इमानी, साळ-
सूद, खातरीचा, खरा.

fall n. पतन n. पडणें n. (२) पानें
गळण्याचा वेळ, शरदॄतु m.

fall v. i. पडणें, पडून जाणें, कोस-
ळणें, ढांसळणें, गळणें (पानें,
आसवें, इ.).

— to fall asleep, झोंपी जाणें.
— to fall upon, भेगावर धां-
वणें-येणें-वर पडणें.
— to fall in, ढांसळणें, आंत
पडणें.
— to fall in with (any one
-thing), भेटणें, (invers.) अढ-

ळणें, गांठ पडणें, गाठणें, सांप-
डणें.
— to fall out, सांडणें, पडणें·
(२) रागें भरणें, फूट होणें, रु-
सणें, (invers.) मन तुटणें.
— to fall away, झिरणें, क्षीण
होणें, रोडका होणें. (२) फितणें,
फितून जाणें.
— to fall down, पडणें.

false a. लबाड, खोटा, लटका, मि-
थ्या, अप्रमाणिक, असत्य, कपटी.

familiar a. सलगीचा, परिचित,
माहीत, निपुण.

family n. कुटुंब n. कूळ n. मौन n.

famous a. कीर्तिवान, नामांकित,
नामदार, विख्यात, प्रसिद्ध.

famously ad. खाशी, नामी.

fan n. पंखा m. विंझुणा m. व्यजन n.

fan v. t. पांखडणें, वारा घेणें-देणें
(पंख्याकडून).

fancy n. कल्पना f. तरंग m. ल-
हर f. भास m.

fancy v. t. कल्पिणें, कल्पना कर-
णें. (२) (invers.) भवडणें.

far ad. लांब, दूर, दूरवर. (२)
पुष्कळ, फार, (लांब, दूर, इ.).
— as far as, पर्यंत, पावेतों.
— so far, इतक्यापर्यंत, एवढ्या-
पर्यंत, स्थवर, तेथवर.
— how far? कोठपर्यंत ? कोठ-
वर?

fare n. भक्ष n. भत्त n. खाद्य n.
(२) भाडें n. हेल m. f. उतार m.

fare v. i. असणें, नांदणें, (invers.)
सोई असणें.

— to fare ill, *or* not well, (*in-vers.*) चांगली सोई नसणे.

— to fare well, नांदणे, (*in-vers.*) चांगली सोई असणे.

farm *n.* शेत *n.*

farm *v. t. i.* खोती करणे, मक्त्या-वर घेणे. (२) शेत करणे, शे-तकरी असणे.

farmer *n.* खोत *m.* (२) शेतकरी *m.* कर्षक *m.* खेती *f.*

farmyard *n.* गोठा *m.*

farther *ad.* अधिक लांब, पलिकडे, पुढें. — farther off, पलिकडे. (२) अणखी, अधिक.

farther *a.* पलिकडचा, पलिकडला, पलिकडील, परता.

fashion *n.* रीत *f.* चाल *f.* शिरस्ता *m.* पद्धति *f.* संप्रदाय *m.* शैली *f.* (२) आकार *m.* डौल *m.* घड-काम *n.* प्रमाण *n.* सांचा *m.* मा-सला *m.* नमुना *m.*

fashionable *a.* रीतीचा, लोकसिद्ध, रीतिप्रमाणें.

fast *ad.* लवकर, जलद, तूर्त, त्व-रित, सत्वर, शीघ्र.

fast *a.* घट्ट, गच्च. (२) जलद. — fast asleep, गाढ झोपीं.

fast *n.* उपास *m.* उपोषण *n.* नि-राहार *m.* — fast day, निराहार, उपवास.

fast *v. i.* उपास करणे, उपासी अ-सणे.

fasting *n.* उपास *m.* उपोषण *n.*

fat *a.* पुष्ट, लठ्ठ, धडाकडा, भष्टपुष्ट

father *r.* बाप *m.* पिता *m.* पूर्वज *m.*

fatigue *n.* कष्ट *m.* श्रम *m.* क्षीण *m.* क्षीणभाग *m.*

fatigue *v. t.* श्रम देणे, श्रमविणे, द-मविणे.

fatigued *a.* दमला, श्रमी, श्रांत, कष्टी, ग्लान.

— to be fatigued, दमणे, श्र-मणे, भागणे, शिणणे, थकणे, (*invers.*) क्षीण येणे.

fatten *v. t.* पुष्ट करणे.

fatten *v. i.* पुष्ट होणे.

fault *n.* अपराध *m.* दोष *m.* गुन्हा *m.* तकसीर *f.* खोड *f.* मर्म *n.*

favor *n.* कृपा *f.* मेहेरबानी *f.* लो-भ *m.* प्रसाद *m.* मर्जी *f.* (२) उपकार *m.* हित *n.* कल्याण *n.*

favor *v. t.* कृपा करणे, अनुकूल होणे-असणे, पक्षपात धरणे, तर-फदारी करणे, मिलाफी होणे, साहाय होणे, अनुकूल पक्ष धरणे.

favorable *a.* कृपाळू, प्रसन्न, शुभ, अनुकूल, हितावह.

fear *n.* भय *n.* धाक *m.* धास्त *f.* भी *f.* भीति *f.* भीउ *f.* झुमान *m.* (२) आशांका *f.* संशय *m.*

fear *v. t. i.* भिणे, भय धरणे, (*in-vers.*) भय वाटणे. (२) सन्मा-नणे, सन्मान करणे. (३) आ-शांका वाटणे, शांका असणे.

feast *v. t.* मेजवानी देणे, भोजन देणे.

feast *v. i.* पुष्कळ खाणे, खाणे, जे-वणे. (२) आनंद पावणे.

feast *n.* जेवणावळ *f.* भोजन *n.* (२) सण *m.*

पणे. (२) नीट करणे, बरोबर करणे-ठेवणे.

flannel *n.* लोंकरी कापडाचा एक प्रकार.

flat *a.* चपटा, सपाट, बरोबर, चापट, समान.

— flat contradiction, निष्ठून नाकार, खसखसीत नाकार, निखालसा *m.*

flat *n.* सपाटी *f.*

flatly *ad.* अगदीं, निखालस, निखालसून.

flatter *v. t.* आर्जव करणे, आर्जवणे, खुशामत करणे, फुसलावणे.

flattery *n.* आर्जव *n.* खुशामत *f.*

flesh *n.* मास *n.* मांस *n.* सागोती *f.* (२) देह *m.*

flew *pret. of* fly.

float *v. i. t.* तरंगणे, तरणे.

flock *n.* कळप *m.* खिलार *n.* थवा *m.* झुंड *f.*

flock (together) *v. i.* कळपांत जमणे, एकत्र जमणे, मिळणे.

floor *n.* जमीन *f.* भूमी *f.* भोंय *f.* भुईं *f.* (घरांतली, खोलींतली, इ.).

flounce *v. i.* धड पडणे.

flour *n.* पीठ *n.* कणीक *f.*

flourish *v. i.* आबाद असणे, भाबादान असणे, सुदामत असणे, वाढणे, (invers.) वृद्धि होणे, यश असणे-येणे.

flourishing *a.* आबादान, आबाद, वाढता, संपन्न, सभाग्य, वृद्धिंगत, बरा, चालता, भद्र, यशस्वी.

— flourishing state, भरभर *f.* भरभराट *m.* बरें, वढती *f.* यश *m.*

flower *n.* फूल *n.*

fly *n.* माशी *f.* मक्षिका *f.*

fly *v. i.* उडणे, उडून जाणे. (२) मोठ्या वेगाने धांवणे-चालणे.

— to fly away, उडून जाणे.

— to fly off, सोडून जाणे.

— to fly at, अंगावर धावणे.

foam *n.* फेस *m.* फेंण *m.* कफ *m.*

foam *v. i.* फेसळणे, फेंसणे.

fodder *n.* वैरण *n*

fold *n.* घडी *f.* (कापडाची). (२) मेंढरवाडा *m.* गोठा *m.*

fold *v. t.* घडी करणे, दुणणे, दुतणे.

folks *n. pl.* लोक *m.* जन *m.*

follow *v. t.* मागें येणे, मागें जाणे, पाठीस लागणे, अनुसरणे, पुढें येणे (शब्द इ.) (२) करणे, (वहिवाट, उद्योग, इ.).

following *a.* पुढील, पुढला.

folly *n.* मूर्खत्व *n.* पोकळी *f.* व्यर्थ पण *n.* व्यर्थ.

fond *a.* प्रियमान, प्रीतिमान, भाविक.

— to be fond of, चाहणे, प्रीति करणे, लालन-लळा करणे, (invers.) चट-चटक-अभिरुचि-भाव असणे, प्रिय-भवउता असणे, भवउणे, संकवणे, शोख-शौक असणे, गोड लागणे.

fondness *n.* शौक *m.* शोख *m.* चट *f.* चटक *f.* रीझ *f.* प्रीति *f.* ममता *f.*

food n. खाणें n. आहार m. अन्न n. पथ m.

fool n. मूर्ख m. निर्बुद्धि m.

fool v. t. ठट्टा करणें, फसविणें, कुचेष्टा करणें.

foolish a. निर्बुद्धि, मूर्ख, वेकूब, पोकळ, व्यर्थ.

foolishly ad. मूर्खपणानें.

foot n. पाय m. पद n. पायगत n. पायतें n. चरण m. पाऊल n. पाया m. बुंध n. तल n. n. (२) एक लांबीच्या मापाचा प्रकार, फूट, बारा इंच.

for prep. -साठीं,-करितां,-ला,-बदल,-पासून,-पर्यंत,-मुळें,-नें. उ. for some days, कांहीं दिवसांपासून. (२) कांहीं दिवसांपर्यंत.
— for the sake of, करितां, मुळें.

for conj. कारण कीं, कांकीं, यास्तव.

forbid v. t. निषेधणें, मना करणें, वर्जणें, नको सांगणें.

force n. बळ n. बलात्कार m. कुवत f. जोर m. n. जोम m. n. जुलूम m.
— to be in force, चालणें. उ. This law is still in force, हा नेम अझून चालत आहे.
— by force of, योगानें, वरून, बळेंकरून.

force v. t. बळानें-बलात्कारानें करणें, बलात्कार-जबरदस्ती करणें-चालणें.
— बळ्ळानें-जोरानें-जुलमानें-इत्यादिक शब्द, प्रयोज्य क्रियापदासीं मि-

ळाले असतां, त्यांकडून force या क्रियापदाचा अर्थ होतो. उ. He forced me to eat, त्याने मोठा आग्रह करून म्या खावें असें केलें. —He forced me to go, त्याने मला जुलमाने चालविलें-पाठविलें-हाकून दिलें.— He forced me to do it, हें त्याने मजकडून जबरदस्तीने करविलें. — He forced me to come, त्याने जबरदस्ती करून मला आणिलें.
— to force down, ठांसणें.

forget v. t. विसरणें, आठवण न धरणें, (invers.) आठवण न राहणें, स्मरण न राहणें, सई न राहणें, विसर पडणें.
— to cause to forget, विसर पाडणें.

forgive v. t. क्षमा करणें, माफ करणें, सोडणें (पाप, अपराध, इ.)

forgot pret. of forget.

forgotten p. p. of forget.

fork n. कांटा n.

form n. आकार m. आकृति f. बांधा m. डौल m. ठेवण f. रूप n. मूर्ति f. विधि m. सांचा m. स्वरूप n.

form v. t. घडणें, बांधणें, काढणें (अक्षरें, आकृती इ.), रचणें, (invers.) वळणें (अक्षरें इ.).

fortnight n. दोन अठवडे, चौदा दिवस, पक्ष m. दोन सप्तकें.

fortune n. दैव n. भाग्य n. (२) वतन n. वित्तविषय m.

— to make a fortune, मोठें द्रव्य मिळविणे.

forty a. चाळीस.

forward a. मोहरला, पुढचा, पुढला. (२) हुशार.

forward ad. पुढें, पुढती, मोहरें.

forward v. t. पाठविणे, धाडणे, रवाना करणे, पहॉंचविणे. (२) पुढें चालविणे.

found pret. & p. p. of find.

four a. चार.

four pence n. एका प्रकारचें नाणे, सुमारें तीन आण्यांच्या मोलाचें.

fourteen a. चौदा, चवदा.

fourteenth n. चवदावा अंश-हिसा, चतुर्दशांश.

fourteenth a. चवदावा, चौदावा.

fourth a. चवथा, चतुर्थ.

fourth n. चतुर्थांश, चवथा हिसा, चौथाई, पाव.

fowl n. पक्षी m. पांखरूं n. कोंबडें n. ग्रामपक्षी m.

fox n. कोल्हाउ f. n. कोल्हा m.

fraction n. अंश m. भाग m. अपूर्णांक m. व्यंगांक m. किंचित.

— vulgar fractions, साधे अपूर्णांक.

— decimal fractions, दशांश अपूर्णांक.

France n. p. देशाचें नाव.

Francis n. p. पुरुषाचें नांव.

Frank n. p. पुरुषाचें नाव.

frank a. साळसूद, सालस, खड-खडीत, भला.

frankness n. साळसुदी f. सालसाई f. भलाई f.

free a. मोकळा, स्वतंत्र, मुक्त, सुटा, सैल, ढील. (२) फुकट.

— at free cost, फुकट.

— free from dirt, &c. स्वच्छ, साफ, मळीन नाहीं, निर्मळ.

— to set free, मोकळणे, मोकळीक देणे, सोडणे, मोकळा करणे, सूट देणे.

free v. t. मोकळणे, मोकळीक देणे, सोडणे, मोकळा करणे.

freely ad. मोकळें, मोकळ्या मनाने, इच्छेप्रमाणे, प्रशस्त, बेधडक, अलग, अचानक, निघोर.

freeze v. i. t. थंडीनें गोठणे-जमणे-सांखणे-थिजणे, गारठणे.

— to freeze to death, गारटून मरणे, थंडीने गोठून मरणे, थंडीने मरणे.

freight n. लादणी f. भरगत f. n. बारदान n.

freight v. t. लादणे, भरगत देणे.

frequently ad. वेळोवेळ, वारंवार.

fresh a. साजूक, ताजा, नवा. (२) खारट नाहीं, गोड (पाणी).

fretful a. चिरउखोर, तिरसट, हसका.

fretfulness n. चीड f. चिरउ f. रूसणें n.

friend n. मित्र m. स्नेही m. सोयरा m. नातलग m. f. सुहृद m. दोस्त m. f.

friendly a. स्नेही, स्नेहाळू, मित्र.

fright n. भय n. भीति f. उचक f.

frighten *v. t.* विचकावणे, भय दा-
खवणे, भेडावणे, उरकावणे.

frightened *a. & p. p.* भयभीत, च-
कीत, घाबरा.

— to be frightened, विचक-
णे, उचकणे.

frightful भयंकर, अघोर, उग्र,
कराल, विकराल, अद्भुत.

frock *n.* अंगरखा *m.* झगा *f.*

frog *n.* बेडूक *m.* मंडूक *m.* बेडकु-
ळी *f.*

frolic *n.* खेळमेळी *f.* ख्याल *m.*
टवाळी *f.* खुशाली *f.* मस्करी *f.*
थट्टा *f.*

frolic *v. i.* बागडणे, खेळणे, वाकु-
डणे.

frolicsome *a.* खेळकर, ख्याली.

from *prep.* -पासून,-हून,-वरून,
-नून,-स्तव.

frost *n.* हिम *n.* बर्फ *n.*

fulfil *v. t.* साधणे, पूर्ण करणे, सि-
द्धीस आणणे.

— to be fulfilled, पूर्ण होणे.

full *a.* पूर्ण, भरला, संपूर्ण, युक्त, उ-
वक, भर.

— full of life, जिवट, तापड,
तापट, जलद.

fully *ad.* पर्के, भगदी, बरोबर, पु-
रा, पुरता, भरून.

fun *n.* मौज *f.* मस्करी *f.* ठठ्ठा *f.*
रंग *m.* तमाशा *m.* खुशाली *f.*

funny *a.* मौजेचा, ठठ्ठेखोर, ठठ्ठेबा-
ज, रंगाचा.

furious *a.* तैसी, साहसिक, मत्त,
तामसी, आवेशी.

furiously *ad.* आवेशाने.

furnish *v. t.* पुरवणे, पुराव करणे,
देणे.

furniture *n.* सरंजाम *m.* साहित्य
n. सामान *n.*

fury *n.* संताप *m.* क्रोधावेश *m.* आ-
वेश *m.* जुलूम *m.* जरव *f.* जो-
र *m. n.* पराकाष्ठा *f.*

G

Gain *n.* लाभ *m.* हित *n.* फायदा
m. नफा *m.* मिळकत *f.* फळ
श्रुति *f.* प्राप्ति *f.* किफायत *f.*

gain *v. t.* मिळविणे, घेणे, संपादणे,
पावणे, (*invers.*) मिळणे, प्राप्त
होणे.

gallery *n.* माडी *f.* (ख्रिस्ती देवळां-
तली).

gallop *n.* चौकी चाल *f.* भरभाव
चाल *f.* दवड चाल *f.*

gallop *v. i.* भरभाव चालणे-पळणे,
चौकणे.

gallop *v. t.* दवउणे, पिटणे, (घो-
ड्याला).

game *n.* डाव *m.* जुगार *m. n.*
(२) शिकार *f.* पारध *f.*

game *v. i.* जुगार करणे.

garden *n.* बाग *m. f.*

gate *n.* दरवाजा *m.* वेस *f.* फाटक
n. द्वार *n.* दार *n.*

gather *v. t.* जमा करणे, जमविणे,
जमावणे, सांवरणे, मिळवणे, अ-
टोपणे,तोडून घेणे (फुलें, फळें, इ.)

— to gather up, गोळा करणे,
भटोपणे.

— to gather together, गोळा करणें, एकत्र करणें, एकवट क-रणें.

gaudily *ad.* देखणाउ प्रकारें, छा-नीनें.

gaudy *n.* देखणाउ, देखाउ, शान-दार, दर्शनीय, शोभायमान, च-कचकीत.

gave *pret.* of give.

generally *ad.* बहुतकरून, प्रायः, बहुधा.

generation *n.* पिढी *f.* पुरुष *m.* (२) उप्पन्न होणें-करणें.

generous *a.* उपकारी, उदार, दा-ता.

Genoa *n. p.* एका शहराचें नांव.

Gentile *n.* मूर्तिपूजक, यहुदी नाहीं तो, विधर्मी.

gentle *a.* कोमळ, गरीब, नरम, भला, शांत, मृदु, सौम्य.

gentleman *n.* भला माणूस *m.* गृ-हस्थ *m.* सभ्य *m.* सुजन *m.*

— old gentleman, झातारा.

— young gentleman, तरुणा.

gentleness *n.* माधुर्य *n.* भलाई *f.* भिमाई *f.* भलेपण *n.* मृदुत्व *n.* सौम्यता *f.* सहनशीलता *f.*

gently *ad.* हळू, हळूच, संभाळून, जोराने नाहीं, सोईसोईने.

geography *n.* भूगोळ *m.*

George *n. p.* पुरुषाचें नांव.

Gertrude *n. p.* स्त्रीचें नांव.

get *v. t.* मिळविणें, घेणें, पावणें, सं-पादणें, (*invers.*) मिळणें, प्राप्त होणें.

— to get done, करविणें, (काम इ.), सिद्धीस आणणें, समाप्तीस आणणें.

— to get up, उठविणें, उचलणें.

— to get down, उतरविणें, पा-उणें, घेणें (पोटांत), गिळणें.

— to get ready, तयार करणें.

— to get away, घेणें, काढून घेणें, हरण करणें, हिसकून घेणें.

— to get off, out, काढणें.

— to get a blow, मार खाणें.

— to get a whipping, शिक्षा पावणें, मार खाणें-घेणें, (*invers.*) शिक्षा मिळणें.

— to get in, आंत घालणें, आं-त शिरें-मावे अर्सें करणें. (२) घेऊन आंत जाणें-येणें.

— to get breakfast, dinner, &c., सैंपाक करणें.

— to get rid of, सांडणें, वाट करणें, मोकळा करणें.

get *v. i.* होणें.

— to get up, उठणें. (२) च-ढणें.

— to get down, उतरणें, खा-लीं येणें-जाणें.

— to get in, आंत येणें-जाणें, शिरणें.

— to get out, बाहेर जाणें-येणें, निघणें.

— to get on the way, वाटेस लागणें.

— to get out of the way, वाट सोडणें, आडून निघणें, निघणें, पलिकडे होणें. (२) वाट चुकणें.

— to get off (a horse, a cart, a table, &c,). उतरणे.

— to get off (*or* start), निघणे.

— to get to (*or* arrive at a place), पोहंचणे, पावणे.

— to get angry, राग भरणे, (*invers.*) कोप-राग येणे.

— to get well, निरोगी होणे.

— to get sick, रोगी होणे.

— to get before, पुढें जाणे -होणे.

— to get behind, मागें राहणे.

— to get through, पार जाणे -येणे.

— to get away, निघून जाणे, जाणे.

— to get ready, तयार होणे.

— to get into difficulty, संकटांत पडणे.

— to get over (a river, &c.), पार-पलिकडे जाणे, उतरणे.

gift *n.* दान *n.* इनाम *n.* बक्षीस *f.* देणगी *f.* वर *m.* प्रसाद *m.* (२) गुण *m.* शक्ति *f.*

gilded *a. & p. p.* मुलामी, सोनेरी.

gill (जिल) *n.* एक प्रकारचें कैली माप.

gilt (gilded पाहा.)

gingerbread *n.* सुंठ भाकर, (ज्या-ने ज्या भाकरींत सुंठ आहे ती.)

girl *n.* मुलगी *f.* कन्या *f.* मूल *f.* पोर *f.* कुवार *f.* पोरगी *f.*

give *v. t.* देणे.

— to give up, सोडणे, सोपून देणे.

— to give place, निघणे, प-लीकडे होणे, जागा देणे.

— to give ear, ऐकणे, कान देणे.

give *v. i.* दबणे, सरणे, सरकणे.

— to give up, दबणे, कबूल होणे.

— to give way, दांसळणे, मो-डणे, तुटणे, दबणे, जाणे.

glad *a.* संतुष्ट, संतोषित, हर्षित, आनंदित.

glass *n.* कांच *f.* भिंग *n.* (२) भार-सा *m.* (३) कांचेची पंचपात्री *f.*

glass *a.* कांचेचा.

glide *v. i.* घसरणे, सरणे, निस-रणे, वाहणे (पाणी).

gloss *n.* चकचकी *f.* ओप *f.* त-कतकी *f.* नितळाई *f.* सफाई *f.*

gloss *v. t.* ओप देणे, चकचकीत करणे.

glove *n.* हाताचा मोजा *m.* पंजा *m.*

gluttonous *a.* खादाड, अधाशी, अधासा, अहोपी.

gnaw *v. t.* कुरकुटणे, करंडणे.

go *v. i.* जाणे, चालणे.

— to go on with (work, &c.) चालविणे.

— to go away, निघून जाणे, उठून जाणे, जाणे.

— She was just going to cry, ती त्याच वेळेस रडणार होती. I am going to tell you, मी तु-झाला सांगणार आहें. I am going to do it, मी तें करीन, *or* करणार आहें.

— to make *or* cause to go, चालविणे.

— to let go, सोडणे, जाऊं देणे.

goat *n.* बकरूं *n.* शेळी *f.* बकरा *m.* बकरी *f.*

God *n.* देव *m.* ईश्वर *m.*

gold *n.* सोनें *n.* सुवर्ण *n.*

gold *or* golden *a.* सोन्याचा, सुवर्णीं.

gone *p. p. of* go. गेला, झाला. (२) हरवला, गमावला, गहाळ.

good *a.* चांगला, योग्य, जोगा, ठीक, बरा, उत्तम, सत्य, भला.

— good morning, सलाम (सकाळीं.)

— good evening, सलाम (सायंकाळीं.)

good *n.* हित *n.* कल्याण *n.* फायदा *m.* बरें *n.* चांगलें *n.* लाभ *m.*

Good Hope *n. p.* एका टोंकाचें नाव.

goods *n. pl.* माल *m.* जिन्नस *m.* सामान *n.* मालमत्ता *f.*

goodness *n.* चांगलेपण *n.* सत्यता *f.* योग्यता *f.* भलाई *f.* (२) कृपा *f.* उपकार *m.* परोपकारीपण *n.* (३) रुचि *f.* चव *f.* रस *m.* कस *m.* छान *f.* गोडी *f.*

goose *n.* हंस *m.*

got *pret. & p. p. of* get.

govern *v. t.* राज्य करणें, अमल करणें, अधिकार करणें. (२) भाटीपणे, भावरणे.

governor *n.* सरदार *m.* सरकार

m. अधिकारी *m.* अधिपती *m.* अखत्यारी *m.*

gown *n.* एक प्रकारचा पोषाक, लुगडें *n.* साडी *f.* पेथ्यवाज *f.* झगा *m.*

grace *n.* कृपा *f.* अनुग्रह *m.* गई *f.* मेहेरवानी *f.* (२) शोभा *f.* सुजनता *f.* छब *f.* सभ्यता *f.* भलाई *f.*

grace *v. t.* शोभणे, साजणे.

Grace *n. p.* स्त्रींचें नाव.

gradually *ad.* उत्तरोत्तर, सोईं-सोईंने.

grain *n.* दाणा *m.* रवा *m.* कण *m.* (२) धान्य *n.* गल्ला *m.* (३) तीळभर, तीळमात्र, तिळप्राय.

— not a grain, बगदी नाहीं, तीळभर नाहीं.

grand *a.* मोठा, ऐश्वर्यवान, वैभववान, थाटमाटी, चांगला.

grandmother *n.* आजी *f.*

grape *n.* द्राक्ष *n.* अंगूर *m.*

grass *n.* गवत *n.* घांस *m.* चारा *m.* हिरवळ *f.*

grateful *a.* उपकारी, आभारी, कृतज्ञ.

gratify *v. t.* संतोषविणे, (*invers.*) भवडणे.

— to be gratified, संतोष पावणे.

grave *n.* प्रेतस्थान *n.* थडगें *n.* स्मशान *n.* कबर *f.*

grave *a.* भरखूम, गंभीर, हास्यमुख नाहीं, भारी, हलका नाहीं.

gravely *ad.* गंभीरपणाने.

graven p. p. & a. कोरींव, खोदींव.

gravity n. भरखुमी f. (२) भार m. गुरुत्व n.

gray a. कसरा, कर्पूर, करडा, पिकलेला (केस).

gray headed n. पांढ्न्या केसांचा, पिकलेल्या केसांचा.

great a. मोठा, फार, भारी, थोर, स्थूळ.

— a great way, लांप, दूर, फार लांप.

— a great deal, many, पुष्कळ, फार, बहुत.

Great Britain n. p. एका देशाचें नाव.

Greece n. p. एका देशाचें नाव.

greedy a. खादाड, अभाशी, भहोंपी, लोभी, लालची.

Greek n. ग्रीक देशांतील माणूस.

Greek a. ग्रीक देशांतील.

Green n. p. एका माणसाचें नाव.

green a. हिरवा, कच्चा, अपक्व, भोळ.

greenish a. हिरवट.

Greenland n. p. एका देशाचें नाव.

grew pret. of grow.

grieve v. t. दुःखावणे, दुःख देणे, खेद देणे.

grieve v. i. शोक करणे, रडणे, पस्तावणे, पश्चात्ताप करणे, हुरहुरणे, खेद करणे, (in vers.) दुःख-खेद भसणे-वाटणे.

grieved a. खिन्न, दुःखित, खेदित.

grind v. t दळणे, चरपणे.

gross a. स्थूळ, रटाळा. (२) नि-

विड, गाढ, घोर. (६) विभत्स.

gross n. बारा dozen, or एकंसें चम्बेताळीस.

ground n. भूमि f. जमीन f. माती f. तळ m. (२) आधार m. प्रमाण n. गमक n. मूळ n.

ground pret. & p. p. of griud.

group n. थवा m. टोळी f. मंडळी f. कळप m. समूह m.

group (together) v. t. मिळविणे, थवा करणे, समूह करणे.

grow v. i. वाढणे, मोठा होणे, हीत होणे, हीत चालणे. (२) होणे. उ.

— to grow warm, गरम-उष्ण होणे. — to grow cold, थंड होणे, थंडावणे, शीतल होणे.

growl v. i. गुरगुरणे, गुरकणे, कुरकुरणे.

grown p. p. of grow.

growth n. वाढ f. वृद्धि f.

guard n. चौकी f. पाहारा m. राखणदार m. f. रखवाली f.

guard v. t. चौकी करणे, राखणे, रखणे, राखण-रखण करणे.

guarded p. p. सुरक्षित.

guess n. अटकळ f. सुमार m. अनुमान m. अनमानधपका m. अजमास m.

guess v. t. अटकळणे, तगदमा करणे, अजमासणे, अजमासाने सांगणे, (invers.) वाटणे.

guide n. वाटाड्या m. मार्ग दाखविणारा m. मार्गदर्शक m. गुरु m.

guide v. t. मार्ग दाखवणे, चालविणे, नेणे.

guiltless *a.* निरपराधी, निर्दोषी.

guilty *a.* अपराधी, दोषी, अन्यायी, गुन्हेगार.

gun *n.* बंदूक *f.* तोफ *f.*

H

Habit *n.* सवई *f.* खोड *f.* सराव *m.* अभ्यास *m.* रीत *f.* चाल *f.*
— bad habit, खोड *f.* व्यसन *n.*

habitation *n.* घर *n.* मंदीर *n.* गृह *n.* मुकाम *m.* (२) वस्ती *f.*

had *pret. & p. p.* of have.

hail *n.* गारा *f. pl.*

hail *v. i.* गारा पडणे.

hail *v. t.* हाक मारणे, हकारणे, हवाटणे, पुकारणे.

hair *n.* केस *m.* बाल *m.* केश *m.*

half *n.* अर्धे *n.* निमें *n.* द्वितीयांश *m.*

half *ad.* अर्धे, अर्धेवट, अर्धा.
— half done, अर्धेवट केला, अर्धे केला, अर्धे कच्चा, अर्धे झालेला.
— half ripe, अर्धे पिकलेला, अर्धे पक्व, अर्धे कच्चा, (फळ.)
— half dead, अर्धे मेला.

half *a.* अर्धा, (in *comp.*) साडे.
— one and a half, दीड.
— two and a half, अडीच.
— three and a half, साडेतीन.
— four and a half, साडेचार, इ.

Hall *n. p.* एका माणसाचें नाव.

halloo *v. i.* हाक मारणे.

halloo *interj.* अरे, अहो.

hallow *v. t.* पवित्र करणे, पवित्र मानणे.

halves *pl.* of half.

Halyard *n. p.* एका माणसाचें नाव.

hand *n.* हात *m.* हस्त *m.* कर *m.* पाणि *m.* (२) गडी *m.* कामकरी *m.*
— at hand, जवळ, सन्निध, शेजारी.

hand *v. t.* हाताने देणे, देणे. उ. Hand me a book, एक पुस्तक मला दे.

handkerchief *n.* रुमाल *m.* हातवस्त्र *n.* छाटी *f.*

handle *n.* मूठ *f.* थरं *n.* मुष्टि *f. m.* दांडी *f.* दांडा *m.*

handle *v. t.* हातीं घेणे, हाताळणे, -वर हात फिरविणे, हात लावणे.

handsome *a.* सुरूप, सुरेख, रूपवान, शोभायमान, भव्य, लावण्य, सुंदर.

handsomely *ad.* चांगलें, सुरेखपणाने, सुंदरपणाने, खाशी.

hang *v. i.* लोंवणे, लटकणे, घोळकंवणे.

hang *v. t.* टांगणे. (२) फांशीं देणे.
— to hang down the head, तोंडें किंवा तोंड खाली घालणे -उतरणे.

happen *v. i.* घडणे, होणे, पडणे, प्राप्त होणे.
— to happen to do, सहज -उगीच करणे, बुद्धिनें-दाटून न करणे.

happiness *n.* सुख *n.* सौख्य *n.* आनंद *m.* स्वास्थ्य *n.* स्वस्थपण *n.*

happy *a.* सुखी, सुखरूप, खुशाल, स्वस्थ.

hard a. कठीण, सखत, मऊ नाहीं, चिकण, षढ, दृढ. (२) अवघड, विकट, सोपा नाहीं, सुलभ नाहीं, कठीण. (३) कठोर, क्रूर. (४) मोठा, जबर, बहुत, फार, भारी, बरब, जोराचा.

— hard time, महागाई, दुका-ळ, संकटाचा समय, विपत्ति, वि-पत्तिकाळ.

— to have a hard time, हा-ल-संकट पावणें, (invers.) मोठा श्रम-भडचण पडणे, हाल-हला-की-संकट असणे.

— hard work, मेहनतीचें-अव-घड-श्रमदायक काम.

— hard labor or work, बहुत श्रम-मेहनत-आयास.

— hard study, बहुत विचार, एकाग्र विचार, अवघड अभ्यास -विद्या. (२) दुर्बोध पुस्तक-शा-स्त्र, अवघड पुस्तक-शास्त्र, दुर्बो-ध्य विद्या.

— hard thought, बहुत विचार. (२) विकल्प. उ. — to have hard thoughts of another, दु-सऱ्याविषयीं विकल्प करणें, (in-vers.) दुसऱ्याविषयीं मनांत वि-कल्प येणे, वाईट वाटणे.

— hard bargain, ठक सवदा, तोटा.

— hard case, दुर्दशा, कठीण गोष्ट.

— hard condition, दुर्दशा.

— hard money, नगद रुपये.

— hard cough, कोरडा खोक-ला.

— hard to digest, (food), अ-पथ्य, पचव नाहीं असा, जड.

— to receive hard treatment (from any one), कोणीएकाचें पुष्कळ सोसणे.

hard ad. फार, पराकाष्ठा, पराका-ष्ठेने, जबर, रगडून, वळकट, षढ, जोराने, वळणे, जबरीने.

— to run hard, v. i. लवकर धांवणे. (२) v. t. दवडविणे, पिटविणे, धांवविणे, पळविणे.

— to study hard, v. i. t. फा-र शिकणे, जीव लावून शिकणे, फार विचार करणे.

— to work or labor hard, v. i. फार श्रम करणे, श्रम घेणे, मेहनतीने काम करणे. (२) v. t. फार कामांत घालणे, -कडून रगडून काम करविणे, -कडून श्रम-मेहनत घेणे.

— to think hard, v. i. फार विचार करणे, जीव लावून विचा-र करणे, मन घालून विचार करणे. (२) (कोणाएकाविषयीं) विकल्प धरणे, मनांत वाईट आ-णणे, वाईट समजणे, विपरित जा-णणे, (invers.) वाईट वाटणे, ब-रें-योग्य केलें नाहीं अर्सें वाटणे, मनांत वाईट येणे.

— to strike or beat hard, v. i. t. वळणे-जोराने-जबर-रग-डून-जबरीने मारणे.

—to pull or draw hard, v. i. t.

5*

चांगलें- वळणे- जोराने- रगडून भोडणे.

— to cry hard, v. i. मोठ्याने -बराकाठा रडणे, भाक्रोश क-रणे.

— to ride hard, v. i. (घोड्या-बर, इ.) बसून पिटीत आणे, रगडून-लवकर चालणे-जाणे.

— to travel hard, लवकर चा-लणे, (अमुक वेळांत) लांब जाणे, रगडून चालणे-जाणे.

— to freeze hard, v. t. i. फा-र गोठणे-थिजणे, गोठून पद्द हो-णे.

— to rain hard, v. i. मोठा पाऊस पडणे, झड लागणे.

— to press hard, v. i. फार चेंपरणे-चेपणे. v. t. फार आ-ग्रह करणे, तगादा देणे-करणे.

— to set hard, (food on the stomach) v. i. अजीर्ण असणे, पचत नसणे, अपथ्य असणे.

harden v. t. गोठवणे, कठीण कर-णे, थिजवणे. (२) घट्ट करणे.

harden v. i. गोठणे, थिजणे, घट्ट होणे, कठीण होणे.

hardened a. & p. p. कठीण, क-ठीण झालेला, निचाडा, घट्ट झा-लेला, सराव पडलेला.

hardly ad. कठीणपणाने, श्रमाने, कष्टाने, आयासाने, जुलमाने. (२) जरूर, बरोबरच नाहीं, थोडें आंत, थोडें कमी, कचा. उ.

It is hardly twelve o'clock बारा वाजण्यांच्या आंत आहे. —

hardly two kos, कचे दोन कोस, अमळसे कमी दोन कोस.

harduess n. कठीणपण n. दार्ढ्य n.

harm n. उपद्रव m. वाईट n. हजा f. नुक्सान n. नाश m. (२) पाप n. दोष m.

harm v. t. उपद्रव करणे, दुःख दे-णे, नुक्सान-नाश करणे.

harmless a. निरुपद्रविक, गरीब, बाळबोध.

harpoon n. शूल m (मोठे मासे धरण्यासाठीं एक हत्यार भाल्या-सारखा.)

harpooner n. शूल टाकणारा m.

Harry n. p. पुरुषाचें नाव.

harsh a. कर्कश, निष्ठुर, कठोर.

harshly ad. निष्ठुरपणाने, कठोरप-णाने, निर्दयपणाने.

harshness n. निष्ठुरपण n. कठोर-पण n. निर्दयपण n.

harvest n. पीक n. फसल f. n. हंगाम m. कापणी f. सुगी f.

has (to have याचा तृतीय पुरुष ए-कवचन,) आहे.

haste n. त्वरा f. घाई f. तांतड f. उतावळी f. जलदी f.

— to be in haste, (inr.) घा-ई असणे.

haste v. i. (hasten, पाहा).

hasten v. i. घाई-त्वरा-जलदी क-रणे, लवकर जाणे-येणे.

hasten v. t. लवकर चालविणे, ल-वकर आणणे.

hasty a. उतावळा. (२) तपट, तामस, रागीट.

hate v. t. द्वेष करणें, द्वेषणें, तिर-स्कारणें, दावा धरणें.

hate n. द्वेष m. अकस m. खुनस m. f. दंश m.

hateful a. द्वेष्य, ओंगळ, ओखटा, वाईट, कंटाळवाणी, भ्रमंगळ, चं-डाळ.

hatred n. द्वेष m. अकस m. f. खुनस m. f. दंश m.

haughtiness n. अभिमान m. गर्व m. मगरुरी f. उन्मत्तपण n.

haughty a. अभिमानी, गर्विष्ठ, म-गरूर, उन्मत्त.

have v. t. बाळगणें, धरणें, (in-vers.) असणें, जवळ असणें. उ. I have a book, मला एक पु-स्तक आहे or मजजवळ एक पु-स्तक आहे. — He has a par-rot, तो राघू पाळतो-बाळगतो. — I have (or keep) a cow, horse, &c. मी एक गाई, घोडा, इ. बाळ-गतों. — I have a book in my hand, मी एक पुस्तक हातांत धरतों.

— to let have, देणें, घेऊं दे-णें. उ. Let me have this book, हें पुस्तक मला दे, or हें पुस्तक मला घेऊं दे.

(२) लागणें, पाहिजे, असणें, प्राप्त असणें, भाग असणें. उ. I have to go to my school, माझ्या शाळेंत मला जावें लागतें,—गेलें पा-हिजे,—जाणें प्राप्त आहे,—जाणें भाग आहे.—She had pills to take, तिला औषधाच्या गोळ्या घ्याया-च्या होत्या. (p. २.) — I had work to do, मला काम करा-याचें होतें.—He had to study his lesson, आपला धडा त्याला शिकायाचा होता.

(३) कोणतें तरी क्रियापद संकेतरू-पाच्या भूतकाळांत असलें, तर या क्रियापदाचा भूतकाळ had हा शब्द कर्त्यांच्यामागें असतां जर असा अर्थ दाखवितो. उ. Had he gone, this thing would not have happened, जर तो गेला असतां तर ही गोष्ट घडली नसती. — This would have been a great shame, had it been quite his own fault, जर हा त्याचाच दोष अ-सता, तर (त्याला) मोठी लाजे-ची गोष्ट असती. (p. ३).— Had I known I would have told you, मला ठाऊक असतें, तर म्या तुला सांगितलें असतें.

have v. a. आहे. उ. I have spo-ken, मी बोललों आहें. — You have said, तुझीं सांगितलें आ-हे. — You have gone, तुझीं गेलं आहां.—They have gone, ते गेले आहेत. — They have said, त्यानीं सांगितलें आहे.— We have spoken, आझों बो-ललों आहों.— He may have gone, तो गेला असेल. — (दुस-रीं उदाहरणें कोणत्या तरी इं-ग्लिश व्याकरणांत पाहावीं).

bay *n.* वाळलेलें गवत *n.* शुष्क तृण *n.* गवत *n.*

haying *n.* गवत कापून तयार कर-णें.

hay-stack *n.* गवताचा गंज *m.*

he *pron.* तो.

head *n.* डोकें *n.* मस्तक *n.* माथा *m.* शिर *n.* डोई *f.* (२) बुद्धि *f.*
— head of the stairs, पायऱ्या-च्या वरतें, जिन्याचें शिखर.
— at the head, पहिला. उ. He is at the head of his class, आपल्या वर्गांत तो पहिला आहे.

head *a.* मुख्य. उ. head-man, मुख्य माणूस, मुकदम.

health *n.* कुशल *n.* आरोग्य *n.* प्रकृति *f.* खुशाली *f.*

healthy *a.* निरोगी, धटाकटा, कुशल, आरोगी, बरा, खुशाल. (२) पथ्य, पथ्यकर, चांगला.

heap *n.* ढीग *m.* रास *f.* पिंड *m.* पुंजा *m.* पुंबी *f.* गंज *m.*
— in a heap, मिळून, एकत्र.

heap (up) *v. t.* ढीग करणें, शि-घेवर-रास करणें, शिगोशिग भ-रणें, सांठवणें, पुंजावणें.
— heaping full, शिघेवर भ-रला.

hear *v. t. i.* ऐकणें, श्रवण करणें, परिसणें, (invers.) ऐकण्यांत येणें, ऐकूं येणें. (२) नानणें.

heard *pret. & p. p. of* hear.

hearing *n.* श्रवण *n.* ऐकणें *n.*
— sense of hearing, श्रोत्र *n.* श्रवणेंद्रिय *n.*

hearken *v. i.* कान देणें, ऐकणें.

heart *n.* अंतःकरण *n.* हृदय *n.* दिल *m. n.* मन *n.* ध्यान *n.* चित्त *n.* (२) काळीज *n.*
— with all the heart, मनोभा-वें, मनोभावेंकडून, मनापासून.

hearth *n.* फरस *m.* फरसबंदी *f.* (चुलीजवळची).

heartily *ad.* मनोभावें, मनापासून, मनोभावेंकरून, अंतःकरणानें, मनाने. (२) पुष्कळ. उ. He eats heartily, तो पुष्कळ खातो.

hearty *a.* धडाखडा, धडाकडा, ट-णक. (२) हृद्य. (३) मिष्टान्न.

heat *n.* उष्ण *n.* उन्हाळा *m.* उ-ष्णता *f.* ताप *m.* दाहा *m.* ग-रमी *f.* ऊन *n.* ऊब *f.*

heat *v. t.* तापविणें, गरम करणें, ऊन करणें, आधण ठाणणें.
— to be hot, तापणें, गरम -ऊन-ऊन भसणें.

heave *v. t.* ढोंकणें, टाकणें, फेंक-णें, उंच करणें, लावणें.
— to heave a sigh, उश्वास टा-कणें.
— to heave to, *v. t.* थांपविणें, उभा करणें (गलबत). (२) *v. i.* थांपणें.

heave *v. i.* —to heave in sight, दृष्टीस पडणें.

heaven *n.* आकाश *n.* आभाळ *n.* अंतराळ *n.* गगन *n.* (२) आ-काशलोक *m.*

heavy *a.* भारी, जड, वजनदार, मोठा, गुरु, जबर, गाढ, घोर,

Hebrew *n. p.* इब्री.

hedge *n.* वे *f.* वही *f.* कुंपण *n.* भोंवार *m.*

hedge (up), *v. t.* बंद करणे, कुं-ठित करणे, कुंठविणे, अडथळा -प्रतिबंध करणे, आडवा लावणे, आडविणे.

held *pret. & p. p. of* hold.

height *n.* उंची *f.* उच्चता *f.* उंचव-टा *m.* डोंगर *m.*

help *n* साह्य *n.* मदत *f.* कुमक *f.* (२) उपाय *m.*

help *v. t.* साह्य करणे, मदत-कुम-क करणे, कामाचा असणे, उ-पयोगी पडणे, अनुकूळ होणे. (२) चुकणे,-पासून राहणे. उ. She could not help crying, तिला रडण्यावांचून राहवत नाहीं. I cannot help doing so, असें केल्यावांचून माझ्याने राहवत ना-हीं. I cannot help it, त्याविषयीं मला उपाय नाहीं.

hen *n.* कोंबडी *f.* कोंबडें *n.*

hence *ad.* एथून, इकडून. (२) यावरून, यास्तव, यामुळें, एकूण.

Henry *n. p.* एका पुरुषाचें नांव.

her *pron.* तिला. उ. Give this book to her, हें पुस्तक तिला दे. (२) तिचा, आपला. उ. Her book is not here, तिचें पुस्तक एथे नाहीं.— She threw away her book, तिने आपलें पुस्तक टाकून दिलें.

herb *n.* भाजी *f.* वनस्पति *f.* औष-धी *f.*

herd *n.* कळप *m.* खिल्लार *n.*

herd (together) *v. i.* कळपांत मिळणे.

here *ad.* एथें, इकडे.

here's, here is याचा संक्षेप.

herself *pron. fem.* स्वतां, आप-णच. (२) आपणाला.

hesitate *v. i.* गुरगुटणे, मुळमुळणे, गुटमळणे, न बोलणे, थांबणे.

hide *n.* चर्म *n.* आधाड *f.* कातडें *n.* चमडें *n.*

hide *v. i.* लपणे, दडणे, छपणे.

— to be hid, गुप्तांत असणे, ल-पणे, छपणे, दडणे.

hide *v. t.* लपविणे, गुप्तांत ठेवणे, झांकणे, दडवून-दडपून ठेवणे.

hidden *p. p. of* hide.

hidden *a.* गुप्त, गुह्य, लपला, ल-पविलेला, झांकलेला.

high *a.* उंच, मोठा, धिपाड, उं-चेला. (२) महाग, फार.

— high language,-words, गौ-ढ भाषण-शब्द.

— the river *or* water is high, पाणी भरलें आहे, पूर आला.

— high tide, भरती.

highest *a.* सर्वांहून उंच, उत्तम, उ-त्कृष्ट, श्रेष्ठ.

— at the highest, निदान, पराकाष्ठा.

highly *ad.* फार.

hill *n.* डोंगर *m.* टेकडें *n.* पहाड *m.*

him *pron.* त्याला.

himself *pron. mas.* स्वतां, आपण, आपोआप, आपलें आपण, आप-

सुख, जातीने. (२) तोच, त्या-
सहि, त्यालाच.

— by himself (*or alone*), ए-
कटा.

hind *a.* मागला, पिछाडी.

hinder (हिन्दर) *a* मागला, पा-
ठीमागला, पाठचा.

hinder (हिन्दर) *v. t.* हरकत
करणे, अडथळणे, अटकावणे,
खोळंबा करणे, विघ्न करणे, न-
उणे, बाधणे, अडचण लावणे.

hindrance *n.* हरकत *f.* अडचण *f.*

hinge *n.* बिजागरें *n.* मिजागरें *n.*

hire *n.* भाडें *n.* मजुरी *f.* मेहनत
f. पोटाला, हेल *m. f.*

hire *v. t.* भाडें करणे, भाड्याने ठेव-
ने-घेणे, ठेवणे (चाकरीस),
चाकरी देणे.

his *pron. mas.* त्याचा, आपला. उ.
This is his book, हें पुस्तक त्या-
चें आहे. He gave his hook
to me, त्याने आपलें पुस्तक म-
ला दिलें.

history *n.* वखर *f.* वर्णन *n.* हकि-
कत *f.* इतिहास *m.* गोष्ट *f.*

hive *n.* मोहळ *n.* मधमाश्यांचें घर.

hog *n.* डुकर *m.* शुकर *n.*

hogshead *n.* एक प्रकारचें केली
माप. (२) मोठें पीप *n.*

hold *n.* घर *m.*

— to get hold, धरणे, (*invers.*)
हात लागणे.

— to lose hold, (*invers.*) हात
निसटणे.

hold *v. t.* भरणे. (२) (*invers.*)

मावणे, राहणे, सांठणे, बसणे.
उ. How much does this vessel hold? या पात्रांत किती मा-
वतें ?

— to hold out, पुढें करणे
(हात, इ.) (२) *v. i.* धैर्य
धरणे, टिकणे.

— to hold the tongue, स्थिर
राहणे, उगीच बसणे.

hole *n.* भोंक *n.* पोखर *n.* पोखारा *m.*
खांच *f.* बिल *n.* बीळ *n.* खळगा
m. विवर *n.*

hollow *a.* पोकळ, भरीव नाहीं.

hollow *n.* दवका *m.* पोखर *n.*
खोलगा *m.* खोलवा *m.*

hollow *v. t.* पोखरणे, खोलवणे.

holy *a.* पवित्र, शुद्ध, सोवळा, नि-
र्मळ, शुचि.

— holy-day, सणाचा दिवस,
सणवार.

home *n.* घर *n.* (२) सदेश.

— at home, घरीं.

— to go home, घरीं जाणे.

— to feel at home, आपल्या
घरीं असें समजणे.

homely *a.* कुरूप, बेढब, सुरूप
नाहीं.

homeward *ad.* घरीं, घराकडे,
आपल्या देशाकडे.

honest *a.* सालस, साळसूद, सरळ,
नीट, नेकीचा, नेतीचा, प्रमाणि-
क, न्यायी, नीतिमान, इमानी,
विश्वासी.

honey *n.* मध *m. f.*

honor *n.* मान *m.* सन्मान *m.*

आदर *m.* सत्कार *m.* प्रतिष्ठा
f. आब्रू *f.* कीर्ति *f.* इमान *n*
यश *m.* पत *f.*

honor *v. t.* सन्मान करणें, मानणें,
भीड धरणें, मर्यादा करणें-राख-
णें, आदर-सत्कार करणें.

honorable *a.* आब्रूचा, पतीचा,
सन्मानास योग्य, सन्मानित,
मोठा, नामदार, नामांकित, सं-
भावित, राजमान्य. (२) प्रमा-
णिक, नेतीचा, साळसूद, सालस.

honored *a. & p. p.* मानलेला,
मान्य.

hoop *n.* कडें *n.* चाक *n.* (पिपा-
चें), चक्र *n.* धांव *f.*

hope *v. i.* उडी मारणें, उडी टा-
कून मारणें, बागडणें.

hope *n.* आशा *f.* अपेक्षा *f.*

hope *v. t.* आशा धरणें, (invers.)
आशा असणें.

horn *n.* शिंग *n.* शृंग *n.*

horse *n.* घोडा *m.* अश्व *m.* वारू
m. तुरग *m.* तुरंगम *m.*

horse-back *ad.* घोड्यावर. — on
horse-back, घोड्यावर, स्वारी.

horse-shoe *n.* नाल *m.*

hospitable *a.* उदार, अतिथिपू-
जक, आतिथ्यसंपन्न, दानशील.

hospital *n.* आजारखाना *m.* धं-
मंशाळ *f.*

hot *a.* ऊन, उष्ण, कढलेला, कढत,
गरम, तीव्र, तीक्ष्ण, तिखट.
— hot-blooded *a.* उष्णरक्ता-
चा, उष्णरगतीचा, तापट, रा-
गीट.

hour *n.* तास *m.* होरा *m.* मुहूर्त
m. घटका *f.*

house *n.* घर *n.* गृह *n.* हवेली *f.*
इमारत *f.* बंगला *m.*

hove *pret. of* heave.

how *ad.* कसें, किती.
— how much? how many?
किती? केवढा?
— how great? how large?
केवढा?
— how little? how small?
किती लहान? किती हलका?
किती थोडे?

however *ad.* तथापि, यद्यपि, तरी,
परंतु, पण.
— however much, many,
कितीतरी.

huff *n.* रुसवा *m.* खीज *f.* चीड
f. रीस *f.*

huff *v. t.* रुसवणें, धिक्कारणें, चि-
डवणें, चिथावणें, खिजावणें.

hug *n.* आलिंगन *n.* कव *f.* मिठी *f.*
खेव *f.*

hug *v. t.* आलिंगणें, कवटाळणें, भे-
टणें, मिठी-कव घालणें.

huge *a.* मोठा, सगीन, खंबीर, अ-
वजड, विशाल, स्थूल.

human *a.* मानवी.

humane *a.* दयाळू, दयापूर्ण, परोप-
कारी.

humble *a.* नम्र, साळसूद, गरीब.

humble *v. t.* नमविणें, नम्र करणें,
भोशाळ करणें, खदा मोडणें,
हलकावणें.

— to humble one's self, भा-
पण नम्र होणे.

humble bee n. भुंगा m. भमर m.
भृंग m.

humor n. स्वभाव m. रंग m. (२)
रक्त दोष m. रक्त विकार m.
— good humor, भलाई.
— bad or ill humor, व्राष्टाई.
(२) रक्त दोष.

humor v. t. लाड करणे, लाडकाव-
णे, लाडावणे, छंदाप्रमाणे चालूं
देणे.

humored a. — good humored,
भलाईचा, भला, सुशील, शांत.
— ill humored, खास्तो, व्रा-
ह, खव्याळ, कैदखोर.

humoredly ad. — good humored
ly, भलाईने.
— ill humoredly, रुसून, व्रा-
ह्याईने.

hump n. कुबड n.

humpbacked a. कुबडा.

hundred a. शें, शंभर, शत.

hung pret. & p. p. of hang.

hunger n. भूक f. क्षुधा f.

hungry a. भुकेला, क्षुधित, उपाशी.

hunt n. शिकार f. पाठलाग m
(शिकारींतला), शोध m. सुदा-
वा m.

hunt v. t. शिकार करणे, पाठ-
लाग करणे, पारध करणे. (२)
शोध करणे-णे, शोधणे, सुदावा
करणे-लावणे.
— to hunt after, शोध कर-
णे, शोधणे, धुंडणे, सुदावा लावणे.

hunting a. पारधी, शिकारी.

hunting n. पारध f. शिकार f.

Hurdle n. p. माणसाचें नांव.

hurry n. घाई f. त्वरा f. उतावळ f.
जलदी f.

hurry v. i. t. घाई करणे, त्वरा
करणे, उतावळीने जाणे-येणे, ता-
भरावणे.

hurt n. जखम f. दुखापत f. उप-
द्रव m. हरकत f. खराबी f.

hurt v. t. दुखवणे, नडणे, बाधणे,
जखम करणे, खोंक-खोंच कर-
णे, उपद्रव करणे, (invers.) ला-
गणे.

hurtful a उपद्रवदायक, द्रोही,
वाईट.

hut n. झोंपडी f. कोपट n खोपट
n खोंपडी f. पर्णशाला f. पर्ण-
कुटी f.

hyena n. तरस m. n.

hymn n. अभंग m. गीत n. स्तोत्र
n.

I pron. मी.

ice n. जमलेलें-थिजलेलें-गोठलेलें
पाणी.

I'd, I would याचा संक्षेप.

idea n. कल्पना f. भाव m. मत
n. भास m.

idle a. रिकामी, कामांत नाही,
भाळशी, सुस्त, निरुद्योगी.

idleness n. आळस m. सुस्ती f.

idly a. आळसाने, सुस्तीने, सह-
ज, उगीच.

idol *n.* मूर्ति *f.* (२) तारंत *m.* जीवाचा तारंत.

if *conj.* जर, जरी.

—(२) कधींकधीं ल्यास या प्रत्ययाच्या योगाने if याचा अर्थ बोधित आहे. उ. I will tell you if he goes, तो गेल्यास मी तुला सांगेन, *or* जर तो जातो, तर मी तुला सांगेन.

—(२) (असतां असला या शब्दानीं if याचा अर्थ होतो). उ. If this story is true, I will tell you, ही गोष्ट खरी असली, तर मी तुला सांगेन, *or* ही गोष्ट खरी असतां मी तुला सांगेन. What will you do if there are none? कांहीं नसलें तर तूं काय करसील? *or* कांहीं नसतां, तूं काय करसील?

—(४) कीं नाहीं, किंवा नाहीं, कीं काय. उ. See if he remembers it, तो याची आठवण करितो कीं काय, (*or* किंवा नाहीं,) हें पाहा. I will see if I can do it, तें मला करितां येतें कीं काय, हें पाहीन. I will try if I can do it, माझ्याने होईल कीं काय, हें पाहीन.

—(५) —as if, यासारिखा, असा, सारिखा. उ. It appears as if the sun rose out of the sea, (p. 55) सूर्य समुद्रांतून उगवतो असें दिसतें, *or* सूर्य समुद्रांतून उगवल्यासारिखा दिस-

तो. He eats as if he liked it, त्याला गोड लागल्यासारिखा तो खातो, *or* त्याला गोड लागे असें खातो. I felt as if I could do no more, आणखी माझ्याने करवत नाहीं, असें मला वाटलें.

—(६) —than if, त्यापेक्षां, पेक्षां. उ. He felt better than if he had not done it, त्याने हें केलें नाहीं *or* नसतें, त्यापेक्षां त्याला बरें वाटलें. I feel better than if I had remained at home, मी घरीं राहिलों असतें त्यापेक्षां आतां बरें वाटतें. He learned faster than if he had staid at home half of the time, तो अर्ध्या वेळ घरीं राहिला असता, त्यापेक्षां त्याने फार अभ्यास केला.

ignorant *a.* अज्ञानी, नेणता, मूर्ख, भटाणी, अभ्यासावांचून, न जाणता.

— to be ignorant of, न जाणणे, (*invers.*) ठाऊक नसणे, न कळणे.

ill *a.* विकारी, रोगी, आजारी, दुखणाईत, बरा नाहीं असा. (२) वाईट, चांगला-बरा नाहीं.

— ill looking, देखण्यांत-पाहण्यांत वाईट, देखणा नाहीं.

— ill tempered *or* natured, द्वाष्ट, खास्तो, खव्याळ, कैदखोर, कर्कश.

— ill will. द्रोह *m.* अकस *f.* खुनस *m.* द्वेष *m.* अढी *m.*

ill *n.* वाईट, वाईटपण *n.* दुष्टाई *f.*

I'll, I will याचा संक्षेप.

I'm, I am याचा संक्षेप.

image *n.* मूर्ति *f.* प्रतिमा *f.* प्रति-
बिंब *n.* प्रतिछाया *f.*

imaginable *a.* कल्पनीय, कल्पित,
मनांत येण्याजोगा.

imaginary *a.* कल्पित, कल्पिलेला,
कल्पनीय.

imagination *n.* कल्पना *f.* कल्-
नासृष्टि *f.* भास *m.* आभास *m*
(२) कल्पनाशक्ति *f.*

imagine *v. t.* कल्पिणे, मनांत आ-
णणे, (*invers.*) वाटणे, मनांत येणे.

imitate *v. t.* अनुसरणे, अनुकरण
करणे, सारिखा-नमुन्याप्रमाणे
-भासल्याप्रमाणे करणे, नकल
करणे, वांकुल्या दाखविणे.

immediately *ad.* लगलाच, तत्का-
ळच, तत्क्षणीं, तावडतोव, भातां-
च, तेव्हांच, याचवेळेस, त्याच-
वेळेस.

impatient *a.* असोशीक, असहन-
शील, अधीर, उतावळा, धीराचा
नाहीं, उत्सुक.

imply *v. t.* दर्शविणे, अधिकारणे,
सुचविणे, अभिप्राय दाखविणे,
दाखविणे, (*invers.*) अभिप्राय
असणे.

importance *n.* भारदस्ती *f.* अ-
गत्य *n.* महत्व *n.* भार *m.*

— of importance, भारदस्त,
भारी, मोठा, अगत्याचा.

important *a.* भारी, भारदस्त, मो-
ठा, जरूर, उपयोगी, अगत्याचा

impossible *a.* असंभाव्य, असंभा-
वित, अघटित, अशक्य, होत ना-
हीं असे.

impress *n.* शिक्का *m.* ठसा *m.*
छाप *m.*

impress *v. t.* बिंबविणे, ठसविणे,
भिनविणे, भरविणे.

— to be impressed (upon
the mind), बिंबणे, ठसणे, बा-
णणे, भिनणे. (२) to be im-
pressed with, (*invers.*) बिंबणे,
ठसणे, बाणणे, भिनणे.

impression *n.* ठसा *m.* छाप *m.*
छापा *m.* (२) भास *m.* आभास
m. कल्पना *f.*

improbable *a.* अघटित, असंभाव्य,
असंभावित.

— This is improbable, ही
गोष्ट खरी नसेल-नसावी.

improper *a.* अनुचित, अयोग्य, गै-
रवाजिबी, बरोबर नाहीं, बरा ना-
हीं, अशुद्ध.

improve *v. t.* अधिक चांगला क-
रणे, सुधारणे, वाढविणे. (२)
चांगल्या कामास लावणे.

improve *v. i.* अधिक चांगला हो-
णे, सुधारणे, अभ्यास करणे,
(*invers.*) अभ्यास होणे.

impudent *a.* दांडगा, अमर्याद,
निलाजरा, निर्लज्ज, धीट.

in *prep.* आंत, -मध्यें, -स, -ीं, -ला. उ.
In the house, घरांत, घरामध्यें.
—in Bombay, मुंबईस, मुंबईम-
ध्यें. — in that day, त्या दिवसीं
-दिवसामध्यें. — in the morn-

ing, सकाळीं. — Bore a hole in that board, त्या तक्तल्याला ए-क भोंक पाडा.

(२)-नंतर,-ने,-प्रमाणें. उ. —in after) three days, तीन दिवसांनीं or दिवसांनंतर. — in this manner or way, या रीतीप्रमाणें -रीतीने. — He went out in disguise, तो मिसाने or मीस करून बाहेर गेला.— in company with or in the company of, बरोबर, छंगर्तीं, संगतीनें, सोबतीने.

—He went out in the dress of a woman, तो स्त्रीचें वस्त्र घालून बाहेर गेला.

— He succeeded in doing it, त्याने तें करणें साधलें, or त्याला तें करण्याचें साधलें, or तो तें करण्यानें निभावला.

— He gave his opinion in writing, त्याने आपलें मत लिहून दिलें.

— He did wrong in doing so, त्याने असें करण्याने वाईट केलें.

— I rejoice in this thing, या गोष्टीमुळें-विषयीं मला संतोष झाला.

— in particular, विशेष, विशेषेंकरून.

— in general, प्रायः, बहुतकरून, सामान्यतः.

— in short, सारांश.

— in fact, खरेंच, वास्तविक, खचीत,

inattention n. उपेक्षा f. हयगय f. हेलसांड f. अवाळ f.

inch n. एका फुटीचा बारावा भाग, लांबीचें माप.

inclination n. झोंक m. कल m. (२) चट f. वळण n. स्वभाव m. सवई f. ओढ f. धोरण m.

incline v. i. झोंकणें, झुकणें, कलणें, वळणें, (invers.) झोंक-चट इ. असणें.

incline v. t. झोंकविणें, वळविणें, वळण लावणें, झोंक देणें.

— to be inclined, सरकणें, झोंकणें, (invers.) झोंक-सवई-चट असणें.

increase n. वाढ f. वृद्धि f.

increase v. i. वाढणें, अधिक होणें, चढणें, (invers.) वृद्धि होणें.

increase v. t. वाढविणें, अधिक करणें, चढविणें, वृद्धि करणें

indeed ad. खरें, खचीत, बरीक.

India n. p. भरतखंड m. हिंदुस्थान m. नरभू f.

Indies n. p.

— East Indies, आशीखंडाचा पुर्वदक्षिण भाग.

— West Indies, आमेरिका खंडाच्याजवळ मेक्षिकोंचें गल्फ यांत कांहीं बेटें आहेत त्याच्या समूहाला हें नांव पडलें.

Indian n. p. आमेरिका देशाच्या प्राचीन लोकांतील माणूस. (२) इंदिया देशांतील माणूस.

indolent a. सुस्त, सुस्ता, आळशी.

industrious a. उद्योगी, मेहनती, कामसू, खटपटी, कष्टाळू.

infant n. तान्हें n. तान्हा m. बाळक n.

infantry n. दळभार m. पायदळ n.

infer v. t. अनुमानणें, अनुमान करणें, अटकळणें, तर्क करणें.

inference n. अनुमान m. अनुमिति f. अटकळ f. तर्क m.

influence n. भारदास्ती f. तोल m. वजन n. वग f. (२) प्रेरणा f. बोध f.

— under the influence of, स्वाधीन, वश्य, ओशाळा. (२) लागलेला, आलेला, (तार, भमल, राग, इ०)

influence v. t. प्रेरणा घालणें, उत्तेजित करणें, मन भरविणें, मथावणें, मनावणें, चिथविणें.

influential a. वजनदार, भारदस्त.

inform v. t. कळविणें, सांगणें, खबर सांगणें, बोधणें, सुचविणें.

inhale v. t. घेणें, (श्वासोच्छ्वास करून).

iniquity n. अन्याय m. वाईटपण n. अनीति f. दुष्टाई f.

injure v. t. उपद्रव करणें, नासविणें, विघडविणें, नडणें, त्रासणें, खराब करणें, बाधणें.

injure v. i. नासणें, खराब होणें.

— to be injured, (invers.) लागणें, नाश-खराबी असणें, खराब होणें.

injurious a. अपकारी, अपकारक, नाशक, नाशी, उपद्रवीक, वाईट.

injury n. इजा f. उपद्रव m. खराबी f. तकस m. अपकार m. तोटा m. नुकसान n. f.

innocent a. निरपराध, निर्दोषी, निरुपद्रवीक, बाळबद, वाईट नाहीं.

inquire v. i. विचारणें, पुसणें, तपासणें, विचार करणें, शोधणें, चौकसी करणें.

insect n. कृमि m. किडा m. किड़ूक n. किडें n. जंतु m. कीट n. कीड f.

inside ad. आंत, मध्यें.

inside a. आंतील, आंतला, मधील.

insist v. i. आग्रह करणें, आड करणें, वजावणें, वजावून सांगणें, हट्ट करणें.

instance n. उदाहरण n. दाखला m. दृष्टांत m.

— for instance, कसें तर.

— in one instance, एकदा, एका वेळेस.

instant n. क्षण m. निमिष m. (वेळेचा.)

instead ad. बदल, ठिकाणीं, जागां, ऐवजी, मुवदला.

instruction n. उपदेश m. शिक्षा f. बोध m.

instructor n. उपदेशक m. शिकविणारा m. पंतोजी m. गुरु m

instrument n. हातेर n. हत्यार n. यंत्र n.

— musical instrument, वाजंत्रें n.

intend v. i. t. मनांत आणणें, बेत

धरणें, कल्पिणें, बेत करणें, हेतु धरणें, अधिकारणें, (invers.) म-नांत असणें, हेतु भसणें.

into *prep.* आंत, मध्यें.

introduction *n.* प्रस्तावना *f.* (पु-स्तकाची), प्रारंभ *m.* सुरवात *f.* प्रवेश *m.*

invitation *n.* आमंत्रण *n.* पाचारण *n.* बोलावणें *n.*

invite *v. t.* आमंत्रण देणें, आमं-त्रणें, पाचारणें, बोलावणें.

irreverent *a.* निर्भीड, निलाजरा, निर्लज्ज, निशशंक, अमर्याद.

Irving *n.* माणसाचें नांव.

is *v. i.* आहे. (am याचा तृतीय पु-रुष.)

Isaac *n. p.* एका पुरुषाचें नांव.

Isabella *n. p.* एका स्त्रीचें नांव.

island *n.* बेट *n.* द्वीप *n.* टापू *m.*

Israel *n. p.* एका पुरुषाचें नांव.

Israelite *n. p.* इस्त्राएली.

it *pron.* तो, ती, तें, हा, ही, हें. उ. It is always best to speak the truth, खरें बोलणें हें सर्वकाल उ-त्तम आहे. — It is wrong to tell lies, लबाड बोलणें वाईट आ-हे. — It is pleasant to see him, त्याला भेटावें हें बरें वाटतें. — (२) कधीं कधीं it याचें भाषांतर होत नाहीं. उ. It rains, पाऊस पडतो. It is light, उजेड आहे -पडला. It is dark, अंधार आहे -पडला. It is two o'clock, दोन वाजले आहेत. It is late, उशीर झाला, दिवस गेला, दि-

वस फार झाला, अस्तमान झाला.

It thunders, गर्जना झाली, ग-र्जतें, वाजतें. It lightens, वीज चमकती, बोबतें, चमकतें, वीज लवती.

Italy *n. p.* एका देशाचें नांव.

italic *a.* तिरकस (अक्षरें).

its *pron. possessive case of it.* त्या-चा, तिचा, आपला.

itself *pron.* स्वता, च, आपण, आ-पल्या आपण, ज्ञातीनें, आपसुख.

I've, I have याचा संक्षेप.

ivory *n.* हस्तिदंत *m. n.*

J

Jacob *n. p.* पुरुषाचें नांव.

Jack *n. p.* पुरुषाचें नांव.

Jamaica *n. p.* एका बेटाचें नांव.

James *n. p.* पुरुषाचें नांव.

jaw *n.* जबडा *m.*

jealous *a.* संशाययुक्त, विकल्पयुक्त, विचक्षण, स्वगौरवतत्पर, आवे-शी, मनस्तेजोयुक्त. — to be jealous, विकल्प-बां-का करणें.

jealousy *n.* विकल्प भाव *m.* विक-ल्प *m.*

Jew *n. p.* यहुदी लोकांतील माणूस.

Jewish *a.* यहुदी.

jockey *n.* चाबुकस्वार *m.*

joke *n.* थट्टा *f.* मस्करी *f.* ठठ्ठा *f.* विनोद *m.*

joke *v. t. i.* ठट्टा-मस्करी करणें.

Jones *n. p.* माणसाचें नांव.

Joseph *n. p.* पुरुषाचें नांव.

journey *n.* प्रवास *m.* मुशाफरी *f.* वाट *f.*

journey *v. i.* प्रवासास जाणे, प्र-वास करणे, मुशाफरी करणे, वाटसरू होणे, देशांतर करणे.

jovial *a.* ठठेखोर, थट्टेखाज, मौजे-चा, रेंगदार, रंगेल, रंगिला.

joy *n.* आनंद *m.* हर्ष *m.* संतोष *m.*

joyful *a.* आनंदयुक्त, संतुष्ट.

judge *n.* न्यायाधीश *m.* (२) जाण-ता *m.* पारखी, परिक्षक.

judge *v. t.* न्याय करणे-ठरविणे, इनसाफ- करणे, निवाडा करणे. (२) तजवीज करणे, अनुमान करणे, विचार-तर्क करणे.

jug *n.* घट *m.*

juice *n.* रस *m.*

Julia *n. p.* स्त्रीचें नांव.

jump *n.* उडी *f.*

jump *v. i.* उडी मारणे, भगडणे.

just *a.* प्रमाणिक, योग्य, सरळ, न्यायी, नीतिमान, सालस, यथा-योग्य, खरा.

just *ad.*-च. उ. — just then, just at that time, तेव्हांच, त्याच वेळेस, तत्काळच. — just so, त-सेंच. — just now, आतांच, आ-तांच्ची, मघांशी. — just right, बरोबरच, ठीकच.

—(२) तेव्हांच,-च, मात्र, केवल, आतांच, जवळ. उ. The sun had just risen, सूर्य तेव्हांच उ-गवला होता. (२) सूर्य केवल उ-गवला होता. —I had just come home, तेव्हांच-त्यांच वेळेस मी

वरी आलों होतों.— He has just food enough, केवल त्याचें पुरतें अन्न आहे. — The work is just done, काम आतांच झालें. — He has just gone, तो आतांच गेला. — She was just going to cry, ती त्याच वेळेस रडणार होती.

—just as good, सारिखाच चां-गला.

-- just by, जवळ.

— you came just in time, तूं बरोबरच-यथाकार्ली-बराच आ-लास.

justice *n.* न्याय *m.* नीति *f.* नीति-मत्त *n.* योग्यता *f.* सरळता *f.* इ-नसाफ *m.*

K

Keep *v. t.* राखणे, बाळगणे, धरणे, ठेवणे, न देणे. (२) पाळणे, सं-भाळणे, बाळगणे, *(invers.)* अस-णे. उ. He keeps a horse, तो एक घोडा बाळगतो *or* त्याला एक घोडा आहे. He keeps sheep, तो मेंढरें पाळीत असतो.

— to keep school, शाला चा-लविणे.

— to keep off *or* away, जवळ येऊं न देणे, दूर ठेवणे-करणे.

— to keep out, आंत येऊं न देणे, बाहेर ठेवणे.

— to keep in, बाहेर जाऊं-येऊं न देणे, आंत ठेवणे-राखणे.

— to keep on (*as* to keep a

horse on grain or hay), खा-
याला देणे-घालणे.

— to keep down *or* under,
दाबणे, दडपणे, खाली ठेवणे. (२)
वर येऊं-जाऊं न देणे.

keep *v. i.* राहणे. उ. — to keep
still, उगीच राहणे.

— to keep out, आंत न येणे,
बाहेर राहणे.

— to keep in, बाहेर न जाणे,
आंत राहणे.

— to keep off, from, away,
दूर राहणे, जवळ न येणे, न येणे.

— to keep on (doing, &c.),
जाणे. उ. — to keep on working, काम करीत जाणे. — to
keep on studying, शिकत शि-
कत जाणे. — to keep on running, धांवत धांवत जाणे.

Kennebec *n. p.* एका नदीचें नांव.

kept *pret. & p. p. of* keep.

key *n.* किल्ली *f.* चावी *f.* (२)
टूक *f.* गुरुकिल्ली *f.*

key-hole *n.* कुलुपाचें भोंक *n.* (चा-
वीसाठीं.)

kick *n.* लात *f.* लत्ता *f.*

kick *v. t. i.* लात मारणे, लथडणे.

kid *n.* करडूं *n.* डोरडूं *n.*

kill *v. t.* जिवें मारणे, वधणे, हत्या
करणे, हिंसा करणे, जीव घेणे,
प्राण घेणे, ठार मारणे.

kind *n.* प्रकार *m.* जात *f.* तऱ्हा *f.*
मत *f.*

kind *a.* मेहेरबान, दयाळू, मायाळू,

कृपाळू, चांगला, प्रीतिमान, हृदय-
वान, भला.

kindly *ad.* दयेने, कृपेने, प्रीतीने,
मेहेरबानीने, कृपा करून, प्रेमाने,
सुजनतेने, माणुसकीने, भलाईने.

kindness *n.* मेहेरबानी *f.* कृपा *f.*
दया *f.* उपकार *m.* परोपकार *m.*
प्रेम *m.* मोहबत *f.*
— with kindness, कृपा करून,
दयेने.

king *n.* राजा *m.* बादशाह *m.* नृप
m. नरपति *m.* भूप *m.* भूपति *m.*
भूपाळ *m.* प्रजापति *m.*

Kingston *n. p.* एका शहराचें नांव.

kiss *n.* चुंबन *n.* मुका *m.*

kiss *v. t.* चुंबणे, चुंबन घेणे, मुका
घेणे.

kitchen *n.* सैंपाकघर *n.* पाकशा-
ला *f.*

kite *n.* पतंग *m.* दावडी *f.* तुक्कल *f.*
(२) घार *f.* गृघ्र *m.*

kitten *n.* मांजराचें पिलूं *n.*

Kitty *n. p.* माणसाचें नांव.

knee *n.* गुडघा *m.* जानु *n.*

knew *pret. of* know.

knife *n.* सुरी *f.* सुरा *m.*
— penknife, चाकू *m.*

knock *n.* ठोक *n.* ठोका *m.*

knock *v. t.* ठोकणे.
— to knock off *or* down, ठो-
कून-मारून पाडणे.

know *v. t.* जाणणे, समजणे, ओ-
ळखणे, (*invers.*) कळणे, माहीत
-होणे-भसणे, ठाऊक होणे-भस-
णे, परिचय-ज्ञान भसणे.

known *p. p. of* know, माहीत, ठाऊक, विदित, उपडा, प्रगट, ज्ञात, प्रसिद्ध, परिचित.

— to be known, कळणे, माहीत असणे, ठाऊक असणे, प्रगट-प्रसिद्ध असणे, विदित असणे.

knowledge *n* ज्ञान *n.* विद्या *f.* परिचय *m.* ओळख *f.*

Kolbe *n. p* माणसाचें नांव.

L

Labor *n.* श्रम *m.* मेहनत *f.* कष्ट *m.* काम *n.* हाल *m.* खटपट *f.* उद्योग *m.*

labor *v. i.* काम करणे, श्रम-कष्ट-मेहनत करणे, खपणे, राबणे, उद्योग-यत्न-खटपट करणे.

lad *n.* मुलगा *m.* पोर *m.* गडी *m.* अडवाप्या *m.*

ladder *n.* शिडी *f.*

lady *n.* स्वामिनी *f.* मडम *f.* बिबी *f.* धनीण *f.* बाई *f.*

laid *pret. & p. p. of* lay.

lamb *n.* कोकरूं *n.* कोकरी *f.* कोकरा *m.*

lame *a.* पांगळा, पंगु, लंगडा.

— to be lame, लंगडणे.

lamp *n.* दिवा *m.* दीप *m.* वत्ती *f.*

lance *n.* भाला *m.* बरची *f.* भाल *f.*

land *n.* जमीन *f.* भूमि *f.* (२) देश *m.* मुलूक *m.*

land *v. i. t.* उतरणे (तारवांतून), कांठावर येणे-आणणे.

lane *n.* पोळ *m.* गल्ली *f.* बोरी *f.* भळी *f.*

language *n.* भाषा *f.* बोली *f.* बोलनें *n.* भाषण *n.* (२) शब्द *m.*

lap *n.* मांडी *f.* ओटी *f.*

lap *v. t.* चाटणे. (२) सरस-अधिक असणे.

large *a.* मोठा, स्थूल, गबदूल.

last *a.* शेवटला, कनिष्ठ, शेवटचा, मागला, मागचा, कडेचा, कडे-शेवटचा.

— at last, शेवटीं, शेवटाखालीं, अखेर, अखेरी.

— last year, गत-गेलें-मागलें वर्ष, गतसाल.

— last night, कालरात्रीं, कालच्या रात्रीं, गेली रात्र.

— last week, गेला अठवडा, मागला अठवडा.

last *v. i.* टिकणे, तमणे, ठरणे, राहणे.

last *n.* शेवटलें *n.* (२) सांचा *m.* (जोडाचा).

latch *n.* अडकण *n.* अडकवण *n.*

late *a.* उशिराने, उशिरां, उशीर करून. उ. Dinner is late to-day, आज जेवण उशिराने-उशिरां आहे. He is late (comes late) to day, आज तो उशिरां-उशीर करून उशिराने आला, *or* त्याला उशीर लागला.

— late in the year, वर्षाच्या शेवटील दिवसांमध्यें.

— late in the day, दिवस फारकरून गेला तेव्हां.

— It is late, दिवस गेला, वेळ गेली,-सरली, उशीर झाला.

— It is too late to do that now, आतां तें करायास अवकाश नाहीं, or तें करण्याची वेळ गेली.

— (२) मागस, मागसलेला. उ. — late fruit, crops, &c. मागस फळें, पीक, इ.

— to be late, मागसणे.

— (३) कालचा, मयत, निर्वांण, परवा. उ. — The late Governor, कालचा सरदार (गवर्नर).

— the late Sir Robert Grant, (झणजे) Sir Robert Grant जो मेला, तो. — the late storm, कालचा वादळ, जो वादळ थोड्या दिवसांमागें होता तो.

late ad. उशिराने, उशिरां, उशीर करून. उ. I come late to day, आज मी उशिराने-उशिरां -उशीर करून आलों, or आज मला उशीर लागला.

lately ad. नुक्ता, अलीकडे, हल्लीं.

laugh n. हास्य n. हसणें n. हसूं n.

laugh r. i. हसणें.

laughing n. हसणें n. हसूं n.

laughing a. हसणारा, हसता, हसरा, हसित, हस्तमुख, हास्यमुख.

law n. नेम m. नियम m. कायदा m. (२) शास्त्र n. नेमशास्त्र n. मर्यादा f.

lay v. t. ठेवणें, घालणें.

— to lay out (money, strength, &c.) खर्चणें, वेचणें, व्यय करणें, पसरणें.

— to lay up, ठेवणें, सांठवणें.

— to lay eggs, अंडें देणें-घालणें.

lay pret. of lie.

lazy a. आळसी, सुस्त, जड, मंद, जडभर्गाचा.

lead n. (लेड) शिसें n.

lead (लीड) n. मुख्यपण n. मुख्यत्व n. मोहरली जागा.

— to take the lead, मुख्य होणे, मुकदम-श्रेष्ठ होणे, पुढें-मोहरें जाणे.

lead (लीड) v. t. नेणें, चालविणें, पोंहचवणें, हात धरून नेणें.

— to lead a life, जगणें, वर्तणे, राहणें.

leading a. मुख्य, श्रेष्ठ, पुढला, मोहरला.

leaf n. पान n. पर्ण n. पत्र n. वरख n. तकट n. (धातूचें).

lean a. रोड, लुकडा, कृश, सडपातळ, पातळ, क्षीण, रोडका, वाळका.

lean v. i. झोंकणें, झुकणें.

— to lean upon, टेंकणें, (invers.) आधार-टेंकण असणे.

lean v. t. झोंकवणें, टेंकवणें.

learned a. & p. p. विद्वान, शिकलेला, ज्ञानी, जाणता.

learning n. विद्या f. विद्याभ्यास m. ज्ञान n.

learnt pret. & p. p. of learn.

least a. सर्वांहून लहान,-थोडा, कनिष्ठ, धाकटा.

— at least, at the least, अलबत्त, कडेहीवट, किमानपक्ष, निदान.

leather n. कातडें n. चामडें n. चर्म n.

leave n. परवानगी f. परवाना m. रजा f. हुकूम m. निरोप m.

leave v. t. सोडणे, सोडून देणे, ठेवून जाणे, ठेवणे, टाकणें, त्याग करणें, अंतरणें, चुकणें, (invers) राहणें.

— to leave off (habit, practice, &c.) सोडून देणे.

— to leave off (a garment, &c.), न नेसणे, टाकून देणे.

— to be left, उरणें, राहणें, शेष राहणें, असणें, बाकी असणें.

leave (out) v. i. (invers.) पानें येणें, (झाडावर). (२) v. t. चुकणें, न धरणें.

leaves pl. of leaf.

led pret. & p. p. of lead.

left pret. & p. p. of leave.

left a. डावा, वाम, (हात, पाय, इ.).

leg n. टांग f. पाय m.

lemon n. निंबू n. लिंबू n.

lend v. t. उसना देणें, उसनवारी देणें.

length n. लांबी f. विस्तार m.

— at length, शेवटीं, मग, अखेर, नंतर. (२) विस्ताराने, तपसीलवार.

lengthen v. t. लांबविणें, विस्तारणें.

lengthen v. i. लांबणें, लांब होणें, उतरणें (तोंड).

leopard n. चित्ता m. चिता m. चित्रक m.

less a. अधिक लाहान, कमी, कम-

तो, उणा, लाहान, न्यून, एवढा नाहीं.

lesson n. धडा m. पाठ f. (२) बोध m. प्रबोध m. उपदेश m.

lest conj. नाहींतर कदाचित, नये झणून. उ. I will tell you again lest you forget, मीं फिरून तुला सांगेन, नाहीं तर कदाचित तूं विसरशील, or त्वां विसरूं नये झणून मी फिरून तुला सांगेन.

let v. t. देणे. उ. Let me come, go, do, &c. मला येऊं-जाऊं-करूं दे. — Let him come, त्याला येऊं दे, or तो येवो, or त्याने यावें, or तो यावा. — Let it be what it may, तें कसेंहि असो.

— to let alone, be, असूं-राहूं देणे.

— to let down, उतरणे, खालीं करणें, ठेवणें.

— (२) to let (a house, garden, horse, &c.) भाड्याने देणें.

letter n. वर्ण m. अक्षर n. हरफ m. (२) पत्र n. कागद m. पान n. चिटी f. लाखोटा m.

level a. सपाट, समान, सुती, सारिखा, एकसारिखा.

level n. सपाटी f.

leviathan n. एका प्रकारचा मोठा मासा.

liable a. जोगा.

— to be liable, (invers.) धोका असणें.

liberty n. स्वतंत्रपण n. मुखत्यारी

f. मोकळीक f. (२) सुटी f.
— to be at liberty, मोकळा
असणे, मुखत्यारी करणे, ऐच्छिक
असणे.
— to take liberties, मुखत्यारी
करणे.
library n. पुस्तकसंग्रह m. पुस्तक-
समुदाय m. (२) किताबखाना m.
पुस्तकशाला f. पुस्तकालय n.
lick v. t. चाटणे.
lie n. लबाडी f. खोटेपण n. लटकी
गोष्ट f.
lie v. i. लबाडी करणे-बोलणे, खोटें
बोलणे. (२) निजणे, पडणे, रा-
हणे, असणे.
lief ad. खुशीने.
life n. जीव m. प्राण m. (२) जन्म
m. आयुष्य n. दिवस pl. m.
lift v. t. उचलणे, उठविणे.
lift n. — to give a lift पाठ देणे,
साह्य करणे.
light n. उजेड m. प्रकाश m.
तेज n. (२) दिवा m. दीप m.
बत्ती f. मशाल f.
— to come to light, उमटणे,
निघणे, दिसूं येणे.
light v. t. पेटविणे, शिलकावणे, ला-
वणे, प्रकाशणे, प्रकाश-उजेड
देणे.
light v. i. बसणे, पडणे.
light a. हलका, भारी नाहीं, लघु,
तुच्छ. (२) चिंचोर. (३) प्र-
काश्ययुक्त, तेजसी, उजेळलेला.
(२) काळा नाहीं, पांढरा, सफेत,
फिका.

— light spirits, मोठें अवसान,
मोठी हुशारी.
lightness n. लघुत्व n. लघिमा m.
हलकेपण n. (२) चिंचोरी f.
like a. सारिखा, तुल्य, अनु-, बरो-
बर, तादृश, -वत्.
— I was like to fall, मी पड-
ण्यासारिखा होतों.
like n. सारिखें n. सारिखेपण n. ब-
रोबरी f.
like v. t. चहाणे, प्रीति करणे, (invers.) आवडणे, चहाणे, मानणे.
likely a. हुशार, चांगला, सुरेख,
सुरूप, देखणा. (२) संभावित,
संभव्य, जोगा, योग्य, सारिखा,
बहुतकरून, फारकरून. उ.
It is likely to fall, तें पडाया-
जोगें-पडण्यासारिखें आहे. — It is
likely he will die, तो फार
करून मरेल.
likeness n. साम्य m. प्रतिमा f. सा-
रिखेपण n. बराबरी f. समानता
f. तुल्यता f. (२) तस्बीर f.
चित्र n.
limb n. फांदी f. फांटा m. फांटी f.
शाखा f. खांदी f. (२) अवयव
m. अंग n.
lime n. चुना m. (२) निंबू n.
जंबीर m. n.
line n. ओळ f. वळी f. रेष f. रे-
षा f. सर m. हार f. पंगत f.
पंक्ति f. (२) दोरी f. रस्सी f.
चन्हाट n. सूत्र n. रज्जू f.
line v. t. मढणे, मढवणे, अस्तर

लावणें. (२) बाजूला लावणें. (३) दोरी टाकणें, बंधणें.

lion n. सिंह m. मृगेंद्र m.

lip n. ओठ m. ओष्ट m. होंठ m.

listen v. i. कान देणें, कानवसा घेणें, ऐकणें, चित्त देणें.

listener n. कानवसा घेणारा m. कानवा m. ऐकणारा m.

listening n. कान देणें n. कानवसा m.

lit pret. & p. p. of light.

litter n. ऐवण f. केर m. कचरा m. (२) वेत n. वीण m.

litter v. t. केर-ऐवण-कचरा करणें.

little a. लाहान, थोडा, थोडका, सूक्ष्म, जरसा, जरा, कांहीं, हलका, थोडुसा, अल्प, स्वल्प, किंचित, तीलमात्र, इलिसा, इवलाला.

little ad. किंचित, थोडें.

live (लैव) a. जिता, जिवंत, सजीव, सचेतन, वांचता.

— live stock, गुरें.

live (लिव्) v. i. वांचणें, जगणें, जिवणें, जिवंत असणें, (invers.) जिव-आयुष्य-असणें. (२) राहणें, नांदणें, वस्ती करणें.

— to live on (food, &c.), खाणें, चरणें, भक्षणें.

lively a. जिवट, चंच, चपल, रंगील, रंगीला, हास्यमुख, हस्तमुख, असुदा, हुशार, तापड, गडबड्या, घटपट्या.

lively ad. चंचपणाने, हुशारीने.

Liverpool n. p. एका शहराचें नांव.

lives pl. of life.

living n. उपजीवन n. उपजीविका f. पोटगी f. चरितार्थ m. दाणापाणी n. उदरनिर्वाह m. पोषण n. जिंदगी f. निर्वाह m.

living a. जिवंत, जिता.

load n. ओझें n. भार m. बारदान n. भरगत n. भारा m.

load v. t. बारणें, भरणें, भरगत करणें, ओझें घालणें, लादणें, चढविणें.

loaf (of bread) n. भाकर f.

lock n. कुलूप n. ताला m. (२) (of hair) वेठाळें n. झुलूप n. (३) चाप m. (बंदुकीचा).

lock v. t. कुलूप लावणें, कोंडणें.

lodge or lodgings n. बिऱ्हाड n. झोपडी f. पर्णशाला f. वास्तव्य n. मुकाम m. वस्ती f.

lodge v. i. बिऱ्हाड करणें, बिऱ्हाड घेणें, राहणें, वस्ती-मुकाम करणें. (२) गुंतून राहणें, अडकणें.

lodge v. t. बिऱ्हाड देणें, जागा देणें (निजण्याची). (२) अडकविणें.

lofty a. उंच. (२) मगरूर, गर्वी.

log n. लाट f. कोंडका m.

London n. p. एका शहराचें नांव.

long a. लांब, दीर्घ.

— long time, फार-पुष्कळ वेळ, वाढोळ.

— not long, थोडा वेळ. (२) लांब नाहीं, अखूड.

— all day long, दिवसभर.

— so long, इतका वेळ, जोंपर्यंत तोंपर्यंत, एवढें लांब.

— how long ? केवढा वेळ ? कि-
तीपर्यंत ? किती लांब ? कोठवर !
— as long as, जोंपर्यंत....तोंप-
र्यंत.

long (for) *v. t.* फार इच्छिणे, उ-
त्कंठित असणे, लुलपणे, खंतावणे.

longer *a.* अधिक लांब, अणखी
(वेळ).

look *n.* चर्या *f.* तोंउवळण *n.* तोंड-
वळा *m.* तोंड *n.* आकार *m.* (२)
अवलोकन *n.* विलोकन *n.* दृष्टि
f. पाहणी *f.* देखणें *n.*

look *v. i.* अवलोकणे, अवलोकन
करणे, पाहणे, देखणे, विलोकणे,
टेहळणे, न्याहाळणे, निरखून पा-
हणे. (२) दिसणे.

— to look (*or* appear) well *or*
ill, चांगला-वाईट दिसणे.

looking *a.* दिसता, दिसणारा.

— to be good looking, चांग-
ला दिसणे, सुरेख असणे.

looking-glass *n.* आरसा *m.* दर्पण
n. भयना *m.*

loose *a.* सैल, ढील, ढिला, सुटा,
पोकळ, लांपट, मुक्त, मोकळा, सु-
टला, सोडलेला.

— to get loose, सुटणे. (२)
ढील होणे.

loose *v. t.* सोडणे, मुक्त करणे,
जाऊं देणे, ढिलवणे.

Lord *n. p.* परमेश्वर *m.* प्रभू *m.* य-
होवा *m.* स्वामी *m.*

lord *n.* प्रभू *m.* धनी *m.* स्वामी *m.*
पति *m.*

lose *v. t.* गमावणे, हरवणे, हरपणे,

मुकणे, उडविणे, बुडविणे, घाल-
विणे, हरणे, (*invers*) जाणे,
हरणे, हरपणे.

— to lose sight of, (*invers.*)
अदृश्य होणे, दिसेनासें होणे.

— to lose temper, रुसणे, रागें
भरणे, (*invers.*) राग-कोप येणे.

loss *n.* तोटा *m.* नुकसान *n.* अपाय
m. हानि *f.* धक्का *m.* जाणें *n.*

— loss of blood, रक्तस्राव *m.*

— to be at a loss, संशयांत
पडणे, (*invers.*) संशय असणे.

lost *pret. & p. p. of* lose.

lost *a.* हरवलेला.

loud *a.* मोठा, उंच, (शब्द, आवा-
ज, इ.).

loud *ad.* मोठ्याने, मोठ्या स्वराने.

louder *a.* अधिक मोठा, (शब्द,
आवाज, इ.)

loudness *n.* मोठेपण, (शब्दाचें,
आवाजाचें, इ.)

louse *n.* ऊ *f.* युका *f.*

love *n.* प्रीति *f.* ममता *f.* माया *f.*
लोभ *m.* (२) लाडका, प्रिय, जी-
वलग, जीवप्राण.

love *v. t.* प्रीति करणे, ममता करणे,
माया करणे. (२) चहाणे, (*invers.*) अवडणे, गोड लागणे, च-
टक-चट-झोंक असणे.

lovely *a.* प्रीतियोग्य, प्रियंकर, प्रिय-
पात्र.

low *a.* नीच, उंच नाहीं, खोल, ल-
हान, हलका, अधम, सखल, ठें-
गणा, चपटा, दस्त.

industrious a. उद्योगी, मेहनती, कामसू, खटपटी, कष्टाळू.

infant n. तान्हें n. तान्हा m. बाळक n.

infantry n. दळभार m. पायदळ n.

infer v. t. अनुमानणें, अनुमान करणें, अटकळणें, तर्क करणें.

inference n. अनुमान m. अनुमिति f. अटकळ f. तर्क m.

influence n. भारदास्ती f. तोल m. वजन n. वग f. (२) प्रेरणा f. भीड f.
  — under the influence of, स्वाधीन, वश्य, ओशाळा. (२) लागलेला, आलेला, (तार, अमल, राग, ६०)

influence v. t. प्रेरणा घालणें, उत्तेजित करणें, मन भरविणें, मथावणें, मनावणें, चित्थविणें.

influential a. वजनदार, भारदस्त.

inform v. t. कळविणें, सांगणें, खबर सांगणें, सोधणें, सुचविणें.

inhale v. t. घेणें, (श्वासोच्छ्वास करून).

iniquity n. अन्याय m. वाईटपण n. अनीति f. दुष्टाई f.

injure v. t. उपद्रव करणें, नासविणें, बिघडविणें, नडणें, त्रासणें, खराब करणें, बाधणें.

injure v. i. नासणें, खराब होणें.
  — to be injured, (invers.) लागणें, नाश-खरापी असणें, खराब होणें.

injurious a. अपकारी, अपकारक, नाशक, नाशी, उपद्रवीक, वाईट.

injury n. इजा f. उपद्रव m. खराबी f. तकस m. अपकार m. तोटा m. नुकसान n. f.

innocent a. निरपराध, निर्दोशी, निरुपद्रवीक, भाळवद, वाईट नाहीं.

inquire v. i. विचारणें, पुसणें, तपासणें, विचार करणें, सोधणें, चौकसी करणें.

insect n. कृमि m. किडा m. किडूक n. किडें n. जंतु m. कीट n. कीड f.

inside ad. आंत, मध्यें.

inside a. आंतील, आंतला, मधील.

insist v. i. आग्रह करणें, आड करणें, बजावणें, बजावून सांगणें, हट्ट करणें.

instance n. उदाहरण n. दाखला m. दृष्टांत m.
  — for instance, कसें तर.
  — in one instance, एकदा, एका वेळेस.

instant n. क्षण m. निमिष m. (वेळेचा.)

instead ad. बदल, ठिकाणीं, जागां, ऐवजी, मुवदला.

instruction n. उपदेश m. शिक्षा f. बोध m.

instructor n. उपदेशक m. शिकविणारा m. पंतोजी m. गुरू m

instrument n. हातेर n. हत्यार n. यंत्र n.
  — musical instrument, वाजंत्रें n.

intend v. i. t. मनांत आणणें, बेत

भरणे, कल्पिणे, बेत करणे, हेतु भरणे, अधिकारणे, (*invers.*) म-नांत असणे, हेतु असणे.

into *prep.* आंत, मध्यें.

introduction *n.* प्रस्तावना *f.* (पु-स्तकाची), प्रारंभ *m.* सुरवात *f.* प्रवेश *m.*

invitation *n.* आमंत्रण *n.* पाचारण *n.* बोलावणें *n.*

invite *v. t.* आमंत्रण देणे, आमं-त्रणे, पाचारणे, बोलावणे.

irreverent *a.* निर्भीड, निलाजरा, निर्लज्ज, निश्शंक, अमर्याद.

Irving *n.* माणसाचें नांव.

is *v. i.* आहे. (am याचा तृतीय पु-रुष.)

Isaac *n. p.* एका पुरुषाचें नांव.

Isabella *n. p.* एका स्त्रीचें नांव.

island *n.* बेट *n.* द्वीप *n.* टापू *m.*

Israel *n. p.* एका पुरुषाचें नांव.

Israelite *n. p.* इस्राएली.

it *pron.* तो, ती, तें, हा, ही, हें. उ. It is always best to speak the truth, खरें बोलणें हें सर्वकाल उ-त्तम आहे. — It is wrong to tell lies, लबाड बोलणें वाईट आहे. — It is pleasant to see him, त्याला भेटावें हें बरें वाटतें. — (२) कधीं कधीं it याचें भाषांतर होत नाहीं. उ. It rains, पाऊस पडती. It is light, उजेड आहे -पडला. It is dark, अंधार आहे -पडला. It is two o'clock, दोन वाजले आहेत. It is late, उशीर झाला, दिवस गेला, दि-

वस फार झाला, अस्तमान झाला.

It thunders, गर्जना झाली, ग-र्जतें, वाजतें. It lightens, वीज चमकती, बोबतें, चमकतें, वीज लवती.

Italy *n. p.* एका देशाचें नांव.

italic *a.* तिरकस (अक्षरें).

its *pron. possessive case of* it. त्या-चा, तिचा, आपला.

itself *pron.* स्वता, च, आपण, आ-पल्या आपण, ज्ञातीने, आपसुख.

I've, I have याचा संक्षेप.

ivory *n.* हस्तिदंत *m. n.*

J

Jacob *n. p.* पुरुषाचें नांव.

Jack *n. p.* पुरुषाचें नांव.

Jamaica *n. p.* एका बेटाचें नांव.

James *n. p.* पुरुषाचें नांव.

jaw *n.* जबडा *m.*

jealous *a.* संशाययुक्त, विकल्पयुक्त, विचक्षण, स्वगौरवतत्पर, आवे-शी, मनस्तेजोयुक्त. — to be jealous, विकल्प-शं-का करणें.

jealousy *n.* विकल्प भाव *m.* विक-ल्प *m.*

Jew *n. p.* यहुदी लोकांतील माणूस.

Jewish *a.* यहुदी.

jockey *n.* चाबुकस्वार *m.*

joke *n.* थट्टा *f.* मस्करी *f.* ठट्टा *f.* विनोद *m.*

joke *v. t. i.* ठट्टा-मस्करी करणें.

Jones *n. p.* माणसाचें नांव.

Joseph *n. p.* पुरुषाचें नांव.

journey n. प्रवास m. मुद्याफरी f. वाट f.

journey v. i. प्रवासास आणे, प्र-वास करणे, मुद्याफरी करणे, वाटसरू होणे, देशांतर करणे.

jovial a. ठठेखोर, थट्टेबाज, मौजे-चा, रंगदार, रंगेल, रंगिला.

joy n. आनंद m. हर्ष m. संतोष m.

joyful a. आनंदयुक्त, संतुष्ट.

judge n. न्यायाधीश m. (२) जाण-ता m. पारखी, परिक्षक.

judge v. t. न्याय करणे-ठरविणे, इनसाफ करणे, निवाडा करणे. (२) तजवीज करणे, अनुमान करणे, विचार-तर्क करणे.

jug n. घट m.

juice n. रस m.

Julia n. p. स्त्रींचें नांव.

jump n. उडी f.

jump v. i. उडी मारणे, बगडणे.

just a. प्रमाणिक, योग्य, सरळ, न्यायी, नीतिमान, सालस, यथा-योग्य, खरा.

just ad.-च. उ. — just then, just at that time, तेव्हांच, त्याच वेळेस, तत्काळच. — just so, त-सेंच. — just now, आतांच, आ-तांशी, मघांशी. — just right, बरोबरच, ठीकच.

—(२) तेव्हांच,-च, मात्र, केवल, आतांच, जवळ. उ. The sun had just risen, सूर्य तेव्हांच उ-गवला होता. (२) सूर्य केवल उ-गवला होता. — I had just come home, तेव्हांच-त्याच वेळेस मी

वरीं भालीं होवीं.— He has just food enough, केवल त्याचें पुरतें अन्न आहे. — The work is just done, काम आतांच झालें. — He has just gone, तो आतांच गेला. — She was just going to cry, ती त्याच वेळेस रडणार होती.

—just as good, सारिखाच चां-गला.

— just by, जवळ.

— you came just in time, तूं बरोबरच-यथाकालीं-बराच आ-लास.

justice n. न्याय m. नीति f. नीति-मत्व n. योग्यता f. सरळता f. इ-नसाफ m.

K

Keep v. t. राखणे, बाळगणे, धरणे, ठेवणे, न देणे. (२) पाळणे, सं-भाळणे, बाळगणे, (invers.) असणे. उ. He keeps a horse, तो एक घोडा बाळगतो or त्याला एक घोडा आहे. He keeps sheep, तो मेंढरें पाळीत असतो.

— to keep school, शाला चा-लविणे.

— to keep off or away, जवळ येऊ न देणे, दूर ठेवणे-करणे.

— to keep out, आंत येऊ न देणे, बाहेर ठेवणे.

— to keep in, बाहेर आऊ-येऊ न देणे, आंत ठेवणे-राखणे.

— to keep on (as to keep a

horse on grain or hay), खा-
याला देणे-घालणे.

— to keep down *or* under,
दाबणे, दडपणे, खालीं ठेवणे. (२)
वर येऊं-जाऊं न देणे.

keep *v. i.* राहणे. उ. — to keep
still, उगीच राहणे.

— to keep out, भांत न येणे,
बाहेर राहणे.

— to keep in, बाहेर न जाणे,
भांत राहणे.

— to keep off, from, away,
दूर राहणे, जवळ न येणे, न येणे.

— to keep on (doing, &c.),
जाणे. उ. — to keep on working, काम करित जाणे. — to
keep on studying, शिकत शि-
कत जाणे. — to keep on running, धांवत धांवत जाणे.

Kennebec *n. p.* एका नदीचें नांव.

kept *pret. & p. p. of* keep.

key *n.* किल्ली *f.* चावी *f.* (२)
टूक *f.* गुरुकिल्ली *f.*

key-hole *n.* कुलुपाचें भोंक *n.* (चा-
वीसाठीं.)

kick *n.* लात *f.* लत्ता *f.*

kick *v. t. i.* लात मारणे, लथडणे.

kid *n.* करडूं *n.* शेरडूं *n.*

kill *v. t.* जिवें मारणे, वधणे, हत्या
करणे, हिंसा करणे, जीव घेणे,
प्राण घेणे, ठार मारणे.

kind *n.* प्रकार *m.* जात *f.* तन्हा *f.*
मत *f.*

kind *a.* मेहेरबान, दयाळू, मायाळू,

कृपाळू, चांगला, प्रीतिमान, हृदय-
वान, भला.

kindly *ad.* दयेनें, कृपेनें, प्रीतीनें,
मेहेरबानीनें, कृपा करून, प्रेमानें,
सुजनतेनें, माणुसकीनें, भलाईनें.

kindness *n.* मेहेरबानी *f.* कृपा *f.*
दया *f.* उपकार *m* परोपकार *m.*
प्रेम *m.* मोहबत *f.*

—with kindness, कृपा करून,
दयेनें.

king *n.* राजा *m.* बादशाह *m.* नृप
m. नरपति *m.* भूप *m.* भूपति *m.*
भूपाळ *m.* प्रजापति *m.*

Kingston *n. p.* एका शहराचें नांव.

kiss *n.* चुंबन *n.* मुका *m.*

kiss *v. t.* चुंबणे, चुंबन घेणे, मुका
घेणे.

kitchen *n.* सैंपाकघर *n.* पाकशा-
ला *f.*

kite *n.* पतंग *m.* बावडी *f.* तुक्कल *f.*
(२) घार *f.* गृभ्र *m.*

kitten *n.* मांजराचें पिल्लूं *n.*

Kitty *n p.* माणसाचें नांव.

knee *n.* गुडघा *m.* जानु *n.*

knew *pret. of* know.

knife *n.* सुरी *f.* सुरा *m.*

— penknife, चाकू *m.*

knock *n.* ठोंक *n.* ठोका *m.*

knock *v. t.* ठोकणे.

— to knock off *or* down, ठो-
कून-मारून पाडणे.

know *v. t.* जाणणे, समजणे, ओ-
ळखणे, (*invers.*) कळणे, माहीत
-होणे-भसणे, ठाऊक होणे-भस-
णे, परिचय-ज्ञान भसणे.

journey *n.* प्रवास *m.* मुशाफरी *f.* वाट *f.*

journey *v. i.* प्रवासास जाणे, प्र-वास करणे, मुशाफरी करणे, वाटसरू होणे, देशांतर करणे.

jovial *a.* ठठेखोर, थट्टेबाज, मौजे-चा, रंगदार, रंगेल, रंगिला.

joy *n.* आनंद *m.* हर्ष *m.* संतोष *m.*

joyful *a.* आनंदयुक्त, संतुष्ट.

judge *n.* न्यायाधीश *m.* (२) जाण-ता *m.* पारखी, परिक्षक.

judge *v. t.* न्याय करणे-ठरविणे, इनसाफ करणे, निवाडा करणे. (२) तजवीज करणे, अनुमान करणे, विचार-तर्क करणे.

jug *n.* घट *m.*

juice *n.* रस *m.*

Julia *n. p.* स्त्रीचें नांव.

jump *n.* उडी *f.*

jump *v. i.* उडी मारणे, बगडणे.

just *a.* प्रमाणिक, योग्य, सरळ, न्यायी, नीतिमान, सालस, यथा-योग्य, खरा.

just *ad.*-च. उ. — just then, just at that time, तेव्हांच, त्याच वेळेस, तत्काळच. — just so, त-सेंच. — just now, आतांच, आ-तांशी, मर्षांशी. — just right, बरोबरच, ठीकच.

—(२) तेव्हांच,-च, मात्र, केवळ, आतांच, जवळ. उ. The sun had just risen, सूर्य तेव्हांच उ-गवला होता. (२) सूर्य केवळ उ-गवला होता. — I had just come home, तेव्हांच-स्यांच वेळेस मी

बरीं आलों होतों. — He has just food enough, केवल त्याचें पुरतें भन्न आहे. — The work is just done, काम आतांच झालें. — He has just gone, तो आतांच गेला. — She was just going to cry, ती त्याच वेळेस रडणार होती.

— just as good, सारिखाच चां-गला.

— just by, जवळ.

— you came just in time, तूं बरोबरच-यथाकाळीं-बराच आ-लास.

justice *n.* न्याय *m.* नीति *f.* नीति-मत्त *n.* योग्यता *f.* सरळता *f.* इ-नसाफ *m.*

K

Keep *v. t.* राखणे, बाळगणे, धरणे, ठेवणे, न देणे. (२) पाळणे, सं-भाळणे, बाळगणे, (invers.) भस-णे. उ. He keeps a horse, तो एक घोडा बाळगतो or त्याला एक घोडा आहे. He keeps sheep, तो मेंढरें पाळीत असतो.

— to keep school, शाळा चा-लविणे.

— to keep off or away, जवळ येऊं न देणे, दूर ठेवणे-करणे.

— to keep out, आंत येऊं न देणे, बाहेर ठेवणे.

— to keep in, बाहेर जाऊं-येऊं न देणे, आंत ठेवणे-राखणे.

— to keep on (as to keep a

horse on grain or hay), खा-
याला देणे-घालणे.

— to keep down or under,
दावणे, दडपणे, खालीं ठेवणे. (२)
वर येऊं-जाऊं न देणे.

keep v. i. राहणे. उ. — to keep
still, उगीच राहणे.

— to keep out, आंत न येणे,
बाहेर राहणे.

— to keep in, बाहेर न जाणे,
आंत राहणे.

— to keep off, from, away,
दूर राहणे, जवळ न येणे, न येणे.

— to keep on (doing, &c.),
जाणे. उ. — to keep on working, काम करीत जाणे. — to
keep on studying, शिकत शि-
कत जाणे. — to keep on running, धांवत धांवत जाणे.

Kennebec n. p. एका नदीचें नांव.

kept pret. & p. p. of keep.

key n. किल्ली f. चावी f. (२)
टूक f. गुरुकिल्ली f.

key-hole n. कुलुपाचें भोंक n. (चा-
वीसाठीं.)

kick n. लात f. लत्ता f.

kick v. t. i. लात मारणे, लथडणे.

kid n. करडूं n. शेरडूं n.

kill v. t. जिवें मारणे, वधणे, हत्या
करणे, हिंसा करणे, जीव घेणे,
प्राण घेणे, ठार मारणे.

kind n. प्रकार m. जात f. तऱ्हा f.
मत f.

kind a. मेहेरबान, दयाळू, मायाळू,

कृपाळू, चांगला, प्रीतिमान, हृदय-
वान, भला.

kindly ad. दयेने, कृपेने, प्रीतीने,
मेहेरबानीने, कृपा करून, प्रेमाने,
सुजनतेने, माणुसकीने, भलाईने.

kindness n. मेहेरबानी f. कृपा f.
दया f. उपकार m. परोपकार m.
प्रेम m. मोहबत f.

— with kindness, कृपा करून,
दयेने.

king n. राजा m. बादशाह m. नृप
m. नरपति m. भूप m. भूपति m.
भूपाळ m. प्रजापति m.

Kingston n. p. एका शहराचें नांव.

kiss n. चुंबन n. मुका m.

kiss v. t. चुंबणे, चुंबन घेणे, मुका
घेणे.

kitchen n. सैंपाकघर n. पाकशा-
ला f.

kite n. पतंग m. दावडी f. तुक्कल f.
(२) घार f. गृभ्र m.

kitten n. मांजराचें पिलूं n.

Kitty n p. माणसाचें नांव.

knee n. गुडघा m. जानु n.

knew pret. of know.

knife n. सुरी f. सुरा m.

— penknife, चाकू m.

knock n. ठोंक n. ठोका m.

knock v. t. ठोकणे.

— to knock off or down, ठो-
कून-मारून पाडणे.

know v. t. जाणणे, समजणे, ओ-
ळखणे, (invers.) कळणे, माहीत
-होणे-भसणे, ठाऊक होणे-भस-
णे, परिचय-ज्ञान भसणे.

known *p. p. of* know, माहीत, ठाऊक, विदित, उघडा, प्रगट, ज्ञात, प्रसिद्ध, परिचित.

— to be known, कळणे, माहीत असणे, ठाऊक असणे, प्रगट-प्रसिद्ध असणे, विदित असणे.

knowledge *n.* ज्ञान *n.* विद्या *f.* परिचय *m.* ओळख *f.*

Kolbe *n. p* माणसाचें नांव.

L

Labor *n.* श्रम *m.* मेहनत *f.* कष्ट *m.* काम *n.* हाल *m.* खटपट *f.* उद्योग *m.*

labor *v. i.* काम करणे, श्रम-कष्ट-मेहनत करणे, खपणे, राबणे, उद्योग-यत्न-खटपट करणे.

lad *n.* मुलगा *m.* पोर *m.* गडी *m.* अडवाप्या *m.*

ladder *n.* शिडी *f.*

lady *n.* स्वामिनी *f.* मडम *f.* बिबी *f.* धनीण *f.* बाई *f.*

laid *pret. & p. p. of* lay.

lamb *n.* कोंकरूं *n.* कोंकरी *f.* कोंकरा *m.*

lame *a.* पांगळा, पंगू, लंगडा.

— to be lame, लंगडणे.

lamp *n.* दिवा *m.* दीप *m.* वत्ती *f.*

lance *n.* भाला *m.* बरची *f.* भाल *f.*

land *n.* जमीन *f.* भूमि *f.* (२) देश *m.* मुलूक *m.*

land *v. i. t.* उतरणे (तारवांतून), कांठावर येणे-आणणे.

lane *n.* पोळ *m.* गल्ली *f.* घोरी *f.* भळी *f.*

language *n.* भाषा *f.* बोली *f.* बोलणें *n.* भाषण *n.* (२) शब्द *m.*

lap *n.* मांडी *f.* ओटी *f.*

lap *v. t.* चाटणे. (२) सरस-अधिक असणे.

large *a.* मोठा, स्थूल, गबदूल.

last *a.* शेवटला, कनिष्ठ, शेवटचा, मागला, मागचा, कडेचा, कडे-शेवटचा.

— at last, शेवटीं, शेवटाखालीं, अखेर, अखेरीं.

— last year, गत-गेलें-मागलें वर्ष, गतसाल.

— last night, कालरात्रीं, कालच्या रात्रीं, गेली रात्र.

— last week, गेला अठवडा, मागला अठवडा.

last *v. i.* टिकणे, तमणे, ठरणे, राहणे.

last *n.* शेवटलें *n.* (२) सांचा *m.* (जोडाचा).

latch *n.* अडकण *n.* अडकवण *n.*

late *a.* उशिराने, उशिरां, उशीर करून. उ. Dinner is late to-day, आज जेवण उशिराने-उशिरां आहे. He is late (comes late) to day, आज तो उशिरा-उशीर करून उशिराने आला, *or* त्याला उशीर लागला.

— late in the year, वर्षांच्या शेवटील दिवसांमध्ये.

— late in the day, दिवस फार एक करून गेला तेव्हां.

— It is late, दिवस गेला, वेळ गेली,-सरली, उशीर झाला.

— It is too late to do that now, आतां तें करायास अवकाश नाहीं, *or* तें करण्याची वेळ गेली,

— (२) मागस, मागसलेला. उ. — late fruit, crops, &c. मागस फळें, पीक, इ.

— to be late, मागसणे.

— (२) कालचा, मयत, निर्वांण, परवा. उ. — The late Governor, कालचा सरदार (गव्हर्नर). — the late Sir Robert Grant, (झणजे) Sir Robert Grant जो मेला, तो. — the late storm, कालचा वादळ, जो वादळ थोड्या दिवसांमागें होता तो.

late *ad.* उद्गिराने, उद्गिरां, उद्गीर करून. उ. I come late to day, आज मी उद्गिराने-उद्गिरां-उद्गीर करून आलों, *or* आज मला उद्गीर लागला.

lately *ad.* नुक्ता, भलीकडे, हल्लीं.

laugh *n.* हास्य *n.* हसणें *n.* हसूं *n.*

laugh *v. i.* हसणें.

laughing *n.* हसणें *n.* हसूं *n.*

laughing *a.* हसणारा, हसता, हसरा, हसित, हस्तमूख, हास्यमूख.

law *n.* नेम *m.* नियम *m.* कायदा *m.* (२) शास्त्र *n.* नेमशास्त्र *n.* मर्यादा *f.*

lay *v. t.* ठेवणें, घालणें.

— to lay out (money, strength, &c.) खर्चणें, वेचणें, व्यय करणें, पसरणें.

— to lay up, ठेवणें, सांठवणें.

— to lay eggs, अंडें देणे-घालणे.

lay *pret. of* lie.

lazy *a.* आळसी, सुस्त, जड, मंद, जडभगाचा.

lead *n.* (लेड) शिसें *n.*

lead (लीड) *n.* मुख्यपण *n.* मुख्यत्व *n.* मोहरली जागा.

— to take the lead, मुख्य होणे, मुकदम-श्रेष्ठ होणे, पुढें-मोहरें जाणे.

lead (लीड) *v. t.* नेणे, चालविणे, पोंहचवणे, हात धरून नेणे.

— to lead a life, जगणे, वर्तणे, राहणे.

leading *a.* मुख्य, श्रेष्ठ, पुढला, मोहरला.

leaf *n.* पान *n.* पर्ण *n.* पत्र *n.* वरख *n.* तकट *n.* (धातूचें).

lean *a.* रोड, लुकडा, कृश, सड-पातळ, पातळ, क्षीण, रोडका, वाळका.

lean *v. i.* झोंकणे, झुकणे.

— to lean upon, टेंकणे, (*invers.*) आधार-टेकण असणे.

lean *v. t.* झोंकवणे, टेंकवणे.

learned *a. & p. p.* विद्वान, शिकलेला, ज्ञानी, जाणता.

learning *n.* विद्या *f.* विद्याभ्यास *m.* ज्ञान *n.*

learnt *pret. & p. p. of* learn.

least *a.* सर्वांहून लहान,-थोडा, कनिष्ठ, धाकटा.

— at least, at the least, अलबत्त, कडेडोवट, किमानपक्ष, निदान.

moss n. शेवाळ f. n.

most a. सर्वांपेक्षां अधिक मोठा, सर्वांहून अधिक मोठा, अधिक, मोठा, फार, विशेष. उ. This is the most of all, हें सर्वांपैकीं-हून अधिक मोठा आहे. He has the most money, त्याला सर्वांहून अधिक पैका आहे.

most ad. पराकाष्ठा, फार, निपट, अति, अतिशयें, मनस्वी.—a most vile person, निपट सोदा, फार दुष्ट. — a most benevolent man, एक फार परोपकारिक माणूस.—a most severe pain, पराकाष्ठेचें दुःख, मोठें दुःख.

(२) most या शब्दाकडून गुणविशेषण आणि क्रियाविशेषण यांची पराकाष्ठा कोटी घडली. उ. He is the most benevolent man among them, त्या सर्वांमध्यें तो परोपकारिक आहे. The most humble, सर्वांहून नम्र.—The most excellent, सर्वांमध्यें उत्तम.—The most learned, सर्वां-पेक्षां विद्वान्.

mother n. आई f. माता f. मातौ-श्री f.

motion n. हलणें n. हालणें n. हालचाल f. हलचाल f. चाल f. गति f.

mount n. पर्वत m. डोंगर m.

mount v. t. i. चढणें, वेंघणें, आ-रूढणें, स्वारी असणें.
— to be mounted, आरूढ भ-सणें, वर बसणें, स्वारी असणें.

mouse n. उंदीर m.

mouth n. तोंड n. मुख n.

move n. हलणें n. हालणें n. चाल-णें n.
— to make a move, सरकणें, कांहीं तरी करावें.

move v. i. हलणें, हालणें, चालणें, जाणें, सरणें, सरकणें.

move v. t. हालविणें, चालविणें, सरकावणें.

Mr. (पुरुषाची पदवी,(साहेब.

Mrs. (विवाहित स्त्रियांनी पदवी,) मडम.

much a. & ad. पुष्कळ, फार, लय, मस्त, बहुत.
— much like, फारकरुन सा-रिखा.
— how much? किती? केव-डा?
— so much, इतका, एवडा, तितका, तेवडा.

mud n. चिखल m. गाळ m.

muddy a. चिखलाचा, गढूळ, चि-खलवट.
— to make muddy, गढुळणें.

multitude n. समुदाय m. जमाव m. मेळा m. पुष्कळपण n.

murder n. हत्या f. खून m. हिंसा m. घात m.

murder v. t. हत्या करणें, वधणें, जिवें मारणें, जीव घेणें, घात करणें.

musical a. स्वराचा, गळ्यावरचा.
— musical instrument n. वाद्य n. वाजंत्र n.

muslin n. मलमल f. मलमली f.

must v. a. (शक्यरूपार्चें सहायका-
री क्रियापद), (invers.) पाहिजे,
लागणे, भगत्य असणे, असणे.
उ. I must go, मला गेलें पा-
हिजे, मी गेलों पाहिजे, or मला
जावें लागतें, or मला जायाचें
आहे, or मला जाण्याचें भगत्य
आहे.
— (२) असेल. उ. He must be
sick, तो रोगी असेल. It must
be so, असें असेल. (२) तसें
झालें पाहिजे.

musty a. उवट.

my pron. possessive case of I.
माझा, आपला.

myself pron. आपण. (२) आप-
सुख. (३) जातीने.
— by myself, एकटा, आपो-
आप, आपलेआप, स्वतः.

my own pron. माझाच, आपलाच,
खासगतीचा.

mystery n. रहस्य n. टूक f. गौप्य
n. गूढ n. गूढत्व n. मर्म n.

N.

Naked a. नागवा, उघडा, नंगा,
नग्न, खुला, सुना, नुस्ता.

nail n. खिळा m. चूक f. शंकु m.
(२) नख n.

name n. नांव n. नाम n. छंझा f.
अभिधान n. (२) आबरू f. की-
र्ति f. प्रतिष्ठा f. आख्या f.
— bad name, बदनाम n. दु-
ष्कीर्ति f. बेआबरू f. अपकीर्ति f.

दुलौकिक m. — in the name
of, भंगर्त्वें, नावानें.

name v. t. नांव ठेवणे, म्हणणे, बो-
लणे, सांगणे.

named p. p. नामक, नार्में.

Nan n. p. शकऱ्याचें नांव.

nap n. डुकली f.

narrow a. अरुंद. (२) एककळी,
एकचाली, (मन).

native a. . मुलकी, स्वभावसिद्ध,
स्वभावीक.

native n. मुलकी.

natural a. सासिद्धिक, स्वभावीक,
स्वभावसिद्ध.
— to be natural (to do, &c.),
स्वभाव असणे, सवई असणे.

naturally ad. स्वभावाने, प्रकृतीने,
प्रकृतिस्वभावाने, स्वभावतः, सह-
ज.

nature n. स्वभाव m. प्रकृति f.
(२) सृष्टि f.

natured a. — good natured,
सुशील, भला, शांत, संथ.
—ill natured, खास्ती, खव्याळ,
कैदखोर, दाष्ट, द्राष्ट.

naughty a. वाईट, दांडगा, उनाड,
कुटील.

navigable a. नाव्य, तारू चालण्या-
जोगा.

nay ad. नाहीं.

near prep. -जवळ,-पासी,-नजीक,
-पासून दूर नाहीं, सन्निध, सर-
सा, शेजारीं. उ. — near the
house, घराजवळ. The village
is near (near this place, near

here, near us), गांव नजीक
-जवळ आहे. — I came near
falling, मी पडण्यासारिखा होतों,
or मी पडणार होतों, or मी पड-
लों असतों, or मी थोडें चुकलों
नाहीं तर पडलों असतों.

near a. जवळचा, जवळ, अलीकड-
चा-कडील-कडला, आरता. (२)
प्रिय, जीवलग. — a near rela-
tive, जवळचा.

nearly ad. सुमारें, सरासरी, सर-
सा, सुमारास, अजमासें, थोडें
आंत, थोडें कमी. उ. It is
nearly ten o'clock, आतां दाहा
वाजनील. I went nearly two
miles, मी सुमारें दोन मैल गेलों.

neat a. स्वच्छ, साफ, चकपक, च-
कचकीत, निर्मळ, नीटनेटका.

necessity n. अगत्य n गरज f.
दरकार f. जरूर n. जरुरी f.

neck n. मान f. गर्दन f. कंठ m.
गळा m.

need n. गरज f. अगत्य n. दर-
कार f.

need v. t. (invers.) गरज-अगत्य
असणें, पाहिजे, लागणें, गरज
लागणें. — You need not fear,
भिऊं नये, तुला भिण्याचें कारण
नाहीं.

needle n. सुई f. दाभण m. सल्ई
f. सुची f. सू f.

needy a. गरजी, गरजवंत, दरि-
द्री, कंगाल, गरीव, विचारा.
— to be needy, (invers.) ग-
रज असणें, अडचण असणें.

ne'er, never याचा संक्षेप.

neglect v. t. विसरणें, लक्ष न देणें,
अनमानणें, उपेक्षा करणें, काळजी
न धरणें, हयगय-अवाळ करणें,
न करणें, चुकणें.

negro n. शिद्दी m. हवशी m.

neighbor n. शेजारी m. शेजारी-
पाजारी m.

neighboring a. शेजारी, जवळचा,
आसपासचा, लगतचा.

neither conj. -हि नाहीं.
—neither...nor, नाहीं...आ-
णि नाहीं. उ. Neither you
nor he, तुझी नाहीं आणि तोहि
नाहीं.

neither a. दोघांतून एकहि नाहीं.

nephew n. भाचा m. पुतण्या m.

nest n. घरटा m. कोटें n. बीळ n.
घर n.

never ad. कधीं नाहीं, कदापि ना-
हीं, कल्पांतीं नाहीं.

new a. नवा, नवीन, नूतन, ताजा,
जुना नाहीं, कोरा, अपूर्ण.

news n वर्त्तमान n. बातमी f.
समाचार m. वार्त्ता f. खबर f.
गप f.

newspaper n. वर्त्तमानपत्र n.

New York n. p. एका शहराचें
नांव. (२) एका देशाचें नांव.

next a. पुढील, दुसरा, जवळचा,
शेजारी, शेजारचा, लगतचा,
पासचा, मोहरचा.

next ad. मग, नंतर, पुढें, मोहरें,
सरसा.

nice a. नामी, चांगला, सरस,

वेंख, नेटका, धोंखट, देखणा. (२) खनखोर, कंटाव्खोर, चिंकन्सखोर.

nickname n. उपाधि m. नांव n.

— to give n nickname, शब्द लावणे, नांव ठेवणे.

niece n. पुतणी f. भाची f.

night n. रात्र f. रात f. रात्रि f निशा f.

— good night, सलाम, (रात्रीं जाते वेळचा).

nimble a. पळका, चपळ, चंचळ, तापड, तीव्र.

nimbly ad. चपळाईने, चपळत्वेक-रून.

ninepins n. एका प्रकारचा खेळ.

ninny n. नंदी, वेकूब.

no ad. नाहीं, नको.

no a° कोणी नाहीं, कोणता नाहीं, कांहीं नाहीं.

— no one, कोणी नाहीं.

— speak no bad words, कोणते वाईट शब्द बोलूं नको.

— no matter, चिंता नाहीं.

noble a. उदार, श्रीमंत, प्रशास्त, नामदार, भव्य, फार चांगला.

nobody n. कोणी नाहीं.

nod n. संकेत m. खूण f (डोक्याने). (२) डुकली f. डुलको f.

nod v. i. डुलणे, डुकल्या खाणे, पेंगणे, झुलणे, तुकावणे. (२) खु-णावणे.

noise n. आवाज m. नाद m. गों-गाट m. गलवला m. कल्ला m. बोभाटा m. ध्वनि m. f. गार्गणे n.

noisy a. गलवला करणारा, गड-बड्या.

— to be noisy, गलवला करणे; गोंगाट करणे, गागणे.

none a. कांहीं नाहीं, कोणी नाहीं.

nonsense n. मूर्खपण n. अटरफट-र n. वेकुबां f. अनर्थ m.

nonsense! interj. छे! छी! थू!

noon n. दुपार f दोन प्रहर m. मध्यान्हकाळ m. बारा वाजतां (दिवसांत).

nor conj. किंवा नाहीं.

— neither this nor that, हें नाहीं आणि तेंहे नाहीं.

north n. & a. उत्तर दिशा f. उ-त्तर f. कौबेरी f. उत्तरेस.

— north star, ध्रुव m.

Norton n. p. माणसाचें नांव.

nose n. नाक n. नासिक n. (२) मुसकें n. मुसकूट n. (जनावरा-चें.)

not ad. नको, नका, नये, नाहीं, न, ना. उ. Do not speak, बोलूं नको-नका-नये. He will not go, तो जाणार नाहीं, or जात नाहीं, or ज.ईना. I did not speak, मी बोललों नाहीं. He was not there, तो तेथे नव्हता.

noted a. & p. p. प्रसिद्ध, नामां-कित, जाहिर, विख्यात.

nothing n. कांहीं नाहीं.

notice n. लक्ष n. चित्त n. (२) जाहिरनामा m. जाहिरात f. जा-हिर बातमी f. मजकूर n. वर्त-मान n. खबर f.

— to give notice, जाहीर क-
रणे.

notice v. t. लक्ष देणे, पाहणे, अव-
लोकन करणे, चित्त देणे.

notwithstanding conj. तथापि,
यद्यपि, तत्रापि, तरी, असें असं-
तांहि. Notwithstanding all I
have said to him he still con-
tinues doing so, म्या त्याला
बहुत सांगितलें असतांहि, तो अ-
झून तेंच करीत जातो.

now ad. आता, सांप्रत, प्रस्तुत, हा-
लीं, एव्हां, सद्या.

— now and then, कर्धीं कर्धीं,
एखादे वेळेस.

nuisance n. उद्रवीक m. f. तरदी
f. उपद्रव देणारा m. उपद्रव-
दायक, पीडा f. पीडा f. इजा f.

number n. अंक m. संख्या f. (२)
गण m. कित्येक. (३)वचन m.
(व्याकरणामध्यें).

— a number of persons, कि-
त्येक जन.

— in great numbers, पुष्कळ.

— a great number, पुष्कळ,
फार, बहुत.

— what number? किती?

number v. t. गणणे, मोजणे, टीर
करणे-घेणे.

nurse n. संभाळणारा m. दाई f.
उपमाता f. बाळगणा m. धार्दी f.

nurse v. t. स्तन पाजणे, संभाळणे,
बाळगणे, पालन करणे.

nursery n. बाळकांची खोली. (२)
लहान झाडांचा याग.

nurture n. बाळमणें n. वाटविणें n.
पालनपोषण n.

nurture v. t. बाळगगे, पोषण क-
रणे, वाटविणे.

nut n. फळ n. (अकरोटाच्या फ-
ळासारिखें, इ.)

O.

O interj. हे, अरे, अहो, अगे, अगा.

O dear! अरेरे! अहाहा! चचच! ओ
ओ! अगेबाई!

Oh that, माझी प्रार्थना असी आ-
हे कीं.

Oak n. एका प्रकारचें झाड.

oar n. वले n.

obedience n. मान m. आज्ञांकित-
पण n. सेवा f. आज्ञा मानणें.

—to yield obedience, मानणें,
मान देणे.

— in obedience, हुकुमाप्रमाणें,
आज्ञा मानून.

obedient c. आज्ञांकित, मान्य,
आज्ञाधारक, मानता.

obey v. t. मानणे, ऐकणे, पाळणे
(आज्ञा), आज्ञांप्रमाणें वागणे
-चालणे.

object n. विषय m. पदार्थ m. वस्तु
f. (२) अर्थ m. उपयोग m.
काम n. हेतु m. वेत m. अभि-
प्राय m. अधिकार m.

object v. i. नाकबुल असणे, ना-
कारणे, दिक्कत धरणे, हुजत-हर-
कत करणे, अडचण सांगणे-मा-
नणे, मान्य नसणे, उलटून गोष्ट
सांगणे.

oblige v. t. जुलूम करणे, जबर-दस्ती करणे, अगत्यांत पाडणे. (२) उपकार करणे, (invers) उपकारी होणे. उ. If you will do this you will much oblige me, (or I shall be much obliged), जर तूं हे करसील, तर मजवर मोठा उपकार होईल. — to be obliged, ऋणी असणे, उपकारी-आभारी होणे-असणे, (inv.)-वर उपकार होणे. — to te obliged (to go, to do, &c.) अगत्य असणे, लागणे, प्राप्त असणे, पाहिजे.

obliging a. उपकारी, उपकार क-रणारा, परोपकारी, उदार.

observe v. t. पाहणे,-कडे लक्ष्य दे-णे. (२) पाळणे, मानणे, मान्य करणे, (आज्ञा, नेम, इ.)

obstruct v. t प्रतिबंध-खोटी कर-णे, अडकावणे, अडथळा करणे, अडचण-हरकत करणे, अडथ-ळणे, कोंडणे, कुंठित करणे, तुंबा-रा लावणे, (invers.) अडचण असणे. — to be obstructed, अडणे, अडकणे, कुंठणे, तुंबणे, कोंडणे.

obtain v. t. मिळविणे, पावणे, सं-पादणे, प्राप्त करणे, (invers.) मि-ळणे, प्राप्त होणे.

occasion n. प्रसंग m. वेळ f सम-य m. वक्त m. कारण n गरज f. — suitable to the occasion, प्रसंगोचित, वेळेनुसार, समयानु-सार.

o'clock (of the clock), वाजतां, वाजले. What o'clock is it? किती वा-जले?

Octavia n. r. स्त्रियेचें नांव. o'er, over याचा संक्षेप. of prep. -चा, -विषयीं, -पैकीं, -भांवील, -भांनून, संबंधी. उ. The Son of man, माणसाचा पुत्र. He spoke of this thing, या गोष्टी-विषयीं तो बोलला. One of them was a Brahman, त्यांतील एक ब्राह्मण होता. — out of, आंनून, बाहेर.

off ad. वरून, पासून. (२) दूर, लांब. — further off, अधिकल वि-दूर. — a great way off, फार लांब -दूर. — to get off, (from a horse -carriage &c.) उतरणे. (२) v. t. काढणे. — to get or go off, निघून जाणे, जाणे. — to take off, काढणे. — to throw off, टाकणे, काढून टाकणे, सोडणे.

offend v. t. राग आणणे-उठविणे, नाखुषा करणे, राग येईल असें क-रणे. (२) उल्लंघणे. (३) अड-खळविणे. — to be offended, रुसणे, रा-गें भरणे, नाखुश असणे, चिड-णे, (invers.) चीड-कोप येणे.

offer *n.* बोली *f.* देऊ.

offer *v. t.* पुढें करणें, देईन अशें सांगणे, बोली-देऊं करणे. (२) अर्पणे.

— to offer to give, to do, &c. देऊं करणे, देण्याचें-करण्याची ह्त्यादिकाची बोली करणे, *or* देईन-करीन ह्त्यादिक सांगणे.

office *n.* अमलदारी *f.* पदवी *f.* पद *n.* अमल *m.* काम *n.* अधिकार *m.* कारभार *m.* (२) भाग *m.* (३) कचेरी *f.*

often *ad.* वारंवार, वेळोवेळ, वरचेवर, बहुत वेळ, पुनःपुनः, मात्क्यान मात्क्यान.

oh! *interj.* हें! आहें!

oil *n.* तेल *n.* तैल *n.* स्नेह *n.*

oil *v. t.* तेल लावणे-चोळणे.

oily *a.* तेलकट, तेलट, स्नेहाळ, बुळबुळीत, मिळमिळीत, औशट.

old *a.* जुना, पुराण, पुराणा, पुरातन, प्राचीन, जीर्ण, चिरकाळचें. (२) ज्ञातारा, वयातीत, वृद्ध, मोठा, थोर, डोकरा. (३) वर्षांचा, वयाचा. उ. — how old? किती वर्षांचा? — five years old, पांच वर्षांचा. — as old as, एवढ्या वर्षांचा, वयाने एवढा.

— to grow *or* become old, वृद्ध-ज्ञातारा-मोठा होणे, वाढणे, जुनावणे.

— old man, ज्ञातारा.

— old woman, ज्ञातारी.

— old age, ज्ञातारपण, वृद्धावस्था, वृद्धापकाळ *m.* वृद्धता.

older *a.* वडील, गौर, मोठा, पूर्वज.

on *prep.*-वर,-ीं. उ. — on the table, मेजावर. — on Monday सोमवारीं. (२)-ने. उ. The snake goes on his belly, सर्प पोटाने चालनो. — He stands on his feet, तो आपल्या पायानीं-वर उभा राहतो.

— to put on (clothes, &c.) नेसणे, लेणे, घालणे. उ. He put his shoes on his feet, त्याने आपल्या पायांत जोडा घातला.

on *ad.* पुढें, मोहरें. उ. Go on, पुढें-मोहरें जा. — Keep on doing so, असें करीत करीत जा.

once *ad* एकवेळ, एकदा, एकवार. (२) अगोदर, एखाद्याभेळेस, पूर्वीं, मागें.

— at once, एकदम, एकाएकी, अकस्मात, एकसमो. (२) एकंदर, लागलाच, तूर्ने, भातांच, तत्काळ.

— once more, फिरून, मात्क्यान.

one *a.* एक.

— some one *or* any one, कोणी एक, अमुक, अमका, फलाणा.

— one another, एकमेक, परस्पर.

— one after another, एकामागें एक, एकानंतर एक, लागोपाट.

— one by one, एकएक, एकामागें एक.

— yourg one, पिलूं n. बचा m. वस्स m. n. धाकटा.

— young ones, पिलें, बच्चे, लें-करें.

— small or little-one, लहान, धाकटा. (२) लेंकरूं, मूल.

— great one, मोठा, थोर, भो-ठाला.

— good one, चांगला.

— bad one, वाईट.

— this one, हा.

— that one, तो.

— You may take the large books and give me the small ones, आपण मोठीं पुस्तकें घेऊन मला लहानसीं द्यावीं.

onion n. कांदा m. पलांडु m.

only ad. केवळ, मात्र,-च, फक्त, नुस्ता.

only a. एकटा, एकुलता.

open a. उघडा, खुला, उघड, विरळ, पातळ, विसकळ.

— to crack open, उलणे, चि-रणे, भेगळणे, (invers) चीर-भेग पडणे.

open r. i. उमलणे, उघडणे, उलणे, खुलणे, विकासणे, भेगळणे, चीर-भेग पडणे.

open v. t. उघडणे, खुलवणे, खुला करणे.

opinion n. मन n. मन n. मसलत f. (२) मान m.

oppose v. t. अडचण-हरकत-विरो-ध करणे, अडथळा लावणे, आड-वा येणे, प्रतिकूळ असणे.

opposite a. समोर, सन्मुख, तोंड-चा, एटच्या, मोहरचा, समोरला. (२) विपरीत, विरुद्ध, आडवा, विरोधी, उलटा.

opposite n. उलटा, विरुद्ध.

opposition n. विरोध m. विरुद्ध-पण n.

or conj. अथवा, किंवा. (२) नाहीं तर.

— or else, नाहीं तर.

orange n. नारिंग n.

orator n. वक्ता m. बोलणारा m.

ordain v. t. स्थापणे, नेमणे, ठर-विणे.

order v. t. आज्ञा देणे-करणे, हु-कूम देणे, सांगणे.

order n. हुकूम m. आज्ञा f. (२) अनुक्रम m. (३) वर्ण m. वर्ग m. प्रत f.

— to put in order, v. t. बरो-बर ठेवणे, रचणे, निटावणे.

— to be in order, बरोबर अ-सणे, नीट असणे, बंदोबस्त असणे.

— to be in good order, (a horse. ox, &c.), ताजा-पुष्ट अस-णे, चांगला दिसणे.

— to keep order (in a school &c.), आटोपणे, आवरणे.

— to keep in order, v. t. बं-दोबस्त करणे, ठेवणे.

— out of order, नीट-बरोबर नाहीं असा, अस्ताव्यस्त, अव्य-वस्थित.

— in order to,-साठीं,-करितां

ordinance *n.* नियम m. रीति *f.* क्रिया *f.* नेम m.

ostrich *n.* एका जातिचें पांखरूं, श्राहामृग m.

other *a.* अन्य, दुसरा, इनर, पलि-कडचा, परका.

— the other day, परवां, माग-न्या दिवसीं.

— every other day, एकांतरा, एक दिवस आड.

otherwise *ad.* नाहीं तर, एरवीं, अन्यथा, दुसऱ्या प्रकारें, वेगळें.

ought *v i* (वर्तमान काळ) पाहिजे, योग्य असणें, भाग-प्राप्त असणें. व. You ought to do this, तु-म्ही हें केलें पाहिजे, *or* तुम्हां हें करावें हें योग्य आहे. You ought not to do so, असें तुम्ही न क-रावें, *or* असें करूं नये, *or* अ-सें करावयाचें नाहीं.

—(भूत काळ) You ought to have done this yesterday, काल तु-म्हीं हें केलें पाहिजे होतें, *or* तुम्हीं काल हें काम करावें हें योग्य हो-तें, *or* काल तुम्हांस हें करायाचें हेंतें. You ought not to have done so, असें तुम्हाला करायाचें नव्हतें.

our *pron.* आमचा, आपला.

ourselves *pl. of* myself.

out *ad.* बाहेर.

— out of,-from, -भांतून,-मा-सून, जदलून,-तकीं.

— inside out, उफराटा.

— to take out, काढणें, का-ढून घेणें, भांतून घेणें.

— to cast out, घालविणें, का-ढून टाकणें, फेंकून टाकणें, बाहेर करणें.

— to put out, काढणें, बाहेर करणें-लावणें. (२) (a lamp &c.) विझविणें.

— to be out, खपणें, सरला अ-सणें, झाला असणें.

— to be out of (employ, work &c.), रिकामा-खालीं अ-सणें, (inv.) उद्योग-काम नसणें.

— to be out of (money, food, clothes &c.) (invers.) सरला असणें नसणें.

— to leave out, सोडणें, खे-रीज करणें, बाद करणें, वर्जणें.

— to make out, साधणें, करूं शकणें, सिद्धीस नेणें. (२) स-मजणें.

outside *n.* बाहेरची बाजू *f.* दर्श-नांग *n.* बाहेरचें अंग *n.*

outside *a.* बाहेरचा, बाहेरील.

outside *ad.* बाहेर, बाहेरच्या बाजूस.

outward *a.* बाहेरचा, बाहेरला.

outward *ad.* बाहेर, उफराटा.

over *prep.*-वर, -वरून, -पार, पली-कडे. व.— over fifty, पन्नासा-वर.

— to go over, beyond, ओलां-डणें, पार-पलिकडे जाणें, उतरणें (नदी).

— to stay over night, रात्री-भर-सकाळपर्यंत राहणें.

over *ad.* वर, ज्यास्त, अधिक, फार. (२) किरून, मक्षयान.

— to say over (prove, lesson &c.), सांगणें, पेंकणे, जपणे.

— to do over (work &c.), फिरून करणे.

— to count over, भरघे मोजणें, मोजणें, फिरून मोजणे.

over *a.* झाला, केला, गेला, सरला. (२) वर, ज्यास्त, अधिक, द्वेष, बाकी.

overbear *v. t* दबावणें, धाक दाख-विणें, दाबणे.

overbearing *a.* उद्दत, गार्विष्ठ, उन्मत्त, मगरूर, उर्मट.

overhear *v. t.* ऐकणें, चोरून ऐकणे, कानवसा घेणे.

overheated *a.* फार उष्ण, तापिन.

overjoyed *a.* अत्यानंदी, फार संतोषित, फार आनंदित.

overset *v. t. i* पालटणें, उलटणे, घासला पडणे-पाडणे

overtake *v. t.* भटणे, धरणे, मिळणे, लागणे (रात्र,) आटोपणे.

owe *v. t.* ऋणी असणे, (invers) देणें-कर्ज असणें, द्यायाचा असणे, देणें प्राप्त असणें, दिलहा पाहिजे, द्यावयास योग्य असणे. उ. I owe you ten rupees, मी तुला दाहा रूपये देण्याचें-देणें आहें. — to owe a duty (invers), धर्म असणे, करणें प्राप्त असणे, कराचें व्ययणे.

owing *present p. p. of owe.*

— owing to, -मुळें, -करून.

owl *n.* घुबड *n.* दिवाभित *m.* डलूक *m.*

own *a.* आपला, स्वकीय, स्व, स्वक, खुद, खास, खासगत, खासगी, खासगीचा.

own *v. t.* (invers.) -ला-चा-जवळ असणे. उ. Who owns this book, or whose book is this? हें पुस्तक कोणाचें आहे? I own it, तें माझें आहे. I own a horse, मला एक घोडा आहे.

— (२) कबूल करणे, अंगीकारणें पत्करणे, स्वीकारणें, माझा म्हणें.

owner *n.* मालक *m.* धनी *m.*

ox *n.* बैल *m.*

oyster *n.* कालव *r.*

P.

Pa *n.* बाप *m.* (लेंकरांचा शब्द).

pack *n.* गठ्ठा *m.* गाठोडें *n.* (२) तफा *m.* थवा *m.*

pack *v. t.* रचणे, खचून रचणे -भरणे.

pagoda *n.* देऊळ *n.*

paid *pret. & p. p. of* pay.

pail *n.* एका प्रकारचें पीप, लांकडाचें भांडे.

pain *n.* दुःख *n.* पीडा *f.* वेदना *f.* बाधा *f.* व्यथा *f.* इजा *f.* व्याधि *f.*

pains *n. pl.* श्रम *m.* कष्ट *m.* काळजी *f.* मेहनत *f.*

pain *v. t.* दुखवणे, पिडणे, दुःख देणे, श्रम देणे.

pair *n.* जोड *m.* जोडा *m.* जोड॰ *f.* जोडें *n.*

— a pair of spectacles, चश्मा *m.* उपनेत्र *m.* भरसी *f.*

— a pair of pantaloons, इजार *f.* पायजमा *m.* तुमान *f.*

— a pair of bellows, भाता *m.*

— a pair of tongs, चिमटा *m.*

— a pair of shoes, जोडें *n.* जुतें *n.*

pale *a.* फिका, पिकूट, निस्तेज, भंधक.

panther चिता *m.*

papa *n.* बाप *m.* (pa पाहा).

paper *n.* कागद *m.* पत्र *n.*

parcel *n* गाठोडें *n.* जुडा *m.* वांटा *m.* वट्कटी *f.* जमाव *m.* ढीग *m.* वेंचका *m.* प्रत *f.*

— a parcel of, अनेक, थोडें बहुत.

parcel (out) *v. t.* वांटा करणे, विभाग करणे, विभागणे.

pare *v. t.* साळणे, (फळ, नख इ. चाकूने इ.) साल काढणे, सोलणे.

parent *n.* बाप किंवा आई.

— parents, आईबाप.

parlor *n.* रंगमहाल *m.* बैठवी वी खोली *f.*

parrot *n.* रापू *m.* रावा *m.* पोपट *m.* कीर *m.*

Parsons *n. p.* माणसाचें नांव.

part *n.* भाग *m.* वांटा *m.* हिस्सा *m.* भंश *m.* कांहां, भंग *n.* अवयव *m.* (२) पक्ष *m.* तरफ *f.*

— in part, कांही प्रकारें, कांही भाग, सगळ्या नाहीं.

part *v. t.* वेगळ्या-निराळ्या करणे, विभागणे, वियुक्त करणे, तोडणे.

part *v. i.* तुटणे, वेगळ्या-निराळ्या होणे, तुटून जाणे.

— to part with, सोडणे, देणे, सोडून देणे.

party *n.* तांडा *m.* तुकडी *f.* टोळी *f.* मंडळी *f.* थवा *m.* ताफा *m.* (२) पक्ष *m.* तरफ *f.* प्रकरण *n.*

party *a.* पक्षाचा, तरफेचा, पक्षाकडील.

particular *a.* एखादा, विशेष, विशिष्ट.

particular *n.* रकम *f.* गोष्ट *f.* कलम *n.*

— in particular, विशेषेंकरून, विशेष.

— in that particular, त्याविषयीं, या गोष्टीविषयीं.

— in this particular, यादिषयीं.

particularity *n.* विशेष *m.* विशिष्टपण *n.*

particularly *ad.* विशेषेंकरून. (२) तपसीलवार, बयादसार.

pass *v. i.* चालणे, जाणे, गमणे, गुजरणे, गमन करणे. (२) चालणे, पटणे, (रुपया, पैका इ.)

— to pass by, -जवळून -वरून जाणे, सोडून जाणे, वाटवणे. (२) सांडणे.

— to pass over (river &c.) उतरणे, ओलांडणे, उतरणे, पार -पलिकडे जाणे.

— to pass on v. i. पुढें जाणे
-चालणे.

— to come to pass, पूर्ण होणे,
प्रत्ययास येणे.

— to pass away, off, हे.ऊन
जाणे, जाणे.

pass v. t. उल्लंघणे, ओलांडणे, उत-
रणे, पार-पलिकडे जाणे, (नदी-
च्या इ.). (२) वाटवणे, जवळून
-वरून जाणे. (३) ठरविणे,
स्थापणे, (नेम, इ.).

pass n. घाट m. (२) परवाना m.
दस्तक n.

passage n. दार n. वाट f. घाट m
(२) जलयात्रा f.

passenger n. उतरकरी m. उता-
रू m f. उतारी m. वाटसरू
m. मार्गस्थ, पांथस्थ.

— to pass on, पुढें पाठविणे-चा-
लविणे-धाडणे.

— to pass (money), चालविणे,
देणे.

past p. p. of pass, गन, गेला, अ-
तिक्रांत, झाला, म.गला, गुदस्त,
पूर्वीचा, आदला. उ. the past
day, गेला दिवस. — past time,
मागला वेळ.

past n. मागला वेळ.

past prep -वरून,-जवळून, शेजा-
रून,पलिकडे. उ. He went
past the house, तो घराजव-
ळून गेला.

— It is past five o'clock, पां-
च वाजून गेले.

pasture n. कुरण n. मैदान n. मा-
ळ m.

pasture v. t. चारणे, चरायाला
घालणे.

pat n थाप f. थापटी f. थापडी f.
चापट f चपेट f.

pat v. t. थापणे, थापटणे, थोपटणे,
चापटणे.

patch n. ठिगळ n. तुकडा m. पडी
f. जोड m.

patch v. t. ठिगळ लावणे, ठिगळ-
णे, तुकडा लावणे, पडी-जोड ला-
वणे.

— patch work,ठिगळाचें काम.

path n. वाट f. रस्ता m. पंथा m.
मार्ग m.

patience n सहन n. धीर m. स-
बुरी f. सोसगूक f. धैर्य n.

patient a. सहनशील, सेबूरीक,
सोसक, धैर्यवान, धीर.

patiently ad. सोसगूकीने, सहना-
ने, धैर्याने, सहनतेने.

Paul n. p. पुरुषाचें नांव.

pause n. अवसान n. अंतर n.

— to make a pause, थांबणे,
अंतर-अवसान करणे.

pause v. i. थांबणे, खळणे, राहणे.

paw n. पंजा m.

paw v. t. i. पंजा लावणे, उकरणे.

pay n. रोजगुरा m. पगार m. त-
लब f. पैसे m. pl. नेमणूक f.
वतन n. नेनात f. मजुरी f. मे-
हनत f. फळ n. प्रतिफळ n.

pay v. t. फेडणे, देणे, चुकविणे,
वारणे, प्रतिफळ देणे.

—to pay attention, चित्त-मन -लक्ष देणे.

peace n. सम्य m. तह m. सस्थता f. (२) समाधान n. शांति f.

— to be at peace, स्वस्थ भसणे.

peaceable a. संथ, शांत, गरीव, भांडखोर नाहीं, भोळ्या.

peach n. एका प्रकारचें फळ.

peacock n. मोर m. मयूर m.

pear n. एका प्रकारचें फळ.

peep n. पाहणें m.
— to take a peep, चोरून पाहणें, टेहळणे, डोकावून पाहणे.

peep v. i. डोकावून पाहणे, डोकावणे, चोरून पाहणे, दडून पाहणे.

pelican n. एका प्रकारचें पांखरूं.

pen n. लेखणी f. कलम n. (२) गोठा m. आवार m. वाडा m.

pen v. t. लिहणे.
(२) — to pen up, कोंडणे, गोठ्यांत ठेवणे-घालणे.

pence n. pl. of penny.

pencil n. एका प्रकारची लेखणी.

penknife n. चाकू m.

penny n. एका प्रकारचें नाणें, सुमारें एका आण्याचे दोन तृतीयांश.

people n. लोक m. जन m. प्रजा f.

pepper v. मिरें n.
— chili pepper, मिरची f.

perch v. i. बसणे.

perceive v. t. पाहणे, समजणे, जाणणे, (invers.) दिसणे.

perfect a. पूर्ण, पुरा, पुरता, पुण्यवान.

perfect v. t. पूर्ण करणे, सिद्धीस आणणे.

perfectly ad. पूर्णतेने, पुरता, बरोबर,-च, अगदी, पुरतेपणीं.

perform v. t. बजावणे, करणे, पूर्ण करणे.

perhaps ad. कदाचित.
— perhaps it is so (or it may be so), असेल.

period n. वाक्याच्या शेवटीं जें पूत्र तें. (२) पूर्ण वाक्य. (३) वेळ f. साक m. (४) शेवट n, मर्यादा f.
— the present period, प्रस्तुत, हल्लीं, आतां, या वेळेत.

periodical a. नियमाचा, नियमित.

permission n. परवानगी f. हुकूम m. निरोप m. रजा f.

permit v. t. देणे, हुकूम-परवाना देणे, होऊं देणे. उ.—to permit to go, जाऊं देणे.

person n. असामी f. जन m. माणूस n. पुरुष m. (२) अंग n. शरीर n. (३) (in grammar.) पुरुष.
— in person, जातीने, स्वतां.

personal a. शारीरी, बाह्य, बाहेरला. (२) खास, खासगत, खासगी. खुद, स्वकीय.

persuade v. t. मनावणे, समजावणे, मन भरविणे, समजूत करणे, मथणे.

pert a. उद्धत, दांडगा, डैलदार, धीट, अविनय.

pet a. n. लाडका, छावडा, डैत, लालित.

Peter *n. p.* पुरुषाचें नांव.

Phebe *n. p.* स्त्रियेचें नांव.

philosopher *n.* ज्ञानी, विद्वान *m.* विवेकी *m.* शास्त्रज्ञ, विचारवंत.

philosophy *n.* विद्याज्ञानं *n.* शास्त्र-ज्ञान *n.* वेद *m.*

— moral philosophy, धर्मज्ञान *n.* नीतिज्ञान *n.* नीति *f.*

— natural philosophy, तत्त्वज्ञान *n.* सिद्ध पदार्थविज्ञान *n.*

pick *v. t.* निसणें, वेंचणें, निवडून घेणे.

— to pick up, वेंचणे, टिपणे, रचलणे.

— to pick out, निवडून घेणे, घेणे, निसणे, वेंचणे.

— (२) तोडणे, कांढणे, (फळ, फूल, इ.).

picture *n.* तसवीर *f.* चित्र *n.* प्रतिमा *f.*

pie *n.* पोळी *f.* पुरणपोळी *f.*

piece *n.* तुकडा *m.* कुटका *m.* खाप *f.* पडी *f.* जोड *m.* (२) नाणे (पैक्याचें). (३) धान *n.* (काप-डाचें).

— pieces *pl.* चूर *m.*

— to dash in pieces, फोडून टाकणे, चूर करणे.

— to break in pieces *v. i.* फुटणे, फुटून जाणे. (२) *v. t.* फोडून टाकणे, फोडणे, आपटून फोडणे.

piety *n.* सत्त्व *n.* धार्मिकपण *n.* धर्मशीलपण *n.*

— a man of piety, धर्मशील माणूस, देवभक्त, साधु.

pig *n.* डुकरीचें पिल्लूं *n.* लहान डुकर *n.*

pile *n.* ढीग *m.* गंज *m.* पुंजा *m.* रास *f.* राशी *f.*

pile (up) *v. t.* रास-ढीग करणे, गंज-पुंजा करणे.

— to pile full, शिगेवरोवर भरणे.

piled *a. & p. p.* शिगेवरोवर भरला.

pill *n.* गोळी *f.* (औषधाची).

pillage *n.* लूट *f.* लुटणें *n.*

pillage *v. t.* लुटणें, लुगारणे.

pimento *n.* कंकोळ *n.*

pin *n.* टाचणी *f.* खुंटी *f.* शल्य *n.* खीळ *f.* भेख *f.*

pin *v. t.* टाचणीने-खुंटीने लावणे.

pint *n.* एकाप्रकारचा कैली माप, (quart याचा अर्धा).

pious *a.* धार्मिक, धर्मशील, भक्तिमान.

pit *n.* खाच *f.* खळगा *m.* खळगी *f.* पोंचा *m.*

pit *v. t.* पोंचें करणे, वण करणे, पोंचट करणे.

— to be pitted, (*inv.*) वण-पोंचे भरणे. व. His face was pitted by the small pox, त्याच्या तोंडावर देवीचे वण होते.

pitiful *a.* करुणाकर, दयाळू, कृपाळू, कृपावंत, दयासमुद्र. (२) दीन, दीनवाणा, कंगाल, करुण.

— in a pitiful manner, काकळूत करून, दीनवाण्या प्रमाणे.

— pitiful tone, कळकळण्या *f.*
pl. काकळूत *f.*

pity *n.* दया *f.* करुणा *f.* कृपा *f.*
कळवळ *m.* कळकळ *f.*

pity *v. t.* कळवळणे, कृपा-दया
करणे, कळवळा करणे, (*invert.*)
कळदला-दया देणे.

place *n.* ठिकाण *n.* जागा *f.* स्थान
n. स्थल *n.* ठार्णे *n.*

— fire place, चूल *f.* चुलवान *n.*

place *v. t.* ठेवणे, स्थापणे, नेमणे,
मांडणे, लावणे.

— to place confidence, वि-
श्वासणे, भरवसा-खातरी-विश्वास
ठेवणे.

plague *n.* पटकी *f.* जरीमरी *f.*
(२) झोंवट *n.* पीडा *f.* उपद्रव *m.*

plague *v. t.* जाचणे, छळणे, सता-
वणे, चाळवणे, त्रास देणे, इजा
-त्रास देणे.

plain *n.* मैदान *n.* सपाटी *f.* भा-
ळजमीन *f.*

plain *a.* स्पष्ट, उघडा, सडक, उघ-
ड. (२) साधा. (३) सपाट,
सम, सारिखा, मैदानाचा.

plainly *ad.* स्पष्ट, उधडें.

plan *n.* युक्ति *f.* मसलत *f.* बेत *m.*
मनसुबा *m.* मनोरथ *m.* (२)
नकाशा *m.* नमुना *m.* प्रमाण *n.*

plan *v. t.* योजणे, बेत-मसलत-म-
नसुबा करणे, चिंतणे, नकाशा
काढणे.

planet *n.* ग्रह *m.*

plank *n.* जाड तकता *m.* फळी *f.*
फळें *n.*

plant *n.* रोप *n.* भाजी *f.* वनस्पति
f. औषधी *f.*

plant *v. t.* लावणे (बी, रोप, इ.)
आरोपणे, स्थापणे, रोवणे.

plate *n.* तबक *n.* थासन *n.* पात्र *n.*

play *n.* खेळ *m.* खेळणे *n.* विनोद
m. क्रीडा *f.* लीला *f.* रमण *n.*
करमणूक *f.* मौज *f.*

play *v. t. i.* खेळणे, विनोद करणे,
क्रीडा-लीला करणे. (२) वाज-
विणे (वाजंत्र).

playfellow *n.* खेळगडी *m.* सव-
गडी *m.*

playful *a.* खेळकर, खिलाडी,
खयाली, बागुका.

playfully *ad.* खेळून, खेळ्ने, वि-
नोदाने, मस्करीने, ठठेने.

plaything *n.* खेळण्याचा पदार्थ *m.*
खेळ *m.* खेळणें *n.*

please *v. t.* भवडणे, संतोष देणे.
(२) इच्छिणे.

— if you please, तुमची खुशी
भसली, जर तुला भवडेल, मर्जी
भसल्यास.

— please to sit down, कृपा
करून बसा.

— please give me that book,
कृपा करून तें पुस्तक मला दे.

pleased *a. & p. p.* संतुष्ट, संतो-
षित, आनंदित, प्रसन्न.

— to be pleased, संतोषणे,
संतुष्ट-खुशी भसणे, मेहेरबानी
करणे.

pleasant *a.* भवडता, रमणीय, रम्य,
संतोषी, भला, चांगला, शांत.

— pleasant weather, चांगला दिवस.

pleasure n. सुख n. आनंद m. खुशी f. संतोष m. मौज f. (२) मर्जी f. इच्छा f.

plenty n. पुरपुराट n. पुरवटा m. पुरें n. अतिशय m. पुष्कळ n. बहुत, फार, बेगमी f.

plough n. नांगर m. हल m.

plough v. t. नांगरणे, उखळणे.

plum n. एका प्रकारचें फळ.

plumage n. पंखवेष्टन n. पंख m.

pocket n. खिसा m. कसा m.

— pocket money, अवांतर खर्चांचे पैसे, खर्ची f.

pocket v. t. खिस्यांत ठेवणे, ठेवणे.

point n. टोंक n. अग्र n. बिंदु m. टांक m. (लेखणीचा). डोंगा m. द्रीवट n.

— to be at the point of death, मरायास टेंकणे-भिडणे, मरणोन्मुख होणे.

— to be on the point of doing, going &c. करायास-जायास इ. भिडणे, करणार जाणार इ. असणे, उन्मुख होणे.

point v. i. बोट दाखवणे, रोखणे.

— to point out to, दाखविणे.

—to point at, towards, (with a stick, finger), काठी-बोट दाखविणे.

poison n. विष n. विख n. जहर n.

poison v. t. विष देणे, विष घालणे, विषयुक्त करणे, विखारा करणे, विखारवणे.

poisonous a. विषयुक्त, विखारा.

pole n. लांब काठी f. दांडी f.

polite a. सभ्य, सभ्योचित, सुजनतेचा, सौजन्याचा.

politely ad. सुजनतेने, माणुसकीने, सभ्यपणाने.

politeness n. सुजनता f. सौजन्य n. सभ्यता f. माणुसकी f. माणूसपण n. गृहस्थगिरी f. गृहस्थपणा m. मुजारत f.

pop v. i. फटफट वाजणे.

— to pop in, फटकर आंत येणे-जाणे, कचकावून आंत येणे-जाणे.

— to pop up, कचकावून-फटकर उठणे,-वर येणे.

— to pop away, off, कचकावून-फटकर जाणे.

Pope n. रोमन् कायोलीक लोकांच्या मंडळीचा मुख्य अधिकारी तो.

poor a. गरीब, दीन, दरिद्री, दुबळा, बापडा, बिचारा, लाचार, द्रव्यहीन. (२) चांगला नाहीं, वाईट, निरुपयोगी, हलका. (३) पातळ, क्षीण, रोड, किडकिडीत.

port n. बंदर n.

portion n. वांटा m. अंश m. अंशांश m. वर्गणी f. हिसा m. तुकडा m.

— a portion, कांहीं.

— a small portion, थोडेंसें.

— a large portion, फारसें.

Portugal n. p. एका देशाचें नांव.

possible a. संभव्य, संभावित, संभूत, जें होईल तें, शक्य.

— as....as possible, शक्तिप्रमा-णें, यथाशक्ति, होईल-येईल तित-की, सर्व शक्तीने. उ. I ran as fast as possible, मी आपल्या सर्व शक्तीने धांवलों. Do it as soon as possible, जितकें लवकर होईल तितकें कर.

— as much as possible, जि-तका होईल-येईल वितका.

— to be possible, संभवणें, शक्य असणें.

— if possible, जर घडेल तर, जर होईल तर, जर संभवेल तर, यथाकदाचित.

possibly ad. अगदीं,-च, (नाहीं). (२) कदाचित. उ. I cannot possibly do it, तें माझ्याने होतच नाहीं. It may possibly rain, पाऊस कदाचित पडेल, पाऊस प-डणार नाहीं असें म्हणतां येत ना-हीं. It may possibly be so, असें कदाचित असेल, नाहीं असें म्हणतां येत नाहीं.

pot n. भांडें n. मडकें n. कुंभ m. घडा m. घागर f.

potatoe n. बटाटा m.

— sweet potatoe, रातालें n. रताळूं n.

pouch n. पीतडी f. पिशवी f. थै-ली f.

pound n. अच्छेर m. (वजनी) एक वजनी माप सुमारें एक रतल n.

pound v. t. कुटणें, खलणें, कांडणें, ताडणें, मारणें, पिटणें.

power n. पराक्रम m. सामर्थ्य n.

शक्ति f. बळ n. ताकत f. जोर m. n. कुवत f. प्रताप m. (२) अधिकार m. अमल m. अख्त्यार m. मुखत्यार m. सत्ता f. ऐश्वर्य n. अधिकार m.

powerful a. पराक्रमी, बळकट, शक्तिमान, वीर्यवान.

practical a. व्यवहारिक, व्यवहार्य. (२) संभव्य, संभाविक, शक्य, जें होईल तें, साध्य, होण्याजोगा, करण्याजोगा, सवघड, सुलभ.

practice n. कसरत f. अभ्यास m. सराव m. करणें n. (२) रीत f. चाल f. संप्रदाय m. धारा m. वहिवाट f. शिरस्ता m. दस्तूर m.

practice v. t. i. अभ्यास करणें, अभ्यासणें, करणें, करीत असणें.

praise n. स्तुति f. स्तव m. वाखाण n. तारीफ f. कीर्ति f. शाबास f.

praise v. t. स्तुति करणें, कीर्ति-कीर्तन करणें, वाखाणणें, तारीफ करणें.

pray v. i. प्रार्थना करणें, प्रार्थणें, मागणें, विनविणें, विनंती करणें.

— Pray tell me, कृपेकरून मला सांग.

— Pray do this, कृपा करून हें कर-करावें.

prayer n. प्रार्थना f. विनंती f. अर्जी f. मागणें n.

precious a. मोलवान, किम्मती, अमूल्य, अपरूप, दुर्मीळ, प्रीय, उंच.

— precious stone, रत्न n.

present n. बक्षीस n. इनाम n. दन

n. भेट f. नजर f. नजराणा m.

present a. हजीर, समक्ष, रूजू.

— at the present time or period, प्रस्तुत, हल्लीं, सांप्रत, आतां, सद्यः; वर्त्तमान काळीं.

— to be present, असणे, हजीर-एर्थे असणे.

present v. t. देणे, पुढें करणे, दाख-विणे, अर्पणे, रूजू करणे, नजर करणे, भेटीस आणणे, वाहणे.

presently ad. थोडे वेळाने, कांहीं वेळानंतर, लवकर, इतक्यांत, आतांसीं, अमळशाने, तूर्त, सत्वर.

preserve v. t. राखणे, रक्षणे, वाचा-वणे, वांचविणे, ठेवणे, संभाळणे, बाळगणे.

preserves n. pl. मुरंबा m. मोरंबा m.

president n. सभापति m. सभाना-यक m. (२) अधिकारी m. मुख्य m. सरदार m.

pretence n. मीस n. बहाणा m. सोंग n. निमित्त n. गतक f. m. फटवण f.

pretend v. t. बहाणा करणे, नि-मित्त-मीस-गतक-सोंग करणे, असें करणे.

prettily ad. सुंदरपणाने, चांगलें, नामी, खूब.

prettiness n. सुंदरपण n. खुबसु-रती f. सुरेखाई f. चिमकुलपण n. नाजकाई f.

pretty a. सुंदर, सुरेख, खुबसुरत, देखणा, छबीला, नीटनेटका, चिमका, चांगला, बरा, नाजूक,

चिमणा, चिमकुला. (२) कां-हींसा, यावत्ततावत.

— pretty soon, थोडे वेळाने.

prevent v. t. निवारणे, निवारण करणे, अटकावणे, टाळणे, दूर करणे, न देणे (होऊ,-जाऊ,-करूं, इ.), मना करणे.

— I do this to prevent his going (to prevent him from going), त्याने न जावें म्हणून मी हें करितों.

prey n. हतवस्तु n. लूट f. जें हरण केलेलें तें.

— beast of prey, श्वापद n. m. घातकपशु m. हिंस्र पशु m. शिकारी जनावर n.

— bird of prey, घातक पक्षी

prey (on or upon) v. i. खाणे, भक्षणे, आहार करणे. m. हिंस्र पक्षी m.

price n. किम्मत f. मोल n. भाव m. धारण f. धारा m. दर m. पाउ m. दरदाम m. निरख m.

prick n. टोंच n. टोंचा m. टोंची f. वेध m. (२) कांटा m.

prick v. t. टोंचणे, खुपणे, बोचणे, रूतणे.

prickly a. कटिरा, काट्यांचा.

pride n. अभिमान m. गर्व m. अ-हंकार m. मगरूरी f. मीपणा m. अहंपणा m.

pride (one's self) v. t. अभिमान धरणे, वाणी बाळगणे, अभिमा-नणे.

primer n. लेंकरांची पहिली पोथी.

principal *a.* मुख्य, पहिला, पुढचा.

principle *n.* तत्व *n.* मूळ *n.* परि-
भाषा *f.* धर्म *m.* नेम *m.* भान *m.*

print *n.* चित्र *n.* तस्वीर *f.* प्रतिमा
f. छाप *m.* छापणें *n.* नकाशा *m.*

print *v. t.* छापणें.

prison *n.* तुरंग *m.* बंदिशाळा *f.*
कारागृह *n.* बंदखाना *m.*

private *a.* एकला, निराळा, एकांत,
गुप्य, गुप्त, अंतस्थ. (२) खास,
खासगत, आपला, स्वकीय.
— a private soldier, शिपाई.

privately *ad.* एकांतीं, गुप्तपणें,
गुप्तपणाने, गुप्तरूपें.

probable *a.* संभाव्य, संभाविक,
संभूत.
— to be probable, संभवणें,
फार करून असणें.
— It is probable, असेल.

probably *ad.* प्रायः फार करून,
बहुत करून.
— He will probably go, तो
जाईल असें वाटतें, *or* तो फार-
करून जाईल.
— It will probably rain, पा-
ऊस येईल असें वाटतें.

procure *v. t.* मिळविणें, घेणें, पावणें,
प्राप्त करणें, जोडणें, (*invers.*)
मिळणें, प्राप्त होणें.

procurable *a.* लभ्य, मिळायाचा,
मिळण्या जोगा, मिळेल असा,
सुलभ.

profane *a.* अमर्याद, निर्भीड, पवित्र
नाहीं, नापाक, वाईट, धर्मंगळ,
अभद्र.

profane *v. t.* विटाळ करणें, विटा-
ळणें.

profit *n.* लाभ *m.* हित *n.* फळ *n.*
नफा *m.* मिळकत *f.* किफाइत
f. प्राप्ति *f.* फायदा *m.* हाशील *n.*

profit *v. i.* (*invers.*) मिळणें, फळ
-नफा-लाभ-मिळकत-हित असणें.

profitable *a.* हितकारक, किफा-
इती, हित, उपयोगी, कामाचा.

promise *n.* वचन *n.* प्रतिज्ञा *f.* क-
रार *m.* बोली *f.* वायदा *m.* भाक
f. भाष *f.*

promise *v. t.* वचन देणें, प्रतिज्ञा
-करार करणें, सांगणें, कबूल
करणें-होणें, देऊं करणें.

proper *a.* योग्य, बरोबर, ठीक,
लायक, वाजवी, नेटका, साजरा,
सत्य, उचित, प्रमाणीक, यथा-
न्याय, यथायोग्य, यथास्थित, नीट,
नीटनेटका, विहित. (२) असल,
खरा. (३) खास, खासगत,
आपला, स्वकीय.

properly *ad.* बरोबर, चांगलें,
यथायोग्य, नीट, तत्वतेनें, वस्तुतः,
जसें व्हावें तसें

property *n.* द्रव्य *n.* धन *n.* माल *m.*
मत्ता *f.* मालमत्ता *f.* हेवज *m.*
पैका *m.* संपत्ति *f.* (२) गुण *m.*
धर्म *m.* तत्व *n.* प्रकृति *f.* स्व-
भाव *m.*

prophet *n.* भविष्यवादी *m.* भविष्य-
भाषी *m.* पैगमबर *m.* भविष्य
सांगणारा *m.*

proportion *n.* प्रमाण *n.*
— in proportion to, प्रमाणें,

तसतसा. उ.— in proportion to its size, त्याच्या आकारमाना-प्रमाणें.

— in the proportion of three to four, तीन चतुर्थींश, तीन आणि चार यांच्या गुणोत्तराने.

propose r. t. घालणे (कोंडें, प्रश्न इ.), सांगणे, बोलणे, पुढें ठेवणे.

proposition n. पूर्वपक्ष m. जें प्रति-पाद्य तें, वाक्य n. पुरवणी f. पुरवार m. बोलणें n. जें म्हटलें तें, बोली f. (२) सिद्धांत m.

prosperity n. कल्याण n. बरें .n भरभर f. भरभराट m. यश m. बरकत f. आबादानी f.

prosperous a. सभाग्य, सभाग्यवंत, भद्र, क्षेम, विशिष्ट, भाग्यवान, श्रीमान, यशस्वी, बरकतदार, आबादान.

protect r. t. वचावणे, वचाव करणे, वांचविणे, संभाळणे, राखणे, रक्षणे, पाळणे, प्रतिपाल करणे.

proud a. गर्विष्ठ, अभिमानी, मग-रूर, अहंकारी, उन्मत्त.

prove v. t. प्रमाण सांगणे, साक्ष देणे, ठरविणे, शाबुत करणे. (२) प्रत्यय-परीक्षा-अनुभव-प्रतीति घेणे -पाहणे, परीक्षणे, पारखणे, ताळ घेणे -पाहणे, (invers.) प्रतीति -अनुभव येणे, प्रतीतीस-अनुभवास येणे, परीक्षा होणे.

prove r. i. निघणे, होणे, ठरणे, उतरणे, दिसं येणे, निपजणे, निभावणे.

provide v. t. पुरवणे, देणे, पुरवटा -तरतूद करणे, सिद्ध -तयार करणे, गरज करणे, बेगमी करणे. (२) बंदोवस्त करणे-ठेवणे.

provider n. पुरवणारा m. बेगमी-करणारा m. देणारा m. जोडता, कमाऊ, मिळविणारा m.

provision n. पुरव m. तयारी f. तरतूद f. बेगमी f. पुरवटा m. उपाय m. (२) अन्न n. खाणें n. अन्नोदक n. आहार m.

provoke v. t. चिथावणे, संतापविणे, राग उठविणे, छळणे, पेटवणे, चेष्टविणे, प्रेरणे, खिजावणे, रुस-विणे, चिडवणे.

— to be provoked, रागें भरणे, रुसणे, चिडणे, चेष्टणे, चिथणे, पेटणे.

pry n. तीर m. उटाळा m. (उच-लण्यासाठीं).

pry v. t. i. उटाळणे, उटाळा देऊन नेटणे, उटाळा देणे.

— to pry up (a weight &c.) उचलणे (तिराने).

— to pry into (secrets &c.) टेहळणे, पाळत लावणे-घेणे-का-ढणे.

— to pry open (a box &c.) उचकटणे.

public n. लोक m. जन n.

public a. प्रसिद्ध, प्रगट, जाहिर, लौकिक, उघडा, (in comp.) लोक.

— public worship, सर्वेंतील भजन.

— public house, धर्मशाळा f.

9*

pucker *n.* सुरकुती *f.* वळकटी *f.* वळी *f.*

pucker *v. i.* सुरकुतणे, अकुसणे, चिंवणे.

pucker *v. t.* सुरकुतिवणे, अकुस-विणे.

pull *v. t.* ओढणे, खेंचणे, ताणणे.
— to pull out *or* off, काढणे.
— to pull up, काढणे, उपटणे
— to pull flowers, फुलें तोडणे, खुडणे,काढणे, वेंचणे.

punish *v. t.* पारपत्य करणे,शिक्षा -शासन देणे, ताडणे, नशीहत देणे, दंड करणे-लावणे, शासणे.

punishment *n.* शासन *n.* शिक्षा *f.* पारपत्य *n.* दंड *m.* नशीहत *f.* ताडन *n.*

pupil *n.* विद्यार्थी *m.* शिष्य *m.* शिकणारा *m.* चेला *m.* छात्र *m.*
— pupil of the eye, डोळ्यां-तील बाहुली-पुतळी-तारा.

pure *a.* शुद्ध,निर्दंम,निर्मळ,निवळ, स्वच्छ, निरा, पवित्र, केवळ.

purple *a.* जांबळा.

purpose *n.* मतलब *m.* इरादा *m.* बेत *m.* हेनु *m.* हेत *m.* मनोरथ *m.* अभिप्राय *m.* विचार *m.* मन-सुबा *m.* (२) काम *n.* विषय *m.* हाशील *m.* प्रयोजन *n.*
— on purpose,-साठींच, हेनूने, मनःपूर्वक, मुद्दाम, तातपुरचा, हुकमा, दाटून, मुद्द्या उद्देशाने, समजून-उमजून.

purpose *v. t. i.* मनांत आणणे, मनावर घेणे, अर्वांकणे, विचार -मनसुबा करणे, बेत-हेतु भरणे, योजणे, (*invers.*) मनांत असणे, बेत असणे, हेतु-मतलब-इरादा -मनसुबा-मनोरथ असणे.

purposely *ad.* (on purpose शहा).

purr *v. i.* कुरकुरणे (मांजर).

purse *n.* कसणी *f.* कसा *m.* बटवा *m.* तोडा *m.* थैली *f.* पिशवी *f.* चंची *f.* पोतडी *f.*

pursue *v. t.* पाठीस लागणे, पाठ-लाग करणे, शोधणे, अनुसरणे, करणे, चालविणे,धरणे (चाल इ.)
— to pursue a study -occu-pation &c. चालविणे, करणे.
— He pursues the same course as before, पूर्वींसारिखा तो करितो-चालतो. — to pur-sue one's way -journey &c. पुढें जाणे.

pursuit *n.* पाठलाग *m.* पाळत *f.* शोध *m.* (२) उद्योग *m.* काम *n.* कार्य *n.*

push *n.* रेंटा *m.* हुंदडा *m.* धक्का *m.* झोंक *m.*

push *v. t.* रेंटणे, रेंढारेंढ करणे, हुंदउणे, ढकलणे, लोटणे, ठेलणे.
— to push along, चालविणे, सरकणे.

push *v. i.* — to push along, पुढें जाणे-चालणे, लोटणे.

put *v. t.* ठेवणे, घालणे, लावणे, मांडणे.
— to put down, उतरणे, ठेवणे, खालीं करणे-ठेवणे. (२)

मांडणे, लिहून ठेवणे· (३)दाबणे, दबावणे.

— to put on (clothes &c.), घालणे, नेसणे, लेणे, बांधणे, लावणे.

—to put out the eyes, काढणे, काढून टाकणे, फुटें करणे. (२) विझविणे (बत्ती, दिवा, इ.). (३) रुसविणे, संतापविणे, राग उठविणे. (४)भाड्याने ठेवणे, व्याजीं ठेवणे-लावणे.

— to put away, ठेवणे, सोडणे, दूर करणे.

— to put in mind, मनांत आणणे, सई देणे, याद देणे.

—to put up, ठेवणे, बांधणे, बंद करणे, घालणे, वर्तें करणे, रचणे.

— to put in fear, भय दाखविणे, भेडावणे, भिवविणे.

— to put in pain, दुखविणे, दुःख देणे, इजा-हाल करणे.

— to put to death, जिवें मारणे, मारणे.

put *pret. & p. p. of* put.

Q.

Quack *n.* (बदकाचा शब्द). क्वां: क्वां: क्वां: (२) चिकित्सक *m.*

— quack doctor, चिकित्सक.

quadruped *n.* चतुष्पद *m. n.*

quality *n.* गुण *m.* स्वभाव *m.* जात *f.* मत *f.*

—good quality, सुगुण, सद्गुण, सद्धर्म, चांगलेपण.

—bad quality, दुर्गुण, वाईटपण.

quantity *n.* मान *n.* माप *n.* परिमाण *n.*

— small quantity, थोडा, जरा, जरासा, किंचित, सल्प, इलिसा.

— great quantity, पुष्कळ, फार, लय, मस्त.

quarrel *n.* कज्जा *m.* तंटा *m.* भांडण *n.* कलह *m.* बखेडा *m.* झगडा *m.* कलगत *f.* खटखट *f.* लढाई *f.* मारामारी *f.*

quarrel *v. i.* भांडणे, कज्जा-तंटा -बखेडा -भांडण करणे, लढणे, झगडणे.

quarrelsome *a.* भांडखोर, भांडगा, झगडाऊ, बखेड्या, कज्जेखोर, कज्जेदलाल, खजाळ.

quart *n.* एका प्रकारचें कैली माप.

quarter *n.* चतुर्थांश *m.* पाव *m.* चौथाई *f.* पाई *f.*

— three quarters, पाऊण.

—a quarter more, सवा, सवाई·

— hue and a quarter, सवा.

— one and three quarters, पाऊणेदोन.

— two and a quarter, सवादोन.

— two and three quarters, पाऊणेतीन. इ.

— (२) तीन महिने, (वर्षांचा चतुर्थांश). (३) कड *f.* बाजू *f.* तरफ *f.* दिशा *f.* (४) खंड *n.* भाग *m.* (५) *pl.* बिन्हाड *n.* मुकाम *m.* छावणी *f.*

— to give quarter, वांचूं देणें.

quarter v. t. चार भाग करणें.
(२) विश्राळ-ठिकाण-बागा देणें.

quarter v. i. उतरणें, मुकाम करणें,
विश्राळ घेणें.

question n. प्रश्न m. सवाल m.
(२) गोष्ट f. बाबत f. खटलें n.
मुकदमा m. (३) शंका f.
दिक्कत f. संशय m. विचार m.
— to call in question, दिक्कत
-संशय घेणें.
— to ask or put a question,
पुसणें, विचारणें.

question v. t. प्रश्न करणें, सवाल
करणें, विचारणें, पुसणें, पुरव्यास
करणें. (२) संशय-दिक्कत घेणें,
(invers.) संशय वाटणें, शंका
असणें.

quick ad. लवकर, जलदी, त्वरेनें,
त्वरित, तूर्त, घाईनें, वेगें, सत्वर,
शीघ्र, लागलींच, आतांच.

quick a. चपळ, चलाक, जलद,
त्वरित, सत्वर, शीघ्र. (२)
जिता.

quickly ad. (quick पाहा) लवकर,
जलदी, तूर्त, घाईनें, त्वरेनें, स-
त्वर, शीघ्र.

quiet a. निवांत, शांत, संथ, साळ-
सूद, उगा, चिप्प, शाल्वद, गरीब,
थंड.

quiet v. t. सथावणें, सस्थावणें,
समजूत करणें, थांबविणें, शांत
मंद करणें, समजविणें.

quietly ad. मुकाट्यां, मुकाट्याने,
निवांत, उगींच, उगा, गुपचिप.

quit v. t. सोडणें, त्यागणें, सोडून
देणें, टाकणें, सोडून जाणें.

quite ad. भगवीं,-च, पुरा, पूर्ण,
निःशेष, निस्तुक, ठार, फार,
झाडून, पार. (२) कांहींसा, थोडें
बहुत.
— not quite, थोड्या अंतराने,
थोडें आंत, थोडें चुकला, वरो-
वरच नाहीं, थोडें राहिलें, थोडें
कमी.

quiver n. तरकश f. m. तूण m.
तूणीर m. भाता m. (तिरांचा).

quiver v. i. थरथरणें, थरकणें,
फुरफुरणें, कांपणें.

quote v. t. काढून दाखविणें, का-
ढून सांगणें, सांगणें, आणणें. उ.
He quoted a verse from the
Bible, त्यानें शास्त्रांतून एक
ओवी काढून सांगितली-लिहिली.

R.

Race n. दौड f. धांव f. धावन n.
धावड f दवड f. (२) वंश m.
गोत्र n. कूळ n. जात f. अवलाद
f. (३) पिढी f.

race v. i. धाव-दौड धावणें, दवड
मारणें.

rag n चिंधी f. चिंधोटी f. चिंभूक
n चिथडा m. चिरगूट n. फडका
m. फडकें n. लंगोटी f.

rage n. राग m. संताप m. आवेश
m. तळतळाट m. तळतळ f.
क्रोध m. क्षोभ m. कोप m.

rage v. i. संतापणें, तळतळणें, ज-

ळणे, क्षोभणे (*invers.*) राग-कोप येणे.

ragged *a.* फाटका, फाटक्या वस्ला-चा, चिंध्या घातलेला-ल्यालेला, ठिगळाचा.

rain *n.* पाऊस *m.* वृष्टि *f.* पर्जन्य *m.*

rain *v. i.* पाऊस पडणे, वृष्टि होणे, पर्जन्य पडणे-लागणे, पाणी पडणे.

raise *v. t.* उचलणे, उंचावणे, उठ-विणे, उभा करणे, उंच करणे. (२) चढविणे, वाढविणे.

ran *pret. of* run.

rank *n.* पदवी *f.* पद *n.* प्रत *f.* पायरी *f.* (२) पंक्ति *f.* पंगत *f.* ओळ *f.* हार *f.* सर *m.*

rank *a.* दाट. (२) घाणेरा.

rank *v. t.* पदवी देणे, मान देणे, मानणे, गणणे, मोजणे.

rank *v. i.* पदवी धरणे, पदवींत राहणे-असणे.

rare *a.* विरळा, दुर्मीळ, अपरूप, असाधारण, लोकोत्तर, थोडका, नादर. (२) कच्चा.

rarely *ad.* विरळा, क्वचित, वारं-वार नाहीं.

rarity *n.* अपरूवाई *f.* विरळें *n.* नादरी *f.*

rat *n.* उंदीर *m.* घूस *f.*

rate *n.* भाव *m.* धारण *f.* धारा *m.* दर *m.* पाड *m.* किंमत *f.* मोल *n.* निरख *m.*

rate *v. t.* भाव-धारण-दर-पाड-किंमत ठरविणे, भावणे, जोखणे. (२) मानणे, मोजणे, गणणे, समजणे, (*invers.*) वाटणे. (३)

धमकावणे, दबावणे, खडखडविणे, दरारा करणे.

rather *ad.* कांहींसा, थोडासा, जरा-सा. उ. — rather a small piece, कांहींसा लहान तुकडा. — This cloth is rather black, हें कापड कांहींसें काळें आहे. (२) पहिलें, वरम. — I had (*or* would) rather go than stay, राहण्यापेक्षां जाणें मला बरें वाटतें. — I had rather not take it, तें घ्यावें हें मला बरें वाटत नाहीं. — I had rather not go there, तिकडे जावें हें मला बरें वाटत नाहीं.

rattle *n.* खुळखुळा *m.* झुणझुणा *m.* घागरा *m.*

rattle *v. t.* खुळखुळावणे, खुळखुळ करणे, खडखडविणे.

rattle *v. i.* खुळखुळणे, गडाडणे, खडखडणे, वाजणे (घागरा).

rattle snake *n.* खुळखुळा साप *m.*

raven *n.* कावळा *m.* कांक *m.* वा-यस *m.*

raw *a.* कच्चा, भाजलेला नाहीं, हि-रवा, अपक्व. (२) अनाडी.

reach *v. t.* पोहंचणे, पावणे, जाणे, येणे, सई करणे, दाखल होणे. (२) देणे. उ. Reach me that book, तें पुस्तक मला दे. (३) (*invers.*) पुरणे (हात, काठी, इ.). उ. I cannot reach it, माझा हात पुरत नाहीं.

— to reach out the hand, हात पुढें करणे.

reach v. i लागणे, लागून ठेपणे, लागू असणे, पोहंचणे, ठेपणे. उ. It reaches the whole length of the bill to the neck, ती चोचेपासून मानेपर्यंत ठेपली आहे. (p. 24). — The procession reached a kos, कोसभर रव लागली.

reach n. भवांका m. सत्ता f.

read (रीड) v. t. i. वाचणे, पढणे, अध्ययन करणे.

read (रेड) pret. & p. p. of read.

reader n. वाचणारा m. पढणेवाला m.

readily ad. खुशीने, तुर्त, लवकर.

readiness n. तयारी f. सिद्धता f. (२) खुशी f. मर्जी f.
— in readiness, तयार.
— with readiness, जलदी, लवकर.

reading n. वाचणे n. अध्ययन n.

reading a. वाचण्याचा. उ. — reading book, वाचण्याचें पुस्तक.

ready a. तयार, सिद्ध, राजी, सज्ज, सज्जित, खुशी, हजीर, रुजू, रोख. (२) हुशार, चतुर.
— ready money, नगद, रोख.

real a. सत्य, वास्तविक, वास्तव, खरा, असल, यथार्थ.

reality n. तत्व n. सत्यपण n. तत्वार्थ m. खरेपण n. आहेपण n.

यथार्थपण n. वास्तविकपण n.

really ad. तत्वतः, खचित, अलबत्त, वास्तविक, यथार्थ.

reason n. कारण n. सबब f. प्रयोजन n. निमित्त n. प्रमाण n. (२) चित्त n. मन n. तर्क m. बुद्धि f.

reason v. i. अनुमानणे, अनुमान करणे, वाद करणे, तर्क करणे.

receive v. t. घेणे, पावणे, ग्रहण करणे, (invers.) पोहंचणे, मिळणे. (२) पत्करणे, मानणे, अंगीकारणे, स्वीकारणे.

recite v. t. सांगणे, देणे (धडा), झाणे.

reckon v. t. लेखणे, गणणे, मानणे, मोजणे. (२) हिशोब करणे, झडती घेणे, धरणे, मोजणी करणे.

recollect v. t. आठवणे, आठवण करणे, स्मरणे, सई करणे, (invers.) सई-याद-स्मरण-आठवण राहणे, मनांत येणे-राहणे-असणे.

recollection n. स्मर m. स्मरण n. आठवण f. याद f. सई f.

record v. t. लिहून ठेवणे, लिहणे, मांडणे, टिपणे, बार करणे.

record n. यादबूद f. याद f. टिपण n. दफ्तर n.

recover v t. फिरून पावणे, परत घेणे-भाणे, (invers.) सांपडणे, पुन्हा मिळणे.

recover v. i. निरोगी होणे, तवाना होणे, बरा होणे, आरोग्य पावणे, (invers.) आराम होणे.

red *a.* तांबडा, लाल, आरक्त, भडक, रक्त.

reduce *v. t.* कमी करणे, संक्षेप करणे, उतरणे. (२) करणे. उ. Reduce twenty rupees to annas, वीस रुपयांचे आणे कर. — to reduce to subjection, वश्य-स्वाधीन-हस्तगत करणे. — to be reduced, रोडका -शुष्क-लंग होणे, भटणे, कमी होणे, उतरणे.

refer *v. t.* लावणे, सोपणे, पुसायाला सांगणे, पाहायाला-जायाला सां- गणे. उ. He referred me to that man, त्याने त्या माणसाला पुसावयास मला सांगितलें. — He referred me to the Bible, त्याने देवाच्या शास्त्रांत पाहावयास मला सांगितलें.

refer *v. i.* लागणे, लागू असणे, विषयीं असणे. (२)-कडे लक्ष देणे, पाहणे, जाणे, येणे, पुसणे, विचारणे.

reference *n.* लागणे *n* संबंध *m.* अनुसंधान *n.* (२) प्रश्न *m.* स- वाल *m.* — to have reference to, ला- गणे, लागू-लागी असणे,-च्या संबंधी असणे, विषयीं असणे. — to make a reference, (re- fer *v. i.* (२) पाहा). — in reference to, विषयीं.

reflect *v. i.* विचार करणे, चिंतणे, मनन-ध्यान करणे, कल्पिणे. (२) परावृत्त होणे, परावर्तन पावणे,

फिरून येणे, (उजेड, किरण इ.)

reflect *v. t.* प्रतिबिंबित करणे, प्रति- बिंब करणे, परावृत्त करणे, (उ- जेड), (*invers.*) प्रतिबिंब होणे -उठणे, परावृत्त होणे. — to be reflected, प्रतिबिंबित होणे, प्रतिबिंब होणे-उठणे, परा- वृत्त होणे, परावर्तन पावणे.

refuse *v. t.* न देणे, नाकबूल होणे, नाकारणे, मान्य नसणे, नाहीं म्हणणे.

regard *v. t.* मानणे, गणणे, सम- जणे, मोजणे, लेखणे, (*invers.*) वाटणे. (२) पाहणे, लक्ष देणे, ऐकणे. (३) लागणे, लानू-लागी असणे.

regard *n.* मान *m.* भीड *f.* प्रीति *f.* नजर *f.* लक्ष *n.* सत्कार *m.* मर्यादा *f.* — in regard to, विषयीं. — to have regard (for) प्रीति -मान करणे, चिंता करणे, मान्य असणे, अभिमान धरणे.

regret *n.* अनुताप *m.* पस्तावा *m.* पश्चात्ताप *m.*

regret *v. i. t.* पश्चात्ताप-पस्तावा -अनुताप करणे, (*invers.*) पश्चा- त्ताप होणे.

regular *a.* नियमाचा, नियमी, बरो- बर, ठीक, यथाक्रम.

regularly *ad.* नेहमी, यथाक्रम, यथानुक्रमें, यथाक्रमाने, क्रमशः अनुक्रमाने, यथायोग्य.

relate *v. t.* निवेदन करणे, सांगणे, कथणे, हकिकत करणे, निरूपिणे.

relate v. i. लागणे, लागू-लागी असणे, संबंधी-विषयीं असणे.

related a. आप्त, नातलग, लगत, गोत्री, गोत्रज, वंशीय. (२) लागी, संबंधी.

relation n. आप्त, नातलग, नातेदार m. f. नातें n. गोत्रज, गोत्र n. सोयरीक f. (२) संबंध m. लाग m. लागीपण n. (३) हकिकत f. कथा f. निवेदन n. निरूपण n.

— in relation to विषयीं.

— to have relation to, लागणे, (invers.) संबंध असणे.

relief n. समाधान n. चैन n. सुख n. आराम m. साह्य n. मदत f. शांति f. विश्रांति f. उपशम m. फुरसत f. (२) बदली f. m. बदल्या m.

relieve v. t. समाधान-शांति करणे, साह्य-मदत करणे, (invers.) चैन-सुख पडणे, आराम पडणे, बरें वाटणे. (२) बदली करणे.

religion n. धर्म m. देवभक्ति f.

religious a. धर्मशील, धार्मिक, भक्त.

relish n. रुचि f. चव f. भावड f. चट f. शोक m.

relish v. i. रुचणे, भावडणे, गोड लागणे, मानवणे.

relish v. t. (invers.) रुचणे, इ.

rely (on) v. i. विश्वासणे, टेंकणे, अवलंब-आश्रय करणे-धरणे, पदर धरणे, आशा-भरवसा धरणे.

remain v. i. राहणे, उरणे, शेष-बाकी असणे, वांचणे. (२) नांदणे, राहणे, मुक्काम-वसति करणे, वसणे, टिकणे, स्थिरावणे.

remainder n. बाकी f. शेष n. उरलेला, शिलक f.

remark n. बोल m. बोलणें n. वचन n. वाक्य n.

remark v. t. बोलणे, सांगणे. (२) पाहणे, लक्ष देणे.

remarkable a. विलक्षण, विशिष्ट, चमत्कारिक, अपूर्व, असाधारण, विशेष, विचित्र.

remember v. t. अठवणे, स्मरणे, अठवण-स्मरण धरणे-करणे, ध्यानांत धरणे, सई-याद करणे, (invers.) मनांत राहणे-असणे, स्मरण-अठवण-सई-याद राहणे-असणे, स्मरण पडणे.

repay v. t. फेडणे, परत देणे, देणे, उतराई होणे.

repeat v. t. घोकणे, फिरून सांगणे, सांगणे, कथणे, झणणे, जप करणे. (२) फिरून करणे, उलटून-परतून करणे, पौनःपुन्य करणे.

reply n. उत्तर n. जवाब m. जाव m. प्रस्युत्तर n.

— in reply, उत्तरें करून, उत्तर देऊन.

reply v. t. i. उत्तर-जवाब-जाव देणे, बोलणे, उलटून बोलणे.

report n. वर्तमान n. खबर f. अवई f. बातमी f. गप f. वदंता f. गोष्ट f. (२) याद f.

report v. t. वर्तमान-खबर सांगणे, जाहेर-प्रसिद्ध करणे, सांगणे.

reproof n. निषेध m. बोध m. बोल m.

reprove v. t. निषेधणे, निषेध-बोध करणे, धमकावणे.

require v. t. हुकूम देणे, मागणे, सांगणे. (२) (invers.) गरज -जरूर-दरकार असणे, पाहिजे, लागणे.

resemble v. t. सारखा असणे, मि-ळणे, (invers.) मेळ असणे.

resign v. t. सोडून देणे, त्यागणे, त्याग करणे, देणे, सोडणे, सोपणे, निरविणे.
— to be resigned, राजी-रजू असणे.

resolve v. i. निश्चय करणे-धरणे.
—to be resolved, निश्चित होणे, निश्चय धरणे, (invers.) निश्चय असणे.

resolute a. धैर्यवान, दमदार, मर्दा, हिमती, शूर, धीर, धीट.

respect n. बहुमान m. आदर m. सन्मान m. सत्कार m. मान m. भीड f. मर्यादा f.
— in other respects, दुसऱ्या गोष्टींविषयीं.
— in this respect, ह्या गोष्टी-विषयीं.
— in respect to, विषयीं.

respect v. t. सन्मान दाखवणे, मानणे, आदर-सत्कार-सन्मान -मान करणे. (२) लागणे, सं-बंधी असणे.

respectable a. मान्य, हुरमती, भला, सन्मानित, प्रतिष्ठित, स-

-न्मान करण्याजोगा, पतिचा, आब्रूदार, संभावित, मातबर.

respected a. & p. p. भला, प्रति-ष्ठित, सन्मानित.

respite n. अंतर n. अवकाश m. फुरसत f. सुटी f. अवधि m. उपशम m. आराम m.

rest n. विसांवा m. विश्रांति f. विश्राम m. दम m. चैन n. शांति f. स्वस्थता f. (२) आधार m. आश्रय m. टेकाव m नेटावा m. (३) बाकी f. उर f. दुसरा, वरकड, उरलेला, राहिलेला, अभ्यं-तर.
— to find rest, शांति-समा-धान पावणे, शांत होणे, (invers.) चैन पडणे.
— to put to rest, शांत करणे, निजविणे. (२) संशय फेडणे.
— to be at rest, शांत-निश्चित असणे.

rest v. i. विसावा घेणे, स्वस्थ राहणे, विरमणे, थांबणे, टेकणे, बसणे, राहणे, असणे.
— to rest assured, खातरी धरणे, निश्चययुक्त होणे, (invers.) शंका-संशय नसणे.

rest v. t. विसावा देणे, टेकणे, ठेवणे.

restrain v. t. अटकावणे, धरणे, दबावणे, आकळणे, आवरणे, आवरण-निरोध करणे, बांधणे, कोंडणे.

return n. परतणें n. माघारें येणें n. परत येणें n. पुनरागमन n. (२) मिळकत f. फळ n. उसने-

10

वाण *n.* प्रतिदान *n.* उलटें *n.*
प्रतिफळ *n.* देणगी *f.* प्रतिक्रिया *f.*
— in return, माघारा, माघारें,
पुनः, उलटें, उलटून.

return *v. i.* परतणे, जाऊन येणे,
परत येणे-जाणे, माघारें येणे-जाणे,
फिरून येणे-जाणे, उलटून येणे
जाणे.

return *v. t.* परत देणे, माघारा
देणे, परतणे, परत पाठविणे, उल-
टून देणे, माघारें लावणे.

revenge *n.* सूड *m.*

revenge *v. t.* सूड घेणे-उगविणे,
उसने घेणे.

reverence *n.* सन्मान *m.* भीड *f.*
मान *m.* आदर *m.* सत्कार *m.*
नमस्कार *m.*

reverence *v. i.* भीड धरणे, स-
न्मान-मान-सत्कार करणे, मान-
णे.

reward *n.* प्रतिफळ *n.* फळ *n.* प्रति-
दान *n.* प्रतिक्रिया *f.* मिळकत *f.*
दान *n.* बक्षीस *f.* प्राप्ति *f.*

reward *v. t.* प्रतिफळ देणे, फळ
देणे, दान-बक्षीस-पैसे देणे (कांही
करण्याबदल).

rhinoceros *n.* गेंडा *m.*

rice *n.* भात *m. n.* तांदूळ *m.* साळ *f.*

rich *a.* द्रव्यवान, पैकेवान, पैकेपूर,
धनवान, दौलतदार, संपत्तिमान,
मातबर, भाळ्या. (२) संपन्न. (३)
खातवट, पिकाऊ, (जमीन, इ.)

riches *n. pl.* द्रव्य *n.* धन *n.* दौलत
f. संपत्ति *f.* लक्ष्मी *f.* माल *m.*
मालमत्ता *f.* मत्ता *f.*

rid *a.* मोकळा, सुटका, सुटा.
— to get rid of, टाकून देणे,
मोकळा-सुटा होणे, सुटका होणे,
(*invers.*) जाणे.

rid *v. t.* निवारणे, टाळणे, निवा-
रण करणे, मोकळा-सुटा करणे,
टाकून देणे.

ride *n.* फेर *m.* फेरी *f.* (घोड्या-
वर, गाडींत, इ.) स्वारी होऊन
जाण्याची खेप *f.* बसून जाण्याची
खेप *f.*

ride *v. t. i* बसून जाणे-येणे, स्वारी
होऊन जाणे-येणे, आरूढ होऊन
जाणे.

right *n.* अधिकार *m.* सत्ता *f.*
मुखत्यारी *f.* इलाखा *m.* मान
m. हक्क *m. n.* (२) न्याय *m.*
इनसाफ *m.* दाद *f.* नीति *f.*
नीतिमत्त्व *m.*
— to put to rights, नीट कर-
णे, निटावणे, सुधारणे.

right *a.* बरोबर, योग्य, नीट, ठीक,
यथार्थिक, यथायोग्य, उचित, उजू,
यथास्थित, ठीकठाक, वाजवी,
युक्त. (२) उजवा, दक्षिण.

right *v. t.* नीट करणे, निटावणे,
सुधारणे.

right *v. i.* नीट होणे, निटावणे.

right *ad.*-च, अचानक, लागलाच
तेव्हांच, नेमका. उ. He went
right away *or* off, तो लागलाच
गेला. — Go right off now,
आतांच जा. — right before
the house, घराच्या समोरच.
— By this road you will go

right to Poona, या मार्गानें अचानक पुण्यास जासील.

ring *n.* कडें *f.* तोंडा *m.* अंगठी *f.* नथ *f.* वेढा *m.* वेढें *n.* चक्र *n.* वर्तुळ्याकार *m.* कौडबुलें *n.*
— to sit-stand in a ring, घेरा घालून बसणें–उभे राहणें.

ring *v. t.* वाजविणें.

ring *v. i.* वाजणें, घुमणें, झणझणणें, झणाणणें, ठणठणणें, ठणाणणें.

rip *n.* उसवणें *n.* फाट *m.*

rip *v. t.* उसवणे, विदारणे, फाडणे, विदारण करणे, विदारित करणे.

rip *v. i.* उसवणे, फाटणे.

ripe *a.* पका, पिकलेला, परिपक्का, तयार, सिद्ध.
— to become ripe, पिकणें.
— not ripe, कचा, हिरवा, अ-पक्व.

ripen *v. i.* पिकणे.

ripen *v. t.* पिकविणे.

rise *n.* उगम *m.* उत्पत्ति *f.* उद्भव *m.* मूळ *n.* (२) चढती *f.* चढ *m.* वृद्धि *f.* तेजी *f.*
— to give rise to, उपजविणे, उत्पन्न करणे, (*invers.*) उत्पन्न होणे, होणे, उपजणे.

rise *v. i.* उगवणे, उठणे, उभा होणे, चढणे, वाढणे, वर येणे–जाणे, निघणे, होणे, उत्पन्न होणे, सुटणे (वारा).

rite *n.* विधि *m.* संस्कार *m.* धर्म-कृत्य *n.* क्रिया *f.* रीति *f.*

ritual *a.* क्रियांसंबंधी, रीतिसंबंधी.

river *n.* नदी *f.* सरिता *f.* ओढा *m.*

road *n.* मार्ग *m.* रस्ता *m.* वाट *f.* पंथा *m.* सडक *f.*

roadside *n.* रस्त्याची बाजू *f.*

roast *v. t. i.* भाजणे.

rob *v. t.* लुटणे, लुबाडणे, लुगारणे, झांबवणे.

robber *n.* लुटारी *m.* लुटारू *m.* वाटपाडू *m.* वाटपाड्या *m.* लुगारू *m.*

robbery *n.* लुटणें *n.* लुंठण *n.* चोरी *f.*

Robert *n. p.* पुरुषाचें नांव.

robin *n.* एका जातीचें पांखरूं. मैना *f.* साळुंकी *f.*

Robinet *n. p.* पुरुषाचें नांव.

rock *n.* दगड *m.* खडक *m.* पाषाण *m.* कातळ *m, n.*

rock *v. t.* हालविणे, डोलविणे.

rock *v. i.* डुलणे, डोलणे, डळ-मळणे, उगागणे, उगणे, उग-मगणे, लडबडणे, हलणे, डुलणे.

rod *n.* छडी *f.* छिपटी *f.* काठी *f.* दंड *m.* गज *m.* (२) एक लां-बीचें माप, सुमारें १२ हात.

rode *pret.* of ride.

Roger *n. p.* पुरुषाचें नांव.

rogue *n.* ठकबाज *m.* ठक *m.* ठग *m.* दगलबाज *m.* सोदा *m.* गु-लाम *m.*

rogueish *a.* ठकवरा, ठकडा, ठ-काड, दगाबाज, ख्याली.

roguery *n.* दगाबाजी *f.* ठक-बाजी *f.* दगलबाजी *f.* सोदेगि-री *f.*

roll *n.* वळकटी *f.* वळी *f.* वळकटी

f. गुंडाळा m. गुंडाळी f. मुरळी
f. विंडा m. (२) पट m. याद f.
नावनिशी f.

roll v. i. लोटणे, उळमळणे, हेल-
कावणे, फिरणे, जुलणे, उळमळ-
णे, लोळणे, गडबडणे.

roll v. t. लोटणे, फिरविणे, डोल-
विणे, लाटणे.

— to roll up, गुंडाळणे, वळ-
कटी करणे, गुंडाळ्य करणे.

— to roll out, लाटणे.

roller n. लाटणी f. लाट f. लाव्या m.

Roman n. p. एका लोकांचें नांव.

romp n. खिदळणारी f. धांगड f.
धांगडधिंगा f.

romp v. i. ख्याल करणें, खिदळणें.

romping n. धांगडणें n. धांगड-
धिंगा m. दांडगाई f.

romping a. खिदळणारी, दांडगी,
धांगड.

roof n. छावणी f. छप्पर n. धाबें n.
छत n. कौलार n.

— roof of the mouth, टाळू f.

room n. खोली f. कोठडी f.
खाना m. (२) जागा f. ठिकाण
n. अवकाश m.

— in the room of, ठिकाणीं,
बदल, बदलीं.

root n. मूळ n. मूळ n. मुळी f. पाळ
n. पाळक n.

root (up) v. t. उपटणे, उपडणे,
काढणे.

rope n. दोर m. चऱ्हांट n. सेल f.
दोरी f. रस्सी f. सउक f

Rose n. p. स्त्रीचें नांव.

rose n. गुलाबाचें फूल n. गुलाब m.

rose pret. of rise.

rot v i. कुजणे, सडणे, नासणे,
कुजून जाणे.

rot v. t. कुजविणे, नासणे, सडविणे.

rough a. खरखरीत, खरखरीत,
खरबडीत, खचरट, उखरखरा-
खर, गुलगुलीत नाहीं, साफ
नाहीं, बरोबर नाहीं. (२) कठोर,
कर्कश. (३) लहरींचा, वाद-
ळाचा.

— a rough sketch or draught,
खरडा m. मसुदा m.

round a. वाटोळा, वर्तुलाकार, मुस-
ळाकार गोळ्याकार, गोल.

round ad. आसपास, आजूबाजूस,
इकडे तिकडे, चहुंकडे, सभोवता,
सभोवतील. उ. I looked all
round, म्या सर्वा ठिकाणीं-इकडे
तिकडे-चहुंकडे-सभोवतें पाहिलें.
He ran all round, तो इकडे
तिकडे-चहुंकडे फिरला-धांवला.
—round about, चहुंकडे, इकडे
तिकडे, आजूबाजूस, सभोवतें,
समंतप्रत. उ. He went round
about (in) the room, तो खो-
लींत-इकडेतिकडे-चहुंकडे फिर-
ला, or तो खोलींत फिरला.
The people stood round a-
bout him, त्याच्या सभोवते लोक
उभे राहिले. — The villages
round, सभोवतील गांवें.
(२) फिरून, मुरडून, मागें, पाठी
मागें, माघारें, उलटून. उ. —
to look round, मुरडून पाहणे,

पाठीमागें -मागें -माघारें पाहणे, फिरून -परतून -उलटून पाहणे, मुरडून पाहणे.

— to turn round v. i. फिरणे, परतणे, मुरडणे, उलटून जाणे, उलटणे. (२) v. t. फिरविणे.

(३) गरगर, गरगरां. उ. — to turn round v. i. गरगर करणे, फिरणे, गरगरणे, गरगरां फिरणे. (२) v. t. गरगरां फिरविणे.

—to whirl round v. i. फिरणे (वेगानें), भ्रमणे, भ्रम-भ्रमण करणे. (२) v. t. फिरविणे, भ्रमविणे, गरगरां फिरविणे.

— to revolve round v. i. फिरणे, भ्रमणे, भ्रम-भ्रमण-फेरा करणे, लोटत जाणे.

— round and round, गरगर.

(४) सर्व. उ. The class read round twice, सर्व वर्गानें दोन वेळां वाचलें, or वर्गानें पाळी पाळीनें दोनवेळां वाचलें.

(५) लांबच्या वाटेनें, जवळच्या वाटेनें नाहीं, तिरपा, वांकडा, चक्र मा- रून. उ. You came round, तुझी जवळच्या वाटेनें आलां नाहीं or तुझी लांबच्या वाटेनें आलां. I came round through Poona, मी पुण्यावरून लांबच्या वाटेनें आलों. Go round, तिर- प्या-वांकड्या वाटेनें जा, चक्र मा- रून-प्रदक्षिणा घालून जा.

— The year round, बारमास, बारा महिने.

round prep. भोंवतें, भोंवता, सभो- वर्तें. उ. — to go round (a tree -house, &c.)-च्या सभोंवर्तें जाणे -फिरणे -हिंडणे, -ला प्रदक्षिणा करणे-घालणे,-ला फेरा करणे -घालणे.

(२) — to tie, wrap, bind round, गुंडाळणे, बांधणे, वेष्टणे. A man came with a rope round his neck, मानेला दोरी बांध- लेला एक माणूस आला. He had a bandage round his foot, त्याच्या पायाला पट्टी गुंडाळली होती.

(३) तिरपा, आडवा. उ. Go round that horse and drive him this way, त्या घोड्याला आडवा जाऊन इकडे हाकून लाव. Go round him, त्याला तिरपा जा.

round n. फेरी f. पाळी f. गस्त f. आवृत्ति f. खेप f. फिरणें उ. — round of the seasons, ऋतूंचें फिरणें.

— to go a round, फेरी-गस्त घालणे, एक खेप करणे.

— The soldiers fired three rounds, शिपायानी तीन वेळां बंदूक सोडली, — or शिपायानी बंदुकी सोडण्याच्या तीन आवृत्ति केल्या.

— They have but one round of cartridges, एकएकापासीं एक एक तीठा मात्र आहे.

round v. t. वर्तुळ-वाटोळा करणे.

rounding *a.* वर्तुळाकार, वाटोळा, गोळ्याकार.

rouse *v. t.* चेतावणे, उत्तेजन करणे, प्रेरणे, सावध करणे, जागा करणे, उठविणे.

rouse *v. i.* उठणे, जागा-सावध -उत्तेजित होणे.

rub *v. t. i.* घांसणे, घर्षणे, पुसणे, खलणे, मळणे, चोळणे, उटणे, रगडणे, लागणे.

ruddy *a.* तांबडा, तांबूस, तुकतु-कीचा, तुकतुकीत, भारक्त.

rude *a.* उद्धत, दांडगा, बेठाक, खलेल, लांठ. (२) हेंगडा, अ-नाडी.

ruin *n.* नाश *m.* हानि *f.* क्षय *m.* खराबी *f.* अनर्थ *m.*

— ruins *pl.* खिंडार *n.* ढीग *m.* दिगार *m.*

— in ruins, ओसाढ, ओस, नाश झालेला.

ruin *v. t.* नासणे, नाश करणे, नासवणे, बिघडविणे, दवडणे, खराब करणे, भंग करणे, (*in- vers.*) नाश होणे, भंग होणे.

ruin *v. i.* नाश होणे, खराब होणे, बिघडणे, भ्रष्ट होणे.

— to be ruined, (ruin *v. i.* पाहा).

rule *n.* विधि *m.* रीति *f.* नेम *m.* कानू *f.* कायदा *m.* मार्ग *m.* प्रमाण *n.* (२) राज्य *n.* हुक-मत *f.* अमल *m.* अधिकार *m.* सत्ता *f.* (३) रेखाटणी *f.*

rule *v. t.* राज्य करणे, अधिकार

-सत्ता-अमल करणे. (२) भाव-रणे, आटोपणे, दाबणे, दबावणे. (३) रेखाटणे, भंकणे.

run *n.* धावण *f.* धावणे *n.* धूम *f.* दवड *f.*

run *v. i.* पळणे, धावणे, धूम मारणे. (२) वाहणे (पाणी), गळणे, निघणे, (अस्तूं). (३) चालणे (घड्याळ), पसरणे, गुज्जरणे, जाणे, (वेळ).

— to run a race, दौड मारणे, धूम मारणे.

— to run off *or* away, निघून पळणे, पळणे, पळून जाणे.

— to run over (water &c.), सांडणे, उचंबळणे.

— to run up, पळत चढणे, व-रतें लवकर जाणे-येणे, वर चालणे (झणी), वाढणे.

— to run down, खालीं चालणे -जाणे, खालीं लवकर जाणे-येणे, खालीं पळणे.

run *v. t.* दवडणे, धावडणे, पिटविणे, पळविणे, (घोड्याला, इ.)

(२) — to run down, पाठलाग करून धरणे, पाठींस लागणे, (पारधीच्या, भिकारीच्या, इ.)

(३) — to run in *or* through, रोवणे, खोचणे, पार पाडणे, भारफार करणे.

rush *n.* दौड *f.* धूम *f.* (वेगाने) रगडा *m.* झपाटा *m.*

rush *v. i.* वेगाने धावणे, रगडून जाणे, रगडणे.

rust n. तांब f. कळंक m. जंग m. मळ m.

rust v. i. कळंकणे, जंगणे, मळीण होणे, (invers.) जंग-तांब चढणे.

S.

Sabbath n. आदित्यवार m. शाबाथ दिवस m.

sacred a. पवित्र.

— sacred book, धर्मपुस्तक.

sacrifice n. यज्ञ m. होम m. पशुयज्ञ m. याग m. यज्ञपशु m.

sacrifice v. t वधणे, यज्ञ करणे. (२) टाकणे, सोडणे, देणे.

sad a. रडका, दिलगीर, उदास, दुःखित, दुर्क्षित्त, रड्या, अभागी.

— sad state or condition, हाल m. दुर्दशा f. विपत्ति f. हलाकी f.

sadly ad. दुःखाने, दिलगिरीने. (२) फार.

safe a. सुरक्षित, निर्भय, बिनधोक, निरुपद्रव, शाबूत, सुदामत, भधोक, निर्धोक.

safely ad. सुदामत, सुरक्षित, निर्धोक, निर्भय, सलामत.

said pret. & p. p. of say.

sail n. शीड m. अवजार n. (२) गलबत n. तारूं n. जाहाज n.

— to set sail, हाकारणे.

sail v. i. हाकारणे, हाकारून चालणे, पाण्यावर चालणे, वाहणे

sailor n. खलाशी m. सफरी m. नावाडी m. दर्यावर्दी m.

saint n. साधू m. संत m. भक्त m.

sake n. कारण n. हेतु m.

— for the sake of, साठीं, करितां. उ. — for the sake of money, पैक्यासाठीं. —for your sake, तुजकरितां. — for my sake, मजकरितां.

— namesake, नावाचा.

salt n. मीठ n. निमक m. खार m. लवण n. (२) धार m.

salt a. खारट, खारा, धार.

salt v. t. मीठ घालणे, खारट करणे.

same a. तोच, तीच, तेंच, एकच, एकसारिखा, सम.

— same... as, जसा··· तसा, जो···तो, दाखल.

sand n. वाळू f. रेति f.

San Salvador n. p बेटाचें नांव.

Sarah n. p. स्त्रीचें नांव.

sat pret. of sit.

satchel n. रुमाल m. पिशवी f. दफ्तर n. थैली f.

satisfy v. t. खातरी करणे, खातरीस आणणे, समजविणे, निशा करणे, संशय फेडणे. (२) पुरविणे, तृप्त करणे, पुरेंसें करणे, (invers.) पुरणे, पुरें असणे.

— to be satisfied, (invers.) खातरीस येणे. (२) तृप्त होणे, खुश-संतुष्ट होणे.

sauce n. बोळें n. कोरडेव्यास, कालवण n. तोंडीलावणें n.

saucer n. एका प्रकारचें तबक, बासन.

saucily ad. बेजबाब, अमर्याद.

saucy a. वेलणारी, उद्धत, उनाड, दांडगा, उद्दत, अमर्याद.

save v. t. तारणे, उद्धारणे, राखणे, तारण-उद्धार करणे, वांचविणे, छोडविणे, जर करणे-पाडणे, (in-vers) तारण-उद्धार होणे. (२) न खर्चणे, ठेवणे, राखणे, संभा-ळणे, वांचविणे.

saw n. करवत m. भरकस n.

saw v. t. करवतणे, भरकसणे, कापणे, चिरणे, (करवताने)

saw pret. of see.

say v. t. बोलणे, ह्मणणे, सांगणे.

scale n. खवल n. खवली f. खपला m. खपली f. उखरवळी f. पोपडा m. पापुदरा m. (२) मान n. (३) pl. तागडी f. तुला f. तराजू f. कांटा m.

scale (off) v. t. पापुदरा-पोपडा काढणे. (२) v. i. पापुदरा -पोपडा-उखरवळी निघणे.

scar n. वण m. किण m. डाग m.

scar v t. वण-डाग पाडणे.

scarred a. p. p. वण-डाग पाडलेला.

scarce a. अलभ्य, दर्मील, विरळा, कमी, थोडा, माहागाईचा, दुर्लभ.

scarce ad. (scarcely पाहा).

scarcely ad. श्रमाने, जुलमाने, कठीणपणाने. उ. I could scarcely speak, मी श्रमाने बोललों.

(२) फारकरून ··· नाहीं. उ. There is scarcely any fruit on the tree, झाडावर फारक-रून फळ नाहीं. There is

scarcely so much there, इतकें तेथें फारकरून नसेल. I had scarcely reached there when, &c. मी तेथें पहोंचलों नव्हतों इतक्यांत इ.

Scarlet n. किरमीज n. कृमि m.

scarlet a. किरमिजी, लाल.

scatter v. t. विसकळणे, विकिरणे, विखरणे, उडविणे, उधळणे, दाणा-दाण करणे, पसरणे.

scatter v. i. पसरणे, फांकणे, दाणा-दाण होणे, विसकळ होणे, चहुंकडे उडणे-जाणे.

scattered a. & p. p. विसकळीत, विकीर्ण, पसरलेले, फांकलेले.

scheme n. उपाय m. बेत m. मन-सुबा m. युक्ति f. तोड f. मसलत f (२) लचांड m.

scholar n. विद्यार्थी m. शाळेंतील मूल n. शिकणारा m. शिष्य m. चेला m. (२) अभ्यासी, जाणता, विद्यासंपन्न, विद्वान, ज्ञानी, शा-स्त्रज्ञ.

school n. शाला f. साळ f.

school v. t. शाळेंत पाठवीत असणे, शिक्षा देणे.

schoolfellow n. शाळेंतील सोबती m. साळगडी m. खेळगडी m.

schoolmistress n. शालेची शिक-विणारीण f.

school room n. शाला f.

scold v. t. i. खरकावणे, दटावणे, कांशा भरऊणे, धमकावणे, दाम-टणे, तडकावणे.

scold *n.* दटावणारीण *f.* कृत्या *f.* कैदाशीण *f.*

scolding *n.* धमकावणें *n.* खरडी *f.*

scowl *n.* अठी *f.* अढी *f.*

scowl *v. i.* अठी घालणें, डोळे उगा-रणें.

scramble *n.* तडकाफडकी *f.*

scramble *v. i.* मिठी करणें, जउ घालणें, तडकाफडकी करणें, (*invers.*) झड पडणें.

— to scramble up (a tree hill &c.) चढणें, वेंघणें, (लवकर).

— to scramble down (a tree &c.), लवकर उतरणें.

scrape *v. t.* खरवडणें, घासणें, छिलणें, तासणें, झाजरणें, खरडणें.

— to scrape together, खळ-वटणें, जमा-गोळा करणें, जोडणें, जथणें.

scratch *n.* ओरखडा *m.*

scratch *v. t.* ओरखडणें, खाजवणें, उकरणें.

scream *n.* भारोळी *f.* किंकळी *f.* किंक *f.*

scream *v. i.* किंकळणें, भारोळी मारणें, ओरडणें, किंकळ्या फोडणें.

scripture *n* लेख *m.* पवित्र लेख *m.*

— scriptures *pl.* ख्रिस्ती शास्त्र *n.* पवित्र लेख *m.*

sea *n.* समुद्र *m.* दर्या *f.* सागर *m.* अब्धि *m.*

— to go to sea, समुद्रप्रवासास जाणें, समुद्रांत हाकारणें.

— to take to sea, घेऊन समुद्र-प्रवासास जाणें.

seam *n.* शिवण *n.* लोड *n. m.* सांधा *m.*

search *n.* शोध *m.* तपास *m.* तलास *m.* चौकसी *f.*

— to make search, शोधणें, धुंडाळणें, खळवटणें, ठिकाण लावणें.

— in search of, शोध करून, शोध करायास.

search *v. t.* शोधणें, शोध करणें-लावणें-घेणें, टुंडणें, हेरणें, खळव-टणें.

season *n.* काळ *m.* ऋतु *m.* वेळ *f.* प्रसंग *m.* समय *m.* दिवस *m.* सुगी *f.* हंगाम *m.* मोसम *f.* — in season, वेळेवारीं, योग्य वेळेस, यथाकाळीं, सुकाळीं.

season *v. i.* वाळणें, पक्का-पीक्का-सुका होणें, (लांकूड), निरवणें, मळगावणें, (*invers.*) सराव होणें.

season *v. t.* वाळवणें, सुकविणें (लांकूड), निर्दंवणें. (२) मीठ-मसाला घालणें.

seasoned *a. & p. p.* सराव झालेला, निरवलेला. (२) मीठ-मसाला घातलेला.

— highly seasoned food, मि-ष्टान्न.

seasoning *n.* मसाला *m.* कालवण *n.* (२) सराव *m.* अभ्यास *m.* निरवणें *n.*

seat *n.* बैठक *f.* आसन *n.* बसक *n.* बसकर *n.*

— to take a seat, बसणे, आ-सीन होणे.

seat v. t. बसविणे, बसूं देणे.

— to seat one's self, or to be seated, बसणे.

second a. दुसरा, द्वितीय, दुजा, अन्य.

second v. एका मिनटाचा साठवा अंश. (२) क्षण m. पळ n. विपळ n.

secret a. गुप्त, अंतस्थ, खोल, गूढ. गौप्य, चोर (in comp.), चोरटा,

secret n. रहस्य n. गूज n. मर्म n. टूक f.

— in secret, एकांती.

secretary n. चिटनीस m. लेखक m. कारकून m. (२) एका प्रकारचें मेज.

see v. t. i. पाहणे, बघणे, विलोकणे, अवलोकणे, (inters.) दिसणे, दृष्टीस पडणे. (२) समजणे.

seed n. बी f. बीज n.

seem v. i. वाटणे, दिसणे, भासणे, लागणे, मनांत-लक्षांत येणे.

seen p. p. of see.

— to be seen, दिसणे, दृष्टीस पडणे.

seize v. t. धरणे, घेणे, हिसकणे, हिसकावणे, घेरणे, पकडणे, छिनावणे.

seldom ad. क्वचित, विरळा, एखादा.

select a. निवडक, चांगला, निवडलेला, परिगणित, वेंचक.

select v. t. निवडणे, निवडून घेणे, काढून घेणे, वेंचणे.

self n. स्व, स्वतः, स्वयें, आपण, बातीनें,-च.

— one's self, आपण.

selfish a. स्वार्थी, स्वार्थपर, आप-मतलबी, आपलपोटाच्या, सहित पाहणारा.

self-schooling n. स्वशिक्षा f.

sell v. t. विकत देणे, विकणे, फरोक्त करणे, विकून टाकणे.

sell v. i. खपणे, विकणे, पटणे, विकत जाणे, (invers.) विकरी होणे-असणे.

semicolon n. लिहिण्यांत ही खूण (;) (अवसान दाखविती.)

send v. t. पाठविणे, धाडणे, जाऊं देणे, पोहंचविणे, पोहंचता करणे, फेंकणे, टाकणे.

— to send away, रवाना करणे, निरोप देणे, जाऊं देणे.

— to send for, बोलावणे, मागणे, आणायाला धाडणे.

sense n. इंद्रिय n. व. — sense of touch, स्पर्शेंद्रिय. — sense of smell, घ्राण, घ्राणेंद्रिय. — sense of hearing, श्रोत्रेंद्रिय. — sense of seeing, नेत्रेंद्रिय, चक्षुरिंद्रिय. — sense of taste, जिव्हेंद्रिय, रसनेंद्रिय. — the senses, इंद्रियग्राम m. (२) बुद्धि f. ज्ञान n. समज f. m. प्राहकता f. अक्कल f.

sensible a. समजदार, समंजस, अकलवंत, हुशार, जाणता, सूज्ञ, प्राज्ञ, बुद्धिवान. (२) चेतन,

देहभानयुक्त. (२) समजण्याजोगा, लक्षांत येण्याजोगा.

sensibly *ad.* समजण्याजोगें, स्पष्ट, हुशारीने, ज्ञानाने, चांगलें, तर्कानें.

sent *pret. & p. p. of* send.

serious *a.* गंभीर, भरकूम, हास्यमुख नाहीं, विचारवंत. (२) ठट्टेचा नाहीं, खरा. (३) भारी, इलका नाहीं, मोठा, फार.

servant *n.* चाकर *m.* सेवक *m.* दास *m.* नौकर *m.* भृत्य *m.* गडी *m.* खिदमतगार *m.*

serve *v. t.* चाकरी करणे, सेवा करणे, सेवणे, मानणे, चाकरीस राहणे. (२) वरें करणे, साह्य करणे. (३) वाढणे, वांटणे.

serve *v. i.* चाकर असणे. (२) उपयोगी-कामास पडणे, पुरणे, निभाव करणे, बरें लागणे, वसणे, मिळणे, जमणे, होणे, चालणे.

service *n.* चाकरी *f.* खिदमत *f.* काम *n.* उद्योग *m.* धंदा *m.* सेवा *f.*

set *v. t.* ठेवणे, लावणे, घालणे, स्थापणे, नेमणे, बसविणे, जडणे, देणे, नीट करणे (हाड).

— to set on fire, पेटविणे, विस्तू-आग लावणे.

— to set up, स्थापणे, घालणे, मांडणे.

— to set down, मांडणे. (२) खालीं ठेवणे, खालों बसविणे.

— to set out (trees &c.) लावणे, रोवणे.

— to set in order, बरोबर

ठेवणे-मांडणे, ठाकठीक ठेवणे, बंदोवस्त करणे, निटावणे.

— to set free, मोकळा करणे, सोडणे, सुटका करणे.

— to set off *or* out, साजणे, शोभणे.

set *v. i.* मावळणे, अस्त होणे. (२) — to set out, forward, *or* off, निघून जाणे, चालटणे, निघणे.

— to set in, लागणे, उठणे, होणे.

set *pret. & p. p. of* set.

set *a.* नेमलेला, ठरविलेला. (२) निश्चयाचा, निश्चित.

set *n.* जोड *m.* प्रत *f.* जोडी *f.*

setting *n.* अस्त *m. n.*

settle *v. t.* ठरविणे, तोडणे, पार करणे, (कज्जा, इ.) नेमणे, जमविणे, मिटविणे, फेडणे, चुकविणे, (हिशोब, खटला, कज्जा, लचांड, इ.). (२) वस्ती करणे, वसाहत करणे, (देश).

— to be settled, वसणे (देश, गांव, इ.). (२) चुकणे, तुटणे, जमणे, मिटणे, फिटणे, (हिशोब, खटला, कज्जा, इ.).

settle *v. i.* बसणे, पडणे, उतरणे.

settled *a.* चुकता. (२) आबाद, आबादान. (३) ठरविलेला, स्थापित, स्थिर, निश्चित, निश्चयाचा, नेमलेला, कायेम.

seven *a.* सात, सर्तें. उ. Seven times seven are forty nine, सात सर्तें एकूणपन्नास.

seventh *a.* सातवा.

seventy *a.* सत्तर.

several *a.* कित्येक, कांहींएक, अ-
नेक, कांहीं, नाना, निरनिराळे,
वेगवेगळे.

severe *a.* क्रूर, निष्ठुर, जड, भारी,
जालीम, सखत, सक्त, कठीण,
तीव्र, तीक्ष्ण, मोठा, पराकाष्ठेचा.

severely *ad.* फार, पुष्कळ. (२)
कठोरपणाने, निर्दयतेने.

sew (सो) *v. t. i.* शिवणे, टांके
मारणे.

shad *n.* एका प्रकारचा मासा.

shaft *n.* दांडा *m.* दांडी *f.*

shake *n.* झटका *m.* कंप *m.*

shake *v. t.* झटकणे, झाडकणे,
झाडणे, हालविणे, कांपविणे.

shake *v. i.* हालणे, कांपणे, हदरणे.

shall *v. a.* हा शब्द भविष्यकाळ
दाखवितो.

shalt *v. a,* shall याचा द्वितीय पुरुष
एकवचन.

shame *n.* लाज *f.* लज्जा *f.* शरम *f.*

shameful *a.* लाजेचा, लाजिरवाणा.

shape *n.* आकार *m.* आकृति *f.*
रूप *n.* स्वरूप *n.*

shape *v. t.* घडणे, आकार देणे, मूर्त
करणे, रूप देणे.

share *n.* वांटा *m.* हिस्सा *m.* विभाग
m. वांटणी *f.* भाग *m.* अंश *m.*

share *v. t.* वांटणे, विभागणे, वांटा
घेणे-देणे, वांटून घेणे-देणे, विभा-
गून घेणे-देणे.

shave *v. t.* तासणे, भादरणे. (२)
मुंडणे, क्षौर-मुंडण-हजामत करणे,
डोई करणे.

shave *n.* सुताराचें एक हतेर *n.*

she *pron. f.* ती.

shear *v. t.* कातरणे, कापणे (कात-
रीने).

shears *n. pl.* कातर *f.* कातरी *f.*

shed *n.* सोपा *m.* बेडें *n.* शाला *f.*
निवारा *m.*

shed *v. t.* गाळणे, टाकणे, (पानें,
केंस, पंख, इ.) (*invers.*) गळणे,
झडणे. (२) पाडणे (रक्त) (३)
— to shed rain, न ठिबकणे,
न पाझरणे, न गळणे, (*invers.*)
न गळणे, न येणे. उ. This roof
sheds rain, हें छप्पर गळत नाहीं,
or या छप्परांतून पाणी येत-गळत
नाहीं.

sheep *n.* मेंढरूं *n.* मेंढें *n.*

shelf *n.* फळी *f.* पूड *m. n.* तक-
ता *m.*

shell *n.* कवच *n. m.*
— egg shell, कवंची *f.* कवंटी *f.*
— cocoanut shell, करोटी *f.*
— (२) नाना प्रकारच्या जंतूचें घर.
उ. कवडी *f.* शंख *m.* —oyster
shell, muscle shell, शिंप
f. शिंपी *f.* कालव *n.* —
pearl shell, शुक्ति *f.* मोतीं *n.*

shell *v. t.* सोलणे, काढणे, (कण-
सांचे दाणे इ.).

shift *v. t.* बदलणे, अदलाबदल
करणे, फिरविणे, उलटा करणे.

shift *v. i.* हालणे, जाणे, फिरणे, ब-
दल होणे. (२) हिकमत-उपाय
करणे, युक्ति करणे.

shift *n.* हिकमत *f.* युक्ति *f.* उपाय

m. उ. — to make a shift, हिकमत-उपाय करणे.

shilling n. एका प्रकारचें नाणें, सुमारें अर्धा रुपया.

shine v. i. प्रकाशणें, उजेड देणें, झळकणें, चमकणें, भडकणें, झकझकणें.

shining a. तेजस्वी, तेजवंत, प्रकाशवंत, प्रकाशक, लखलखीत.

ship n. गलबत n. तारूं n. जहाज n.

ship v. t. गलबतावर लादणें, गलबताकडून पाठविणें, गलबतांत घालून धाडणें.

shirk v. i. काढतें घेणें (आपणाला), पाठ काढणें-चोरणें, अंग राखणें, अंग काढणें.

shiver v i. हुडहुडणें, कांपणें, थरथरणें, (invers.) हींव वाजणें.

shock n. धक्का m. (२) धस m. धसका m. आंच f.

shock v. t. धसका घालणें, (invers.) पोटांत धसकण भरणें. (२) धक्का लावणें-देणें, (invers.) धक्का होणें.

— to be shocked (invers.), पोटांत धसकण भरणें. (२) (invers.) धक्का लागणें-होणें.

shocking a. घोर, अघोर, उग्र.

shoe n. जोडा m. जुति f. पादुका f. नाल m. (घोड्याचा).

shoe v. t. नाल बांधणें-लावणें.

shone pret. of shine.

shook pret. of shake.

shore n. कांठ m. तीर n. तड f.

किनारा m. कड f. (नदीची, समुद्राची, इ.)

short a. तोकडा, अखुड, उणा, कमी, लांडा, लांब नाहीं, पुरा नाहीं, र्‍हस्व, वामन, ठेंगणा, भग्रा, खुजा, थोडा (वेळ). (२) भरवार.

— in short, सारांश.

should v. a. शक्यरूपाचें साहाय्य क्रियापद, योग्यता आणि धर्म, असे अर्थ फारकरून दाखवितें. उ. Children should obey their parents, लेंकरानीं आपल्या आईबापांचें ऐकावें हें योग्य आहे. — You should not do so, तुझीं असें करूं नये. — You should have done this yesterday, तुझीं हें काल करायाचें होतें. — I said you should not go, जाऊं नये असें म्या तुला सांगितलें.

— (२) अवश्यता दाखवितें. उ. I said you should go, तूं जासीलच जासील or तुला गेलेंच पाहिजे असें म्या सांगितलें. I said you should not go, तूं जाणारच नाहींस or तूं जाऊंच नये असें म्या सांगितलें.

— (३) भविष्यार्थ दाखवितें. उ. I told you I should go, मीं जाईन असें म्या तुला सांगितलें. I said you should go, तूं जासील (or येसील) असें म्या सांगितलें.

— (४) संशयार्थ दाखवितें. उ. Should it rain (or if it should rain) I shall not go, जर पाऊस

पडेल तर मी जाणार नाहीं. If I should tell you, (or should I tell you) you would not let me go, जर मी तुला सांगीन तर तूं मला जाऊं देणार नाहींस, or जर मी तुला सांगतें तर तूं मला जाऊं न देतास.

—(५) संकेतार्थ दाखविर्तें. उ. I should think not, नाहीं, असें मला वाटतें. —I should not say so, असें मी न बोलतों.— Were I in your place I should not do so, जर मी तुझ्या ठिकाणीं असतों, तर असें न बोलतों.

shoulder n. खांद m. खांदा m. स्कंध m.

shoulder v. t. खांद्यावर घेणे.

shout n. अरोळी f. हाक f. हर-ळी f. जयजयकार m.

shout v. i. हुर्यो हुर्यो करणे, भ-रोळी करणे, हाक-हर्ळी मारणे, पुकारणे.

show n. तमाशा m. (२) टुमटाम f. टामटूम f. ज्ञान f. डौल m. छांछूं n.

show v. t. दाखविणे, पाहूं देणे, नजरेस पाडणे, दृष्टीस पडूं देणे.

— to show one's self -itself, दृष्टीस पडणे.

shown pret. of show.

showy a. छानदार, दर्शनी, देख-णाऊ, घवघवीत, भव्य.

shrug n. आकर्षण n. (खांद्यांचें).

shrug v. t. आकर्षणे (खांदि).

shun v. t. चुकविणे, टाळणे, वर्जणे, वर्जित करणे, जवळ न जाणे-येणे.

shut v. t. मिटणे, लावणे, बंद करणे, झांकणे.

— to shut up, कोंडणे, कैदेंत घालणे, बंद करणे.

shut v. i. मिटणे, बंद होणे, लागणे.

shut pret. & p. p. of shut.

shy a. बुजरा, मुरका, बुजरा.

sick a. रोगी, आजारी, विकारी, दुखणाईत.

— to be sick, (invers.) ओका-री येणे. (२) (invers.) कंटाळा -चिलस-किलस येणे.

sickness n. रोग m. आजार m. दुखणें n. विकृति f. वाखा m.

side n. बाजू f. तरफ f. अंग n. कड f. किनारा m. (२) कूस f. (३) पक्ष m. तरफ f. फळी f.

— by the side of, जवळ, शे-जारीं, लगत, सरसां.

— on this side, अलिकडे.

—on the other side, पलिकडे, पार.

— on all sides, चहुंकडे, चौ-फेर, आसमंतात, सभोंवतें, आजू-बाजूस, अवरसचवरस.

sigh n. सुसकारा m. उसासा m. उच्छ्वास m.

sigh v. i. सुसकारणे, शोचणे, उ-सासा देणे-टाकणे.

sight n. दृष्टि f. नजर f. पाहणी f. अवलोकन n. दर्शन n. (२) चक्षुरिंद्रिय n. डोळे m. pl. नेत्रें-द्रिय n. लक्ष n. (३) विचार m. लक्ष n. उ. This is wicked in the sight of God, हें देवाच्या

लक्षांत वाईट आहे, *or* हें देवा-
समोर वाईट आहे.

— to be in sight, दिसणे, दिस-
ण्यांत-दृश्य भसणे.

— to be out of sight, अदृश्य
-दिसेनासें भसणे, दिसण्यांत न-
सणे.

— at first sight, पाहतांच, प-
हिल्याने, दृष्टीस पडतांच.

— at the sight of, पाहतांच,
नजरेस पडतांच, दर्शनीं, पाहून.

— to take sight, रोखणे, नेम
धरणे.

— in the sight of, देखतां,
समोर. (२) विचारांत, लक्षांत.

—(४)—of a gun, माशी *f.*

—(५)—कौतुक *m.* मौज *f.* उ. I
never saw such a sight in my
life, असी मौज म्या कधीं पाहिली
नाहीं, *or* यासारिखें म्या कधीं
पाहिलें नाहीं.

sign *n.* खुण *f.* चिन्ह *n.* लक्षण
n. इंगित *n.* निशाणी *f.* (२)
चमत्कार *m.* अद्भुत *n.* उत्पात
m. कौतुक *m.* (३) राशि *m.*
नक्षत्र *n.*

sign *v. t.* सही करणे.

signify *v. t.* दाखविणे, बोधणे, कळ-
विणे, (*invers.*) बोध होणे, अर्थ
असणे. It does not signify,
(*invers.*) त्यांत हाशील-फळ-अर्थ
नाहीं. (२) (*inv.*) त्याविषयीं
चिंता नाहीं.

silent *a.* उगाच, चिप्प, अबोल.

silly *a.* वेडूब, बावळा, गयाळ, या-

याळी, मूर्ख, भोळा, अचरट
निर्बुद्धि, वेडसर, खुळसर. (२)
हलका.

simple *a.* साधा, एकेरीं, नुस्ता,
शुद्ध. (२) सोपा, सोपारा, सव-
पट, साहजिक. (३) भोळा,
साळसुद, सालस, साळदाळ.

sin *n.* पाप *n.* दोष *m.* पातक *n.*

sin *v. i.* पाप करणे.

since *prep.* पासून. उ.— since
morning, सकाळपासून.

since *ad.* मागें. उ. Three days
since, तीन दिवस मागें. How
many days since he came,
तो येऊन किती दिवस झाले, *or*
तो आल्यावर किती दिवस झाले.

since *conj.* ज्यापेक्षां····त्यापेक्षां,
कारण कीं, झणून, असें असतां.
उ. Since God is my friend
I am not afraid, मला भय
वाटत नाहीं कारण कीं देव माझा
मित्र आहे, *or* देव माझा मित्र
आहे झणून मला भय वाटत नाहीं,
or देव माझा मित्र असतां मला
भय वाटत नाहीं.

sincere *a.* भावार्थी, निष्कपट अदां-
भिक, खरा, अनन्य, सालस.

sincerely *ad.* मनोभावें, मनोभावें-
करून, कपटरहित, अदांभिक-
पणानें.

sincerity *n.* भावार्थ *m.* अनन्यभाव
m. मनोभाव *m.* सत्यता *f.* खरे-
पण *n.* साळसाई *f.*

sing *v. i. t.* गाणे, गायन करणे,
मंजूळ शब्द काढणे-करणे.

single a. एकला, एकटा, एकच, एकाकी, एकेरा, दुहिरी नाहीं.
— a single man, सडा.

single (out,) v. t. निवडणे, काढणे, बहुतांतून एक घेणे-दाखविणे.

singly ad. एक एक, पृथक, एक-ट्याने.

singular a. एकाज, तऱ्हेचा, तऱ्हे-वाईक, निराळा, असाधारण, अपूर्व, एककल्ली, नवल.
— singular number, एकव-चन.

sink n. मोरी f. नाहणी f.

sink v. i. बुडणे, डुबणे, उतरणे, बसणे, फसणे, गळणे, खचणे, खालीं जाणे, रुतणे. (२) शिणणे, ठसणे, भिनणे, (मनांत).

sink v. t. बुडविणे, डुबविणे, रेवविणे, ठसविणे, फसविणे, गाडणे, खणणे, खालीं करणे, उडविणे (पैका).

sip n. भुरका m.

sip v. t. i. भुरकणे, ओरपणे, पिणे, पान करणे.

sir n. a. महाराज, साहेब, जी, दादा.

sit v. i. बसणे.

six a. साहा, सकें. उ. Six times six are thirty six, सहा सकें छत्तीस.

sixpence n. पैक्यांचें एक नाणें.

sixth a. साहावा, षष्ठ.

sixth n. षष्ठांश.

sixty a. साठ.

size n. परिमाण n. मान n. मोठे-पण n. आकारमान n. बिस्तार

m. लांबीरुंदी f. भवरसचवरस.

skate n. पादुका f. (पायांला लावून मोठलेल्या पाण्यावर घसरत चाल-ण्यासाठीं).

skate v. i. घसरत चालणे (गोठ-लेल्या पाण्यावर).

skill n. कौशल n. युक्ति f. कसब n. हिकमत f. हुनर f. हातोटी f. वस्तादगिरी f.

skilled a. प्रवीण, निपुण, वस्ताद, अभ्यासी, जाणता, पारखी, शार्त-गत, तरवेज.

skillful a. युक्तिमान, परिज्ञाता, पुरा, कसबी, कुशल, हुशार.

skin n. सालटी f. चर्म m. चामडी f. कातडी f. त्वचा f. (२) तर-फल n. खल f. सालपट n. त्व-चा f.

skin v. t. कातडी काढणे, साल काढणे, त्वचा काढणे, सोलणे, छिलणे.

skip v. i. भगडणे, खिदडणे, उडी मारणे, चपळाईने उडी मारणे.

slap n. धपका m. धण्णा m. धमाटा m. धप्पल f. चपराक f. चडक f. चटकणी f.

slap v. t. चपराकणे, धमाटणे, चपराक मारणे.

slate n. पाटी f. (दगडाची).

slave n. दास m. गुलाम m. लॉंज f. लवंडी f.

slay v. t. जिवें मारणे, वधणे, हत्या करणे, घात करणे, प्राण-जीव घेणे.

sled n. घसरण्याचें वाहन n.

sleek n. गुळगुळीत, मऊ, नरम, ताजा.

sleek v. t. मऊ करणे.

sleep n. झोप f. नीज f. निद्रा f. शयन n.

sleep v. i. झोप येणे, निजणे, (in-vers.) झोप येणे.

slept pret. of sleep.

slice n. फांक f. फांकळी f. काप m. ड्याकल m. खाप f. फोड n.f.

slice v. t. फांकणे, कापणे, फांक-फोडी करणे.

slid pret. of slide.

slide v. i. घसरणे, सरकणे, सरणे, ढळणे, निसटणे, निसरणे, सर-कटणे, फरकटणे.

slide v. t. सारणे, सरविणे, सरका-वणे.

slight a. कांहींसा, हलका, किर-कूळ, जरासा, थोडासा, बारी-क.

slight n. अनादर m. अव्हेर m हेलना f. हेलसांड f. अनमान n. भमर्यांदा f.

slight v. t. अनादर करणे, हेलना-हेलसांड-अनमान करणे, अबाळ करणे, अनमानणे, उपेक्षणे, उ-पेक्षा करणे, लक्ष न देणे, चां-गलें न करणे, हयगई-कसवचोरी करणे.

slightly ad. किंचित, यत्किंचित, थोडेंसें, जरासें, जरा, कळतन-कळत.

slip n. संचार m. सरकणें n. सरणें n. घसरणें n. (२) पढी f. फडकें

n. फडका m. लंगोटी f. चिर-फळी f. फळी f.

— to give the slip, झुकणे, झुकाटणे, झुकांडी देणे.

slip v. i. निसरणे, सरणे, सरकणे, घसरणे, ढळणे, निसटणे, खिसणे, झुकणे, निघणे, हालणे. (२) चोरून जाणे-येणे, हळू जाणे-येणे.

— to slip off or away, झुकणे, झुकाटणे, झुकाटी देणे.

slip v. t. सारणे, सरविणे, निसर-विणे, सरकावणे, ढळविणे, खुप-सणे.

slow ad. & a. सावकाश, हळू, भिमा, मुस्त, मंद.

sly a. नजरचोर, दृष्टिचोर, दृष्टि चुकविणारा, धूर्त, चोर (in comp).

slily ad. गुप, गुपचिप, गुप्तरूपें, हळू, चोरून, दृष्टि चोरून.

small a. लहान, सूक्ष्म, क्षुद्र, अल्प, हलका, स्वल्प, थोडका, धाक-टा.

— small pox, देवी f.

smart a. हुशार, चपल, कुशाळ, चुण-चुणीत, चणचणीत, सुज्ञाण, तड-कफडक.

smart v. i. चुरचुरणे, चुणचुणे, खुपणे, सलणे, दुखणे, झोंबणे.

smart n. चुणचुण f. चुरचूर f. दुःख n.

smatterer n. किंचिज्ञ m. अर्ध-वाट m. वाडी m. f.

smell n. वास m. गंध m.

— a bad smell, घाण f. दुर्गंध.

— to take a seat, बसणे, आ-
सीन होणे.

seat v. t. बसविणे, बसूं देणे.

— to seat one's self, or to be
seated, बसणे.

second a. दुसरा, द्वितीय, दुजा,
अन्य.

second n. एका मिनटाचा साठवा
अंश. (२) क्षण m. पळ n.
विपळ n.

secret a. गुप्त, अंतस्थ, खोल, गूढ,
गौप्य, चोर (in comp.), चोरटा,

secret n. रहस्य n. गूज n. मर्म n.
टूक f.

— in secret, एकांती.

secretary n. चिटणीस m. लेखक
m. कारकून m. (२) एका
प्रकारचें मेज.

see v. t. i. पाहणे, बघणे, विलोकणे,
अवलोकणे, (inters.) दिसणे,
दृष्टीस पडणे. (२) समजणे.

seed n. बी f. बीज n.

seem v. i. वाटणे, दिसणे, भासणे,
लागणे, मनांत-लक्षांत येणे.

seen p. p. of see.

— to be seen, दिसणे, दृष्टीस
पडणे.

seize v. t. धरणे, घेणे, हिसकणे,
हिसकावणे, घेरणे, पकडणे, छिना-
वणे.

seldom ad. क्वचित, विरळा, एखादा.

select a. निवडक, चांगला, निवड-
लेला, परिगणित, वेंचक.

select v. t. निवडणे, निवडून घेणे,
कादून घेणे, वेंचणे.

self n. स, .स्वतः, स्वयें, आपण,
जातीने,-च.

— one's self, आपण.

selfish a. स्वार्थी, स्वार्थपर, आप-
मतलबी, आपलपोटाच्या, सहित
पाहणारा.

self-schooling n. स्वशिक्षा f.

sell v. t. विकत देणे, विकणे, फरोक्त
करणे, विकून टाकणे.

sell v. i. खपणे, विकणे, पटणे,
विकत जाणे, (invers.) विकरी
होणे-असणे.

semicolon n. लिहिण्यांत ही खूण (;)
(अवसान दाखविती.)

send v. t. पाठविणे, धाडणे, जाऊं
देणे, पोंहंचविणे, पोंहचता करणे,
फेंकणे, टाकणे.

— to send away, रवाना करणे,
निरोप देणे, जाऊं देणे.

— to send for, बोलावणे, मागणे,
आणायाला धाडणे.

sense n. इंद्रिय n. व. — sense of
touch, स्पर्शेंद्रिय. — sense of
smell, घ्राण, घ्राणेंद्रिय. — sense
of hearing, श्रोत्रेंद्रिय. — sense
of seeing, नेत्रेंद्रिय, चक्षुरिंद्रिय.
— sense of taste, जिव्हेंद्रिय,
रसनेंद्रिय.

— the senses, इंद्रियग्राम m.
(२) बुद्धि f. ज्ञान n. समज f. m.
ग्राहकता f. अक्कल f.

sensible a. समजदार, समंजस,
अकलवंत, हुशार, जाणता, सूज्ञ,
प्राज्ञ, बुद्धिवान. (२) चेतन,

देहभानयुक्त. (२) समजण्याजोगा, लक्षांत येण्याजोगा.

sensibly *ad.* समजण्याजोगें, स्पष्ट, हुशारीनें, ज्ञानानें, चांगलें, तर्कानें.

sent *pret. & p. p. of* send.

serious *a.* गंभीर, भरकूम, हस्यमुख नाहीं, विचारवंत. (२) ठट्ठेचा नाहीं, खरा. (३) भारी, इलका नाहीं, मोठा, फार.

servant *n.* चाकर *m.* सेवक *m.* दास *m.* नौकर *m.* भृत्य *m.* गडी *m.* खिदमतगार *m.*

serve *v. t.* चाकरी करणें, सेवा करणें, सेवणें, मानणें, चाकरीस राहणें. (२) बरें करणें, साह्य करणें. (३) वाढणें, वांटणें.

serve *v. i.* चाकर असणें. (२) उपयोगी-कामास पडणें, पुरणें, निभाव करणें, बरें लागणें, बसणें, मिळणें, जमणें, होणें, चालणें.

service *n.* चाकरी *f.* खिदमत *f.* काम *n.* उद्योग *m.* धंदा *m.* सेवा *f.*

set *v. t.* ठेवणें, लावणें, घालणें, स्थापणें, नेमणें, बसविणें, जडणें, देणें, नीट करणें (हाड).

— to set on fire, पेटविणें, विस्तु -आग लावणें.

— to set up, स्थापणें, घालणे, मांडणें.

— to set down, मांडणें. (२) खालीं ठेवणें, खालीं बसविणें.

— to set out (trees &c.) लावणें, रोवणें.

— to set in order, बरोबर

ठेवणें-मांडणें, ठाकठीक ठेवणें, बंदोवस्त करणें, निटावणें.

— to set free, मोकळ्या करणें, सोडणें, सुटका करणें.

— to set off *or* out, साजणें, शोभणें.

set *v. i.* मावळणें, अस्त होणें. (२)— to set out, forward, *or* off, निघून जाणें, चाटणें, निघणें.

— to set in, लागणें, उठणें, होणें.

set *pret. & p. p. of* set.

set *a.* नेमलेला, ठरविलेला. (२) निश्चयाचा, निश्चित.

set *n.* जोड *m.* प्रत *f.* जोडी *f.*

setting *n.* अस्त *m. n.*

settle *v. t.* ठरविणें, तोडणें, पार करणें, (कज्जा, इ.) नेमणें, जम-विणें, मिटविणें, फेडणें, चुकविणें, (हिशोब, खटला, कज्जा, लचांड, इ.). (२) वस्ती करणें, वसाहत करणें, (देश).

— to be settled, वसणें (देश, गांव, इ.). (२) चुकणें, तुटणें, जमणें, मिटणें, फिटणें, (हिशोब, खटला, कज्जा, इ.).

settle *v. i.* बसणें, पडणें, उतरणें.

settled *a.* चुकता. (२) आबाद, आबादान. (३) ठरविलेला, स्थापित, स्थिर, निश्चित, निश्च-याचा, नेमलेला, कायम.

seven *a.* सात, सर्त. उ. Seven times seven are forty nine, सात सर्तें एकुणपन्नास.

seventh *a.* सातवा.

spiteful *a.* अकसी, अकसखोर, उंशी, द्रोही.

splendid *a.* तेजस्वी, शोभायमान, शोभिवंत, उमदा, फार चांगला, देखणा, भव्य, विलसित.

split *v. t.* चिरणे, फोडणे, तडके असें करणे.

split *v. i.* फुटणे, चिरणे, उकलणे, तडकणे, तणणे, तडा पडणे, उम- लणे, उलणे, (*invers.*) चीर -भेग-चिरण होणे.

split *pret. & p. p. of* split.

split *a.* तुफाड, फुटला, चिरले- ला.

spoil *v. i.* नासणे, खराब होणे, बिघडणे, सडणे.

spoil *v. t.* नासविणे, सडविणे नाश्ट करणे, खराब करणे, बिघडविणे, नाडणे. (२) लुटणे.

spoke *pret. of* speak.

spoken *p. p. of* speak.

spoon *n.* चमचा *m.* पळी *f.*

sport *n.* मौज *f.* मस्करी *f.* विनोद *m.* मनोरंजन *n.* खेळ *m.* खेळ- णी *f.* खेळकुडीं *f.* थट्टा *f.* तमा- शा *m.*
— in sport, मस्करी-विनोदें करून, थट्टेकरून, मस्करीने.

sport *v. i.* बागडणे, विनोद करणे, मस्करी-थट्टा करणे, खेळणे.

sportive *a.* खेळकर, थट्टेखोर, थट्टेबाज, विनोदी, ख्याली.

spot *n.* ठिकाण *n.* जागा *m. f.* स्था- न *n.* थांग *m.* (२) डाग *m.* ठि- पका *m.* कलंक *m.* खोड *f.*

spot *v. t.* ठिपके -डाग -कलंक देणे, डाग पाडणे.

spot *v. i.* डाग पडणे-होणे.

spotted *a.* चित्रविचित्र, डागील, डाग्या, ठिपक्याठिपक्यांचा.

spout *n.* तोटी *f.* पन्हळ *m.* नळी *f.* नळा *m.*

spout *v. t.* उडविणे, सोडणे, (पा- णी इ.).

spout *v. i.* उडणे, सुटणे, निघणे, (पाणी इ.)

sprawl *v. t. i.* फांकणे, पसरणे, (हात, पाय, इ.).
—sprawling, हात पाय पसरून, पसरट, पसरलेला, पसरता.

spread *v. t. i.* पसरणे, विस्तारणे, अंथरणे, हांतरणे, चालणे.

spring *n.* उडी *f.* उसळी *f.* झपाटा *m.* (२) झरा *m.* (३) वसंत *m.* वर्षांचा एक ऋतु. (४) कमाण *f.* (यंत्राची). (५) मूळ *n.* कारण *n.*

spring *v. i.* उडी मारणे, उडणे, उसळणे, फांदणे, झपाटा मारणे. (२) उठणे, निघणे, उपजणे, उग- वणे, रुजणे, फुटणे, होणे, उत्पन्न होणे.

sprout *n.* अंकुर *m.* कोंब *m.* कोम *m.* कोंवरा *m.* मोड *f.*

sprout *v. i.* अंकुरणे, रुजणे, उग- वणे, फुटणे, (*invers.*) अंकुर-मोड येणे.

spur *n.* नांगी *f.* (पांखरांची). (२) कांटा *m.* टोंक *n.*

spur *v. t.* चेतविणे, टांचळणे, कांटा मारणे (घोड्याला), प्रेरणे.

spy *n.* हेर *m.* गुप्तदूत *m.* टेहळ्या·

spy *v. t.* पाहणे, टेहळणे, (*invers.*) दिसणे.

— to spy out, हेरणे.

square *a.* चौरस, बरोबर.

square root *n.* द्विघातमूळ *n.* वर्गमूळ *n.*

square *n.* चौकडी *f.* चौंक *m.* (२) गुणा *m.* (३) द्विघात *m.* वर्ग *m.*

square *v. t.* चौरस करणे. (२) द्विघात-वर्ग करणे.

squeal *v. i.* किंकळणे, किंकळी फोडणे.

squirrel *n.* खडी *f.* खार *f.* चानी *f.*

St. *or* saint, संत *m.* साधु *m.*

stain *n.* डाग *m.* ठिपका *m* कळंक *m.* ठपका *m.* बट्टा *m.*

stain *v. t.* रंगणे, भरणे, डाग-ठिपका पाडणे-करणे.

stained *a. & p. p.* डागील, भरला.

stair *n.* पायरी *f.*

—stairs *pl.* जिना *m.* शिडी *f.* पायऱ्या *f.*

— up stairs, माडीवर.

— down stairs, खालीं, (माडीवरून).

stake *n.* खुंटा *m.* सुळका *m.* डांभा *m.* सूळ *m.* मेढ *f.* (२) पण *n.* पैज *f.*

— to be at stake, (*invers.*) जोखीम-पण-पैज असणे.

stake *v. t.* पण-पैज पाडणे-घालणे

-ठेवणे-करणे, जोखीम करून ठेवणे.

stalk *n.* देंठ *m.* तांट *n.* काठी *f.* सड *m.* कडवा *m.* ऊंख *n.* (२) अकड *f.* डौल *m.* मिरवणूक *f.*

stalk *v. i.* मिरवणे, ठमकणे, ठमकत चालणे, झुमकणे.

stall *n.* गव्हाण *f.* ठाण *n.* (२) दुकान *n.*

stammer *v. i.* तोतरें बोलणे, बडबड करणे, अडकळत बोलणे.

stamp *n.* शिक्का *m.* मोहर *f.* मुद्रा *f.* छप्पा *m.* छाप *m.* ठसा *m.* मोर्नंब *n.* (२) आपट *f.* पायाचा दणका *m.*

stamp *v. t.* छापणे, शिक्का ठोकणे-मारणे, मुद्रा करणे, छापा करणे. (२) तुडविणे, दणदण करणे, पाय आपटणे.

stand *n.* स्थिति *f.* स्थीत *f.* स्थान *n.* (२) अड्डा *m.* अखाडा *m.* (३) घडीची *f.* चवरंग *m.* तिवई *f.* (४) निश्चय *m.*

—to come to *or* be at a stand, थांबणे, उभा राहणे, अटकणे, तकूब होणे, खुंटणे, प्रतिबंध होणे.

stand *v. i.* उभा राहणे, राहणे.

— to make stand up, उभा करणे, उभारणे.

— (२) थांबणे, राहणे. (३) असणे. उ. The lamp stands on the table, दिवा मेजावर आहे. (४) टिकणे, राहणे, ठरणे.

— to stand for, बदल असणे, झणजे,-च्या ठिकाणीं असणे.

— a tear stood in her eye, तिच्या डोळ्यांत असूं आलें.

start *n.* उचका *m.* धक्का *m.* (२) गमन *n.* प्रस्थान *n.* निघणें *n.*

start *v. i.* उचकणें, विचकणें, तुजणें. (२) निघून जाणें, निघणें, चालूं लागणें, उठणें, जाणें. (३) हलणें, ढळणें, सरणें, न राहणें.

start *v. t.* विचकावणें, तुजविणें. (२) वाटेस लावणें, रवाना करणें, मुरू-आरंभ करणें, उठविणें, चालविणें, चालू करणें. (३) हालविणें, ढळविणें, सारविणें.

starve *v. i.* उपासीं मरणें, भुकें मरणें.

starve *v. t.* उपासाने मारणें, उपासीं ठेवणें-राखणें.

state *n.* अवस्था *f.* दशा *f.* स्थिति *f.* स्थीत *f.* (२) राज्य *n.* खातें *n.* मुलूक *m.* (३) टामटूम *f.* टुमटाम *f.*

— in a bad *or* sad state, दुर्दशेंत, हालांत, हलाकींत, अडचणींत, विपत्तींत, बरोबर नाहीं.

— in a good state, सुस्थित, बरा, चाबूत.

state *v. t.* सांगणें, निवेदणें, निवेदन करणें.

station *n.* पदवी *f.* अमल *m.* हुद्दा *m.* अधिकार *m.* (२) ठाणें *n.* ठिकाण *n.* स्थान *n.* जागा *m. f.*

station *v. t.* ठेवणें, उभा करणें, नेमणें.

stay *n.* रहिवास *m.* वास्तव्य *n.*

मुकाम *m.* खोळंबा *m.* उशीरं *m.* नांदणूक *f.* स्थिति *f.*

stay *v. i.* राहणें, थांबणें, वसणें, टिकणें, मुकाम-वस्ति-स्थिति-खोळंबा करणें, (*invers.*) मुकाम-वास -स्थिति इ. असणें.

stay *v. t.* राहविणें, थांबविणें, भटकावणें, आकळणें, आवरणें.

steal *v. t.* चोरणें, चोरी करणें, चोरून घेणें, उचलणें.

steal *v. i.* चोरून येणें-जाणें, लपून -दडून जाणें-येणें.

— to steal away, चोरून-लपून जाणें.

steel *n.* पोलाद *n.* तिखें *n.*

stem *n.* देठ *m.* डेंख *n.* काठी *f.*

stem *v. t.* आडवा येणें जाणें.

step *n.* कदम *n.* पावला *m.* डेंग *n.* डांग *f.* पाऊल *n.* (२) पायरी *f.* पायंडी *f.* पायटा *m.*

— He is coming for I hear his steps, तो येत आहे, कां कीं मी त्याची चाहूल ऐकतों.

step *v. i.* पाय टाकणें, पाऊल टाकणें, डांग टाकणें, चालणें.

stew *n.* पक्वान्न.

stew *v. t.* शिजविणें, पाक करणें.

stew *v. i.* शिजणें.

stick *n.* काठी *f.* दंड *m.* लाकूड *n.* छडी *f.* शिपटी *f.* फोक *m.* सोटा *m.* काडी *f.*

stick *v. i.* चिकटणें, लागणें, लगटणें, डसणें, टिकणें, राहणें, ठरणें, हतणें, अडकणें, फसणें, जडणें, न सोडणें.

— to stick out *or* up, बाहेर
-वर निघणे.

stick *v. t.* चिकटावणे, उकविणे,
लावणे, जडविणे, जोडणे. (२)
खोंचणे, टोचणे.

— to stick in, टोचणे, रोवणे,
भोंसकणे, खुपसणे, दुसणे.

— to stick out, बाहेर काढणे
-घालणे, पुढें करणे. उ. He
stuck (put) his head out of
the window, त्याने खिडकीबा-
हेर आपलें डोकें घातलें, *or* त्याने
खिडकींतुन डोकावलें. — He
stuck (put) out his foot, त्याने
आपला पाय पुढें केला.

stiff *a.* ताठ, ताठर, निबर, लवचीक
नाहीं.

— to be stiff, ताठरणे.

— to become stiff, ताठणे.

still *a.* उगा, उगाच, निर्वात, नि-
श्चळ, स्वस्थ, अचळ.

still *ad.* उगाच, निमूट, गुप, गुप-
चिप, सुमसाम, सामसूम, मुका-
ठाने, हळू. (२) अजून, अजून-
पर्यंत, आतांपर्यंत, तोंपर्यंत, इत-
क्यावरहि. (३)उ. — still more
or more still, अणखी, त्यापेक्षां
-यापेक्षां अणखी, विशेषेंकरून.
(४) असतांहि, तथापि, तरी.

still *v. t.* शांत करणे, शांतविणे,
समजविणे.

still *n.* अर्क काढण्याचें यंत्र *n.*

stilt *n.* काठी *f.* (पायाला लावून
चालण्याकरितां).

sting *n.* नांगी *f.* अंकडा (विंचाचा),

कांटा (गांभणीचा, माशीचा.).

sting *v. t.* उसणे, नांगी मारणे,
कांटा मारणे (गांभण, इ.)

stir *n.* गडबड *f.* खटपट *f.* धाम-
धूम *f.*

stir *v. i.* हालणे, हलणे, ढळणे, स-
रणे, चालणे.

stir *v. t.* हालविणे, ढवळणे, काल-
वणे, घाटणे, सरविणे.

— to stir up, उठविणे, चिथा-
वणे, चिढविणे, प्रेरणे, उत्तेजित
करणे.

stock *n.* भांडवल *f.* विशात *f.* केवा
m. पुंजी *f.* मालमत्ता *f.* (२)
ताणा *m.* वंश *m.* मूळ *n.* (३)
ग्रामपशु *m.* (४) खोड (झाडा-
चें). (५) दांडी *f.* कुदा (बंद-
कीचा).

— stocks, *pl.* खोडा *m.*

stock *v. t.* लावणे, पुरविणे, सांठ-
विणे, भरणे.

stocking *n.* पायाचा मोजा *m.*

stole *pret.* of steal.

stolen *p. p.* of steal.

stone *n.* दगड *m.* धोंडा *m.* पा-
षाण *m.* शिला *f.*

— grindstone, सहाण *f.*

— whetstone, निशाणा *m.*
निश्णा *m.*

— hewn stone, चिरा *m.*

(२) बी *f.* (फळाची). उ. stone
of the mango, कोय *f.*— stone
of the jack fruit, date, &c.
आठी *f.*

stone *v. t.* धोंडे-दगड मारणे.

12

stood *pret. of* stand.

stool *n.* पाट *m.* घडवंची *f.* धडोंची *f.* चौरंग *m.* तिवई *f.*

stoop *v. i.* लवणे, झुकणे, ओणवणे, ओणवा होणे, वांकणे, नमणे, दब-णे, उतरणे.

stop *n.* विराम *m.* अवसान *n.* अंतर *n.* विश्रांति *f.* विसांवा *m.* (२) प्रतिबंध *m.* अटकाव *m.*
— to put a stop to, बंद करणे, कुंठित करणे, प्रतिबंध करणे.

stop *v. i.* थांबणे, राहणे, अवसान करणे, उभा राहणे, खोळंबणे, भ-रणे, बंद होणे-पडणे-राहणे, कुं-ठणे, खुंटणे.

stop *v. t.* थांबविणे, अटकावणे, खोळंबा करणे, उभा करणे, आड-विणे, प्रतिबंध-बंद करणे, खुंट-विणे, कुंठित करणे.
— to be stopped, बंद होणे -पडणे-राहणे. (stop *v. i.* पा-हा).

store *n.* सांठा *m.* सांठवण *n.* ठेव *f.* जमाव *m.* (२) केवा *m.* भांड-वल *n. f.* पुंजी *f.* (३) भांडागार *n.* दुकान *n.* वखार *f.*

store *v. t.* सांठवण करणे, सांठविणे ठेवणे, जोडणे, भरणे.

storm *n.* तुफान *n.* वादळ *m. n.* चंडवात *m.*

storm *v. i.* वादळणे, तुफान सुटणे, पाऊस पडणे. (२) झाडणे, वाद-ळणे, चवताळणे, आदळआपट करणे, दणकावणे, दणदणणे.

storm *v. t.* छप्पा मारणे-करणे.

stormy *a.* तुफानाचा, वादळण्याचा, पाऊस पुष्कळ पडण्याचा (दिवस).

story *n.* गोष्ट *f.* कथा *f.* बखर *f.* इतिहास *m.* हकिकत *f.* नकल *f.* फरदूक *n.* चुटका *m.* बात *f.* गप्प *f.* (२) मजला (घराचा).
— an upper story, मजला *m.*
— second story, माडी *f.*

stout *a.* मजबूत, बळकट, भक्कम, धबदूल, धबवती, कणखर, घ-रमर, ठोसर, जाड. (२) लठ्ठ, कडा, धमकट, टणका, मोठा, धष्टपुष्ट, धडाकडां, धडसा.

straight *a.* सुती, नीट, सरळ, सुर-ळीत, उन्नू, सडक, वांकडा नाहीं, तंग, समोर, सम.

straight *ad.* तडक, अचानक.

strange *a.* विचित्र, चमत्कारिक, अजप, अपूर्व, नवल, अद्भुत, विलक्षण, अचाट. (२) परका, परकी, पर, अन्य.

stranger *n.* पाहुणा *m.* ओळखीचा नाहीं, परका *m.* परदेशी, फिर-स्ता *m.* आगंतुक.
— to be a stranger to, न समजणे, न जाणणे.

straw *n.* काड *f.* पेंडा *m.* (२) काडी *f.*

strawberry *n.* एका प्रकारचें फळ.

stream *n.* ओघ *m.* धार *f.* प्रवाह *m.* ओत *m.* नदी *f.* ओढा *m.* ओहळ *m.*

stream *v. i.* (*impers.*) धारा पडणे -निघणे-वाहणे.

street n. रस्ता m. वाट f. मार्ग m. (गांवांतला), गल्ली f. अळी f.

strength n. बळ n. जोर m. शक्ति f. कुवत f. सामर्थ्य n. जीव m. देठ m. (२) कस m.

stretch v. t. ताणणे, ताठ-तंग करणे, लांबविणे, पसरणे, वाढविणे.

— to stretch out (the hand, &c.), लांब करणे, पुढें करणे.

stretch v. i. लांबणे, पसरणे, लागणे, लागून ठेपणे.

stretched a. & p. p. वाढर, ताठ, तंग, ताणलेला.

strike v. t. मारणे, हाणणे, ताडणे, लयणे, ठोकणे, पिटणे, बडविणे, प्रहार करणे.

— to strike with admiration, आश्चर्य वाटे असें करणे, (invers.) अनुमोदणे, अनुमोदन करणे.

— a thought strikes me, एक विचार माझ्या मनांत आतांच आला.

— to strike out, न घेणे, न भरणे, वर्जणे. (२) काढणे, खोडणे, रद्द करणे.

strike v. i. लागणे, ठेपणे, वाजणे.

string n. दोरी f. तंतु m. तंत्र n. सूत्र n. सूत n. तार f. सुतळी f. रज्जु f. रस्सी f. बंद m. कसा m. (२) माळ f. हार m. पंगत f. ओळ f. सर m.

string v. t. पटवणे, ओवणे.

strip n. चिंधोटी f. चिंधी f. पट्टी f. फटकें n. लंगोटी f. चिरफळ्वी f. तंतु m.

strip v. t. सोलणे, नग्न करणे, लुटणे, खालीं करणे.

— to strip off, काढणे.

stripe n. पट्टा m. धारी f.

stripe v. t. पट्टा ओढणे-काढणे.

striped a. पट्टाईत, पट्टापट्टीचा, पट्ट्या पाडलेला.

stroke n. धपका m. पटका m. ठोका m. दणका m. धका m. टोला m. रट्टा m.

strong a. मजबूत, कणखर, बळकट, जबर, पक्का, खंबीर, घसमर, ठोसर, भक्कम, जोराचा, धडवती, तवाना, मोठा, भारी, ताठर. (२) गुणवान, कसाचा.

strongly ad. बळकटीने, कम्याने, जोराने. (२) आग्रहाने.

struck pret. & p. p. of strike.

stuck pret. & p. p. of stick.

study n. अभ्यास m. अध्ययन n. शिकणें n. व्यासंग m. विद्याभ्यास m. (२) चिंतन n. तजवीज f. विचार m. लक्ष n. (३) शिकण्याची खोली.

study v. t. i. शिकणे, अभ्यास करणे, चिंतन करणे, लक्ष देणे.

stuff n. पदार्थ m. सामान n. संच m. जिन्नस m. f. माल m. खटलें n. (२) अगडतगड n. भलतेंसलवें.

— of good stuff, हाडाचा चांगला.

stuff v. t. भरणे, ठासणे, घालून भरणे, खचणे, दपटणे.

stung pret. & p. p. of sting.

stupid a. मंद, गयाळी, मूर्ख, जड, बेकूब, निर्बुद्धि, सुस्त, सुस्ता, स्तिमित.

stye n. बुकरांचा गोठा. (२) रांझ-णवाडी f. आंजिणी f.

subdue v. t. जिंकणे, हस्तगत करणे, स्वाधीन करून घेणे, जेर करणे, वश्य करणे, नरम करणे, दबावणे. (२) शांत करणे.

subject n. गोष्ट f. मजकूर m. हाशील n. विषय m. (२) तावें-दार. (३) कर्ता m.

—subjects, pl. रयत f. प्रजा f. लोक m.

subject a. अंकित, वश्य, अधीन, तावेदार, स्वाधीन, खालीं, आज्ञां-कित, सत्तेचा.

subject v. t. वश्य करणे, स्वाधीन करणे, हस्तगत-अंकित करणे. (२) पाडणे (अगत्यांत, संकटांत इ.) (invers.)-कडून होणे-पडणे-लागणे. उ. This subjects me to inconvenience, याकडून मला अडचण होती-पडती.

submission n. अधीनत्व n. स्वाधी-नता f. अंकित होणे, हस्तगत होणे.

submissive a. दीन, वश, हुकमी, आज्ञांकित, आज्ञाधारक, नम्र, दबेल, दैन्यवाणा, गरीव.

submissively ad. दैन्याने, नम्रतेने, नम्र होऊन, मान्यतेने.

substance n. सारांश m. तात्पर्य n. गोडोरा m. हाशील n. सार m. मजकूर m. (२) कस m. तत्वार्थ m. तत्व n. अर्क m. सत्व n.

जीव m. (३) पदार्थ m. द्रव्य n. (४) धन n. संपत्ति f. दौलत f.

succeed v. i. निभणे, बरें चालणे, चालणे, सिद्धीस जाणे, पार पडणे, निघणे, लागणे, निभावणे, (in-vers.) निभाव असणे. (२) मार्गें येणे-जाणे, पुढें-नंतर होणे.

succeed v. t. -च्या मार्गे येणे,-चा हुदा घेणे,-च्या बदल येणे,-च्या जाग्यावर-ठिकाणीं येणे. (२) निभावणे, सफळ करणे, सिद्धीस आणणे, बरकत देणे, पार करणे.

success n. निभाव m. भाग्य n. सही f. बरकत f. n. यश m.

such a. असा, असला, तसा, तसला, इतका, एवढा, त्यासारिखा, या-सारिखा. उ. He was such a good man that every body loved him, तो इतका चांगला होता, कीं त्यावर सर्व प्रीति करीत असत. I never saw such a large one before, एवढा मोठा म्या कधीं पाहिला नाहीं. Such persons should be punished, असें मनुष्य शिक्षा देण्यास योग्य आहेत, or अशा मनुष्यांस शिक्षा द्यावी.

— such as, जो···तो, सारि-खा, जसा···तसा. उ. Such as obey God will be happy, जे देवाला मानितात ते सुख पाव-तील. Give me such a book as you have, एक पुस्तक तुझ्या-सारिखें मला दे.

— such a one, अमुक, अमका, फलाणा.

suck v. t. स्तन पिणे, चोखणे, ओढणे (तोंडाने), चुंखणे, चुंफणे.

sudden a. अकस्मात्‌चा, अवस्तां-चा.

suddenly ad. अकस्मात्‌, एकाएकी, अचानक, अवचित, अवस्तां.

suffer v. i. t. सोसणे, भोगणे, सा-हणे, सहन करणे, दुःखित-हलाक असणे. (२) देणे. उ. He suffered me to go, त्याने मला जाऊं दिल्हें.

sufficient a. पुरा, पुरता, चुटपुटता, टापासटीप, पाहिजे तितर्के, बस.
— to be sufficient, पुरणे, पुरा असणे.

sufficiently ad. पुरें, बस.

suffocate v. i. गुदमरणे, (invers.) दम कोंडणे.

suffocate v. t. श्वास-दम कोंडणे.

sugar n. साकर f. श्र्करा f. सा-खर f.

suit n. जोड m. जोडा m. (२) खटला m. परिवार m. स्वारी f. (३) अर्जी f. विनंती f. प्रार्थना f. (४) मुकदमा m. खटला m.

suit v. t. i. भवणे, पटणे, सोईं-वार असणे, पसंत पडणे, सोईस पडणे, मनास उतरणे, पचणे, मानवणे. (२) साजणे, शोभणे, जमणे, मिळणे, जोडी असणे.

suitable a. सोईवार, सोईचा, यथा-योग्य, यथास्थित, यथोचित, योग्य, हलाल, विहित.

sum n. रकम f. संख्या f. (२) बेरीज f. जमा f. (३) इत्यर्थ m. सारांश m. तात्पर्य n. तत्वार्थ m.
— what sum, किती.
— a large sum, पुष्कळ.
— a sum of money, पैका.

sum (up) v. t. बेरीज करणे, जमा करणे, एकंदर करणे, सारांश सांगणे, मजकूर सांगणे.

summer n. उष्णकाळ m. उन्हाळा m.

sun n. सूर्य m. आदित्य m. रवि m. प्रभाकर m. यभस्ति m. भास्कर m. दिनकर m. (२) ऊन्ह n.

Sunday n. आदित्यवार m. रविवार m. शाब्बाथ दिवस m.

sung pret. & p. p. of sing.

sunk pret. & p. p. of sink.

sup v. i. जेवणे (संध्याकाळीं).

superior a. मोठा, उत्तम, चांगला, उंचा, सरस, श्रेष्ठ, फार चांगला, नामी. (२) मुख्य, अधिकारी.

supper n. जेवणें, खाणें, (सांजचें).

supply n. पुरव m. पुरवटा m. पुरें n. भरती f.

supply v. t. पुरवणे, देणे, भरती करणे.

support n. रक्षण n. जिंदगी f. उप-जीवन n. पोषण n. फळणपोषण n. पाळण n. (२) आधार m. टेंट m. टेंकणे n. गमक n. प्रमाण n. पाठ f. आश्रय m. पुष्टीकरण n.

support v. t. रक्षणे, संभाळणे, पो-षण करणे, पाळणे, (invers.) पदरीं असणे. (२) आभार देणे,

लोसणे, आश्रय-गमक देणे, प्रमाण
देणे.

suppose *v. t.* समजणे, कल्पिणे,
अटकल करणे, मानणे, (*invers.*)
वाटणे, ध्यानांत-मनांत येणे-अस-
णे.

sure *a.* निर्भांत, खचीत, निश्चयाचा,
निश्चित, निश्चययुक्त.

— to be sure, खचीत समजणे,
न चुकणे, (*invers.*) खचीत
वाटणे, संशय नसणे, निश्चयें
असणे. (२) बरीक, खरें.

sure *ad.* निश्चयें, खचीत.

surface *n.* पाठ *f.* (पृथ्वीची, समु-
द्राची). क्षेत्रफळ *n.* पृष्ठ *n.* पृष्ठ-
भाग *m.* पातळी *f.* दृश्य अंग *n.*
बाहेरचें अंग, दर्शनांग *n.*

— below the surface, अंतरीं,
आंत, वरच्या भागाखालीं.

— near the surface, वरतें ज-
वळ, (पाण्यांत) खोल नाहीं.

— on the surface, वर, वरतें,
पाठीवर, वरवर.

surprise *n.* विस्मय *m.* आश्चर्य *n.*
अचंबा *m.*

— by surprise, अचानक, अ-
कस्मात, अवचित, अवस्तां.

surprise *v. t.* दंग करणे, गांठणे,
अकस्मात भेटणे.

— to be surprised, दंग अ-
सणे, चकित होणे, आश्चर्य वाटणे,
अचंबा वाटणे.

Susan *n. p.* स्त्रियेचें नांव.

sustenance *n.* भक्ष *m.* अन्न *n.*
आधार *m.* आहार *m.* उपजीवन

n. उपजीविका *f.* उदरनिर्वाह *m.*
जिंदगी *f.*

swallow *n.* घांस *m.* ग्रास *m.* (२)
एका प्रकारचें पांखरूं.

swallow *v. t.* मिळणे, ग्रासणे, पो-
टांत घेणे, (*invers.*) घशाखालीं
उतरणे-उतरून जाणे, पोटांत येणे
-जाणे.

swam *pret. of* swim.

swan *n.* राजहंस *m.*

sweep *v. t.* झाडणे, केर काढणे.

sweep *n.* झोंक *m.* झपाटा *m.*

sweet *a.* गोड, मधुर, मिठा, मिष्ट,
गुळचट, मंजूळ, मधुर. (२)
प्रिय, लाडका, ममतेचा.

sweetmeat *n.* मिठाई *f.* खाऊ *m.*

sweetness *n.* गोडी *f.* माधुर्य *n.*
मधुरता *f.* मधुरिमा *m.*

swell *n.* हेलकावा *m.* (समुद्रांतील).

swell *v. i.* सुजणे, फुगणे, फुलणे.
(२) मोठा होणे, चढणे, वाढणे.

— to cause to swell, फुगविणे.

swell *v. t.* वाढवणे, फुगविणे, मोठा
करणे, चढविणे.

swift *a.* पळका, त्वरित, जलद,
शीघ्र, चपळ, तीव्र.

swiftly *ad.* वेगें, त्वरित, जलदी,
लवकर, त्वरेनें, शीघ्र.

swiftness *n.* वेग *m.* जलदी *f.* त्वरा
f. शीघ्रपण *n.*

swim *v. i.* पोहणे, तरणे, तरंगणे,
पोंवणे.

swim *n.* झुलणा *m.* झुला *m.* झोंका
m. झोंक *m.*

swing *v. i.* झोका घेणे-खाणे, झुलणे, झोळकंवणे, हिलगणे.

swing *v. t.* झोका देणे, हालविणे.

sword *n.* तरवार *f.* खड्ग *m.*

syllable *n.* अक्षर *n.*

T.

Table *n.* मेज *n. m.* चवरंग *m.* घडोंची *f.* (२) कोष्टक *n.*

— to sit down to the table (to eat), मेजावर बसणे.

tail *n.* शेपूट *n.* शेप *f.* पुच्छ *n.*

take *v. t.* घेणे, धरणे, नेणे, घेऊन जाणे.

— to take away, काढणे, नेणे, घेउन जाणे.

— to take (to eat *or* drink), खाणे, पिणे.

— to take turns, फेरपाळीने करणे, दम मारून करणे.

— to take care of, संभाळणे, रक्षणे, पाळणे, शाळगणे, राखणे.

— to take care, खबरदारी ठेवणे, जपणे, जतन-पालन करणे, संभाळणे, जपणे. (२)—Take care ! खबरदार!

— to take off, काढणे.

—to take out, काढणे, उपटणे

— to take up, उचलणे, उठ-विणे, उपटणे, वरतें घेणे. (२) घेऊन वर जाणे, वर नेणे.

—to take up room, (*invers.*) जागा लागणे-पाहिजे, जागा भरणे -अटणे-गुंतणे.

— to take a walk *or* ride

फिरणे, हवा खायाला जाणे, स-हेला करणे, करमणे, गमणे.

— to take pleasure, सुख पा-वणे, (*invers.*) सुख वाटणे.

— to take place, होणे, घडणे.

— to take a path *or* road, एका वाटेने जाणे, वाट धरणे.

— to take hard *or* ill, वाईट मानणे,-विषयीं रागें भरणे, रुसणे, चिडणे, (*invers*) वाईट वाटणे.

— to take time, उशीर करणे, (*invers.*) वेळ लागणे.

— to take notice of,-कडे लक्ष देणे, नजर-चित्त देणे.

— to take liberties (p. 73.) अभिमान धरणे, मोकळीक घेणे.

— to take the liberty to do, to ask, to say, प्रशस्त-मोकळे-पणाने करणे-मागणे-बोलणे.

taken *p. p.* of take.

tale *n.* गोष्ट *f.* कथा *f.* नकल *f.*

talent *n.* बुद्धि *f.* तर्क *m.* युक्ति *f.* गुण *m.*

—a man *or* person of talents, बुद्धिमान, युक्तिमान, तर्कबाज.

talk *n.* संवाद *m.* जावसाल *m.* संभाषण *n.* वात *f.* गोष्ट *f.* गप्प *f.*

talk *v. i.* जावसाल करणे, संभाषण करणे, बोलणे, संवाद करणे, गोष्ट सांगणे-करणे.

tall *a.* उंच, घिपाड.

tallow *n.* चरबी *f.* (गुरांची).

tame *a.* माणसाळलेला, ग्राम्य, पाळ-लेला, दमित, माणसाचा सोकील.

— to be tame, मणसळणे, मा-णसवणे, सर्वकणे.

tame *v. t.* पाळणे, पोसणे, माणस-ळविणे, दमित करणे, दमन कर-णे.

taste *n.* चव *f.* रुचि *f.* स्वाद *m.* (२) चट *f.* चटक *f.* चव *f.* हौस *f.* गुण *m.*

taste *v. t.* चाखणे, रुचि घेणे, गोडी घेणे. (२) अनुभव घेणे, (*invers.*) प्रत्ययास-प्रचितीस येणे.

taste *v. i.* लागणे, (*invers.*) रुचि असणे.

— to taste good, रुचणे, गोड लागणे.

tattle *v. i.* गपा झोकणे, गप मारणे, चहाडी सांगणे, थात फेंकणे.

tattling *n.* कानगी *f.* चहाडी *f.* चुगली *f.* गप *f.* गप झोंकर्णे.

tattling *a.* चहाड, चहाउखोर, गप्पी.

taught *pret. & p p. of* teach.

teach *v. t.* शिकविणे, उपदेशणे, उपदेश सांगणे, बोध करणे, बोध-विणे, दाखविणे, पढविणे.

teacher *n.* शिकविणारा *m.* उपदे-शक *m.* गुरु *m.* शिक्षक *m.* पंतोजी *m.*

tear (तीर) *n.* असूं *n.* अश्रु *m. n.*

tear (तेर) *v. t.* फाडणे, चिरणे, विदारणे, टरकणे, चरकणे.

— to tear in pieces, फाडून-तोडून टाकणे, तुकडे करणे, वि-दारण करणे.

tear *v. i.* फाटणे, चिरणे.

tearing *n.* विदारण *n.*

teeth *pl. of* tooth.

tell *v. t.* सांगणे, कथणे, निरूपिणे, निवेदन करणे.

temper *n.* स्वभाव *m.* वासना *f.* प्रकृति *f.* मनोवृत्ति *f.* देहस्वभाव *m.* (२) पाणी *n.* (धातूचें).

temper *v. t.* नीट करणे, यथायोग्य-तयार करणे. (२) पाणी देणे, (धातूला).

temple *n.* देऊळ *n.* (२) कान-शील *n.* आंख *m.*

tempt *v. t.* मोहणे, मोहनी करणे, मोह लावणे, उत्तेजन देणे, चिथ-विणे, प्रचीति-परीक्षा पाहणे-घेणे-करणे.

temptation *n.* मोह *m.* मोहन *n.* उत्तेजन *n.* परीक्षा *f.* प्रचीति *f.*

ten *a.* दाहा, दहा, दशक, दहम, दाही.

tend *v. t.* पाळणे, संभाळणे, राखणे, चारणे, वळणे.

tend *v. i.* वळणे, तोलणे, पडणे, कामास पडणे, (*invers.*) वळण-झोक-तोल असणे, होणे.

tender *a.* कोवळा, कोमल, नाजूक, सुकुमार, नरम, मृदु. (२) मा-याळू, हृदवान, दयाशील. (३) वर्मी.

— a tender point *or* spot, वर्म *n.*

tender *v. t.* नजर करणे, बोली करणे, दाखविणे, देणे.

tenderly *ad.* मायेने, करुणेने, मम-तेने, नाजकाईने, दयेने.

tenderness n. माया f. ममता f. करूणा f. नाजकाई f. नरमाई f. कोवळीक f.

terrible a. अघोर, घोर, भयंकर, क्रूर, उग्र.

testament n. करार m.
— Old Testament, ख्रिस्ती शास्त्राचा पूर्व भाग.
— New Testament, ख्रिस्ती शास्त्राचा उत्तर भाग.

testimony n. साक्ष f. प्रमाण n. ग्वाही f. शाहिदी f. गमक n.

than conj. -पेक्षां, -हून. उ. —less than twenty, विसांपेक्षां कमी, विसांच्या आंत. — more than twenty, विसांपेक्षां अधिक, विसां- वर.
— than if, असल्यापेक्षां. उ. She felt better than if she had eaten the whole, सर्व खाल्ल्यापेक्षां तिला अधिक आनंद झाला.

thank v. t. आभार मानणे, उप- कार मानणे, उपकारी असणे.

thanks n. pl. स्तुति f. उपकारस्तुति f. आभार मानणें.

thanksgiving day n. उपकारस्तुति करण्याचा दिवस.

that pron. तो, ती, तें. (२) जो, जी, जें.

that conj कीं. उ. I think that he will come, मला वाटतें कीं तो येईल, or तो येईल असें मला वाटतें.

that's, that is याचा संक्षेप.

theft n. चोरी f. तस्करी f.

their a. त्यांचा, आपला.

them pron. त्यांस, त्यांला, आप- णांस.

themselves pron. pl. of himself, herself, & itself.

then ad. तेव्हां, तेव, मग, तर, नं- तर, त्यावर, त्यावेळेस, झणजे.

thence ad. तेथून.

there ad. तेथें, तिकडे.
— there is, आहे.
— there was, होता, होती, होतें.

therefore ad. यास्तव, यामुळें, या- दरून, सबब, झणून, त्यास, त- स्मात्.

these pron. pl. of this.

they pron. pl. of he, she, it.

they're, they are याचा संक्षेप.

they've, they have याचा संक्षेप.

thick a. जाड, दाट, गाढ, जाडा, निविड, घट्ट, गउद, ठॉसर, पातळ नाहीं.

thicken v. t. अळणे, दाट करणे, घट्ट करणे, थिजविणे.

thicken v. i. अळणे, घट्ट-दाट होणे, जमणे, अटणे, जाड होणे, थिजणे.

thickness n. जाडी f. दाटण f. दाटणी f. घट्टाई f.

thief n. चोर m. तस्कर m. उच- ल्या m.

thieves n. pl. of thief.

thigh n. मांडी f. फरा m.

thimble n. टोपण n. अंगुस्तान n.

thin a. पातळ, जाड नाहीं, रोड,

रौडका, क्षीण, बारीक, किडकि-
डीत, सडसडीत, सडपातळ, चि-
वळ.

thin v. t. पातळ करणे, विसकळ
-विरळा करणे.

thine pron. तुझा.

thing n. पदार्थ m. वस्तु n. वस्तु f.
गोष्ट f. चीज f. जिन्नस m. f.
(२) pl. सामान n. सामोग्री f.

think v. t. i. कल्पिणे, चिंतणे, वि-
चार करणे, मनांत-ध्यानांत आण-
णे, मनन करणे, समजणे, मनांत
म्हणणे, न विसरणे, स्मरणे, (invers.) वाटणे, मनांत येणे-असणे.

thinly ad. थोडक्याने, थोडें, थोड-
कें.

—thinly dressed, थोडकीं वस्त्रें
घातलेला-नेसलेला.

thinner a. अधिक पातळ-थोडका.

third a. तिसरा, तृतीय, तिजा.

third n. तृतीयांश m. तिजाई f.

thirst n. तान f. तान्ह f. तृषा f.

thirsty a. तान्हेला, तृषित, तान्हाळू,
तृषाक्रांत.

— to be thirsty, तान्हणे, (invers.) तान लागणे.

thirteen a. तेरा, त्रयोदश.

thirteenth a. तेरावा, त्रयोदश.

thirty a. तीस.

this pron. हा, ही, हें.

—this morning, आज सकाळ,
आज सकाळीं.

— this evening, आज संध्या-
काळ-ळीं.

— this day, आज.

Thomas n. p. पुरुषाचें नांव.

thorn n. कांटा m. कंटक m.

thorough a. पुरा, पूर्ण, पक्का.

those pron. plu. of that.

thou pron. तूं.

though conj. जरी.

thought n. कल्पना f. विचार m.
मनोवृत्ति f. चिंता f.

thought pret. & p. p. of think.

thousand a. हजार, सहस्र.

thread n. दोरा m. सूत n. सूत्र n.
धागा m. तंतु m. तंत्र n. तार f.

thread v. t. ओंविणे, गोंविणे, (सु-
ईला.)

threaten v. t. भेडावणे, भेडसा-
वणे, धमकावणे, भिववणे, धाक
दाखविणे. उ. He threatened
to strike, त्याने मारण्याचें भेडा-
वणे केलें or मी मारीन असें त्याने
सांगितलें.

three a. तीन, तिषे, तिहीं, त्रिक.
Three times three are nine,
तीन त्रिक नव.

threw pret. of throw.

throat n. कंठ m. गळा m. घसा m.

through prep. मधून, पार, आर-
पार, सर्व, पहिल्यापासून शेवटा-
पर्यंत, अर्थेती, भर. उ. Through
the village, गांवामधून -पार
(जाणे), गांवभर (पसरणे, गोष्ट,
इ.) Through a board, तक्त्याला
आरपार (भोंक पाडणे, जाणे. इ.)
To get or go through (with
work, difficulty, duty, &c.),

समाप्त करणें, पार जाणें-पडणें, सिद्धीस-तडीस नेणें.

— (२) कडून, में, आंतून. उ. The letter came through the Post office, डांकेतून पत्र आलें. He did it through another, त्याने दुसऱ्याकडून केलें.

throw v. t. टाकणें, फेंकणें, झुगारणें, झोंकणें, ढकलून देणें, ढकलणें.

— to throw away, out, off, टाकून देणें, ढकलून देणें.

— to throw down, पाडणें, आपटणें.

thrust v. t. खोंचणें, खुपसणें, रोवणें, टोंचणें, भोंकसणें, भसकणें, ठुसणें, ठुसकणें.

— to thrust out or away, ढकलून-काढून देणें, घालविणें.

thrust n. खुपसणें n. ठुसकी f.

thus ad. असें, तसें, याप्रमाणें, त्याप्रमाणें.

thy pron. तुझा, आपला.

thyself pron. आपण, आपणाला, स्वतां, ज्याच्या.

tidings n. pl. वर्त्तमान n. बातमी f. खबर f. समाचार m.

tie n. बंद m. बंध m. बंधन n.

tie v. t. बांधणें, बंद करणें, तांगणें, बांधून ठेवणें, गांठ मारणें.

tiger n. वाघ m. व्याघ्र m.

tight a. ताठ, गच्च, भउच, तंग, ताण, घट्ट.

— to pull or make tight, ताणणें, तंग-ताठ करणें, ओंवळणें.

— to be tight, भउचणें, ताठ तंग, असणें.

tighten v. t. ताठणें, गच्च करणें, ताठ तंग, करणें, ओंवळणें, ताणणें.

till conj. पर्यंत, पावेतों, पूर्वी, अगोदर, वर. उ. Do not go till I tell you, मी संगेन तोंपर्यंत-तोंवर जाऊं नको. — till now, अजून, आतांपर्यंत, आजपर्यंत.

time n. वेळ f. समय m. वखत m. n. काळ m. मुदत f. दिवस m. उ.— at that time, तेव्हां, तेव, त्या वेळेस -समयीं-वखतावर -काळीं-मुदतीवर-दिवसीं. — at what time, केव्हां, कर्धीं, कोण त्या वेळेस.

— (२) अवकाश m. वेळ m. फुरसत f. फावणें n. फावत. उ. I have not time to do that, तें करावयास मला अक्काश-वेळ -फुरसत-फावत नाहीं.

— a hard time, महागाई, दुकळ, दुकाळ, विपरीति, विपत्तिकाळ. — to have a hard time, हाल -संकट पावणें, (invers.) मोठा श्रम-अडचण पडणें, हाल-हलाकी -संकट असणें-होणें, संकट पडणें.

— (३) इहलोक m. उ. — in time or eternity, इहलोकीं किंवा परलोकीं. — time of life or life-time, आयुष्य n.

—(४) pl. -दा, -पट, -वेळां, -वेळ, -वार, -ने, बारी. उ. — a second time, दुसऱ्याने. — three times, तीनदां-वेळां-वेळ-वार. (२)

तिपट. उ.—This number is three times that, ही संख्या त्या संख्येची तिपट आहे. (३) उ. Three times three are nine, तीन त्रिक नऊ आहेत. — often times, बहुतवेळां, वारंवार.

timid a. भेकड, भित्रा, भिकट, भिरू, भिऊस्त, बुजीर.

tin n. कथील n. वंग n. कल्हई f.

tin v. t. कल्हई करणे-लावणे.

tired a. दमळ, थकला, श्रमी, कंटाळला, भागला. (२) कंटा- ळळा.

— to be tired, दमणे, थकणे, श्रमणे, कंटाळणे, भागणे.

tis, it is याचा संक्षेप.

to prep. -ला, -स, -कडे, -जवळ, -ीं. उ. — to the house, घराला, घरास, घराकडे, घरीं. —come to me, माझ्याजवळ -कडे ये. Give it to him, तें त्याला दे.

—(२)-पर्यंत,-पावेतों,-वर, तागाईत. उ. to this place (as far as this place), एथेपर्यंत-पावेतों. — to this day, आज-आतां पर्यंत -पावेतों. He went to (as far as) Poona, तो पुण्यापर्यंत-पावेतों गेला.

—(३) प्रमाणें. उ. I made it to his order, त्याच्या आज्ञां-सांगि- तल्याप्रमाणें म्या केलें.

— This is not to my taste, हें मला भावडत नाहीं.

— He beat the horse to death, त्याने घोड्याला असें मा- रिलें कीं तो मेला.

— They all consented to a man, सर्वांनीच कबूल केलें.

— Listen to me (hear me), माझें ऐक, माझ्या गोष्टीकडे कान दे.

— Attend to your work, आ- पल्या कामावर लक्ष ठेव-लाव.

— He told me to my face, त्याने माझ्या तोंडावर सांगितलें.

— as to this, या गोष्टीविषयीं.

— It broke to pieces, तें फु- टून गेलें, or त्याचे तुकडे झाले.

—(४) to हा शब्द क्रियापदाच्या मागून असतां सामान्यरूप दाख- वितो. उ.—to go, जाणे, जाऊं, जायाला, जायास, जायाचा, जाया- चें, जाणार, जावें ह्मणून. I go to school to learn English, इंग्लिश शिकायाला मी शाळेंत जात असतों.

toad n. बेडकुळीचा एक प्रकार.

to-day n. ad. आज.

toe n. बोट n (पायाचें), नख n. m. (पाखरांचें).

together ad. एकत्र, एकवट, मिळून, एकंदर, बरोबर, संगें, संगतें.

told pret. & p. p. of tell.

Tom n. p. पुरुषाचें नांव.

Tommy n. p. पुरुषाचें नांव.

to-morrow ad. & n. उद्यां, उद- यीक.

— to-morrow morning, स-काळ, सकाळीं.

tone n. नाद m. सूर m. आवाज m.

tongs n. pl. चिमटा m. गावी f.

tongue n. जीभ f. जिव्हा f. (२) धूर f. (गाडीची). (३)भाषा f. बोली f. (४)कांटा (तायडींचा).

to-night ad. आज रात्रीं.

too ad. हि. ज. I will read this book too, मी हें पुस्तकहि वाचीन, or मीहि हें पुस्तक वाचीन. (२) अधिक, फार, अति, पराकाष्ठेने, पराकाष्ठा, यथायोग्य त्यापेक्षां, पाहिजे यापेक्षां (अधिक, थोडा). उ. This is too much, जें पाहिजे-योग्य त्यापेक्षां हें अधिक आहे, or हें फार आहे.

took pret. of take.

tool n. श्राउत n. हतेर n. हस्त n. साधन n. सामग्री f. (pl).

tooth n. दांत m. दाढ f.

torn p. p. of tear. विदारित, फाटका, फाडलेला.

torpid a. निचेतन, निष्चेत, अचेतन, मंद, जड, स्तिमित.

touch n. स्पर्श m. शिवणें n.

—sense of touch, स्पर्गिंद्रिय n.

touch v. t. स्पर्श करणे, शिवणें, हात लावणे. (२) ठेवणें, लागणें, पहोंचणें, पावणें.

—to touch the heart, (invers.) कळवळणे, कळवळा येणे, मनांत दया येणे.

tough a. चामट, चेंचट, वातड, चिकट, मजबूत, कठीण.

tow n. ताग m.

tow v. t. ओढणे, चालविणें, (तारू इ. पाण्यावर).

towards prep. कडे.

town n. गांव m. n. शहर n. नगर n.

toy n. खेळ m. खेळण्याचा पदार्थ m. खेळणें n.

trade n. उद्योग m. व्यवहार m. काम n. कसब n. (२) व्यापार m. वाणिज्य n. उदीम m. देणें घेणें n.

trade v. i. व्यापार-उदीम करणे, व्यवहार करणे, विकत घेणे-देणे.

translate v. t. तरजुमा-भाषांतर करणें, उतरणें. (२) वाहणें, नेणें.

translation n. भाषांतर n. तरजुमा m.

trap n. सांपळा m. फांसा m.

trash n. भ्लतेंसलतें n. ऐलपैलवस्त f. n. निष्टारें n. खेरमेर f. फांसफूस f. अयडतगड n. केर m.

travel v. i. चालणे, कंठणे, जाणे, खेटणे, प्रवास करणे, देशांतरास जाणे, देशाटन करणे.

traveller n. वाटसरू m. बाटमार्गी m. पांथस्थ m. पथिक m. यायी m. फिरस्त m. फिरस्ता m. उतारी m. मार्गस्थ m.

travels n. pl. प्रवास m. चालणी f. फिरणें n. हिंडन n. देशाटन n. (२) प्रवासाची बखर.

treat v. t. -सीं वामणे, -चें करणे, -चा उपचार करणे. उ. — to treat one well, एकार्चे चांगलें करणे, एकासीं चांगलें वागणे. — to treat one ill *or* shamefully, एकार्चे वाईट करणे. — to treat one with kindness, एकाला प्रीति-ममता दाखविणे, बरें-दया करणे. — to treat with contempt, तुच्छ मानणे, तिरस्कार -अनादर करणे, फजिती करणे. (२) — to treat of (a subject, science, &c), -विषयीं बोलणे -लिहिणे-कळविणे-दाखविणे, (*invers.*) -विषयीं असणे. उ. He treated of the subject of Astronomy, खगोलाविषयीं त्याने कथा सांगितली -लिहिली. This book treats of plants, हें पुस्तक झाडांविषयीं आहे. — Etymology treats of the different sorts of words, &c. Etymology हें शब्दांचे वेगळेवेगळे प्रकार इत्यादिक दाखविते.

treatment *n.* वागणूक *f.* वागणें, करणें.

— good treatment, चांगलें करणें (दुसऱ्याचें).

— bad *or* ill treatment, वाईट करणें (दुसऱ्याचें).

tree *n.* झाड *n.* वृक्ष *m.* तरु *m.* झाडमाड *n.*

tremble *v. t.* कांपणे, स्फुरणे, डगणे, उगमगणें, थरथरणे, थरारणे.

trembling *a.* उगउगीत, थरथरत, कांपत.

trembling *n.* कंप *m.* कांप *m.* थरथरी *f.* थरथराट *m.* स्फुरण *n.*

trembling *ad.* थरथर, थरकन.

tribe *n.* वर्ण *m.* वर्ग *m.* गोत्र *n.* जात *f.* ज्ञात *f.* वंश *m.* कूळ *n.*

trick *n.* खोड *f.* चटक *f.* संवय *f.* खतखोड *f.* (२) चेष्टा *f.* ख्याली *f.* विनोद *m.* धिंगामस्ती *f.* (३) टूक *f.* युक्ति *f.*

trick *v. t.* ठकविणे, फसविणे.

trickle (down) *v. i.* गळणे (पाणी, इ.), झरणे, पाझरणे.

tried *pret. & p. p. of* try.

trifle *n.* हलकी गोष्ट *f.* अल्पगोष्ट *f.* थौडकें *n.* हलकें *n.* जरा.

trifle *v. i.* उगीच बोलणें -करणें, व्यर्थ बोलणें-करणें, गमणे.

— to trifle away time, वेळ निरर्थक घालविणे.

trifling *a.* हलका.

trifling *n.* उगीच बोलणें-करणें, व्यर्थ -निरर्थक बोलणें -करणें, निरर्थक घालविणे, गमणें.

triumph *n.* विजय *m.* जय *m.* फत्ते *f.* जयजयकार *m.*

triumph *v. i.* जय मिळविणें-करणें, जयास जाणें.

troop *n.* टोळी *f.* झुंड *f.* स्वारी *f.* तांडा *m.* थवा *m.* ताफा *m.*

—troops *pl.* सेनभार *m.* स्वारी *f.* दळ *n.* फौज *f.*

trot *n.* दुडकी चाल *f.* दउदउणें *n.*

trot *v. i.* दुडदुड चालणे, दउदउणें, तुरुतुरू चालणे.

trot *v. t.* दउदउविणे, दुउदुउ चाल-
विणे.

trouble *n.* श्रम *m.* मेहनत *f.* खट-
पट *f.* तारंबळ *f.* लचंड *n.*
तस्दी *f.* कष्ट *m.* उपद्रव *m.* त्रास
m. इजा *f.* छळणूक *f.* (२)
संकट *n.* अडचण *f.*

trouble *v. t.* उपद्रव देणे, दुखविणे,
त्रास देणे, श्रम देणे, सतावणे,
छळणे, जाचणे, गांजणे, चालवणे,
त्रासणे, इजा देणे.

—to be troubled, दुखणे, घाव-
रणे, संकटांत पडणे, (*invers.*)
अडचण-दुःख वाटणे.

troublesome *a.* उपद्रव देणारा, उप-
द्रविक, श्रमदायक, त्रासक, पीडा
करणारा, छळणारा, चेष्टेखोर,
खोडकर.

trout *n.* एका प्रकारचा मासा.

trudge *v. i.* वणवण करणे, जाये
करणे, फिरणे, फांस्टाफांसटीने
चालणे, पायपिटीने चालणे, हेल-
पाटा घेणे.

true *a.* खरा, सत्य, असल, वास्त-
विक, ठीक, खोटा नाहीं, लबाड
नाहीं, यथार्थ, प्रमाणिक, इम्रानी.

trumpet करणा *m.*

trunk *n.* संदूक *f.* पेटी *f.*
— trunk of a tree, कांड *n.*
खोड *n.*
—trunk of an elephant, सोंड
f.

trust *n.* विश्वास *m.* भरवसा *m.*
इतवार *m.* खातरी *f.* (२)

अनामब *f.* हवाला *m.* दिम्मत *f.*
जिम्मा *f. m.*

trust *v. t.* विश्वासणे, खातरी-विश्वा-
स-भरवसा ठेवणे, (*invers.*) खात-
री असणे.

trust *v. i.* आशा धरणे, (*invers.*)
वाटणे, भ्रवशा-खातरी असणे.

trusty *a.* विश्वासू, खातरीचा,
विश्वासी, इमानी, पतीचा.

trustworthy विश्वासू, विश्वासी, इ.
(trusty पहा).

truth *n.* खरेपण *n.* सत्यवा *f.* सत्व
n. सत्य *n.*

try *v. i.* यब-प्रयत्न करणे, झटणे,
हात लावणे, लागणे, उद्योग करणे.

try *v. t.* परीक्षा करणे-पाहणे-घेणे,
पारखणे, पाहणे. (२) अनुभव
घेणे, (*invers.*) प्रत्ययास-प्रतीतीस
येणे.

tub *n.* पीप *n.*

tug *v. i. t.* श्रमाने वाहणे-चालणे,
श्रमाने नेणे.

tumble *v. t.* उलकटणे, उलटा-
पालट करणे, लोटणे, पाडणे,
घीटाळा करणे, अस्ताव्यस्त करणे,
गोंधळणे, ढकलुन-लोटून पाडणे.

tumble *v. i.* पडणे, लोटून पडणे,
कोसळणे, ढांसळणे.

tumbler *n.* पंचपात्री *f.* (कांचेची).
(२) भोरपी *m.*

turn *n.* पाळी *f.* पालट *m.*
— by turns, फेरपाळीने, आ-
ळीपाळीने, दमादमाने, दम मा-
रून.

—to take turns, फेरपाळीने करणे, दम मारणे.

— (२) फेर m. फेरी f. फेरा m. पलाटन n. उ. — to take a turn, फेरी इ. घालणे, फिरणे.

— (३) वळण n. वांकण n.

— the road made a turn, रस्ता वळला.

— (४) खेप f. पाऊठ f.

— (५) (of mind), सवई f. शौक m. वळण n. धौरण n. स्वभाव m. कल m.

— (६) — a good turn, एखादें बरें करणें. — a bad turn, एखादें वाईट करणें.

turn v. i. फिरणे, मुरडणे, वळणे, वांकणे, कलणे. (२) बदलणे, उलटा होणे, बदलून होणे.

— to turn over, उलटणे, उलटा होणे, पालटणे.

— to turn out, निघणे, निप-जणे. (२) वाट सोडणे, बाजूला जाणे, फुटणे (वाट, रस्ता, इ.)

— to turn away, सोडून जाणे, फिरुन जाणे, मुरडून जाणे, मुर-का करणे, मुरकणे.

— to turn in, आंत जाणे.

—to turn to account, कामास -उपयोगी पडणे.

turn v. t. फिरविणे, उलटणे, उलट करणे, पालटणे, उफराटा करणे, कलथणे, लावणे, (मन, डोळे, इ.) (२) कातणे.

— to turn over, उलटणे, पाल-टणे, उलटापालट करणे, लोटणे.

— to turn out, बाहेर काढणे -घालविणे, हाकलून देणे, घाल-विणे. (२) ओतणे, रिचावणे.

— to turn away, रजा देणे, घालविणे, दूर करणे, बरतफं करणे.

— to turn to account, कामास लावणे.

turnip n. शलगम m.

'twas, it was याचा संक्षेप.

twelve a. बारा.

twenty a. वीस.

twenty-five a. पंचवीस.

twice ad. दोनदां, दोन वेळ, द्विवार. (२) दुपट.

twig n. टहाळ m. टहाळा m. टहाळी f. डाहळी f.

'twill, it will याचा संक्षेप.

twitch n. हिसका m. हिसडा m.

twitch v. t. i. हिसकणे, हिसडणे.

— to twitch away, हिसकून घेणे.

twitch v. i. स्फुरणे.

two a. दोन, दोघे, दोन्ही, दोहो.

tyrannical a. जबरदस्त, जालीम, जुलुमाचा.

tyrannize v. t. जुलूम करणे, जुलु-मदस्ती करणे, जबरदस्ती करणे.

tyranny n. जुलूम m. जुलूमदस्ती f. जबरदस्ती f.

tyrant n. जुलूम करणारा m. जबर-दस्त m. जबरदस्ती करणारा m.

U.

Ugly a. उग्र, कुरूप, भेांगळ, विरूप,

विद्रा. (२) वाईट, खोडकर.

unable *a.* अशक्त, शक्तिमान नाहीं, शकत नाहीं.

— I am unable to read, मला वाचतां येत नाहीं, *or* माझ्याने वाचवत नाहीं.

uncle *n.* चुलवा *m.* मामा *m.* काका *m.*

uncommon *a.* असाधारण, असामान्य, विरळ, अपरूप, विशेष, भलता नाहीं.

uncommonly *ad.* फार, विशेष.

under *prep.* खालीं, आंत, खालतें,
— to be under water, पाण्यांत बुडलेला असणे.

under *a.* खालचा.

understand *v. t.* समजणे, जाणणे, उमजणे, (*invers.*) ध्यानांत-लक्षांत-समजण्यांत येणे, समज पडणे, कळणे, कळूं येणे.

understanding *n.* समजूत *f.* बुद्धि *f.* ज्ञान *n.* मन *n.* समज *f.* अक्कल *f.*

understood *pret. & p. p. of* understand, विदित, अवगत, ठाऊक, माहीत, गतार्थ.

undertake *v. t.* हात लावणे-घालणे (कोणीएका कामास), आरंभ करणे, आरंभणे, लागणे.

undertook *pret. of* undertaken.

undress *v. t. i.* वस्त्र काढणे, पोषाक काढणे.

uneasiness *n.* असुख *n.* चळवळ *f.* असमाधान *n.* अशांतपण *n.* अस्वास्थ्य *n.*

uneasy *a.* अस्वस्थ, अशांत, असुखी.

unfortunate *a.* अभागी, देवहीन, हतभाग्य, करंटा, दुर्दैव, भाग्यहीन.

unfortunately *ad.* दुर्दैवाने.

unhappy *a.* असुखी, असमाधानी, दुःखित, अस्वस्थ, उदास, सुखी नाहीं, दुःखाचा.

United States *n. p.* एका देशाचें नांव.

unkind *a.* कृपाळू नाहीं, प्रियमान नाहीं, मेहरबान नाहीं, निर्दय, कठोर, क्रूर.

unjust *a.* अन्यायी, अनीतिमान्, बेइनसाफी, जबरदस्त, ठीक नाहीं.

unless *conj.* जर नाहीं तर. उ.
I shall go unless it rains, जर पाऊस पडत नाहीं तर मी जाईन.

unlike *a.* सारिखा नाहीं, वेगळा, निराळा, विषम, समान-बरोबर नाहीं.

unpaid *a.* फिटला नाहीं, फेडला नाहीं, न चुकवलेला, उतराई नाहीं.

unpleasant *a.* नावडता, आवडता नाहीं, गोड नाहीं, चांगला नाहीं, ओंगळ, कंटाळायुक्त, कंटाळवाणा.

until *conj.* पर्यंत, पावेतों, तोंवर, तोंपर्यंत, वागाईत. उ. —until death, मरणापर्यंत -पावेतों. —
Do not go until I tell you, मी सांगीन तोंपर्यंत, जाऊं नको.

unto *prep.* -पावेतों, -पर्यंत, -ला, -स, -कडे. (to *prep.* 1. & 2. पाहा).

up *prep. & ad.* वर, वरतीं, खालून.

— up to, -जवळ, -कडे, -पाशीं, -स,-ला,-गावेतों,-पर्यंत.

— up in the air, भास्मानीं, अधांतरीं, उंच, अंतरिक्षांत.

— up stairs, माडीवर, वर, वरतीं.

— to eat up, खाऊन टाकणें, अवघें खाणें, झाडून खाणें.

— to cover up, *v. t.* झांकणें, झांकून ठेवणें, लपवून-दडवून ठेवणें.

— to lay up, *v. t.* ठेवणें, साठवून ठेवणें, सांठवणें, जोडणें, मिळविणें.

— to shut up, *v. t.* कोंडणें, बंद करणें, कोंडून ठेवणें-टाकणें.

— to get up, *v. i.* उठणें. (२) चढणें, वर जाणें. (३) *v. t.* उठविणें.

— to burn up, *v. t.* जाळून टाकणें. (२) *v. i.* जळून जाणें.

— to wind up, (thread, &c.) गुंडाळणें.

— to wind up (a watch, &c.) किल्ली देणें.

— to wind up (business, work, &c.) समाप्तित आणणें, संपविणें, आटोपणें.

— to turn up, *v. t. i.* उलटून करणें, कलथणें, उठविणें.

— to bring up (children), वाढविणें, शिक्षा देणें.

— to root *or* pluck up (weeds &c.) उपटणें, खुरपणें, वखरणें, वेणणें.

upon *prep.* वर. (२) विषयीं. उ. — upon this subject, या गोष्टीविषयीं.

— upon the whole, सारांश पाहून, सारांश.

upper *a.* वरचा, वरला, वरील.

upright *a.* उभा. (२) प्रामाणिक, सात्विक, खरा, सालस, नीतिमान, न्यायी, नेतीचा, नेकीचा, सचोटीचा, विश्वासी, सरळ, इमानी, साळसूद.

upset *v. i.* उलटा होणें, लवंडणें.

upset *v. t.* उलटणें, उलटा करणें.

upset *pret. & p. p. of* upset.

upward *or* upwards *ad.* वरतीं, वर, आकाशाकडे, खालून. उ. He looked upward, त्याने वर -आकाशाकडे पाहिलें.

— (२) -वर, -अधिक,-पेक्षां, -हून, ज्यास्त. उ. — upwards of twenty, विसांवर, विसांपेक्षां अधिक, इ.

urge *v. t.* आग्रह करणें, ताघरावणें, चिथावणें, प्रेरणा करणें, उत्तेजित करणें, दामटणें, पिटविणें, (घोड्याला, इ.).

us *pron.* आम्हाला, आम्हास.

use *n.* (युस) उपयोग *m.* काम *n.* गरज *f.* फायदा *m.* लाभ *m.*

— of use, उपयोगी, कामाचा.

— to be of use, लागणें, लक्षभणें, कामास पडणें, (*invers.*) गरज असणें.

— of no use, निरुपयोगी, कामाचा नाहीं, व्यर्थ, फुकाच.

— to make use of,-चा उपयोग करणे, कामास लावणे. (use v. t. पाहा).

— (२) रीत f. चाल f. दस्तूर m. वहिवाट f. रूढि f. सराव m. अभ्यास m.

use v. t. (यूज) व्यापारणे, कामास लावणे,-चा उपयोग करणे-घेणे, वापरणे.

— (२) खर्चणे (पैका, अन्न, इ.), खाणे (अन्न, इ.), नेसणे, लेणे, घालणे (वस्त्रं इ.), पिणे (पाणी, द्राक्षरस इ.), घेणे, घालणे. उ. He uses sugar in his tea, तो आपल्या चहांत साखर घालीत असतो.

— (३) बोलणे, घेणे, (शब्द इ.). उ... He uses bad language or words, तो वाईट शब्द बोलत असतो.

use v. i. (यूज) (भूतकाळांत मात्र) असणे, (invers) रीत-चाल-दस्तूर असणे. उ. He used to go, तो जात असे. That horse used to kick, तो घोडा लात मारीत असे, or त्या घोड्याला लात मारण्याची खोड-सवई होती.

— to be used to (a work, thing, &c.), संवकणे, (invers.) सवई-सराव-अभ्यास-रीत-चाल असणे.

useful a. उपयोगी, कामाचा, कामी, बहुगुणी, हिताचा, हितकारक.

usual a. रीतीचा, रीतिप्रमाणे, नियमित, नेमस्त, चालीचा.

usually ad. बहुधा, बहुतकरून, प्रायः.

V.

vain a. व्यर्थ, निष्फळ, निरर्थक, पोकळ. (२) अभिमानी, डौलदार, पत्राजी, थलबेला, पोकळ. — in vain, व्यर्थ, वांयां, उगीच, एरवीं, निष्कारण.

valuable a. मोलवान्, अपरूप, किम्मतीचा, फार चांगला.

value n. मोल n. किम्मत f.

value v. t. मोल-किम्मत ठरविणे, -ठेवणे -सांगणे. (२) किम्मतीचा मानणे, मानणे, मोजणे, गणणे, चांगला मानणे.

vast a. फार मोठा, विशाल, अपार, अपरंपार, प्रचंड.

vegetable n. वनस्पति f. भाजी f. तरकारी f. शाक f. हिरवळ f. भाजीपाला m.

vehicle n. वहन n. यान n. गाडी f. गाडा m. पालखी f. रथ m. मेना m. द्वार n. (२) अनुपान n.

venture v. i. t. धजणे, धीर करणे.

venture n. जोखीम f. — at a venture, उगेंच, नेम न धरून.

verse n. ओवी f. श्लोक m. — in verse, पद्याचा.

versed a. निपुण, हुशार, अभ्यासी,

कुशल, तयार, जाणता, माहित-
गार.

very *ad.* फार, अति, पुष्कळ,-च.
— the very one, तोच, तीच,
तेंच.

vessel *n.* पात्र *n.* भांडें *n.* कोठा *m.*
वासन *n.* (२) तारूं *n.* गलबत
n. जाहाज *n.* नाव *f.* नौका *f.*
—bloodvessel, नाड *f.* नाडी *f.*
रग *f.*

vex *v. t.* त्रासणें, दुःख-त्रास देणें,
सतावणें, छळणें, जाचणें, गांजणें,
चाळविणें, चिडविणें, दुखविणें.

vexed *a. & p. p.* चिडला, दुःखित,
नाखूश, रंजीस.
— to be vexed, चिडणें, इ-
सणें, रंजीस येणें, (vexed पाहा).

victim *n.* यज्ञपशु *m.* यज्ञ *m.*
वध्य *m.* हार्य *m. n.* वधण्याचा,
भक्ष्य.

victuals *n. pl.* भन्न *n.* खाणें *n.*
भक्ष्य *m.* आहार *m.* खाद्य *n.*

vile *a.* ह्लाड, पामर, कुत्सित, कुटील,
भोगळ, अमंगळ, नीच, वाईट,
दुष्ट, चांडाल.

village *n.* गांव *m. n.* ग्राम *m.* पुरी
f. पुर *n.* खेडें *n.* मौजा *m.*

vine *n.* वेल *f.* लता *f.* (२) द्राक्षी
f. द्राक्ष *f.*

violence *n.* बलात्कार *m.* जबर-
दस्ती *f.* जबरी *f.* जुलूम *m.* जुलू-
मदस्ती *f.* साहस *n.* खलेली *f.*
जोर *m. n.*

violent *a.* साहसिक, जबरदस्त,

जोराचा, खलेल, लांठ, सखत,
मनस्वी.

violently *ad.* बलात्काराने, जबर-
दस्तीने, जबरीने, पराकाष्ठेने,
जुलूम करून, साहसाने, जोराने,
बळाने, मनस्वी.

virtue *n.* नेक *f.* नेव *f.* भलाई *f.*
गुण *m.* नीति *f.* चांगलेपण *n.*
सद्गुण *m.* सत्व *n.* सचोटी *f.*

virtuous *a.* नीतिमान्, चांगला,
सत्वशील, सत्वधीर, सद्गुणयुक्त.

visit *n.* भेट *f.* मुलाखत *f.* दर्शन
n.
— to make a visit, go on a
visit, भेटायाला जाणें-येणें.

visit *v. i.* भेटणें, भेट घेणें, जाणें,
पाहण्याला -भेटायाला जाणें-येणें.
(२) झडती घेणें, फळ देणें, (पा-
पार्चे इ.)

visitor *n.* पाहुणा *m.* भेट घेणारा
m.

voice *n.* सर *m.* वाणी *f.* शब्द *m.*
आवाज *m.* ध्वनि *m.*

volume *n.* पुस्तक *n.* ग्रंथ *m.*

voracious *a.* खादाड, अधाशी.

voyage *n.* प्रवास *m.* (जलमार्गाने),
जलयात्रा *f.* सफर *f.*

W.

waddle *v. i.* डुलणें, झुलणें, चालणें
(बदकासारखा), डोलणें, भिर-
कांडी मारणें.

wag *n.* थट्टा करणारा *m.* थट्टेबाज
m. मौज्या *m.* विनोदक, विनोदी,
फरदुष्या.

wag v. t. हालविणे, डोलीवणे, (डोकें, डेपूट).

wagon n. गाडी f. गाडा m. (चार चाकांचा), रथ m.

waist coat n. बंडी f.

wait v. i. थांबणे, राहणे, खोळंबा करणे, खोळंबणे, बसणे, सबुरी करणे, वाट पाहणे.

— to wait upon,-ची खिदमत -चाकरी करणे.

wake v. i. जागा होणे, उठणे.

wake v. t. जागा करणे, उठविणे.

Walden n. p. पुरुषाचें नांव.

walk n. फलांटी f. पर्यटन n. परि-क्रमन n. सहल f. हवा खायाला जाणें n. (पायानीं). (२) पाऊल-वट f. वाट f. (३) चाल f. वर्तणूक f.

— to take a walk, फिरणे, फिरायाला जाणे, (पायानीं.)

walk v. i. चालणे, जाणे, (पायानीं), पायीं पायीं चालणे. (२) वर्तणे.

wall n. भिंत f. दिवाल f. कोट m. परिघ m. कुंपण n. भावार m. कुसूं n. गावकुसूं n.

— tent-wall, कनात f.

wall (in or up) v. t. -भोवतें भिंत घालणे-बांधणे.

wallow v. i. लोटणे, लोळणे, लोट-पोट करणे.

walnut n. अकरोट m.

want n. गरज f. प्रयोजन n. द-कार f. अगत्य n. जरूर n. (२) कमती f. उणें n. कसर f. अभाव m. अडचण f.

— to be in want of, (invers.) पाहिजे, गरज असणे, अगत्य असणे, लागणे.

want v. t. (invers.) पाहिजे, गरज असणे, लागणे. (२) इच्छिणे, मागणे, (invers.) इच्छा असणे. (३) (invers.) उणा-कमी असणे, नसणे.

ware n. जिन्नस f. माल m. सौदा m.

warm a. गरम, उष्ण, सोमळ, कोमट.

warm v. t. शेंकणे, गरम करणे, उष्ण करणे, तापविणे, वाफ देणे, ऊब देणे, ऊबेत आणणे.

warmly ad. आग्रहतेने, तप्तपणाने, संतापाने, रागाने.

warn v. t. सुचविणे, बोध करणे, जतावणे, जगावणे, जाणविणे, सां-गणे, खबर देणे. (२) झाक दाखविणे, भेजावणे.

warning n. बोध m. बोधन n. ख-बर f. सुचना f. संदेश m.

— to give warning, सांगणे, (warn v. t. पाहा).

was pret. of be, होतों, होता, होती, होतें.

wash v. t. धुणे, धुऊन घेणे, धा-लन -प्रक्षालन करणे, धाळणे, नाहणे, स्नान करणे, अंघूळ कर-णे, अचवणे.

— to wash off, धुऊन टाकणे.

— to wash away v. i. धुपून जाणे. (२) v. t. धुपून नेणे.

watch n. घड्याळ n. (२) पहारा m.

चौकी *f.* गस्त *f.* (२) प्रहर *m.*

watch *v. t. i.* चौकी करणे, जपणे, टपणे, पहणे, वाट पहणे, निरखून पाहणे, जागा राहणे, पहारा -जागरण करणे, सावध होणे, जागणे.

watchful *a.* सावध, जागरा, जपणारा, हुशार, जागणारा.

water *n.* पाणी *n.* जल *n.* उदक *n.* नीर *n.* आप *n.* पानीय *n.*— *in comp.* जल. उ. — a water animal, जलचर.

water *v. t.* पाजणे, पाणी देणे.

wave *n.* लाट *f.* तरंग *m.* लहर *f.* लहरी *f.* जलतरंग *m.*

wave *v. i.* हालणे, फडफडणे.

wave *v. t.* हालणे, पालवणे, हालविणे.

— to wave (*or* waive) a subject, गोष्ट सोडणे.

wax *n.* मेण *m.* मोम. *n.* लाख *f.*

wax *a.* मेणाचा.

wax *v. t.* मेण लावणे.

wax *v. i.* होणे, वाढणे. उ. — to wax stronger, बळकट होत जाणे.

waxen *a.* मेणाचा.

way *n.* वाट *f.* मार्ग *m.* रस्ता *m.* रहदारी *f.* पंथ *m.*

— highway, राजमार्ग *m.* सडक *f.* हमरस्ता *m.*

— a little way, थोडें अंतर, लांब नाहीं, थोडी वाट.

— a great way, लांब, दूर.

— to get *or* be on the way,

चालूं लागणे, वाट धरणे, मार्गावर -वाटेवर असणे, वाटेस लागणे.

— to be out of the way, वाट चुकणे, चुकणे. (२) गहाळणे, पहकणे, गहाळ असणे, हरपणे.

— to be in the way, आडवा येणे, अडचण-अडथळा करणे, वाटेंत-मध्येंच उभा राहणे, (*in vers.*) -कडून अडचण-अडखळ होणे.

— to get out of the way *v. i.* वाट सोडणे, पलिकडे-दूर होणे, आडवाटेने जाणे, आडून निघणे, निघणे. (२) *v. t.* काढणे.

(२) रीत *f.* चाल *f.* पद्धत *f.* तऱ्हा *f.* शैली *f.* प्रकार *m.* संग्रदाय *m.* परिपाठ *m.* शिरस्ता *m.* उ. Do this way, या प्रकारें -या रीतीनें-असें कर.

(३) दिशा *f.* कड *f.* उ. — this way, इकडे.— that way, तिकडे. — which way, कोणीकडे. — every way, चहुंकडे.

— I came this way, that way, मी या वाटेने-त्या वाटेने आलों *or* मी इकडून-तिकडून आलों.

(४) उपाय *m.* इलाज *m.* उ. There is no other way to prevent it, हें न पडावें याविषयीं दुसरा उपाय नाहीं.

(५) छंद *m.* उ. He will have his way, तो स्वछंद करील.

we *pron.* आम्ही.

weak *a.* अशक्त, दुर्बळ, निर्बळ, निर्जीव, दुबळा, अर्धं, कमकुवत,

बळकट नाहीं, शक्तिमान नाहीं, निरस, कस नाहीं थसा, पोकळ.

weakness *n.* अशक्तपण *n.* दुर्बळता *f.* (२) पोकळ्याई *f.* (३) क्षुद्र-क *n.* अवगुण *m.* दुर्गुण *m.* खोड *f.* मर्म *n.*

wean *v. t.* थान तोडविणे, थान तोडणे.

weaned *a.* पारठा, थान तोडलेला. — to be weaned, स्तन सोड-लेला असणे.

weapon *n.* शस्त्र *n.* हत्तेर *n.* आयुध *n.*

wear *v. t.* नेसणे, घालणे, लावणे, पांघरणे, (वस्त्र, इ.), (*invers.*) असणे. (२) झिजविणे, वदल-करणे. — to wear out, जीर्ण करून टाकणे, झिजविणे. — to wear away *or* down, झिजविणे, घासणे. —he wears a cheerful coun-tenance, त्याला हास्यमुख असतें.

wear *v. i.* टिकणे, तगणे, राहणे. (२) झिजणे, घासणे, (*invers.*) वदळ होणे-लागणे. — to wear out, जीर्ण होणे, झिजणे जुना होणे. — to wear away, झिजणे.

wear *n.* वदळ *f.* घासणी *f.*

weather *n.* हवा *f.* दिवस *m.*

weave *v. t.* विणणे.

wedding *n.* वऱ्हाड *n.* लग्न *n.* शादी *f.*

weed *n.* निदण *n.* रान *n.*

weed *v. t.* निदणे, वेणणे, चोखलणे, निदण काढणे, खुरपणे, ओख-रणे.

week *n.* अठवडा *m.* सप्तक *n.* सात दिवस.

weep *v. i.* रडणे, शोक करणे, अश्रुपात-आक्रोश-रोदन करणे.

weigh *v. t.* तोलणे, तुलणे, वजन करणे, तुकणे, ताडून पाहणे, जोखणे.

weigh *v. i.* (*invers.*) वजन अस-णे, भारी असणे.

weighing *n.* तुलना *f.* वजन क-रणे *n.* उन्मान *n.*

weight *n.* वजन *n.* तोल *m.* ग-रिमा *f.* ओझें *n.* उन्मान *n.* जोख *n.* बोज *m.* गुरुत्व *n.* जडत्व *n.* भार *m.* — of weight, वजनी, वजन-दार, भारी.

weighty *a.* वजनदार, वजनाचा, भारी, मोठा.

welcome *n.* आगतस्वागत *n.* स्वागत *n.* उ. He gave me a hearty welcome, त्याने माझें आगत-स्वागत चांगलें केलें.

welcome *a.* उ. — You are welcome to this, तूं हें खु-शीने घे. — You are welcome here, तूं बरें आलास. — You are welcome to stay as long as you please, खुशी वाटेल तोंपर्यंत सुखरूप राहा.

welcome *v. t.* भागतस्वागत कर-
णें.

well *a.* बरा, चांगला. (२) निरो-
गी, खुशाल, कुशल, हुशार.

well *ad.* बरें, चांगलें, ठीक.

— as well as not, श्रमावांचून,
श्रनायासानें, अडचण नाहीं. उ.
Mary said they could let
him go as well as not, तो
जावा यांत कांहीं अडचण नाहीं,
असें मेरीने सांगितलें. — I can
do it as well as not, मला हें
करण्यास अडचण नाहीं.

— as well as, एवढा चांगला,
सारिखा जसें,···तसें. उ. I
can do this as well as you,
जसें तुला तसें मला हें करितां
येतें, *or* मला तुझ्यासारिखें-
एवढें हें करितां येतें. — (२)
हि, आणि हि. उ. He came as
well as his father, तो आणि
त्याचा बापहि आला. I am
pleased to hear of your
good behaviour as well as
your progress in study, (*or* I
am not only pleased to hear
of your good behaviour but
also of your progress &c.)
तूं चांगला अभ्यास करितोस हें
केवळ ऐकल्याने संतोष वाटतो
असें नाहीं, तर चांगल्या आचर-
णानेहि संतोष वाटतो.

well *n.* विहीर *f.* आड *m.* कूप *m.*
कुवा *m.* बारव *f.* वापी *f.* बाव *f.*
बावडी *f.*

went *pret. of* go.

wept *pret. of* weep.

were *pret. of* be, (बहुवचन).

west *n. & a.* पश्चिम *f.* पश्चिमेक-
डला.

western *a.* पश्चिम, पश्चिमेचा, पश्चि-
मेकडला.

West Indies *n. p.* अमक्या बेटांचें
नांव.

wet *n.* ओलें *n.* पाणी *n.*

wet *a.* ओला, भिजलेला.

— a wet day, पावसाचा दिवस.

— a wet nurse, उपमाता.

— to be wet, भिजणें.

— to make wet, भिजविणें.

wet *v. t.* भिजविणें.

whale *n.* माशाची एक जात.

what *pron.* काय, कोणता, जें-तें.

— She did not know what it
was to be sick, रोगी पडणें
काय आहे, हें तिला ठाऊक नव्हतें.

when *ad.* केव्हां, जेव्हां···तेव्हां,
असतां, वर, ज्यावेळेस····तेव्हां,
तेव्हां. उ. When will you
come ? तुझीं केव्हां याल ?

— I will do this when
he comes, जव्हां तो येईल,
तेव्हां मी हें करीन *or* तो आल्या-
वर मी हें करीन.—When he
saw me he ran off, मला पाहून
तो पळत गेला.—When I was in
the house I saw him, मी घरा-
मध्यें असतां त्याला पाहिलें. — I
met him when I was walking
in the street, मी रस्त्यामध्यें

चालत असतां तो मला भेटला, _or_
मी रस्त्यामध्यें चालत होतों तेव्हां
तो मला भेटला.

whence _ad._ कोठून.

whenever _ad._ जेव्हां तरी···तेव्हां,
कोणत्यांहि वेळेस.

where _ad._ कोठें, जेथें, जेथें···तेथें,
कोणीकडे.

—any where, कोठें तरी.

—no where, कोठेंहि नाहीं.

—every where, सर्व ठिकाणीं,
सर्वत्र.

whereas _ad._ असें असतां.

wherever _ad._ कोठें तरी, जेथें तरी,
कोणत्याहि ठिकाणीं.

wherefore _ad._ यास्तव, यासाठीं.
(२) कां? कशासाठीं? कशाला?

whereupon _ad._ त्यावर, मग, तेव्हां.

whether _ad._ कीं काय? (२) को-
णता.

—whether or not, किंवा
नाहीं. उ. I do not know whether he will come or not, तो
येईल किंवा नाहीं हें मला ठाऊक
नाहीं.

which _pron._ कोणता-ती-तें, कोणचा.
उ. which man, कोणता माणूस.

—Which is the best, this or
that? हें किंवा तें कोणतें चांगलें?
(२) जो···तो, जो···असा, तो, जो.
उ. I have read the book
which you gave me, जें पुस्तक
तुझीं मला दिलें तें म्यां वाचलें, _or_
तुझीं दिलेलें पुस्तक म्यां वाचलें.
I saw a snake which was

three feet long, तीन फूट लां-
बीचा साप म्यां पाहिला, _or_ म्यां
एक साप पाहिला, तो तीन फूट
लांब होता. I received a letter
which is well written. मज-
कडे एक चांगलें लिहिलेलें पत्र
आलें, _or_ एक पत्र मजकडे आलें तें
चांगलें लिहिलें आहे, _or_ चांगलें
लिहिलें आहे असें एक पत्र मज-
कडे आलें. There was no fruit
on the trees which were near,
जवळच्या झाडांवर कांहीं फळें न-
व्हतीं.

while _n._ वेळ _m._ काळ _m._

— a long while, वाटोळ _m._
बहुत वेळ.

— This is not worth while,
यांत हित-हाशील नाहीं.

while _ad._ जोंपर्यंत···तोंपर्यंत, इत-
क्यांत, असतां. उ. Sit still
while I read, जोंपर्यंत मी वाच-
तों, तोंपर्यंत उगींच बैस. I came
in while he was speaking, तो
बोलत होता, इतक्यांत मी आंत
आलों. They used to do so
while they were small, ते
लहान असतां असें करीत अ-
सत.

whim _n._ विकल्प _m._ तरंग _m._ ल-
हर _f._ कुतर्क _m._

whimsical _n._ लहरीदार, एककली,
उचलचावडा.

whip _n._ चाबूक _m._ कोरडा _m._
असूड _m._ शिपटी _f._ छडी _f._

whip *s. t.* मारणे, (चावकाने, छ-
डीने).

whiskers *n. pl.* डवे *m.*

whisper *s.* कुचकूच *f.* कुबचूब *f.*
कुसफूस *f.*

whisper *v. i.* कुचकुचणे, कुज-
तुबणे, कुसफुसणे.

whistle *n.* शीळ *m.* शेळ *m.*

whistle *v. t* शीळ बजावणे, शेळ
घालणे, सणसणणे.

white *a.* पांढरा, शुभ्र, सफेत,
धवळ, भवळ, बेत, गोरा, कोरा
(कागद).

whither *ad.* कोणीकडे, जिकडे....
तिकडे, जेयें, नेयें... वेयें, तेयें,
कोठें.

whittle *v. t.* वासणे, क्षाचणे, (चा-
कूने).

who *pron.* कोण. उ. Who are
you ? तूं कोण आहिस? (२) जो
...जो, जो...भसा, जो, वो. उ.
The man who came here yes
terday is a bad man, जो मनु-
ष्य काळ आला तो वाईट आहे.—
A man came yesterday who
told me so, काल एक माणूस
आला त्याने मला असें सांगितलें.
A woman who had three
children died this morning,
जिला तीन लेंकरें होतीं असी एक
स्त्री आज सकाळीं मेली, or आज
सकाळीं एक स्त्री मेली जिला तीन
लेंकरें होतीं. I saw a man who
had broken his leg, मोडक्या
पायाचा माणूस म्या पाहिला, or

ज्याचा पाय मोडला असा एक
माणूस पाहिला.

—Ann was a child five years
old who was good and kind
to all (p. 4), आन नामक
सर्वांवर कृपाळू व चांगली असी
पांच वर्षांची एक मुलगी होती.

—A man who came that way
said &c. (p 5), त्या वटेने एक
माणूस येऊन झणाला इ.

— He is a man who has been
in the service of many people, तो बहुत लोकांची चाकरी
केलेला माणूस आहे.

— There was a man there
whose name was Rama, राम
नामक असा माणूस तेयें होता or
रामा या नांवाचा माणूस तेयें होता.

— Those who stood near
heard the voice, जवळ उभे
राहणाऱ्यांनी वाणी ऐकली, or जे
जवळ उभे राहिले त्यांनी वाणी ऐ-
कली.

— Where is the man who
owns this horse, या घोड्याचा
मालक कोठें आहे?

— Where is the man who
brings the water, पाणीवाला
कोठें आहे?

— Where is the man who
owns this cart, गाडीवाला कोठें
आहे?

whoever *pron.* जो कोणी....जे,
जे....ते सर्व.

whole *n.* सगळें, भवतें, साकल्य *n.*

whole a. सगळा, सर्व, संूर्ण, पूण, सारा, समडा, समस्त, अवघा, भर. (२) धड, धडसा, बदा, मात्र, शाबूत, आखा.

—whole number, पूर्णांक.

wholesome a. पथ्य, पथ्यकर, पुष्-कारक, हितकारक, चांगला.

wholly ad. अगर्दीं, निइशेष, निपट, निस्तूक, पस्त, तमाम, धाडून.

whose pron. कोणाचा, ज्याचा, त्याचा.

why ad. कशासाठीं, कां, कां बरें.

wicked a. दुष्ट, वाईट, दुर्जन, कुजन, पापी, पापिष्ट, पातकी, अभर्मी.

wickedness n. दुष्टपण n. दुष्टाई f. वाईटपण n. पाप n. अभर्म m.

wide a. रुंद, मोठा, प्रशस्त, विस्ता-रित.

widow n. विधवा f. रांड f. बीडकी f. रेंडा f.

wife n. बायको f. पत्नी f. स्त्री f.

wigwam n. झोंपडी f. खोंपट n.

wild a. रानवट, रानटा, जंगली, वन्य, रानांतील, वनचर, वन. (२) अचाट, बेकैद, उनाड. — to run wild, रानांत राहणे. (२) वरळणे, अचाट होणे.

wild n. रान n. वन n.

wilderness n. रान n. वन n. बंगल n. अरण्य n.

wildness n. उनाडकी f. बेकैद f. (२) वनपण n.

will n. इच्छा f. खुशी f. मर्जी f. छंद m इरादा m. — with good will, खुशीने, संतोषाने.

(२) मृतपत्र n. मृत्युलेख m.

will v. t. इच्छणे, ठराव -निश्चय करणे, (invers.) इच्छा-मर्जी -खुशी असणे.

will v. a. हा शब्द भविष्यकाळ दाखवितो. उ. He will go, तो जाईल. — He will not go, तो जाणार नाहीं.

William n. p. पुरुषाचें नांव.

willing a. खुशी, खुश, राजी, रजू, तयार.

willingly ad. खुशीने, आपसुखाने.

Wilson n. p. माणसाचें नांव.

wilt v. a. will याचा द्वितीय पुरुष, एक वचन. उ. Thou wilt go, तूं जासील.

wilt v. i. कोमणे, कोमजणे, सुकणे, वाळणे, सुकून -वाळून जाणे.

wilt v. t. कोमजविणे, सुकविणे, काळविणे.

win v. t. जिंकणे, मिळविणे, बोम्पणे, संपादणे, पावणे, प्राप्त करणे.

wind (उइंड) n. वारा m. वायु m. हवा f. यात m. वाव m. अनिळ m. मारुत m.

wind (वैंड) v. t. गुंडाळणे, वेष्टणे, फिरविणे.

— to wind up (a watch, machine), किल्ली देणे. (२) —to wind up (business, &c.)

अटोपणे, समाप्त करणे, गुंडा-
ळणे.

wind v. i. वळणे, फिरणे, वांकणे,
सर्पटणे, सर्पटत चालणे.

winding a. वांकडा, सर्पटत, नीट
नाहीं, बरोबर नाहीं.

window n. खिडकी f. झरोका m.
धारें n.

wine n. द्राक्षरस m.

wing n. पंख m. पक्ष m.

wink n. निमिष m. पलख m. n.

wink v. i. डोळा घालणे, डोळ्यावर
कानडें मोडणे. (२) काणा डोळा
करणे. (३) खुणावणे.

winter n. हिंवाळा m. शीतकाळ m.

winter v. i. हिंवाळ्याचे दिवस रा-
हणे.

winter v. t. हिंवाळ्याचे दिवसांत सं-
भाळणे (ग्रामपशूळ इ.).

wipe v. t. पुसणे.

— to wipe away, off, पुसून
टाकणे.

wisdom n. ज्ञान n. शहाणपण n.
विवेक m. अक्कल f. समज m. f.

wise a. ज्ञानी, विवेकी, चतुर, बुद्धि-
मान, सुज्ञ, शहाणा, भूर्त, समं-
जस.

wish n. इच्छा f. मनोरथ m. वां-
च्छा f. इरादा m.

wish v. t. i. इच्छिणे, इच्छा धरणे
-करणे, (invers.) इच्छा-खुशी
असणे. (२) मागणे.

wished (for), इच्छित, इष्ट.

with prep. संगतीं, संगातें, संगें,
संगीं, संगट, सहित, सहवर्त-
मान, बरोबर, सुद्धां, निशीं. उ.
Come with me, माझ्यासंगतीं
-बरोबर या.— He came with
his horse, तो आपल्या घोड्या-
सुद्धां आला, or तो आपला घोडा
घेऊन आला.

—(२)-जवळ,-ला,-कडे,-पासीं. उ.
I have ten rupees with me,
माझ्याजवळ -माझ्यापासीं -मला
दाहा रुपये आहेत.

—(३) -ने, -कडून, -योगाने. उ.
He did it with his hand, त्याने
आपल्या हाताकडून -हाताने हें
केलें. — with difficulty, श्र-
माने.

—(४)-विषयीं,-चें. उ. What will
you do with this? याचें-या-
विषयीं काय करसील?

—(५) असतां. उ. He came to
school with dirty hands, तो
आपले हात मलकट असतां शा-
ळेत आला.

—The man with a hat on,
टोपीवाला. The man with the
cart, गाडीवाला.

withdraw v. i. हटणे, मागे सरणे,
निघणे, उठून जाणे.

withdraw v. t. काढणे, येऊन
जाणे, माघारें घेणे.

wither v. i करपणे, कोमजणे,
कोमणे, वाळणे, सुकणे.

wither v. t. सुकविणे, वाळविणे.

withered a. & p. p. करपलेला,
वाळलेला, सुकलेला, शुष्क,
वावका.

within *prep.* आंत, मध्यें, आंतून.

without *prep.* -वांचून, -शिवाय, -खेरीज, -विरहित, -विगर, विन्न, बिन, बिना, नाहीं, सोडून, न घेउन, निं -(in comp.)

— He has been out begging all day without getting any thing, दिवसभर भीक मागत फिरला परंतु कांहीं मिळालें नाहीं. —I can do without it, हें नसलें तरी निभाव होईल.

without *ad.* बाहेर.

witness *n.* साक्षी *m.* साक्षीदार *m.* *f.* ग्वाही *m.* पाहणारा *m.* शा-हिदी *m.* (२) साक्ष *f.* साक्षी *f* शाहिदी *f.* ग्वाही *f.*

wolf *n.* लांडगा *m.* वृक *m.*

wolves *pl. of* wolf.

woman *n.* स्त्री *f.* बायको *f.* बाई *f.* भाड *f.*

women *pl. of* woman.

won *pret. of* win.

wonder *n.* आश्चर्य *n.* अद्भुत *n.* चमत्कार *m.* कौतुक *m.* नव-लाई *f.* (२) आश्चर्य *n.* विस्मय *m.* अचंबा *m.*

wonder *v. i.* आश्चर्य करणें, विस्मय करणें, (invers.) आश्चर्य वाटणें, विस्मय-अचंबा होणें.

wonderful *a.* चमत्कारिक, आश्चर्य-कारक, विचित्र, अपूर्व, अपरूप.

won't, will not याचा संक्षेप.

wood *n.* लांकूड *n.* काष्ठ *n.* (२) वन *n.* जंगल *n.* झाडी *f.* रान *n.* भरण्य *n.*

wood *a.* (wooden पाहा).

wooden *a.* लांकडी, लांकडाचा.

woods *n. pl.* वन *n.* रान *n.* भ-रण्य *n.* झाडी *f.*

wool *n.* लोंकर *f.* लंव *f.* लोंहकर *f.* ऊर्णा *f.*

wool-comber *n.* लोंकरीचा पिंजा-री *m.*

woollen *a.* लोंकरी, लोंकरीचा, पश्मी.

word *n.* शब्द *m.* पद *n.* (२) वा-र्तमी *f.* गोष्ट *f.* वाक्य *n.* भाषा *f.* बात *f.* खबर *f.* समाचार *m.* वर्तमान *n.* संदेश *m.*

wore *pret. of* wear.

work *n.* काम *n.* धंदा *m.* उद्योग *m* करणें *n.* कार्य *n.* कृत्य *n.* कर्म *n.* कारिगिरी *f.* (२) मेह-नत *f.* श्रम *m.* कष्ट *m.* (३) ग्रंथ *m.* पुस्तक *n.*

work *v. i.* काम करणें, खपणें, उद्योग चालविणें. (२) चालणें, वाहणें, वाहता असणें. (३) गो-कळ -सैल होऊन हलणें. (४) फसफसणें.

work *v. t.* कामास लावणें,-कडून काम करविणें.

— to work hard (oxen &c.) घुसडणें, दामटणें, कष्ट देणें, -कडून फार काम करविणें. — (२) ढवळणें, कालविणें.

working *a.* उद्योगी, काम कर-णारा, मेहनती, खटपट्या, कमाऊ.

world *n.* जग *n.* पृथ्वी *f.* दुनया *f.* (२) लोक *m.* जन *n.* आलम

f. भाल्यदुनया *f.* (२) संसार *m.* प्रपंच *m.* भव *m.*

worldly *a.* प्रपंची, संसारी, संसारिक.

wormwood *n.* संताप *m.*

worn *p. p. of* wear.

— worn out, जीर्ण, जुना. (२) थकला, भागला, शिणला.

worse *a.* अधिक वाईट-खराब, एवढा चांगला नाहीं. (२) अधिक रोगी.

— He becomes worse, तो अधिक वाईट होत चाल‍तो. (२) तो अधिक रोगी होत भाहे.

worship *n.* भजन *n.* पूजा *f* भक्ति *f.* उपासना *f.* अर्चा *f.* अर्चन *n.* आराधना *f.*

worship *v. t.* भजणे, पुजणे, उपासणे, अर्चणे, भजन-पूजा करणे.

worst *a.* सर्वांहून वाईट-खराब.

— at the worst, पराकाष्ठा, निदानीं.

worth *n.* किम्मत *f.* मोल *n.* चांगुलपण *n.* उपयोग *m.* योग्यता *f.* गुण *m.*

worth *a.* किम्मतीचा, मोलाचा. (२) योग्य, जोगता, जोगा.

worthy *a.* योग्य, जोगा, जोगता, पात्र. (२) चांगला, भला.

would *v. a.* व्यक्यरूप सुचवितो, इच्छा व निश्चय भसे अर्थ फारक-रूम दाखवितो. उ. He would not hear me, तो माझें ऐकेना.—

He said he would go, मी जाईन, असें त्याने सांगितलें.— He said he would not go, मी जाणार नाहीं, असें त्याने सांगितलें.

— I would tell you if I knew, मला ठाऊक असतें तर मी सांगतों.— Had I known I would have told you, म्या जाणलें असतें तर म्या तुला सांगितलें असतें.

— If you would be a good child I would not punish you, तूं चांगलें लेंकरूं असतास तर मी तुला शिक्षा न करितों.— He would go, तो जाईच.— She would eat (used to eat) unripe fruit, ती हिरवीं फळें खात असे.

would'nt, would not, याचा संक्षेप.

wove *pret. of* weave.

wound *n.* जखम *f.* घाव *m.* वार *m.* व्रत *n.*

wound *v. t.* जखम करणे, वार करणे, घाव मारणे, जखम पाडणे.

wound *pret. & p. p. of* wind.

wrap (round, up) *v. t.* गुंडाळणे, वेष्टणे, वेढणे, लपेटणे.

wretch *n.* रंक *m.* कंगाल *m.* बिचारा *m.* (२) दुष्ट, नीच, चांडाळ *m.*

wretched *a.* फार असुखी, त्रेडी, दीन, बिचारा, भिकार, दुःख पावलेला, कृपापात्र.

— wretched state *or* condition, दीना *f.* दैन *n.* दुर्दशा *f.* दुरवस्था *f.*

wretchedness *n.* दैन *n.* दैना *f.* दुःख *n.*

wrinkle *n.* सुरकुती *f.* आठी *f.*

wrinkle *v. t.* सुरकुतविणे.

wrinkle *v. i.* सुरकुतणे.

write *v. t. i.* लिहिणे, लेखणे.

—to write down, मांडणे, लि-
हून ठेवणे.

writing a. लिहिण्याचा.

writing n. लेख m. खत n. लिहिणें
n. लिपि f. अक्षरें n. pl.
— hand-writing, दस्तूर n.
लिपि f. दस्तखत n.

written p. p. of write.

written a. लिहिलेला, लिखित.

wrong a. वाईट, अन्यायी, ठीक
नाहीं, बरें नाहीं, बरोबर नाहीं,
अयोग्य, अनुचित, अशुद्ध.
— to be wrong, चुकणे, (invers.) चूक असणे.

wrong n. वाईटपण n. अन्याय m.
अपराध m. अधर्म m. नुकसान
n. f.

wrong v. t. -चा अन्याय करणे, -चें
वाईट करणे, दगलबाजी करणे.

wrote pret. of write.

wry a. वांकडा, वक्र, विडा, (तोंड).

Y.

yard n. वाडा m. अंगण n. (२)
एक लांबीचें माप सुमारें चोवीस
तसू इतकें, यार्ड.

year n. वर्ष n. साल f. संवत्सर
m. (२) सन n. शक m.
— He is ten years old, तो
दाहा वर्षांचा आहे.

yellow a. पिवळा, पीत.

yellowish a. पिवळट.

yes ad. होय, हो, हां, जी.

yesterday n. ad. काल n.

yet conj. तथापि, तरी, असतांहि.

yet ad. अजून, आजपर्यंत, अद्यापि,

तोंपर्यंत. (२) अणखी.

yield v. t. देणे, (invers.) उत्पन्न
होणे, उपजणे, होणें, येणे, (फळ).
(२) देणे, सोडून देणे.

yield v. i. हटणे, दबणे, नमणे
वळणे, ऐकणे, कबूल होणे.

yonder ad. तेथें, तेथतेथे, तिकडे.

yonder or yon a. तेथचा, तेथला,
तो दुरचा, तिकडील, तिकडचा.

you pron. तुझी, तुझाला, तुझास,
तूं, तुला.

you'll, you will याचा संक्षेप.

young a. तरुण, जवान, कोवळा,
लाहान, नवतरुणा.
— young one, बच्चा m. पिलू
n. बाळ n.

young n. बच्चे m. pl. पिलें n. pl.

younger a. अधिक तरुणा-जवान
-लाहान, धाकटा.

youngest a. सर्वांहून तरुणा-लाहा-
न, कनिष्ठ, धाकटा.

your pron. तुमचा, आपला, तुझा.

yours pron. तुमचा. (नामाशिवाय).
उ. This is my book, that is
yours, हें पुस्तक माझें आहें तें तुझें.

yourself pron. आपण, स्वतां,
जात्या, जातीने, आपणाला.

you've, you have याचा संक्षेप.

you're, you are याचा संक्षेप.

Z.

Zeal n. आस्था f. आस्थिकपण n.
आवेश m. हौस f. भगत्यसाद m.

zealous a. आस्थिक, आवेशी, भ-
गत्यवादी, हौसदार.

Zero n. शून्य n. पूज n.

Lightning Source UK Ltd.
Milton Keynes UK
UKHW031426280119
336340UK00010B/590/P